# RED TIGER HUNTING

ALEXANDER C. JUDEN

5points
press

E-book ISBN: 979-8-9867905-0-3

Print ISBN: 979-8-9867905-1-0

JudenBooks@gmail.com

5points
press

# CONTENTS

# 1

---

**The Hook**

It was the home opener for the New York Yankees. My seat at the Polo Grounds was down the third baseline, four rows back from the grass, halfway between the bag and the ten-foot fence that made up the left field wall. The Yankees fans around me were mercilessly razzing the poor Red Sox left fielder.

The Yankees had been sharing the Polo Grounds with the Giants since about 1912. I'd only been there once, and that was before the fire, so I'd never really seen this ballpark. I think it was called Brush Stadium then. I'd watched the Giants play the Reds, but I couldn't remember who had won the game. That failing seemed fitting.

It was a beautiful day, and my seat was in the sun. I had my jacket off, my tie loosened, and my hat pulled down to shade my eyes. Like most of the men in the crowd, I reckoned I'd have sweat rings under my arms in a bit.

I'd bought a beer before sitting down. I wasn't much of an afternoon drinker, but with all the talk about temperance and prohibition, I decided that if I didn't have this afternoon beer, I'd someday regret it. I don't much like regrets. Since the war, I didn't risk having any.

Prohibition, now there's an idea that only a woman or Woodrow Wilson could love. The world was changing and not for the better, but at least the beer was cold.

By the time I reached my seat, the Red Sox were up three to nothing. The game was already in the bottom of the third inning, and there was a pretty good crowd.

I didn't mind missing the first few innings because I wasn't a Yankees fan. How could anyone be? No one should like a team stolen from another city even if that city was Baltimore. I felt that way without even considering the Yankees' name changes, and once I did, well, I just couldn't understand how even a New Yorker could root for them. Orioles, Highlanders, Yankees, I didn't care what you called them. They should be shunned as the vagabond baseball carpetbaggers they were. But hell, that's why they fit so well in New York City. A town full of people from somewhere else. A hell of a way to live.

I shook my head. Most importantly, they weren't my team.

For that matter, neither were the Red Sox. But at least I knew some of the Sox players. They'd beaten the Cubs to win the World Series last year. Of course, I hadn't really been following baseball then. The last time I followed baseball, Amos Strunk was an Athletic, but here he was in a Red Sox uniform. It seemed like nobody stayed put anymore, no loyalty—not that I blamed Amos for leaving Philadelphia. He was probably getting paid more. Nothing wrong with that.

Looked like Harry Hopper was in the outfield too. Well, there's an exception to every rule. It seemed like he'd been with Boston forever.

The left fielder, Ruth, seemed pretty good-natured about the ribbing, and frankly, I think the crowd kind of liked him. I'd heard of him, but I didn't know if he'd been playing when I'd left for England.

I chuckled. Hell, I thought Ruth was a pitcher, but the people in the stands were talking about him as if he were a better hitter than Cobb. A fan one row behind me explained that he'd hit a two-run home run in the top of the first with two outs. Just what the American League needed, somebody better than Cobb—who didn't play for the Senators.

Thinking about the Senators made me smile. I was a longtime fan. After my family left Texas for Washington, I became an eleven-year-old baseball fanatic, even sleeping with my glove. I used to make the trip over to League Park to watch the team play. It was a great park. Where else did the centerfield wall wander around a bunch of houses and a few trees? Walter "the Big Train" Johnson, Clyde Milan, George McBride, I loved those guys. It seems now like some cruel joke that, while growing up, I rooted for a guy named Germany Shaefer, but I did.

After a whipping or a fight, or whenever something really bothered me, if I could, I'd go to the ballpark. If there was no game, I'd sneak into the park and just sit. Somehow the ballpark had always soothed me. It filled my need to feel like I was part of something big and important. A need that had cost me in recent years.

I never scored the games. Frankly, I never learned how. Instead, it was enough to just sit in the stands and be part of the crowd. The sameness of it, the routine, was reassuring, soothing.

One of my best memories was the day I dragged my sisters to a Senators doubleheader against the Naps—they're the Indians now. We trounced them the first game, seven or eight to nothing. It was wonderful. My sisters actually enjoyed it, laughing and giggling at the young men in the crowd, cooing over one of the Naps players, I can't remember which, and teasing me whenever I cheered. Cy Young pitched the second game for the Naps. I remembered not because he pitched particularly well, but because, even as young as I was, I knew I was seeing someone special. My sisters didn't think so. They left in the third inning. But I stayed. The Naps won 5–2. I remember standing and applauding at the end. Applauding in part for the split, which was better than I expected, but really applauding for Young, who won his five hundredth game that day. As I stood there, alone in a crowd of three thousand, I realized I was happy. It was a nice feeling. There wasn't anywhere else in the world that I wanted to be or anything else I wanted to be doing. It was a feeling I've had only twice. Well, one of these days, the Senators would win the pennant, and I suppose I'd be happy that day too.

Today, despite the comforting, unchanging sameness of the game, I was anxious. This was a new feeling for me, an addition to the perpetual pall of depression that had hung around me since my return from the war. When I thought about it, I was sure the depression sprang from my inability to comprehend what I had seen and done and become and maybe—however much I might want to deny it—from my disfigurement. Why had we bothered? So that I could be embarrassed about the holes in my socks? It was disrespectful of the men, many my friends, who had died. My prewar worries were at best trivial, and my postwar worries were no different.

Not that my friends had died so that I could worry about which of my two ties to wear. In truth, they died for no reason at all. But I still connected the dreary existence of peacetime life to their sacrifice. How could the humdrum, meaningless, contemptible lives of so many of the people I saw daily—hell, at this damn game—warrant the extinction of the men I knew? They couldn't. Just as those men shouldn't have paid for the continuation of my own pathetic existence. But the pointless sacrifice of the dead and my continued habitation of this new, colorless peacetime world remained my only certainties.

Sitting around me, the young guys, guys my age, looked like I felt, haunted and miserable, some with coat sleeves pinned up around missing arms.

Thank God I hadn't been wounded that badly. I might be ugly, but I could still work if I just had the heart for it.

Despite the apparent soundness of my limbs, and please forgive my whining, I had my life-changing deformities.

I don't mean the physical scars, although God knows those were obvious enough.

No. I was different now. I'd always been prone to bouts of moodiness and short temper. In truth, before the war, these had probably come from immaturity.

But the war. The war.

It had opened a door in me. Or maybe it's better to say it lifted a veil from my eyes. At twenty years of age, I began to realize something profoundly disturbing yet unavoidably obvious. Civilization was a sham. Duty, honor, loyalty, religion, obedience, respect—all the invisible chains that had bound me, unknowing and blind, to a society shaped and benefiting others. Words forging link after link of the chains that held me tight. Chains that bound millions of men to each other, both as comrades and as enemies. Perhaps my own instinct for survival had convinced me of this fraud, for survive I did.

The war cut the links to what I'd been raised to believe. Childhood stories of brave men locked in battle at sunken roads, wheat fields, and peach orchards paled beside real life. Now etched into my bones like filigree work on a fine hunting gun was a disgust with society and with myself. I'd sacrificed my own good self-opinion, whether warranted or not, and any hope of living in civilized society on behalf of that very civilized society.

The anger that seemed to live just below my heart began to boil.

I could not live in peace anymore.

For if you just scratched this thin coating we call civilization, even with a baby's soft fingernail, you would see the flyblown dead in France. And I had a perpetual need to scratch. Because just outside the edge of civilized society, in the darkness beyond the new electric lights, was a world more alive where each minute, each second, could be of the most profound importance. Did that dear girl pining away the day in the munitions factory worrying about poor Tommy in France cut the fuse length right? For if she didn't, that exact shell she built might kill her cherished sweetheart. A world at war, in all its gruesomeness, has a vibrant, vivid truth to it that civilized society could never hope to offer.

"Griffin," I remember my particular friend Mitchell telling me, "war is life boiled right down to the bone, and bone don't make much of a meal."

While I agreed with Mitchell, I worried that I'd acquired a taste for bone.

For in France, I had learned to see a whole new range of colors previously beyond my perception. Those new colors made the old peacetime colors seem faded and drab. I missed the new colors, and that realization horrified me. I believed that such colors could only be seen in a place where I had entirely abandoned any thoughts of hope or joy and resigned myself to live in terror. I didn't understand how I could miss such a life, but I did. And despite my recently changed circumstances, the bleak, disturbing world in which I lived promised to continue unchanged.

The crack of the bat brought my mind back to the game. Ruth ran under a shallow fly ball, fielded it cleanly, and threw it in. He moved well for such a big guy. I sighed, leaned back, and sipped my beer.

I sought the unchanging serenity of the baseball diamond because I was hoping the magic of the game would give me some peace, for today at least. I needed the sort of calm that could only come from immersion in something beyond myself. The gloom I now carried with me daily was deepened by the fact that I'd done something that I was sure to regret.

Last night, I'd taken a job.

I'd accepted a job that would immerse me in the trivial problems of people I didn't know and couldn't possibly care about. I'd taken the job because I was generally an extremely practical person, and I had to do something between today and the day I died. Taking the job was the best option I had.

Anyway, there appeared to be some possibility, however small, of getting killed while doing it. That quality alone made it attractive to me. And in the meantime, I secretly hoped to feel that surge of life that comes with the possibility of death. I hoped I would see those novel, brighter colors again.

I had miscalculated, for last night my nightmares had changed.

I think my dreams changed because the job promised to take me back to England. Not a place I would choose to go.

Since returning stateside, my nightmares had been of the war. I would be caught in no-man's-land under a descending flare or slowly suffocating as I struggled to claw my way from the mud of a collapsed trench. The worst dream was the one closest to the truth. The lieutenant's whistle blows the advance, and my mates swarm up the trench ladders, but I don't move. I stand frozen, unable to follow. Despite the mocking, the screams, and the pleas for help, I remain unmoving, crying, and shaking with fear. My friends go on to die without me.

But last night, to my dismay, I discovered a new, more disturbing chapter to this familiar dream, one that left me weak and trembling. Really, it wasn't so different from standing frozen in the mud as my friends advanced. The message was the same. But this dream was by far more frightening to me because within it lay a tiny kernel of possibility and truth.

As innocuous as it sounds, I dreamed of being recognized in a London crowd. Not that some former comrade would recognize me. Those who knew me were likely dead. But consistent with the confused and indefinable logic of dreams, in this new nightmare, I was indeed recognized.

*As people stream by me with Nelson's column overhead, I feel a sudden gut-wrenching fear when Henry Strong calls out my name. Henry still wearing the shredded British khaki he died in, his sunken eyes questioning and hurt.*

*"Jack, we missed you, Jack, we could have used another man, Jack," he gently chides.*

*And, as he sees me, more men appear; all long dead, and they too turn to me and speak my name.*

*"Why weren't you with us, Jack?" they ask, hurt and abandoned.*

*"I lived through two years with you," I whine in answer.*

*Then the living people moving through the square turn to see me too. And they recognize me. Not by name but by character. They see me for what I am. They know me to be a deserter and a coward. With anguished sobs of remembrance of their loved ones, they rush upon me all mute yet murderous. The dead men, my friends, look on without either satisfaction or understanding.*

*As the writhing mass closes on me, I wake.*

Waking was a relief, but the relief quickly faded with the realization that the crowd only sought to give me my just deserts, for I truly was a deserter and a coward. I'd learned to live with my cowardice and to ignore, if not forgive, that weakness. But the possibility of returning to England, to Europe, was too much for my sleeping mind to accept.

I don't mean to say that I am incapable of what are, objectively, feats requiring some bravery. Far from it. I'd proven again and again that I could carry my load. Even when wearing English khaki, I had stepped out to face the machine guns and endured the crushing shelling without outward complaint.

No, my cowardice came from taking an exit when my mates could not. At the first chance, I'd run home and left my friends to die. I don't want to overstate my responsibility for their deaths. They would have died anyway, but it was my obligation to see it through, and that's what I hadn't had the nerve to do.

I only returned to fight after my remorse and self-loathing had entirely burned away the callow, asinine boy I had been in 1914. By 1917, when I enlisted in the Marine Corps, all that was left was a husk of a man seeking absolution by shellfire. Bravery is overcoming fear. By that time, I simply had no fear. I embraced the possibility of the gruesome wound and the painful death. Obviously, I remained an ass even in 1917.

With the marines, I had done my penance. A penance so brutal that I should have dreamed only of seraphim. Instead, my nagging conscience remained my own harshest accuser, and while I slept, the possibility of returning to English soil awakened the old bone-deep guilt, which created shades to haunt me. Shades that should long ago have been banished by blood. Despite seeking death, I did not find it. I lived to return home in late 1918, recovering from wounds, empty and without purpose.

But at least it was now baseball season.

At the outbreak of the war, I was preparing for my second year at the University of Durham in England. I'd come the previous year seeking that dash of European leavening that would set me apart from and above others when I returned to America. The university had accepted me, no doubt with some reservations, to take a course in Latin and ancient history. In the middle of June 1914, I came back to England before the school term started to tour the Continent, socialize with my English friends, and most crucial of all, to woo my friend Bert Williams's lovely sister, Evelyn.

It was a wonderful time. Even now, I smile at the thought of those uncomplicated days. It was the best summer of my life. As with so many young men, I had my well-laid plans for life. In my case, they included a degree from an English University and the practice of law in New York, despite it being the home of the Yankees, and marriage to Evelyn Williams. It was my profound desire for Evelyn that started my transformation.

With Germany's invasion of Belgium and the English declaration of war on August 4, England erupted in a patriotic paroxysm that swept men and boys to recruiting stations without thought. To me, it seemed like the last day of school for an entire nation. I felt no differently. I entirely sympathized with my English friends and wished it were my last day of school too.

Of course, my friends all determined to enlist. How could any man (they were boys really) refuse the call to arms that the entire nation felt? They spent an enormous amount of energy, arguing about what regiment to join. One simply didn't want to go to war with the wrong crowd. As the "neutral" American, they ignored me during these debates. Williams and the others eventually settled on the Artists Rifles, which had some history of taking public school and university men. The flush on Evelyn's cheeks at their determination and her frank adoration of George Moore was too much to bear. I insisted I would join with them. At first they sought to dissuade me, declaring in that superior English way that "it was not my fight." Their meaning, of course, was that it was their war and they weren't sure I was invited. That objection lasted just as long as it took me to insist that Germany's unpardonable violation of defenseless Belgium mandated that any moral, honorable man take up arms against the faithless Kaiser. Of course, I insisted not for moral reasons but selfish ones.

My fervor to fight positively glowed, and we all enlisted together. When the Rifles were transferred to France as part of the Officer Training Corps, a unit intended for officer training, I, with my focus ever on Evelyn, asked for a transfer out of the battalion, ostensibly for the purpose of joining one that would see combat sooner. Really, having no interest in becoming an officer, my hope was to remain in England with Evelyn a little longer. My plan worked even better than I could have hoped. Not only was I not transferred to France in October 1914, but I remained in England until March 1915. I had Evelyn to myself. With the start of the war, English society's rigid conventions relaxed, and Evelyn was mine. Of course, much to my dismay, I also managed to get to the front sooner than my peers.

I was a fool. My friends were right. It wasn't my fight. I frankly didn't care one way or the other whether Belgium was invaded or the Kaiser ruled France. I just wanted Evelyn Williams.

Well, I got her. I also got to see her newly gazetted brother cut in half by Maxim fire. He didn't die alone. Advancing with their men, Cecil Thomkins and John Franklin died that same day. When I visited Tippy Fredrickson in the trenches, I saw him killed by a sniper's shot—while making tea. Quite a good shot it was too. Tony Beecham, who had also been promoted to subaltern, disappeared in a geyser of mud made by a German 77. Billy Jones, my closest friend, vanished without a trace during an assault in a nameless Flanders field. Finally, after serving twenty-one months in France and after being reluctantly promoted to corporal, I was, mercifully, shot in the head while standing watch. My good luck.

At first I was horrified, for it was hardly the "blighty" I'd secretly hoped for. The sniper's bullet had struck me after deflecting off wooden trench supports, and I'd been blinded in both eyes. The seriousness of my wound meant that I was evacuated to England and Evelyn. As often as she could, she visited me in the hospital. My head was swathed in bandages during her early visits, and my temper was frayed beyond breaking. I was terrified then, but she was so proud of her man's sacrifice. Initially she forgave me my temper. Over time, she started to imagine living a lifetime with an angry, blind man, and I could sense her ardor waning.

After the bandages came off, she would walk me around the hospital grounds, and we would sit on a bench while she held my hand in hers. Her small, soft delicate hand was a reminder of a world that no longer existed for me. She talked of honor and noble sacrifice and her prayers for my sight to return. If she knew what I'd been through, she should have prayed that it did not. While she would ask about the front, she really had no desire to hear about it, and I was in no condition to describe it. I knew that I was not going back. It was the past. My wound gave me the opportunity to flee, and I would flee. Evelyn was not part of the future. She might have sensed that, deep in my soul, I felt both blessed and ashamed to have survived.

For by then, my vision was returning. I studiously hid this fact from the doctors and the nurses and Evelyn. The doctors expressed surprise that I had no sight at all, despite the reaction of my eyes to their examinations. They chalked it up to trauma and spoke optimistically about the return of my vision. The improvement was slow, but I knew that, when it returned, I would have to go back to the front. That possibility was too terrible to contemplate, and I was willing to pay any price to avoid it. If blind, I could not fight. I was free of the crushing obligation to return to the front. To hell with honor, obligation, friendship, and love. I was not going back to France. Evelyn no longer figured in my plans. She no longer could.

I asked to be returned to the United States to recover. I was, after all, an American volunteer. Evelyn did not object. By then, she wanted me gone too. The British Army discharged me, and still feigning blindness, I took a steamer home.

Ironically, I garnered more sympathy than the average wounded man. As an American, I'd done my part, and my nation was not even at war. My pretense was despicable, but it got me out of the British Army and back to the States. I was home just after Christmas 1916.

Only after I returned did the dreams, the remorse, and the self-loathing truly begin. I would read about the war in the newspaper, and I would be wracked with guilt and shame, enduring sleepless or nightmare-ridden nights. By April of 1917, I was a wreck. I was drinking more meals than I was eating, a beer for breakfast, graduating to whiskeys by midafternoon. Finally, mercifully, the United States' declaration of war against Germany roused me from my stupor. In America's war with Germany, I believed I found the road to my redemption.

I took a bath, brushed my clothes clean, walked down to the post office, and enlisted in the Marine Corps. "First to Fight" was their motto. At the time, I damn well hoped so. Unfortunately, they were. With the marines, I paid my debts to those I'd left behind. Despite the current nightmares, in my heart, I believed I owed no more. I had no more to give. I tried to die, but whether because of God, which I doubt, or because of fate and all its fickle cruelty, I did not die.

I fought a different war with the American Expeditionary Force than I had with the English. In the trenches, with the English, I lived in constant fear of the random shell, the sniper's bullet, and the gas attack. I lived an animal's life in waist-deep, freezing muck, always wet, covered with lice, neighbor with cat-sized rats, and tired beyond expression. With the American Second Division, rather than just the likelihood of death, I lived with its certainty. There was simply no way to avoid that inevitable result. Ignoring the lessons learned by our allies in the first four years of war, Pershing and his generals ordered us to execute frontal assaults against entrenched machine guns. We met with the same harrowing results as the English and French earlier in the war. Yet we still took ground, and we still beat the Germans.

And I did not die.

Instead, I returned to the States where Harry Armistan found me and convinced me to find his daughter.

## 2

### A Damsel in Distress

Patricia Kingsbury née Armistan, Tricia or Trish to her friends, daughter of Harry Armistan, had traveled from New York City to Liverpool, arriving on March 16, 1919. With her was her husband of seven days, Gavin Kingsbury. Together they had accompanied Gavin's sister, Sarah, home to England. After leaving Sarah in England, the couple was to travel on to Italy for their honeymoon. The Kingsburys, including Sarah, took the train to London and a cab to the Hotel Savoy. The couple took a room, paying for three nights. Armistan had received letters from both Patricia and Gavin on Savoy stationery. He hadn't seen fit to give me the letters. I'd asked, but he said they were "personal and there's nothing in them anyway." After spending two nights, they simply failed to reclaim their room key on the evening of the third. Their room was empty of luggage and personal belongings.

It was not an exceptional or even unusual circumstance for young lovers to spontaneously venture somewhere new and unplanned. One night's room price could be easily forgotten in the romantic rush toward a new, shared experience. The mysterious and worrying fact was that Gavin had promised his new father-in-law that, as part of his job working for Armistan, he would visit certain businessmen while in London. He never made the promised visits. Armistan refused to reveal the purpose of Gavin's planned visit to the city. Armistan was determined to find them, but whether this urge arose from paternal concern or a capitalist's avarice, I was unsure.

Armistan had contacted me indirectly through General Neville.[1] He'd found Neville through mutual contacts in Washington. General Neville commanded me and about two thousand other men in France. Why Neville remembered me or even knew how to contact me, I couldn't say. But somehow he did. He sent a terse note to my parents' house asking that, as a favor to him, I contact Harry P. Armistan of New York City. I got the letter only because I stopped off in San Francisco to finalize the sale of my parents' home. Neville's letter was lying on the floor in the foyer after being pushed through the mail slot. I'd come to the house to collect the few belongings my sisters had left for me. It was a miracle that it had only been mailed a few weeks before.

I had recovered from the wounds that sent me home in November. I had no job and no real qualifications for one. I wasn't particularly interested in finishing my university degree.

So, with nothing better to do, I went to New York and found Harry Armistan, which was not difficult.

Armistan was a millionaire, who appeared well on his way to making his second, fifth, or tenth million. I went to his office off Wall Street, but his secretary directed me to phone back the next morning. The next day, I dropped a nickel in a public telephone and arranged to meet Armistan over breakfast at his club. We spent the meal talking about the "business of investing" as he called it. Oddly, he was convinced the future of the armaments industry was bright despite the war ending.

Armistan was a small man, but he had great energy and an engaging personality. In meeting him, the first thing that struck me was the complete absence of the reserve one expects of a New York City financier.

"Good God, I'm glad I found you! Which one of the many lines I put in the water reeled you in?" he asked with a smile.

"General Neville found me."

"Where?"

"San Francisco," I answered.

"Didn't interrupt anything, did he?"

"A wake," I answered tersely. He chose not to pry.

He was charming and friendly, not particularly forthcoming about why he sought a meeting, but he fed me and didn't raise an eyebrow when I ordered a vodka and tomato juice with my breakfast.

"Prohibition's coming," I explained anyway.

He smiled, which made me like him. He insisted he wanted to get to know me better before we discussed business, so he invited me to dinner at his home the next evening.

He lived in an impressive brownstone west of Central Park. A butler answered the heavy wood-and-leaded-glass door. He showed me through the expensively decorated foyer into a library, where he left me. Across a great expanse of Persian carpet, a large window with the drapes drawn faced a fireplace under a luminous oil painting of a storm at sea. A low fire burned, taking the April chill from the room. Leather-bound volumes trapped in floor-to-ceiling dark wood shelves covered the remaining two walls. Ancient histories seemed to predominate. I found books by Pliny, Caesar, Plutarch.

I discovered a copy of the *Agricola* and pulled it from the shelf. I sat in one of the four wing-backed chairs to flip through the pages. To my delight, the book was in Latin.

I was still parsing my way through the first page when Armistan arrived.

"Mr. Griffin," he said, his enthusiasm and charisma filling the room. "Good of you to come. Please let's eat." He gestured me into the dining room.

At a dinner of lobster and very rare porterhouse steak, we talked about his work, the fast-approaching ban on alcohol, Bolshevism, and a little bit about the war and the developing peace. He was discreet, never asking directly about my experiences. No doubt he could read at least some of them from the scar on my face. When I say "we talked," really he did the talking, but his waiter poured the wine with a heavy hand, so I had no complaint about my role as listener.

Ultimately, he told me of his daughter, her marriage, her husband, and her disappearance. I'd passed whatever test he'd set for me. After his servant laid out coffee and brandy for us in the library, he asked if I would go to Europe to find his missing daughter. He said he was heartbroken, and I believed him.

I thanked him for the meal but told him no.

To his credit, he was undeterred.

"I would answer no differently if I were in your shoes," he said, reaching into a drawer in the small table between us, "but I'm serious. I won't take no for an answer. I need your help."

From the drawer, he took a package wrapped in butcher's paper and tied with string.

"Open it," he said, holding it out to me with two hands. "It's for you, if you'll take the job."

I hesitated, but I didn't want to be tossed out on the street before I finished my brandy. I took the package. My stomach roiled as I felt the weight of it.

"Unless there's a gold bar in here instead of a gun, I don't think this little package is going to convince me to take your job," I said as I placed the package unopened on the table next to me.

Armistan grinned.

"Damn, Neville's right. He said you were clever. Come on, open it. Trust me, it'll be worth your while."

I wondered what Neville could have possibly told Armistan to recommend me. But I was curious.

"What sort of job requires a pistol, Mr. Armistan?" I said as I tugged the wrapping strings.

Inside the thick paper lay a heavy pistol nestled in a cotton rag. It was an English Webley .455 revolver. I knew because I'd carried one for a year and a half in France. Packed around it were bricks of money. English, French, Italian, and, of course, US dollars. Apparently he expected me to encounter some difficulties during my search.

"As you can see, I'm serious about this, Griffin. I'll not send a man on a job without every advantage. I know you're no fool or Win Neville wouldn't have recommended you."

Again, I wondered how Neville knew him and exactly what Neville had told Armistan about me. Somehow I doubted Neville thought any more of me than any other Fourth Brigade Marine who'd managed to survive the war.

"Why Neville? How did you even know him?" I asked.

"Oh, that was just good luck. I contacted my friends in Washington and told them I needed someone like you, and they told me General Neville was staying in New York at the time. With their recommendation, I contacted him. He was extremely helpful. Discreet, but helpful. Did you know he told me he would have made you an officer if you'd wanted to be one? He seemed to have quite a bit of faith in your decision-making under fire. He did say that you were a hopeless romantic and that all the men looked up to you because you fought with the English."

Well, perhaps not so discreet if he labeled me as a romantic.

"Look, Griffin, I don't know what happened to Trish. I just know she's missing. She's my daughter, and I love her. I want her found. I don't think she'd just disappear without telling me something. I..." He appeared shaken by emotion. "I need her back. I need to know she's okay."

"And if she's not... okay, Mr. Armistan? What then?" I asked.

"I'm a rich man," Armistan continued, "but that doesn't mean I don't love my daughter. I've often turned a blind eye to her choice in men. I didn't forbid her anything, and as a result, I got Kingsbury as a son-in-law. To be honest, he didn't seem like a bad sort considering some of the other men she's known. But if she's been hurt, then I want my pound of flesh from whoever hurt her!"

I said nothing, weighing the package in my hands.

"Griffin, I'm not some sort of crackerjack who can go out and rescue Trish. I'm an old man. I couldn't have rescued her even when I was young. I talked to Win Neville, and he told me to get you to do it." He leaned toward me. "He told me you're a merciless, unrelenting man. I can't go to England and bring my daughter back. I need you. My daughter needs you. And if you're going to go for me, then dammit I'm going to make sure you've got the tools to get the job done. Win told me you might go if the mood took you. Well, look, here's a picture of my daughter. She's a beautiful girl, and she needs your help."

Armistan handed me a picture of his daughter. She *was* a beautiful girl. In the picture, she was standing behind a wicker chair, smiling for the photographer. Her light hair framed her face as she looked through the camera. Like Armistan, she was small. It was then that it occurred to me that Neville might have thought of me as soon as he knew a woman was involved. I'd spent more than a little time in France in the stockade for wandering off to find a mademoiselle or two. That trouble had all occurred before Neville took over the brigade, back when he still commanded the Fifth Regiment. We were still training with the French, learning the French way of doing things. I'd already learned the English way. I was bored and burning for the absolution that prompted me to join the marines.

"Mr. Armistan, you don't know she needs any help at all," I answered. "She's probably fine. They're on their honeymoon. They took a little detour. It's nothing more than that."

In truth, even then, the thought of going back to England horrified me.

Then Armistan told me about the black valise containing "business papers" that Kingsbury never delivered to certain "contacts" in the London financial district.

"I have wide-ranging commercial interests and investments,

John. With the end of the war and the victory of the Allies, there will be enormous opportunities in Europe, and it's imperative that I strengthen my relationships with my resources in Europe. Why, there's now the possibility of countries being organized in Europe that haven't existed for hundreds of years. This is the opportunity of a lifetime. The papers I sent with Gavin included a list of European contacts for my representatives in London to establish. They included a listing of projects I was considering. John, I believe one of my competitors has kidnapped Trish and maybe Gavin. God help us if Gavin is working for one of my enemies."

Despite my fear of returning to Europe, the lure was too tempting. He wanted me, an out-of-work, jaded, directionless former marine with no peacetime skills at all, to bring home his daughter and save his business. The one thing I had not expected before meeting Armistan was to feel genuinely needed. That was something I was just not prepared to resist, but the thought of returning to England made my stomach knot.

"Win warned me you might balk at chasing down a couple on their honeymoon. If that were all this was, I wouldn't waste your time, but the contents of that valise are worth a lot of money, not to mention lives. Griffin, I want my daughter home safe and sound, and I need that briefcase back."

"Mr. Armistan, I've only been home a few months. You hand me a pistol and tell me you want me to go to Europe to hunt down your daughter—while she's on her honeymoon. That's got to sound a little strange, even to you."

"How about you just consider this a fully paid trip to Europe, on me, with a little $10,000 bonus at the end of the trip? Surely you've had some desire to go back as a civilian," suggested Armistan.

No! I wanted to shout. Even without the possibility that I'd be recognized, I had no urge to return to Europe. Revisiting memories of shelling, gas, gut-gnawing fear, and the putrefying stench of the week-old dead held no attraction for me.

"Look, why don't you just wait a few weeks? I'll stay in touch, and if they don't turn up, I'll do as you ask," I said.

That was when I saw how truly afraid and desperate he was. His fear was more tangible than mine.

"Griffin, I beg you. Go to Europe and find my daughter. I'll give you any damn thing you want. I've got a bad feeling about waiting, and I've learned to trust my instincts. Neville tells me I couldn't get anyone better. He says you've got guts and luck and you don't scare. Go to England, Italy, or wherever the hell she is, and bring back my daughter."

I looked again at the picture of Patricia Kingsbury, General Neville's secondhand praise warming me. Without any deliberation, I felt myself mentally commit to finding Patricia. The image of a fisherman setting the hook after a red drum hits his bait came to mind. I was the redfish, and Patricia was the bait. Armistan had set the hook well.

"All right, but if I find them and nothing's wrong, I'm coming right back," I promised.

His relief was obvious.

"And one more thing, Mr. Armistan. I'll want help. If I can find him, I want to bring along a man I knew in France. His name is William Mitchell. He speaks a little French and a couple of other languages." I stretched the truth about Mitchell's linguistic skills. "He's smart and tough, and I think he could make the difference in finding your daughter," I finished.

"Fine. I trust your judgment. I'll pay him too. Five thousand dollars. Just find them and get the valise from Gavin. I'll have someone else take it to my contacts in London. Make sure Patricia is safe. That's the important thing."

As he spoke, I broke open the pistol and looked down at the cylinder holding six fat cartridges and thought of the Colt .45 automatic in the bottom of my suitcase. I immediately decided to shave down the Webley's cylinder so that, with half-moon clips, it would take the same bullet as the Colt.

I looked up at Armistan and smiled. "I'll want more ammunition."

Armistan laughed. "You'll have it."

Armistan then told me what he knew of Kingsbury and his relationship with Patricia.

Gavin Kingsbury was ten years older than Patricia, which made him eight years older than me. He was, according to Armistan, born of a Swiss mother and an English father. He was well educated, literate, and charming in an English public school way. In hiring him, Armistan saw him as a useful tool in expanding his business interests in Europe. Armistan had hired Gavin as his English solicitor, and Gavin met Tricia while on a business trip to see Armistan in New York just prior to the start of the war. According to Armistan, Tricia was immediately taken with him. Kingsbury was an ardent pacifist who refused to support the English war effort. He ultimately moved to New York in 1916 to avoid the English universal call-up. His family was relatively wealthy, but he was somewhat frugal in his habits. Armistan frankly admitted that he didn't understand what his daughter saw in the man.

I asked if Armistan had a picture of Gavin. He produced what was obviously a wedding photograph of Gavin and Patricia arm in arm. He stood tall and straight next to his new wife. His hair, longish on the top, was combed back, displaying a prominent widow's peak. He was a handsome man with a charm that was apparent even in the photograph.

"Hmm. A tall, handsome Englishman. I can't see why your daughter would be attracted to him."

Armistan laughed, nodding his head. "I guess I expected my only daughter to fall in love with someone a little more like her dad. Really, the only thing I ever saw him get passionate about was the futility and wastefulness of the war."

I had to agree with Kingsbury on that, but I kept the thought to myself. "Why'd the war come up?"

"We were talking about investing in certain companies that

were involved in wartime production, and that got his back up, I guess," Armistan said.

"What exactly did he say?"

Armistan shook his head. "I don't remember his exact words, but it was clear that he thought the war was solely for the purpose of protecting the status quo. Defending the interests of the rich and royalty, that sort of thing. He was vehement about it. I let it drop, thinking he was sensitive because as half Swiss, maybe he felt some sympathy for the Kaiser."

"Does he speak any languages other than English?" I asked.

"French, Italian, German, maybe Spanish, but I'm not sure. I think he knew a little Russian too. With his skills, he really would have been a tremendous asset in my business," answered Armistan.

I noticed Armistan's use of the past tense. It seems that, where business was concerned, Armistan wasn't afraid to cut his losses.

Armistan then relayed what he understood to be the couple's itinerary for their honeymoon. After visiting Sarah, the sister, at her home west of London in a town called Weybridge, they were to spend a few days in London and then travel by train to Dover and take the ferry to Calais. Once in Calais, they were to travel to Paris, spend two nights and then board a night train bound for Florence. He handed me a handwritten copy of the itinerary, which included hotel names and addresses.

"Were they going to stop in and see his parents?" I asked.

"Both dead," Armistan said bluntly. "Happened before the war."

Briefly I felt a strange kinship with Gavin Kingsbury. I knew what it was like to lose both parents. It made me feel very alone. It was odd for a grown man to think of himself as an orphan, but some ties outlast childhood. I wondered if Gavin felt the same way.

Armistan had little more to tell, and I finished my brandy and stood to leave. At that moment, there was a knock at the library door.

"Come in," Armistan called.

A thickset man wearing a well-made suit pushed open the door. His eyes met mine briefly, and he appeared to catalog me as unimportant. I did the same, finding in his pale regular features, brown hair, and eyes nothing either remarkable or memorable.

"Mr. Armistan, the message you were expecting has arrived," he reported.

"Thank you, Reynolds. Mr. Griffin was on his way out."

Reynolds made no move to shake hands.

I picked up the money and the Webley and turned to Armistan.

"Thanks for the hospitality," I said. "I'll be catching the first ship I can to England, so if you think of anything else I need to know, I'll only be here a short while. I'm staying at the Pennsylvania."

"Yes, opposite the station. A fine choice. I prefer the Ritz-Carlton myself. Smaller and quieter."

"And a bit more exclusive," I finished for him. Armistan laughed. "By the way, Mr. Armistan," I said, looking down at him, "why not have your local help do this job?" I nodded to Reynolds. I caught a tightening around Reynolds's eyes but nothing else.

Armistan seemed undisturbed by the question.

"What? Morgan?" Armistan gestured to Reynolds. "He's a friend of the family, and I have grown quite reliant on him and need him here for now. And, as you say, he's local, but when you find Gavin and Patricia, you shouldn't be surprised to see him. I'll likely send him over to arrange their return."

"Wouldn't they just finish out their honeymoon?" I asked.

"Oh, I think they have used up all the leash I'm willing to give them," Armistan answered with a cold smile.

God help Patricia and Gavin when they finally did get back.

We shook hands, and I turned to leave.

"Griffin," Armistan called after me, "I expect you to succeed. And hurry. Time is of the essence."

I nodded my understanding.

Armistan's butler had offered to ring for a cab, but I decided to walk. I determined that the security of the Webley balanced rather nicely with the danger of the banknotes stuffed in my pockets. I needed to walk and to think—about returning to England.

Obviously I needed more than just last night's walk to think things through. Otherwise, I wouldn't have retreated to the ballpark.

I'd taken a job I didn't want that was sending me to a place I didn't want to go. The attraction was Patricia, a girl in danger. A damsel in distress. Maybe. Despite knowing myself for a blackguard and a coward, I couldn't resist the lure of a girl I'd never met. Of course, the money didn't hurt.

As the Sox came up to bat, I finished my beer and stood. Time to hit the head, grab another beer, a hot dog, and a pretzel. I'd said I'd go, so nightmares or not, I was going. It'd be good to see Mitchell again anyway.

# 3

## Blood and Wheat

I first met William Mitchell at Belleau Wood. I learned later that the wood was the historical hunting preserve for the wealthy. It was heavily wooded, dark, and before the war, I was sure it must have been serene, even magical.

At the time, I was a corporal in the Forty-Ninth Company, which was part of the First Battalion, Fifth Marine Regiment of the Fourth Marine Brigade, which made up half of the Second Infantry Division of the American Expeditionary Force. That's a lot of words to say "I was a marine." The Fourth Brigade was the only Marine Brigade in the whole AEF.

I met him late in the morning, but it's a morning worth describing: a beautiful spring day, just outside of Paris. Bucolic, that's the word. Except for the war. It was June 6, 1918. Neither of us knew then that it would be the deadliest day in Marine Corps history, which was filled with deadly days.

In the company, we knew the Germans were on the move, and we'd all heard the scuttlebutt about the collapse of the French lines. We believed it. The brass must have thought the Germans were going to take Paris because they were rushing the

Americans forward. They had to be desperate if they needed Americans. We were trucked up near the ever-approaching front in French camions. The trucks had excruciatingly hard bench seats, no suspensions, and were driven by little, insanely reckless Asian drivers who spoke no English and swore in French.

After we left the trucks, we marched. We passed retreating poilus and entire extended French families—grandma, grandpa, daughter, and squalling kids, all pulling, pushing, or carrying their valuables. No men and few boys were to be seen. The families clogged the roads and were both tired and terrified.

The day had a different feel from those I'd seen with the British. This was no static war. There were no trenches. Instead, at a designated spot, we were told to stand fast and allow the retreating French to pass through our lines. Around us lay green fields divided by dark shady woods. At any other time, I would have found the countryside very pretty, but truth be told, I was a bit distracted. The other fellas were anxious: time to see the elephant. I'd seen the elephant. I knew what was coming, and the captain seemed to know it. I suppose that's why I had the corporal stripes.

For two days, we waited, hearing the nearing crump and rumble of artillery fire. Occasionally a shell would land nearby, killing a cow or knocking down a tree. The smell of dead livestock gave it all an air of authenticity that had the boys' eyes sparkling with excitement. The men in my company couldn't wait to fight. They were convinced that we were genuinely superior to the Germans in courage and strength and truly armed with a just cause. *Gott mit uns*[1]—not the Boche. I waited with an odd combination of growing dread and feverish desire for the terror I knew would come.

After midnight on June 6, the company received orders to prepare to attack at dawn. Despite stumbling through the dark to find our jump-off point, we managed to get in position. As the night gave way to the increasing light, the whistles blew, and in four waves, the Forty-Ninth stepped out of the cover of the woods where we had marshaled. As the sun broke red over the horizon, we moved into the open wheat field a half mile from our objective, Hill 142. Two hundred yards to our front stood an intervening wood, shaded and dark, looking cool and inviting on the already warm day. We just had to wade through the wheat, and we'd be in that shade.

The first wave was splendidly aligned as the officers' canes went up and pointed to the hill. For the first time since being trucked to the front, my dread receded and I was at home. Was it courage, innocence, or faith that allowed these men, unrelated to the French by blood or common experience, to cross an ocean and step into this unknown field with bayonets fixed? My company, along with the Sixty-Seventh to our left, moved into the field. Poppies dotted the knee-high wheat. A splendid day for a walk in the fields. I could smell the wheat in the heat.

Sporadic shells broke black against the brightening sky.

The Germans, mostly invisible shadows in the green-blue shade of the wood, let us get very, very close before they opened fire. Thanks to my freakish luck, I was in the third wave.

The hail of fire was so thick that the lines of marines ahead of me bent forward as if walking into a strong wind. The machine-gun fire cut huge swaths through our ranks. In the strong summer daylight, the blood was bright against the wheat stalks, as bright as the poppies covering the field. Within minutes, whole files of marines lay dead or dying. Despite the murderous drumming of the Maxims, the rifle fire from our advancing waves was steady.

Without thinking, I found myself flat on the crushed wheat and poppies. Maxim bullets tugged at my combat pack and kicked dirt into my eyes.

Time lost meaning.

The captain was up, shouting us forward—he pulled on my pack on his way toward the wood shielding the Germans. We followed.

Somehow we got into the woods.

"Damn it, we're supposed to take some prisoners," I heard someone shout as my Springfield barked, knocking down a fleeing German. I moved through the trees and stumbled into a tangled ravine, my bayonet leading the way. A German jumped toward me, thrusting his bayonet-tipped rifle, and a second man behind him snapped off a wild rifle shot. I felt a sting along my side and fired my Springfield. The big .30-06 bullet knocked the first German backward into the undergrowth. I didn't even think to work the action. Instead, I jumped aside the barrel of the second German's Mauser, savagely slamming my rifle butt into his head below the ear. He dropped. I pulled myself out of the ravine and joined the company as it formed to cross the next field, to take the next wood.

Again, we formed in waves, but this time, because we were too few to make up four waves, we formed into two. The remaining officers decided to put any marine carrying a Chauchat,[2] the French automatic rifle, in the second wave. No point in having them all killed first I supposed.

As part of the first wave, I moved out of the woods into the next field. We moved in this way for what seemed like hours, from field to wood to field, rooting out Fritz's hidden machine guns.

At one point, I don't recall why, I was suddenly knocked flat, my rifle gone. Bullets hummed and whined by my face, snapping off wheat stalks near my eyes. The fire was so intense that crouching was impossible.

I crawled, really squirmed, forward.

The wounded, some sobbing or crying, some pale and silent, tried to lie flat without curling around their wounds because even the width of their bodies was too high. With mechanical precision, the machine-gun fire painted the field, hitting wounded, unwounded, and dead. The meaty smack acted as a terrifying spur to all of us lying before the murderous guns. We had to move. The cries, smells, heat, and my own fear and frustration destroyed my ability to think. I would die in this field. On the left, some marines rose to rush the tree line, but the Boche fire quickly turned on them and scythed them down. But as they fell, the rest of us rose, and their fatal rush allowed us to reach the German guns. In the melee that followed, I found another Springfield.

Although we had reached our objective, no one knew it at the time. Most of the officers were gone, and so we moved out of cover, across more fields, and into more tangled squares of wooded brush, hunting Germans.

Eventually the staggering casualties and an entire lack of support convinced the survivors to withdraw through more killing fire back to the edge of the hill. By 0900, our advance was complete. The Forty-Ninth and Sixty-Seventh, which advanced with us, were decimated. The exhausted marines from the two companies were hopelessly intermingled along the line. It was just as well. With our officers dead, the commander of the Sixty-Seventh took command of the whole bunch. We dug in and waited for the Boche to try to drive us out.

They counterattacked four times that day. We broke them every time, not with machine guns, for we had none, but with rifle fire. As the heat of the day increased, the wounded throughout the woods could no longer contain their agony.

"First aid!" they cried. "First aid, God, please. Help me."

Others, unable to speak, would bleat animal-like, with an awful, unpredictable rhythm.

I met Mitchell after our original advance. It was not a formal meeting with a handshake and a fake smile. Instead, before we spoke, I got to know him very well indeed.

It was between German counterattacks just after 1000 in the morning. I was already dog-tired. My platoon, as far as I knew at the time, consisted of me and one other man. I think we were on the far right of our line, and I know we had no liaison with other units to the right. Our only contacts on the left were some guys from fourth platoon. I was busy trying to scrape out a firing hole in the root-laced dirt when I heard one of the Maxims in front of me open up. Expecting another attack, I flattened my body to the ground and looked past the man-sized rock that provided the keystone of my cover.

In front of me, I saw a thin man in the US Army khaki we'd been issued, dashing across the open ground. The clearing was littered with the bodies of marines from our morning advance. He moved from body to body as geysers of dirt exploded around him, with the crack of Mausers punctuating the barking of the Maxims. I swear he quartered the field like a good hunting dog. The corpsman, for he could only be a corpsman, would check each marine for maybe half a second. Then he'd either move on or haul the body onto his back and stumble like hell for the cover of the trees near me. Once, while carrying a wounded man across his back, he was knocked down by machine-gun fire. The bullets kicked puffs of dust from the wounded marine's khaki tunic as they impacted. I cringed and pulled my knees up into my stomach as my testicles tried to pull themselves inside me. But the corpsman got up, leaving the now-dead marine, and moved on. I couldn't stand watching anymore, so I started firing into the general vicinity of the machine guns.

"Willis, damn it, give the poor bastard some covering fire," I yelled to the man nearest me. Other marines down the line added their fire too, but I'm not sure it really made any difference.

It seemed like he was in that field for hours, but it couldn't have been more than a minute or two. He had worked his way back toward the wood where we were sheltered. Every few feet, he would dive for whatever cover he could find. As he neared, I could see his wild-eyed face. He levered himself off the ground not far from me and launched himself behind my broken rock shelter. He landed in a heap next to me.

"Thanks for the help," he panted as he handed me a musette bag filled with cartridge belts. Somehow he'd had the presence of mind to collect the bag from one of the casualties.

I took the ammunition.

"I doubt it did much good," I said. I hissed down the line and tossed the musette bag to Willis. "Pass it down."

I turned back to the corpsman. The right side of his face was caked with dried blood and etched by tears or sweat. His right eye was bruised almost shut.

"How many of those guys are still alive," I asked.

"A couple. I only tried to move the ones that I didn't think could wait till dark."

"You're one crazy son of a bitch," I said.

He didn't answer. Instead, he handed me a French two-liter canteen.

I looked back over the field, still dotted with khaki-clad bodies, and drank. The watered wine in my canteen was long gone.

"Where'd you take the guys who you brought back?" I asked.

"There are two other hospital apprentices just inside the wood line. They'll get them to an aid station."

"How come you drew the short straw and had to go out there?" I asked.

"There was no draw to it," he answered. "I was just kinda out there without thinking about it, and they stayed in the woods. No luck to that draw at all."

"Are you the Forty-Ninth's pharmacist mate?"

"The Forty-Ninth? Shit, I thought this was the Sixty-Seventh." He gave a chuckle that was part sob. "Nope, hospital apprentice. Hell, I haven't even been promoted once. That should tell you how long I've been in the navy."

"Well, if you ever need anything from anyone in the Forty-Ninth, buddy, you just have to ask. My name's John Griffin." I rolled toward him and offered my hand. He frowned and held out his right hand. The hand was wrapped in a blood-soaked field dressing.

"Sorry. I'm Will Mitchell. When the mam'selles start cooing at you about how brave you must have been to have fought here, don't forget to mention that the navy was here too."

"I won't forget," I promised.

That's how I met Mitchell. In a division blessed with very brave men, Mitchell was the bravest I knew. He was also the smartest and luckiest man I've ever met. Being quick-witted and utterly cold-blooded about his job made him an incredibly good corpsman. The men in the regiment loved him. He was my best— and probably only—friend in the world.

I last saw him near the Meuse River. It was still dark, but the blackness was broken by the constant malevolent flashing of artillery and mortar fire promising nothing but more dead and broken men. I was moving with my column down the bank toward the river when a shell burst knocked me down. I couldn't move, and it seemed like hours that I lay facedown, numb and disoriented, the tip of my nose in the freezing mud, hearing the zip and ping of the battlefield alive around me. Someone rolled me over. I found Mitchell looking me in the eye. I don't know what he saw, but he pulled me onto his back. My head dangled down by his elbow, and in the flashing light of exploding shells, I could see that his right boot was filled with blood. He got me to the shelter of the trees above the river and moved back out into the maelstrom without a word.

That was the last time I saw him. I would need to contact him as soon as I could.

THE NEXT MORNING, AS I WAS ENJOYING BREAKFAST AT THE Pennsylvania's café, Morgan Reynolds entered the restaurant, carrying a small package. He caught my eye and came directly to my table.

Despite an unreasonable desire to be rude, I stood as he arrived and offered my hand.

"Mr. Reynolds, good morning. What brings you to the world's largest hotel?" I asked with a smile, determined to resist my impolite urges.

After hesitating slightly, he took my hand.

"Mr. Griffin, I have a package for you."

"Please join me," I offered. I sat and sipped my coffee, ignoring the outstretched parcel.

He sat across from me and set the small paper-and-twine-wrapped box on the table. I waved the waiter over and sent Reynolds a questioning look.

"Coffee, black," he told the waiter. "Nothing else." He turned to me. "This is the ammunition Mr. Armistan promised," he explained succinctly.

"I'm impressed," I said. "I had joked about needing more ammunition, but I certainly hope I won't need it." With a box of .455 ammunition, there was no point in cutting down the Webley's cylinder now.

"What Mr. Armistan promised, you will get," Reynolds said emphatically. "He is a man of his word. Scrupulously so."

"I would have thought that would be a disadvantage in the business world," I noted.

"For most men it is, but with Mr. Armistan, those who deal with him know that if he promises something, he delivers it. Good or bad," Reynolds said.

I wasn't sure whether Armistan intended to send Reynolds as a warning, but I didn't want there to be any doubt that, if so, his warning was useless.

"Mr. Reynolds, don't be coy please," I said in as civil a tone as I could manage. "Are you here to warn me that there is a downside for me if I can't find the Kingsburys?"

Reynolds watched me for a moment, his bland features showing no emotion. "As Mr. Armistan said himself, he expects you to succeed. He does not expect, reward, or appreciate failure."

"No wonder you didn't volunteer for the job then," I said.

"I would have gone had he asked me. But he insists on the right tool for each job, and he believes you are the right tool," Reynolds assured me.

"That's good to hear," I said, doing my best to keep all sarcasm out of my voice. "I do have a question that you may be able to help me with though." I waited for his permission to continue.

He nodded.

"Why is there such urgency in finding the missing couple? I understand Mr. Armistan is a worried father, but in a few weeks, he will almost certainly hear from Gavin or Patricia. Why does he need to hire me to hunt them down?"

Reynolds nodded again. "Mr. Armistan is not used to being in the dark. He does not accept being ignored. He has cabled them several times with no response. He is driven and successful in his business, and these traits bleed over into his private life. But right now, most of all, he is afraid."

I suddenly found myself very glad that I invited Reynolds to join me.

"And why is that? Surely he can't be that worried about Patricia," I said.

"No, it's not Patricia. Although I wish it were," Reynolds stated. "Mr. Armistan invests in various industries. He invests heavily and makes a lot of money. At times, he will create informal partnerships with specific investments in mind. He will contact various investors in his circles who he thinks will be interested in the specific venture. He runs the venture and makes money for all his partners. He takes a substantial but fair commission for his efforts."

"Sounds like he's good at identifying opportunities. So why is he afraid?" I asked.

The waiter's arrival with the coffee carafe gave Reynolds time to marshal his thoughts.

"He gave Gavin Kingsbury a substantial sum to be deposited in certain bank accounts in the city of London. These are not formal financial transfers traceable to anyone. These funds are primarily contributions from his partners. These funds were to be invested on their and Harry's behalf. He is convinced that Gavin has absconded with these funds, kidnapped Patricia, and fled to Switzerland."

"But Gavin has only been gone a few weeks. And he's on his honeymoon."

"True," Reynolds answered, "but Gavin knew the funds needed to be delivered immediately. And it is more money than Mr. Armistan can afford to lose. His partners would not be... understanding."

"So why are you telling me this?" I asked.

"As Mr. Armistan said, I am an old friend of the family. So old, in fact, that I had thought at one time that I would marry Patricia. My father is one of Harry's silent partners. Harry decided the business opportunities Gavin offered were better than those that would be offered by closer ties with the Reynolds family. My father agreed. But if my father learns that his money has been stolen..." Reynolds shook his head. "Hell hath no fury like my father when he thinks he's been taken advantage of. And the other partners are no more forgiving. It is imperative that you find the valise that Gavin was tasked to deliver. And if you don't find it, Harry's problems will be bigger than just a missing girl."

"But why do you care, Mr. Reynolds?" I asked, suspecting I knew the answer.

"I still care about Patricia. She's been a good friend to me. If that money isn't recovered, my father and his circle will find Gavin and Patricia. Even in Switzerland. I don't want anything bad to happen to Trish," he answered sincerely. "And to be frank, my father's business will one day be my business. I want that valise found as well."

I wired Mitchell immediately after my breakfast chat with Reynolds. I sent only a few details with a promise of payment and a note about the urgency to come. I received a reply the next day that included a time and place to meet in London. Mitchell wasn't due in London until the twelfth of April. Before then, I needed to track down the sister-in-law. I certainly hoped to have some leads to share with Mitchell before he arrived. Despite myself, I was beginning to feel a little of the urgency Armistan and Reynolds felt. Life threatened to become interesting.

**4**

---

**The Hunt**

A few days after my dinner with Armistan and shortly after
the Sox drubbed the Yankees, I took the RMS *Mauritania*
from New York. She was the same ship the newlyweds had taken
the month before. Traveling on the luxurious four-funnel liner—
the fastest commercial vessel crossing the Atlantic—made for a
very different trip from the last time I crossed the Atlantic west
to east on the USS *Henderson*. Using Armistan's money, I had no
hesitation about traveling first class. Really, I had no choice
considering that the Kingsburys had traveled first class, and if I
wanted to learn anything about their voyage, I'd have better luck
as a first-class passenger myself.

As it turned out, I did have some luck. I spoke with the Kingsburys' steward, their waiter, and even the ship's first officer. The
waiter and the steward remembered the couple and the sister.
Both said that the ladies were quite pretty and near enough in
coloring and looks to be sisters. They often played bridge with
two widows, and they enjoyed walks on the deck and never
missed their afternoon cocktails. Gavin appeared to spend most
of his time, when not with Patricia or Sarah, with two "foreign

gentlemen," smoking and talking. This choice bit of information came from their former steward, a Geordie from Newcastle, whom I could barely understand.

"You said they were foreign gentlemen?" I asked him. "Foreign like me or foreign like a Frenchman."

He'd laughed. "Even more foreign than the French. Rude they were. Slavs or Germans I'd wager, but they spoke in English."

I'd asked him to describe them and scribbled notes in a small notebook as he did. The steward said both men were average height, which according to him, was four inches shorter than me. He also thought both were about ten stone. Two Slavs weighing around one hundred forty to maybe one hundred and fifty pounds, both five feet, six inches tall. Although one was younger than the other, both men appeared to be no older than forty. The older of the two always paid. Their clothes were not of English cut, but then they wouldn't be if the steward was sure he was looking at two Germans.

"Did they share meals with the Kingsburys?" I asked.

"No. The men would sit smoking for hours, speaking with their heads close together."

"What would they talk about?"

He smiled. "Now, sir, what makes you think I'd even know?"

I dug a fiver out of my pocket, which immediately disappeared into the steward's.

"I can't say with certainty," he confided, "but they mentioned needing a dealer or broker or something like that, a trader of some sort they hoped to find on the Continent. And some names that made no sense to me… Baby something or other. And Frank, whoever that is. Curious sorts of names."

"Did the three men seem to know each other when the voyage started?" I asked.

"Ah," he said. "I could not say for sure, but they did seem very friendly from the start."

"Did the two women ever speak to these men?"

"The wife did. She smiled her pretty smile at them, but I don't think the other lovely miss had much use for them. She avoided them after the first day."

"Did they disembark together?"

"You mean the young couple and the sister with the men?"

"Yes," I said.

"No, no. The sister would have had none of that. The foreigners left the ship quickly. The Kingsburys took their time."

The *Mauritania* arrived in Southampton, and I caught the train to London. The city was still full of men in uniform. The irrational part of my mind was convinced that someone would recognize me. The rational part was confident that my scarred and more mature face would go unnoticed. Of course, that did nothing to dry the perspiration on my brow or calm the butterflies fluttering in my stomach. As I pushed my way through the crowds, I kept my hat pulled down low.

I went to the Savoy Hotel. Since that was where Patricia and Gavin had stayed, I decided to stay there myself. But succumbing to my suspicious nature, I signed the register as John Smith.

When asked, the staff didn't remember the newlyweds or the sister. After proper financial lubrication, the concierge let me look at the guest register, which confirmed the couple's arrival. He also said they had paid for three nights but were gone after the second night.

It was possible that Patricia and Gavin had simply decided to spend their last night in London with Sarah, assuming Sarah had stayed in London. Unfortunately, after a few days of canvassing posh London restaurants and bars with two photographs from the couple's wedding set, I'd had no luck in finding anyone who remembered them.

Instead of searching, last night I'd gone to a pub and drank my fill. Although my head ached and my mouth was dry, discontinuing the fruitless searching had improved my disposition. Perhaps my luck was changing.

Today I would try finding the sister, Sarah.

It was still dark, not half past four. I threw off the sheet. I dressed quickly, quietly. I left some money on the nightstand. The girl never stirred as I eased the door open and left the anonymous flat. The London air was chill as I stepped on to the street.

I stretched my legs during the walk back to the hotel and started to warm to the idea of the hunt.

# 5

## Larkspur Fencing

When I got back to the Savoy, I took my time bathing and shaving. I pulled out the new suit I had gotten courtesy of Armistan. I'd had it pressed just for today. No point in driving a motorcar if you're not going to look your best. As an afterthought, I put the Colt in my small carryall. I felt good, healthy, and strong. For a moment, as I shrugged into my jacket, I felt young again. It made me want a cigarette, which caused me to remember the ominous words of the navy doctor who had put me back together after the Meuse.

"Griffin," he'd said, "somewhere along the line, you inhaled some gas, phosgene, if I had to guess. The chest wound and the leg wound look okay, ugly, but okay. But son, you got phosgene in your lungs. You probably won't live past forty. If you smoke, you'll be dead by thirty. I'm sorry, son."

Doc Watson was a cantankerous cuss, but he was a square guy. I took him at his word and quit smoking. What a miserable time that was. By then the war was pretty much over. If he'd told me the same thing after Belleau Wood, I'd probably have laughed and lit one up. Even with the war over, I didn't expect to reach forty, but thirty was just around the corner. Perhaps General Neville knew that I expected to go west[1] soon, and that was why he had recommended me to Armistan: a final favor for a former marine.

Whether I lived one year or another fifteen, today I was going for a drive in an automobile. I gave the bellman my name and told him I was expecting a car. My plan was to drive out to Weybridge and see Kingsbury's sister. My hope was that she might give me at least the whiff of a scent of where to find her brother and his bride.

The car was perfect. A 1917 Model T touring car. I believe it cost about $250 in the United States. With steel wheels, $260. The throttle was on the column and the gear shifter on the floor. Low gear toward me, high gear away, I reminded myself. Clutch pedal on the left, reverse in the center, brake on the right. Child's play. I smiled.

With the smell of leather and gasoline mingled, I struggled with the clutch and gears as I left the Savoy. The traffic in London was a brutal reminder of how little I had driven. Nevertheless, even though I was not a good driver, I thoroughly enjoyed the experience despite the shouted obscenities from the drays and carriages I blocked each time I stalled the engine. I hadn't really driven much since before the war, and even then, not on any consistent basis. The day was wonderful with the wind blowing through the cab and the bright sunlight warming the car's interior. I had to take off my hat to keep it from blowing out of the car.

Armistan had advised me that Sarah Kingsbury had a home outside London in one of the many small towns that dotted the river Thames to the west. The truth was, it would have been easier to take the train, but I planned on taking all day to get there by motorcar. Frankly, I wanted to do a little touring on Armistan's nickel.

As I left the Savoy, I turned right onto the Strand and crossed the Thames over Waterloo Bridge. From there, I just followed my nose south and west along the river. Since it was Sunday morning as I left the city, most people were off the roads, which was just as well because I was completely lost almost immediately after crossing the river. Once out of London proper, I did have to share the way with a few carriages, but for the most part, it was quiet and peaceful. Around noon, I ended up in a village called Balham. I stopped at a pub and had lunch. I had no choice but to ask directions before I set out again.

I folded my jacket onto the passenger seat, loosened my tie, and rolled up my sleeves, in effect, girding my loins for the remaining drive. Although I knew it wouldn't be dark for five or six more hours, I was starting to worry that I wouldn't get to Weybridge until after sunset. The last thing I wanted to do was knock on Sarah Kingsbury's door in the dark.

So armed with my new directions, I weaved my way more west than south with one small village running into the next, eventually reaching a bigger town with the reassuring name of Kingston on Thames.

In Kingston, I got directions from a one-legged veteran attended by his small daughter. I pulled up next to them as they walked through town. There were others out walking, but I stopped by the crippled young man on crutches and his child. I suppose he was the only one on the street with whom I knew I had something in common. When he saw me, there seemed to be a flicker of recognition in his eyes. For a brief, horrible instant, I thought I knew him, but the glint I saw in his eyes was acknowledgment not recognition. In me, in my disfigured face, he saw a brother-in-arms. His little fair-haired daughter smiled up at me as I stood by the car and asked for directions to Weybridge.

"Yank?" he asked before answering. I nodded, and he didn't seem to need any other information. He recommended that I cross the Thames to what he assured me was the west side of the river and cross back at the next bridge upriver at Hampton Court.

"That way you'll see King Henry's palace," his little daughter promised me solemnly.

"After you cross at the palace, turn right and follow the river," her father advised me. "You will come to Walton and shortly after that Weybridge."

I waved as I pulled away, pleased that I didn't stall the car. He'd get a wooden leg eventually. There were just too many others who needed them too. I thought about the way his daughter's small hand rested on his arm as he manipulated his crutches and about the strength in his pale blue eyes. Although I was tempted to pity him, I knew he neither needed nor wanted my pity. He had survived and was home. Home with his little girl, who was probably born the same year he went to the front. Home when so many others weren't. Home where he had something important, something valuable, something worth surviving for.

Not long after Kingston, I drove parallel to a long, high brick wall. I passed framed gateways into the grounds of the palace, and as I turned south and crossed the river, I could see the palace over my left shoulder. It seemed to me that the most striking feature of the place was the number of chimneys it had. It looked like there were hundreds, each with a different brickwork design. I slowed as I drove. Carriages and a motorcar rolled across the bridge with me. Up and down the river, couples and families strolled along the banks in the late-afternoon sunlight.

I turned west to follow the river away from the palace. The road seemed straighter than any since I had turned off the Strand, and I drove for some time with what looked like a levy rising on my left. I passed a sign that read SOUTHWARK AND VAUXHALL WATER COMPANY, and I remembered going through Vauxhall earlier in the day. I began to worry that somehow I'd backtracked, but shortly after the reservoir ended, I came to Walton.

By mistake, I had crossed the Thames and found myself in yet another small town, the name of which I didn't recognize from my earlier directions. I had to stop and ask for directions again. A preacher pointed me back across the bridge and to the right. I recrossed the bridge, and as I drove, trees and hedges crowded the narrow track running south and west. I knew the direction only because the setting sun was shining in my face. I had long ago lost any independent sense of direction. Generally, I have an extremely good sense of direction, but the English countryside had thoroughly defeated it.

Shortly after turning back along the river from Walton, I rolled into Weybridge, tired, grimy, and relieved. Realizing I would not make it back to London and the Savoy that night, I stopped at the first place that looked like it could put me up for the night: the Ship Inn, an old pub that had served as a recruiting depot for sailors during one of England's many wars with France. It stood on the north side of a small triangular green called the Bull's Ring after the old animal baiting days. At least that's what George Howell, the very friendly owner of the inn, told me. He gave me a room overlooking the green. As he handed me the key, I asked him if he knew where Sarah Kingsbury lived.

"No, no. Can't say I do." He looked over my shoulder as the door to the pub opened behind me. "Now I don't know her, but maybe Mr. Forester does." He nodded past me at a thin middle-aged man who had followed me into the pub. "Mr. Forester, do you know a Sarah Kingsbury who's supposed to live hereabouts?"

Forester ignored the innkeeper and looked at me.

"Is that your motorcar?" he asked sharply.

"I'm driving it, but it's not mine," I answered.

"Bloody nuisance," he said.

"Tough to argue with you there," I answered. "It would've been quicker to take the train." I gave a small smile. It would be dark soon, and I needed to know where Sarah Kingsbury lived. I didn't see any point in arguing with a Luddite about motorcars when he might have the information I needed. Also, after a day in the automobile, I was not nearly so enthusiastic as I had been that morning.

He stared at me as if weighing my sincerity and seemed to come to a decision.

"Do you know Sarah?" he asked with some skepticism.

"No sir, but I promised her family I'd look her up while I was here. And I try to keep my promises." I hoped that sounded enough like American frontier philosophy that he'd take me at my word.

Forester nodded. "Kingsbury..." He lingered over the name. "Yes, she lives in the Willoughby cottage across the Wey Bridge down beyond the lock. It's not too far. Stay on the road through town, and as it turns left up the hill, turn right. You will see the bridge in front of you. Cross the bridge and turn left at the lock. After that, just follow the road."

Unsure whether Sarah let the cottage from the Willoughbys or the name was another charming anachronism in a country riddled with them, I quickly forgot the appellation but not the directions.

After following Forester's advice, I was soon driving across the bridge. The road to the left was almost hidden on the far side, and I nearly drove past it. Only the quaint little lock warned me that the overgrown road was my turn. To stop in time to make the turn, I had to stomp on the brake. I forgot to clutch, and the engine died.

Rather than restart the engine, I let the car roll down the slope below the lock and steered it to the side of the road. After having wrestled with the car all day, I really wanted to walk. Unfortunately, the narrow dirt track wandered off through the woods roughly parallel to the river, and it had no end in sight. Reluctantly I restarted the automobile and drove down the trail. Shortly I came upon a narrow gravel pathway barred by a picket gate. There was just enough room to turn the car around. With the low sun reflecting orange off the high, fluffy white clouds, I had found my excuse to abandon Ford's contraption.

Although the town sat just across the bridge, I truly felt like I was out in the English countryside. A sluggish little stream ran beside the lane, and I washed my hands and face, shaking the water from my hands. I paused at the gate and felt an unaccustomed sense of well-being flow through me. The gate had no latch, and I pushed it open, hoping Sarah Kingsbury was not fond of large dogs. A dozen paces down the walk, I came to a small cottage with a thatched roof. Perhaps because of the description of Sarah I had gleaned from my inquiries on the *Mauritania*, I had expected something grander. I was pleasantly surprised to find a comfortable, welcoming little home. Larkspur and daisies intermingled with the strawberry and lavender that crowded around the red front door.

I used the old bronze knocker and waited. I knocked again, and I heard the pad of feet inside. I resisted the urge to peek through one of the small square windows set high in the stone on each side of the door.

A young woman pulled open the door. She was tall and slim with sandy-blond hair pulled back from the sharp angles of her face. She had that pale skin that thinly covers the bones and shows the veins underneath while still browning in the sun. Her wide-set gray-blue eyes were slightly surprised.

In seeing her, I was struck by the simple changes in women's clothing. Her skirt showed her bare feet and shapely ankles—a sight I would have been denied before the war. Despite having her hair pulled up in a tangle and a slight paint smudge on her chin, she was quite lovely. Over her blouse and skirt, she wore a large man's frayed white shirt mottled with paints of assorted colors.

Oils, I thought, as the smell of linseed oil and turpentine reached me. An odd perfume for a young woman, but I welcomed it. It reminded me of my mother, who would pull on one of Dad's old uniform shirts as a smock when she painted. Sarah Kingsbury had the same idea.

"Can I help you?" The words, said in a lovely English accent, were polite, but the tone was not. She no longer looked surprised, only annoyed.

"I hope so," I answered. "My name is John Griffin. Are you Sarah Kingsbury?"

She watched me for a few seconds, as if waiting for more. I waited with her, a hint of a smile on my face. Her sharp eyes studied me. She looked candidly from my eyes to my face to the new suit.

"In a manner of speaking," she finally answered.

I decided to press ahead despite her equivocal answer. "I'm trying to locate your brother."

"He is on his honeymoon; he was recently married."

"Yes, I know. His father-in-law, Harry Armistan, asked me to make sure he and his wife were all right. Apparently they've been missing for some time."

She showed no surprise. "Isn't that the idea of a honeymoon, to get away from the prying of families and family lackeys and to spend time alone together?" she asked.

"I wouldn't know, Miss Kingsbury. I've never been married. I just know that Mr. Armistan is a very worried father."

"Actually, my proper surname is Willoughby, and I do know the purpose of a honeymoon, having married Captain Willoughby." For a moment, I thought I caught a barely discernible twinkle in her eye. "I'm sorry, I can't help you. My brother is not here," she finished.

"Is Captain Willoughby in?" I asked, not willing to be put off. I looked over her shoulder into the cottage.

"No, I'm afraid he's not. He had the bad sense to get himself killed in France. Something about the premature detonation of a Mills bomb," she said unsympathetically.

"I'm very sorry to hear that, ma'am."

She waved a hand, dismissing my half-hearted condolences.

"He was something of an ass. Funny, he looked a bit like you. Not so big or rough around the edges, but he had the same air of unwarranted confidence." Her face softened into what I almost took for a smile.

"Unwarranted, Mrs. Willoughby? It seems to me I've never misjudged a Mills bomb," I said meanly.

She laughed, a light infectious sound, and I smiled.

"Well, you certainly misjudged something," she said as she looked pointedly at the scars on my face. For the first time, she looked at me with something approaching warmth.

Self-consciously I reached up and touched the ridges of the scar running into my eyebrow.

"I suppose I did. A woman really," I said truthfully. "And myself."

"Really?" she said with interest. "Well, Mr. Griffin. I get few visitors, and none are as forthright as you. Come in. But I warn you, I will do nothing to help you find my brother or sister-in-law for that odious little man, Armistan."

She backed away from the door, inviting me into the cool interior of the cottage. I stepped into the shade and followed her toward the rear of the house. She took off her makeshift smock and stretched up to hook it on an open door. As she stretched, I studied her figure under the light cotton blouse and skirt, and I felt a bit like a wolf in the chicken coop.

We walked through her home, and she tried to be civil.

"Are you staying in London then?" she asked.

"Yes, the Savoy."

"That's where Gavin and Tricia stayed," she answered.

"Yes, I'd hope to catch them there, but it seems they've moved on."

She led me into the kitchen, which overlooked a small, fenced garden.

"Have you met Gavin, Mr. Griffin?" she asked as she busied herself lighting a wholly unnecessary but cozy fire in the kitchen hearth.

"No. I never have. In fact, I hadn't met Mr. Armistan until after your brother and Patricia were married. Mr. Armistan was worried about his daughter and worried about your brother," I added as an afterthought. "He asked me to come over and make sure they were all right."

"Pardon me if I'm a little skeptical, Mr. Griffin. Somehow I doubt Harry Armistan cares a fig about my brother. And you hardly look like one of Armistan's groveling shop clerks."

"Mrs. Willoughby, if I may ask, you appear to dislike Mr. Armistan. Why is that?"

"Because he is a meddlesome little man who sees my brother as a useful tool and little more. He thinks because he is wealthy, he can have anything he wants." A slight flush rose to her cheeks. She pointed to a wicker-backed chair by a scarred wood table. I sat. She put water on to boil for tea, assuming, as the English always do, that tea was a necessary social lubricant.

"Have you known Mr. Armistan long?" I asked.

"Long enough to know he viewed Patricia as a possession, Gavin as an asset, and me as a potential conquest," she answered sharply.

"Pardon me?" I said with a disbelieving laugh. She gave me a hard look, and I cut off my laugh midbreath. I worried that I had just lost all the ground I'd gained with her, but if what she said was true, I found it hard to fault Armistan's taste. "I'm sorry, Mrs. Willoughby, I don't doubt your word, but as Patricia's father, I would have thought Mr. Armistan might consider himself a little old for you," I said as sincerely as I could.

"Well, he did not," she said haughtily. "He seemed to think that I would be flattered by his interest."

"I gather that you weren't?"

"He is a despicable little man who has only two favorable attributes that I have been able to find: he has a perfectly lovely daughter, and he can recognize talent when he sees it. My brother is a good example."

I wondered how Armistan would feel about that assessment.

"Did your brother know of Mr. Armistan's advances?" I asked.

"Mr. Griffin," she said in a tone that indicated the depth of the stupidity underlying my question, "I would not be so foolish as to tell my brother that his soon-to-be father-in-law made improper advances. The only possible result of such a conversation would be to cause unnecessary pain to two people I love very much. Armistan won't change simply because some snip of a girl or her brother confronts him about his conduct."

I found it hard not to smirk at her description of herself as a snip of a girl.

"Instead," she continued, "he would smoothly lie, causing my brother and Patricia confusion and doubt. I simply refused to allow that. Now, any other questions you may have must wait. You are my uninvited guest, and so you will have to answer my questions first." She waited for my assent.

I hesitated before I answered. "That will depend on the questions, Mrs. Willoughby."

Apparently my answer was agreement enough.

"I don't suppose old Harry's heart was acting up when you saw him?" she asked hopefully.

"I hate to disappoint you, but he seemed perfectly healthy when I last saw him," I said.

"When was that?" she asked.

"About two weeks ago."

"Damn!" She surprised me with the oath—another change brought by the war. "God has no trouble slaughtering millions of young men, but he can't seem to kill one randy old man with a heart condition," she concluded bitterly.

While I believed it a bit unfair to blame God for the killing that I saw only men do, I thought it best not to comment.

"You fought in the war, of course," she said with certainty.

"I'm an American. Why would you assume I fought in the war?" I asked.

"Well, aside from the frightful scar on your face," she said bluntly, "you're young enough, fit enough, and have the proper look in your eyes, all combined, of course, with the unwarranted air of confidence."

"Of course there is that unwarranted air," I said lightly, fearing where her questioning would lead. I was quickly learning that Sarah Willoughby was not bound by the fundamental social restrictions on polite conversations with strangers, and she said or asked whatever pleased her. I supposed that I'd waived any right to expect restraint or tact by appearing uninvited at her door.

"Tell me," she demanded as she leaned over me to pour my tea. "Are you a brave man, Mr. Griffin?"

I watched her pour, congratulating myself on restraining my natural desire to peek down her blouse, not thinking myself so much brave as virtuous for averting my eyes.

"No, Mrs. Willoughby. No, I'm really not," I answered honestly.

She looked up with interest. "What an odd admission for a man to make. Surely you know that as a veteran of the *Great War*, you must be brave, strong, and loyal," she said sarcastically.

"Just as you, as a young English matron, are gentle, nurturing, and kind?" I asked.

"Well, I suppose we are both disappointments." She laughed. "But I am very loyal," she said. "Very loyal. Milk?"

"Please."

"My brother is very brave. Perhaps the bravest man I know," she said with certainty. "Tell me, where did you fight, Mr. Griffin?" She asked the question as a challenge.

The interview was not going as I'd planned. But I found her intriguing, and, to my surprise, I found I wanted to talk to her—just not about the war.

"I didn't so much fight as survive," I said as I sipped my tea.

"My husband fought in Flanders," she said. "He would tell me of the most awful conditions there."

I hoped he hadn't been too graphic in his descriptions of the appalling physical conditions and the mental torture of life in the freezing, flooded trenches.

"Wait, don't answer! Let me think," she said, as if she were involved in some intriguing guessing game. "As an American, you must have fought in the Argonne Forest."

"I'm very impressed with your knowledge of American operations in France, but I didn't fight in the Argonne. How long have you lived here?" I asked, hoping to divert her from her chosen topic.

She ignored my question. "I need a hint. Are you sure you fought with the Americans?" She said it as a joke, but I felt my stomach turn over. It was time to put a quick end to her curiosity.

"I was a marine. An American marine. I fought at Belleau Wood, Soissons, where I was wounded. I returned to fight at Blanc Mont and the Meuse, where I was wounded again. That was in November," I said, hoping that would satisfy her.

"How long did you spend at the front?" she asked.

I found that I didn't want to lie to her, but I couldn't answer honestly without including my time in the British Army.

"Do you mean in quiet sectors, training with the French?" I asked, hoping for a better question to answer.

"No," she said decisively, "from the first battle you mentioned to the last, how long?" She watched me intently as if my answer were of great importance.

"June, July, August, September, October, and a little bit of November." I counted out the six hellish months on my fingers. "Part of that time, I was in hospital."

"Really six months?" she said. "James, my husband, served for three years and five months before he was killed. It almost doesn't seem fair that he would survive for so long only to die near the end. How could the bloody fool live so long only to die in the last month of the war?" It was clear from the heat of her words that she missed her dead husband.

I waited, not sure she wanted me to answer. She looked up from her tea.

"Is that one of your questions, Mrs. Willoughby?" I asked softly. "Because it happens to be one that I can answer."

53

She nodded.

"Your husband isn't to blame. Just unlucky."

She waited for me to continue, and I did.

"You know how unpredictable everyday life is," I said. "The unexpected rain shower, a random gust of wind, a stumble on an unnoticed root. Hell, even the lucky coin toss." I smiled. "Well, war is really just another aspect of life. With surprises too. Except all the repercussions are magnified. The rain postpones an attack. The gust of wind decides where a shell lands and who dies. It can decide the direction and spread of gas, the point of impact of a sniper's shot." I gestured to my temple. "The unplanned stumble can save you or kill you. The coin toss may decide who takes watch, who has watch where, who goes first, and ultimately who dies. There is no consideration for good, evil, need, hope, prayers, or often the skill of the soldier. I saw no divine plan as to who lived or who died. It was luck. Blind, indifferent luck, and when your time was up, your time was up. Your husband had three and half years of luck. That's a lot of luck. It just wasn't enough."

She watched me with large eyes.

"You seem to have learned a lot in such a short time at the front," she said, almost whispering.

"Oh, I had plenty of time to learn. A man at the front ages like a mayfly: every day a lifetime," I noted with a smile.

"Hah!" She barked out the laugh, and the somber mood was broken.

"Why are you helping Armistan?" she asked.

"Because I have nothing else to do, and I'm waiting for my luck to run out."

"You should find something different to do, Mr. Griffin," she said quietly. "Or I fear your luck just might."

I watched her as she spoke. I sensed that she wanted to say more, but she didn't.

"Tell me about your brother, Mrs. Willoughby," I said.

She studied me, considering my request. "He hated the war

from the very beginning. You can't imagine what it was like in England in 1914."

If you only knew, I thought.

"Everyone was ecstatic that we were finally going to fight the Hun. After decades of having the nerve to challenge British supremacy, old Fritz was going to get his comeuppance. Of course, we were all inflamed by their horrid treatment of Belgium. Honestly, you can't burn villages, rape nuns, and murder civilians and expect civilized people to ignore it."

I wondered if this was a thinly veiled rebuke of America's delayed entry into the war, but she continued without pausing to judge her comment's effect.

"I was always close to my brother, and we shared the same friends. My God, we were all so excited, so damned happy. It was disgusting. Frankly, I was as bad as the rest of our crowd."

She paused, looking inward at the memories, and so did I.

"The same people who'd been complaining against the government not a month before the war went out and enlisted the day it was declared. Our good sense just left us. It happened to everyone. Everyone except my brother. He didn't change a bit. He'd been against the government and the empire before the war, and he saw nothing in the start of the war to change his view. At first I thought he simply didn't appreciate what was happening. At the time, Germany seemed so evil. You must understand"—she looked at me, almost pleading—"everyone supported the war. Everyone knew we had to fight the Germans. It was the right thing to do."

I understood all too well.

"My brother was the only one who was unashamed of his opposition to it. We shunned him. Called him coward and mocked him. He bore it all without a foul word or complaint."

She stood and walked to the windows, looking out into her garden.

"Several girls and I actually gave him white feathers. He accepted them with great dignity. I remember, when he took mine, he smiled and shook his head. He said: 'I'm like Cassandra, Sarah. I see the future, but no one will believe me.'

"I hated him then. He seemed so smug in his certainty, acting sad, as if we were the ones who really didn't understand. He was impervious to the condemnation of our friends, our family, everyone he knew. Eventually he left for America. He didn't leave because of his ostracism. He left because he simply refused to fight, and by then the government had instituted universal call-up. He left before my wedding. But I think he knew I didn't want him to come. He was always sensitive to my needs."

She walked back to the table and cleared our now-empty cups.

"You see? My brother is the bravest person I know. I can't imagine resisting the tidal wave of pressure he must have felt. That's real bravery, not putting on a lieutenant's uniform like some brainless sheep and marching off to be slaughtered."

While I didn't doubt the moral courage of Gavin Kingsbury, it seemed that Sarah Willoughby was angry with her husband for not taking the same course. I found that I wanted to comfort this beautiful young widow, and I didn't like her anger at her dead husband with whom I sympathized.

"Mrs. Willoughby, during the war, how often did your husband come home on furlough?" I asked.

She looked at me with slightly knitted brows.

"How often?" I asked again.

"I don't know, several times, why?"

"Don't you think that after having been to the front, your husband knew the truth that your brother had predicted before the war? Because your husband lived it. Don't you think that each time he had to leave you he was crushed by the futility of it all and the inevitability of his death? Yet he was always brave enough to go back. He was as brave as your brother, braver, if you ask me. He kept returning out of loyalty to his men and his mates. To do that, to leave you, his beautiful young wife, time after time without any hope of survival, that's courage."

She turned to the sink in her cozy kitchen. "Is that how it was for you, so brave and loyal despite your earlier disclaimer?" she asked acidly over her shoulder but with tears in her voice.

I laughed out loud at the thought. "Not in the slightest. I had entirely different motivation."

Surprised by my reaction to her question, she turned back to me. "And what motivation was that?"

"That is not one of the questions I will answer," I said with a smile. "But I knew men like your husband and respected them. You should too."

"What is it you want from me, Mr. Griffin?"

"Honestly, I don't want much at all. I want to see your brother and Patricia and make sure they're all right. I don't want to interrupt their trip. Mr. Armistan is genuinely worried. No matter what you may think of him, I think he loves and cares about his daughter." I left out the slight detail of the missed London meeting and the valuable valise.

"I sincerely doubt that, Mr. Griffin, but I last saw them in London," she said. "I believe they'd decided to go to Germany instead of Italy. Although I think they'll get to Italy eventually. Gavin has some friends in Berlin from before the war. They were all against the Kaiser, but I think that some of them succumbed to the same madness that swept England. Some died in the war. I'm not sure where Gavin and Patricia will stay, but if I know Patricia, it will be as nice a place as they can find."

Wonderful, I thought. Germany.

"I don't know much more than that," she finished.

"Thank you. And thank you for the tea and allowing me to intrude," I said as I stood.

"Do you have plans for dinner, Mr. Griffin?" she asked quickly. A slight blush crept up her neck. "I don't often have visitors, and when I do, they are never as refreshing as you have been. I'd be pleased if you could stay."

"Mrs. Willoughby, you've been more than kind already," I said, despite wanting to stay.

"I'm a fine cook, and I've some fresh vegetables from my garden."

I hesitated briefly, listening to my better side futilely argue for an immediate retreat.

"I would love to stay, but I have certain conditions." She raised her eyebrows expectantly. "First, I help you cook and clean up, and second, we don't talk about the war anymore."

She gave a relieved smile. "Fine. You can cut the onions."

# 6

---

## Unwelcome Guests

As I'd asked, we spoke no more of the war but instead shared stories of our childhoods. Whenever she spoke of Gavin, it was clear that growing up she loved and respected him. I felt like a scoundrel for listening to her private memories of a brother I was hunting, but I ignored the feeling and enjoyed what turned out to be a very good meal of steamed fresh vegetables, a pheasant stuffed with sausage, and a good bottle of light white wine.

As we ate, Sarah told me of the itinerant life that she and Gavin shared. They had moved back and forth between England and the Continent, sometimes Switzerland, sometimes France or Italy. It sounded like her father was some sort of banker. Like her brother, she was fluent in several languages, but unlike her brother, she appeared to be apolitical except for her extreme contempt for all forms of patriotism. In 1912, her family had settled permanently in London, and tragically, the next year both her parents died. She had grown quite attached to Gavin until his "inexplicable stubbornness" about the war.

I found that my time with her was well spent. I'd learned a lot about her brother and a lot about her.

Finally it grew late, and Sarah showed me to the front door of the cottage. As I turned back to say goodbye, she stepped forward and kissed me on the cheek, giving me a brief hug. I smiled down at her, still smelling the scent of her hair.

"Good night, Mrs. Willoughby," I said.

"Shh, my name is Sarah, John," she said.

I found I was oddly pleased she had remembered my first name from my original introduction.

"Of course. Sarah, good night."

"Should you happen to visit Surrey in the future, John, you're always welcome here for tea," she said, seeming to enjoy the sound of my name.

"I'll remember that," I promised, "and if you happen to be in London, I'm at the Savoy, remember."

I left her in the doorway. As I walked down the darkened garden to the wooden gate, I found myself enjoying thinking about Sarah Willoughby.

Down the path, I could see the deeper shade of the car on the road below outlined against the hedges. Something about the silhouette made the skin on my forearms and the back of my neck prickle. Without breaking stride, I scanned the outline of the car, searching for movement. I wished for the Colt in my bag back at the pub.

As I reached the driver's door, a shape rose from the front of the car. I sensed a second person behind me. Ignoring the natural urge to run like hell, I rushed the man in front. I saw a flash of steel in his right hand. I kicked out with my hard-toed shoe, and I felt the tip strike the bone in his shin or knee. He screamed. I swung a hard overhand right punch into the center of his shadowy face. I felt and heard bone snap, whether in my hand or his face, I wasn't sure. At the same time, I felt a sharp tearing along my left arm. I stepped past him, hoping to put some space between me and the man behind me. Instead, a hand grabbed my

60

collar, and I was pulled backward. I spun around, sweeping my left arm between my body and the man behind me. I pinned his knife hand against the body of the car, and I threw an ineffectual elbow into the side of his head. His knee exploded into my hip. He was aiming for my groin.

"Bugger," he hissed.

I started to panic at the thought of his friend somewhere behind me. I snapped my head forward, headbutting him, once, twice. He gasped in pain. My left arm was on fire, but it remained wedged against his, pressing to hold the knife from me. Realizing he was eventually going to work the knife free, I grabbed his ear with my right hand and spun him toward the front of the car. I heard a tear and felt a tug along my suitcoat as the man behind me stabbed down at me. The two men collided. The second man fell against the bonnet of the car, and I punched the first under the ribs. I heard the breath rush out of him, and I hit him again. He stumbled and fell to the ground. The second man started to rise off the car, and I kicked him as hard as I could in the side. He tumbled off the hood, dropping his knife. The first came off the ground with his head down and his knife forward. My knee took him in the face at the cost of a slash across my leg. I hooked my elbow into the side of his head and punched down into his face again and again, feeling my knuckles split as they bounced off bone. Suddenly my head seemed to explode, and I fell back into the car. I tried to get my hands up to protect myself.

"John," I heard Sarah call from the garden walk, and I saw her framed in the weak light of an oil lamp she carried in her hand.

Terror surged through me. I pushed off the car and rammed my attacker backward.

"Sarah, get to the house and lock your door," I shouted.

Both men were up, but I could see only one knife. I glanced back toward the cottage. Sarah's slim figure stood in the open gate.

"Damn." I heard one of the men hiss. They both turned and

ran through a break in the hedges. I fell back against the car. Sarah rushed over.

"Are you all right?"

"This is a tough neighborhood. You ought to be in the house," I said, gently prodding the side of my head with my fingers.

"I'm not leaving you out here," she said firmly. She pulled me off the motorcar and moved me toward the path.

"I hope you've got good locks, Mrs. Willoughby," I said softly.

"My locks are fine, and so is my husband's shotgun," she said calmly.

"Now that's a reassuring thought," I said as I stumbled after her.

I waited by the front door as Sarah slid home the large iron bolt, and again, I followed her through the house to the kitchen. I was conscious of the blood dripping from my forearm and leg, and out of a misplaced sense of politeness, I tried not to drip anywhere.

"Damn," I swore as we entered the kitchen. Sarah moved over to inspect my wounds.

"No, no." I tried to wave her off. "Look at what those bastards did to my suit. Say what you want about Harry, but he buys a fine suit. I think this one is ruined," I said as I fingered the rent in the sleeve. I looked up at Sarah and saw her staring at me with a sort of stunned curiosity.

"I apologize for my language, but it's the first nice suit I've owned since before the war," I said defensively. The burning in my arm and leg demanded my attention.

I peered through the rip in my sleeve and saw a long, straight slash through the meat on the underside of my left forearm. Then I looked at the wound, more of a vee-shaped tear, in my leg. Both were bleeding freely, and I found myself performing a rather curious juggling act, trying to keep the blood off Sarah's kitchen floor. Damn they hurt.

"I don't suppose you have any alcohol, a needle, thread, and a bit of clean linen you won't miss, do you?" I asked.

She opened a cabinet in the kitchen and produced a bottle of rum. She then hurried from the room only to reappear with the needle, thread, and linen.

"Any experience as a nurse?" I asked hopefully.

"Not a bit," she said emphatically.

I poured some rum on a bit of cloth and pressed it into the wound on my arm, tying the cloth in place with a strip of linen. In order to appear properly stoic and manly, I managed to avoid crying out or, for that matter, crying.

"Can you tear me some more?" I asked.

I rolled up my pant leg and poured rum directly on the leg wound. The pain was incredible but endurable. Fortunately, no big veins were cut or bones broken. Thank God for small mercies.

Sarah watched me closely, not offering to help after tearing several strips of linen.

"All right," I said with what I hoped was a touch of humor, "as an English lady, you must be able to sew."

"Oh no!" she said with more than just a little horror.

"Look, I'll sew up the one on my leg, but I really can't do the one on my arm."

She shook her head without answering.

"Would you mind threading the needle?" I asked as sweetly as I could. I continued to press my makeshift compress into the leg wound.

I was surprised to find that I took a certain masochistic pleasure in the thought that I was going to have to sew myself up. Growing up, my father had told me a story about my grandfather, who was a notorious alcoholic and womanizer. Despite his negative attributes, he was in the words of my father "one tough old son of a bitch, mean too." I always wondered how much of his toughness and meanness were the result of the bottle. As my father told the story, my grandfather, after a rather vicious fistfight with a neighbor, found himself with his lip split almost to his gum line. As a country doctor with few friends, he had no choice but to sew it up himself, which he did, much to my grandmother's dismay, before the mirror in the family parlor.

I'd always wondered if I'd have the guts to do the same. Of course, I never considered until now that my grandfather was very likely drunk at the time he did it. With that in mind, I picked up the bottle of rum and took a healthy swig directly from the bottle.

I struggled to keep the rum down, gagging at the memories that the taste of the drink brought back. The tot of rum poured from the earthen jar as the lieutenant and the company clerk looked on. A jar labeled RUM D. S. Eight ounces per man served before going over the top. It brought back memories of a fatalistic terror that death and dismemberment were inevitable yet unpredictable certainties.

After winning the fight with my stomach, I soaked the needle and thread in rum. Then I pressed the bleeding lips of the leg wound together and began to sew, the tiny prick of the needle almost unnoticeable against the burning of the alcohol and of the wound itself.

As I finished, Sarah took a swig of rum, poured some onto her hands, and rubbed them together. She gently pushed my hand away and tied off a knot on my rough stitching. She rethreaded the needle and began to sew up my arm.

By the time she finished, I was feeling light-headed. She bound up both the leg and arm.

"I'm going to cut off your clothes so you don't have to disturb the bandages when you undress," she declared.

"Why would I want to undress?" I asked.

"You certainly can't go anywhere in the clothes you're wearing, and I doubt very much you're fit enough to go anywhere anyway."

"This must be part of your conspiracy to keep me from finding your brother," I said weakly. For just a second, her hands stopped moving as she cut the shirt from my back.

"Nonsense. People are poor, dissatisfied, and the war

suspended their ordinary respect for authority, and I suppose Americans are as likely targets for assaults these days as any foreigners."

I watched her face, noticing for the first time the almost purple flecks in her irises. I wondered briefly if it was a guilty conscience that caused her hesitation. I certainly didn't want to believe that she was an accomplice in the attack. I didn't really see how she could have been, considering that there was no telephone, and since arriving at her house, I'd spent every moment in her company.

She cut away my clothes, leaving me in my undershorts. If she were part of a conspiracy to prevent my finding her brother, I was truly in trouble.

She threw my clothes in a waste bin by the back door and left only to return with a blanket and a second pile of clothing. I said a mental farewell to the suit Armistan's money had bought.

"Here," she said as she wrapped the coarse wool around my shoulders. I thanked her, thinking that the room had grown quite cool.

She looked down at me slumped in her kitchen chair.

"Mr. Griffin," she said formally, "judging by your well-used skin, you appear to have fought in two wars, not just one." I followed Sarah's eyes to my chest where the pink scarring caused by the Meuse River shrapnel wounds showed vividly even in the dim light of her kitchen.

Knowing that the truth is best hidden when openly acknowledged with good humor, I laughed weakly.

"If you only knew," I said, secure in the belief that she in no way accepted that possibility.

"Frankly, I don't see how you survived," she finished.

I pulled the blanket around me. "Mrs. Willoughby, as a man who often but not always considers himself a gentleman, I have a delicate and difficult favor to ask..." I waited for at least some tacit approval before I continued.

"What could possibly be more delicate than sitting in my kitchen all but naked, Mr. Griffin?" she asked.

"Well, ma'am, that's exactly it. I honestly don't want to have to try to change into your husband's clothes and drive back to the pub tonight. Is it possible for me to sleep here in the kitchen? Please don't feel obligated to say yes," I rushed to add.

"John, you are welcome to stay. My reputation is already so blemished I have nothing to fear from your remaining," she answered.

She really was a very beautiful woman.

In truth, I was afraid to go back out into the night. The possibility that the two men remained outside waiting was too daunting a prospect. Also, I wanted to try to learn a little more about Gavin, which was a self-deceiving way of saying I wanted to learn a little more about Sarah. I felt an indescribable attraction, a truly magnetic pull. I'd felt that magical tug since she'd answered her door. I couldn't remember ever being more entranced by a woman. I thought of my puerile longing for Evelyn. That pull, while certainly very real, was not the same sort of primal need I felt for Sarah Willoughby. Despite the pain of my wounds, my stomach rolled at the thought of touching her.

She left the room and returned with an over/under shotgun that looked to be a 12-gauge. With an interesting glint in her eye, her experienced hands broke it open and she checked the loads. Satisfied, she closed it and leaned it against a cupboard across from the fireplace.

"If we need it," she said as she turned toward me.

"You know what you're doing," I stated.

"Yes, shotgun or rifle. I've been shooting most of my life," she explained.

I shifted in my seat and knocked my newly bandaged leg into the kitchen table. The sudden agony, if not the shotgun, sobered me from my romantic reverie.

"Come," she said, reaching down with a helping hand. "You can sleep on the couch in the parlor."

I stood and shuffled after her.

Unfortunately, Sarah would speak no more that night. She insisted, quite reasonably, that she was exhausted.

I was exhausted too.

Shortly after she bedded me down on the parlor couch, I drifted off to sleep. It was a troubled sleep, and in the very early morning, I jerked awake. Whether I woke because of some unremembered dream or because I was sleeping in an unfamiliar place, I wasn't sure. I winced as I pulled Sarah's blanket off my legs. I stood and picked up the clothing Sarah had brought me. I pulled on the trousers and a shirt. Her husband's clothing fit well enough. With my shoes in my hand, I padded through the house in my stocking feet, looking for what woke me. I'll admit I hoped to run into Sarah. I searched the small house and found her bedroom, the door ajar. The room was empty, the bed unslept in. I wondered if Sarah's leaving had woken me.

I dismissed the thought. She had to be around the house somewhere.

"Sarah," I called softly.

I stepped into the kitchen. The shotgun remained leaning against the cupboard. I glanced through the back window into the garden. A shadow flickered through the yard more imagined than real. My heart began to pump uncomfortably fast. I saw a second shadow move in the moonlight. Quickly I stepped over to the shotgun, picked it up, and moved deeper into the house. Out of habit, I checked the loads and moved into the hallway off the parlor. I found myself worrying that the shells were bird shot, which wasn't likely to stop anyone determined to come in the house.

I waited in the hallway. I reviewed in my mind Sarah's form and height. It's poor form, even for a coward, to shoot one's hostess.

If nothing else, I had learned patience in the war. After seeing the second shadow, I was certain someone had been in the garden, moving toward the house. I ignored the aches in my arm and leg and held the shotgun across my body.

I heard a distinct whistle, and then boots hammered simultaneously into the front and back doors. The front door gave way first, followed shortly by the back. I took a deep breath to steady myself. With my back to the front wall, I peered around the doorjamb toward the front door. A large shadow appeared. It looked to be pointing a pistol at the couch where I'd slept. A second shadow appeared in the kitchen doorway. I held very still. I was in trouble if he could distinguish my shadow from the darkness of the hallway.

"Where is he?" one of them hissed.

Without warning, the shape by the kitchen door raised its arm toward me. More on instinct than thought, I dropped into a crouch and raised the shotgun. I felt the stitches in my leg tug, and I hoped the wound hadn't reopened.

With a stunning roar and flash, which outlined the three of us, he fired a pistol at me. The wood doorframe above me splintered, and I fired one barrel into his shadow. He fell back into the kitchen door. The deafening blast of repeated pistol shots roared through the room as the first man fired into the hallway where I hid. I felt more than heard the bullets slam into the wall near me. I fired a second time. The roar in the enclosed space was almost a physical blow. The blast knocked the man from his feet. I hobbled across the room, looking for a pistol. I found one by the kitchen door. On the darkened floor, neither man moved.

I stepped over the body in the kitchen doorway, and I found Sarah's abandoned lamp and a match. I lit the lamp and turned to see that I'd made an awful mess of Sarah's house. Both men were unmistakably dead. Judging by their wounds, Sarah was not a bird hunter. I couldn't be sure if these were the same men who had attacked me earlier. I was able to examine the face of one body. It might have been bruised, but I couldn't be certain. The shotgun blast to the chest or the subsequent fall might have caused what little evidence I found. To the extent I could without stepping in the blood pooling under them, I checked their bodies and hands for evidence of a fight, but I found nothing conclusive.

Looking down at the men, I was struck by two things: first, the incongruity of two gruesomely dead bodies in a tidy English cottage; and second, the utter lack of remorse I felt at their deaths. These men hadn't been soldiers fighting for the Kaiser. Yet in Sarah's quaint little home, I had cut them down without hesitation. The war had diminished me. It had winnowed out all superfluous notions and emotions, changing me from a gentleman to an animal. I shook my head and pushed those thoughts from my mind. Careful not to step in the blood, I took the time to put on my shoes.

Magnetic attraction to Sarah or not, I had the uncomfortable feeling that she hadn't been completely honest with me. She had left the house for a reason, leaving me alone and exposed to the killers. I found that I didn't want to be in the house when she came home. I suspected that she wouldn't be alone. With the empty shotgun in one hand and a dead man's pistol in the other, I limped through the house, searching each room. I found a second pistol by the front door and more shotgun shells in a hall cabinet. I filled my pockets and reloaded the shotgun.

I had a rushed sensation of time closing in on me. The nightmare I'd been dreaming since taking this job threatened to come true. If the English authorities found out that these men were dead, at this place, and if they talked to Howell at the pub, which was likely, they would hunt for me. I couldn't let that happen. Images of English newspapers describing an American named John Griffin swam through my panicked mind. I would hide the bodies and clean the house as well as I could. It didn't matter that I killed these men in self-defense. If my name ended up in the English papers, all the people I didn't want to know about me would read in their morning newspaper that I'd returned to England.

I looked at my watch. Three thirty. If Sarah didn't return before dawn, I would have time. If she was an accomplice to my attempted murder, my hope was that she wouldn't return tonight because she would want her friends to have time to dispose of my body.

I limped through the broken front door and out to the motor-car. No one jumped from the shadows. After several nerve-racking minutes, I got the car started and pulled it up next to the path leading to the front door. Back in the cottage, in the tiny bathroom, I found an armload of towels. Using the towels, I wrapped the wounds, one man's head and the second man's torso. With the extra towels, I wiped the walls and floor clean of the most obvious blood and tissue.

I found a second blanket. Using it and my sleeping blanket, I cocooned both bodies and, one at a time, dragged them out to the car, careful to use my left arm as little as possible. I went back into the house and found a mop and bucket in the kitchen pantry. Taking my time, I mopped the wood floors from the parlor to the front of the house. I dumped the water bucket on Sarah's straw-berries. After muscling both bodies into the back of the car, I put the bucket and the mop on top of the stacked bodies.

Then I went back through the house with the lamp in one hand and a clean damp towel in the other. I forced myself to work methodically, making sure that other than the splintered door jamb and the shotgun pellets in the plaster wall, nothing remained of the brief gunfight. Satisfied with my cleaning, I dug through Sarah's trash for my old clothes, picked up the shotgun, and went out the front door, pulling it shut on its splintered frame as best I could.

After putting the clothes and the gun on the front seat, I walked out past the car and looked for some edging stones that I could pull free without it being too obvious. I piled four large stones on the floor of the passenger side of the car. I blew out the lamp and turned back toward the cottage. In the moonlight, it looked serene and peaceful.

I drove down the hill back toward town. As quietly as I could with the motorcar running, I stopped in front of the pub and used my key to open the front door. Taking the stairs two at a time, feeling warm blood trickling down my leg, I hurried up to my room and grabbed my still-packed bag. I quickly opened it, tossed in both new pistols, and pulled the Colt from the bottom of the carryall. I dropped a five-pound note and the key on the bed, and without a backward look, climbed down the steps for the drive back to London.

I needed to find Mitchell. He'd be in London, waiting for me. He'd know what to make of Sarah Willoughby and her deceased houseguests.

But first I had to find a bridge over a nice, deep river.

# 7

## Bangers and Bruises

Mitchell was to meet me in Trafalgar Square, next to the lion under Nelson's remaining arm. Although that plan had seemed melodramatic when Mitchell had proposed it via telegram, after my experience in the Surrey countryside, I was glad that he had suggested we meet in a public place rather than at the hotel. Mitchell had chosen Trafalgar Square because it was an easy, central location. He was supposed to be there at one in the afternoon. Although exhausted from my early-morning adventures, I had returned to the Savoy only to drop off the motorcar. I didn't stay for fear of more of Sarah's friends. I had wandered the West End of London until it was near the time to meet. I was as jumpy as a cricket as I limped toward the square.

I was early, but as I walked through the fluttering pigeons, I saw Mitchell leaning on the wall supporting the left front lion, his hat pulled down over his eyes, a cigarette dangling from his lips. He had already seen me, which was, of course, why he was waiting by the wrong lion. He had the same big, crooked grin I remembered.

"Black Jack Griffin!" He shouted the unwelcome nickname as

he pushed off the granite toward me. He knew Pershing was not a general I respected, but few were.

"It's been a long time, Will," I said as we shook hands. And it had been.

"Yes, it has. You're still a big ugly bastard. How do you feel? 'Cause you look terrible."

"Then I look better than I feel," I answered, my heart slowing.

He laughed.

"Come on, we have a lot to talk about. Where's your bag?" I asked.

"Let's go get something to eat," he suggested. "Left my bags at Charing Cross. I'll send for them once I get to where we're staying. Is it the Savoy?"

"Maybe. There's a pub just over by the church." I nodded toward St Martin's. "They'll have something to eat, and I can tell you what I know."

"Is that a new limp, Griff?" Mitchell asked.

"Yes, it is. I'm afraid I might need a little of your sewing," I answered with what I hoped was a brave smile.

Mitchell looked over at me. "Seriously?" he asked.

"'Fraid so."

"Are you sure it can wait, John?"

"Yup. Come on."

We walked across the square and crossed between the carriages and speeding black taxis. The pub was relatively quiet. It seemed like the wartime hours had taken their toll on afternoon drinking. As far as I knew, pubs still closed from two p.m. to five p.m. and had to shut down by eleven at night.

"Pint of bitter?" Will asked.

I nodded. "And steak-and-kidney pie."

I took a seat at a corner table, and Mitchell went to the bar and ordered two pints, my food, and a ploughman's lunch with an order of bangers. The barkeep pulled our pints, and Mitchell brought them to the table.

"Cheers," he said. We touched glasses and drank. "Okay, tell me what's going on."

"Did you bring a gun?" I asked in a hushed voice.

"Damn, Griffin!" he scoffed. "You've been in this country for less than a week. Why the hell should I need a gun?"

"Did you bring a gun?" I asked again.

Mitchell met my look and smiled. "One or two."

I explained to Mitchell what I'd learned from Armistan and that he wanted us to find his daughter and his black valise. Then I described my visit to the English countryside.

"I went out to see the sister, Sarah, west of London. Pretty girl by the way. I ran into trouble. I think she sent it my way."

"John, my good friend," Mitchell said, "she didn't need to send trouble after you. You're a magnet for it." He sipped his beer. The barkeep brought the food, and Mitchell forked a bite of Stilton cheese closely followed by a piece of sausage into his mouth. "Well, hell, tell me what happened," he demanded through a mouth stuffed with food.

As he ate, I finished detailing my visit with Sarah Willoughby. I left out the part about my physical and emotional attraction to her, hoping Mitchell would accept my objective assessment of the visit more easily without the addition of what was in my view, unnecessary information.

When I'd finished, Mitchell nodded. He was entirely undaunted by the fact that I'd already killed two men and been attacked by possibly another two.

"Would you recognize the men if you saw them again?"

"Which ones? The dead ones, probably," I answered sarcastically, "but I doubt we'll see them. Them being dead with rocks in their pants and a river over their heads." The pain of the knife wounds was making me irritable.

"Whoa, sorry. What I mean is, do you think the guys you killed were the guys who beat the tar out of you in front of your lover's house?"

"I never said they beat the tar out of me," I said quickly. "And Sarah is not my lover."

He waved my protests away with his fork. "Sure, sure, just like you never said you think Mrs. Willoughby is a lot more than just a *pretty girl*." He laughed.

I laughed with him. "Yeah, I suppose I didn't say exactly how attractive she is, did I? I don't know if the men who attacked me at the motorcar were the same ones I killed in Sarah's house. I hope so, but I don't know." There was one question that I was reluctant to ask Mitchell, but I wanted some confirmation that Sarah Willoughby was not some sort of human black widow slaughtering prospective mates. "Why do you think she left the gun for me?"

As he took a drink, Mitchell looked over the rim of his pint glass at me. "She probably liked you," he answered. "I hope that makes you happy. She didn't want to kill you outright. Hey, you two might have a future."

"I knew I shouldn't have asked."

"Well," Mitchell said, "I'll just have to go to Weybridge and see what sort of hornet's nest you've stirred up."

"I'm not sure that's a good idea. If they find the bodies, any American will be suspect. They might just decide to search you, and if they find a gun, you're in deep trouble."

"Look, John, I won't bring a gun. I'll stop and buy a nice, sturdy umbrella. Hell, I'll pretend I'm a Spaniard. And I'm not half as ugly as you, so there's no chance I'll be confused for the American who was sleeping with Mrs. Willoughby," he finished.

I felt my face flush. "All right. That should work. Don't take the motorcar though. Take the train."

"I can't even drive. Why the hell would I want to take a godforsaken automobile anywhere?" He drained his pint and stood. "But did I mention that I've learned to fly?" He laughed at the look on my face. "We need to go to your hotel so that I can look at your scrapes."

I looked up sharply at the description of my knife wounds as "scrapes."

"I'll get my things sent there," he continued with a smile, completely aware of my outrage at his description of my wounds. "If there's anything else we need, we should be able to get it in London, and as I said, I'm going to want a good, sturdy umbrella."

Although I was reluctant to return to the hotel, I couldn't muster the energy to suggest that we find a new one. With a groan, I pulled myself out of the chair. The cuts, bruises, and sleepless night had taken their toll, and I wasn't looking forward to more stitches.

"I know you can find an umbrella in this town," I said. "Learned to fly, huh? I never would have guessed you'd do that."

He laughed as we pushed through the door into the afternoon sunlight.

<hr />

LATE THE NEXT MORNING, MITCHELL INSISTED I ACCOMPANY HIM to buy that sturdy umbrella. Somehow he knew of an establishment called Brigg & Sons, located in Covent Garden. Mitchell picked over the canes and umbrellas in the shop the way my mother used to pick over fruit. The poor shopkeeper was confused by the fact that Mitchell never actually wanted to open the umbrellas. He kept trying to tell Mitchell how to operate each one he picked up.

Their interaction developed into a kind of comic dance. Mitchell would comment, "I need a heavier one." The shopkeeper, clearly never having heard that a heavy umbrella was better than a lighter umbrella, would say something like, "Sir, I assure you that these umbrellas, despite their light weight, are quite sturdy. For example..." He would start to open the umbrella, and Mitchell would turn away, continuing his hunt through the various umbrellas and canes on display.

Mitchell didn't really want an umbrella at all. What he wanted was a good stick that he could carry around without appearing to be carrying a good stick. I'd asked him why he didn't just buy a sturdy cane, and he had insisted that canes were a ridiculous affectation that should only be carried if truly needed. I didn't think it prudent to mention that carrying an umbrella on a cloudless day was a ridiculous affectation even if one was in rainy England.

While he shopped, Mitchell began to tell me one of his outlandish stories. He was in the habit of routinely telling outrageous lies with a straight face. Then when I would doubt him, he would get mad. In this story, he was describing his study of the secret art of Filipino stick fighting.

Mitchell's father had been a navy doctor, and his family had spent nearly seven years in the Philippines. So the story had at least a kernel of truth. Will had been young but not too young to learn to fight, according to him.

It sounded absurd to me, but I'd seen him in a brawl before, and there was no doubt he could more than hold his own. Being accustomed to his stories that often began with the most ridiculous statements like, "While growing up, I routinely smoked opium with Chinamen," I nodded at the right spots as he spoke and tried to relax into the shop's leather armchair. While Mitchell's tending my various "scrapes" was helpful, I still needed rest.

"Escrima, that's what the Filipinos call stick fighting. Now, there are many different styles. Almost as many styles as teachers. Illustrisimo, caballero... I only had the opportunity to study actual stick fighting for a year. Our houseboy's uncle knew a great master, and he agreed to take me for training."

By this time, the shopkeeper merely followed Mitchell through the store without comment, a frozen half smile on his face as Mitchell twirled and twisted his umbrellas.

"Master Rodriguez stressed body placement and movement," Mitchell continued.

Despite the trance into which I'd fallen, I couldn't help a snort of disbelief at hearing Mitchell sincerely claim training by "Master Rodriguez." I don't think Mitchell noticed.

"The trick," he continued, "is to correctly judge the distance between you and your opponent." He raised an umbrella in his fist. The shopkeeper's smile disappeared, and he began to look alarmed. "And you've got to cross that distance at the right time and in the right manner." Mitchell flowed forward, rapping an imaginary opponent on the head.

I closed my eyes.

"Aha!"

I looked up. Mitchell was holding what had to be the ugliest umbrella in the shop. It was thick and heavy, and unlike many of the umbrellas in the store, there was absolutely nothing graceful about it. It had a black handle, and the tip was shod in metal.

"This will do," he said as he swished it through the air. "Mahogany?" he asked the clerk.

"Yes, sir."

"I'll take it." The proprietor looked distinctly relieved as Mitchell counted the purchase price into his palm.

Mitchell twirled the umbrella once more as I stood, and we stepped out onto the sidewalk.

"John, I'll go straight on to Weybridge," Mitchell said, lighting a cigarette. "No point in waiting for the trail to grow cold. You ought to go back to the hotel and get some rest."

"I like the sound of that," I said weakly. As he turned toward Charing Cross Station, I called out, "Be careful."

Without turning back to me, he waved a hand in the air as he jauntily stuck the tip of his umbrella into the pavement, treating it very much like a cane.

# 8

### Goose Feather Shower

I went back to the hotel, undressed, and stretched out on the bed. Mitchell wouldn't be back for at least a day, and I felt too worn out to do anything else. I tried to sleep, but the disturbing feeling that I'd forgotten something important prevented sleep from coming. Finally, in frustration, I pulled the Colt from the bottom of my suitcase where I'd stowed it and pushed it under my pillow. Eventually I drifted off.

When I woke, it was dark outside. I'd been dreaming of Sarah, which was quite a nice dream. Then I dreamed of Sarah's house without Sarah, which was not a nice dream.

I picked my watch off the nightstand and read the luminous hands, the dim light coming through the room's window offering little help. Four in the morning.

The disturbing feeling had returned. It was the dream. And it was not the dream. I heard Sarah asking, "Are you staying in London then?" And my answer, "Yes, at the Savoy."

Suddenly I realized I'd been an idiot to return to the Savoy. I'd told Sarah where I was staying. If she truly wanted me dead, all she had to do was send her thugs to the Savoy. They would describe me to the concierge, and they would find me. My heart began to race, and I started to sweat. Quickly I dressed. I left the light off and stumbled around the room, packing my bag. I pushed the .45 into my belt and sat on the bed to pull on my shoes.

I stopped. What was I thinking? Nothing Sarah had said or done showed that she wanted to hurt me. Yes, but someone wanted me gone, and just because it might not be Sarah, she might have told someone about my visit. Obviously, someone knew. Gavin, perhaps. No, I told myself. I was jumping at shadows. The men in Surrey were in Surrey. They'd be looking in Surrey. No one was hunting me at the Savoy.

I almost lay back on the bed, but at that moment, shadows broke the light coming under the door, and a second later a heavy blow landed on the wood around the knob, and at a second blow, the door splintered open. I got a quick glimpse of the shadowy figures in the doorway. I felt a rush of fear, and with one shoe on and one shoe off, I kicked myself backward, somersaulting over and behind the bed.

Gunshots exploded into the room. I felt bullets slap into the bed and the wall behind me, goose feathers erupting from the bedclothes and slivers from the headboard slicing the air as they zipped past my ear. I looked under the bed, and past the bed skirt, I saw three sets of feet outlined by the light of the hallway. I pulled the .45 from my belt and racked the slide. I fired through the bed skirt, the boom and flash of the Colt almost deadening my senses. A man screamed and fell to the floor, thrashing. The bed sagged as one intruder jumped onto it. Without looking, I raised the Colt over the edge of the bed and fired twice. I'd be damned if I'd die under a goddamn bed. A third man stepped around the end of the bed, and we fired simultaneously. I felt his shot pass by my face. Blindly, I fired again.

Beyond the foot of the bed, one man sat in a crumpled, boneless heap against the wall, a German broomhandle Mauser automatic pistol clutched in his hand. Even in the relative darkness of the room, there was no doubt he was dead. With my numbed ears, I tried to listen for movement in the room, but there was only the whimpering and ragged breathing of the first man who fell. I could hear distant shouts from beyond my doorway but no other sounds. I stood. A second man lay sprawled across my bed. His blood was in the process of staining the sheets and mattress.

I found my other shoe and pulled it on. It took a little time to tie with shaking hands. I pushed the Colt behind my belt and picked a Mauser up off the floor, a red *nine* carved in its wooden handle. I stepped to the door and peered out. There was no movement yet.

The third man whimpered on the floor, cradling his right leg, which was shattered just above the ankle. I was surprised he wasn't shrieking. He would be soon enough.

"Don't kill me," he begged in a hysterical whisper. "Please don't kill me."

It seemed like the shouts from beyond the door grew louder, but it was difficult to tell after the deadening thunder of the gunshots.

It didn't matter. I couldn't take the chance of being questioned by the English authorities. I would not be. The chance of recognition was too great.

I crouched by the stricken man, careful of the blood pooling around him.

"Why?" I asked.

"Go home, you bloody Yank," he sobbed. "Oh God, I'll lose my leg fer sure."

"Where did Sarah Willoughby find you? What did she tell you?"

"Sod off," he hissed, his courage returning. "You have no bleedin' idea what you're doing. You need to leave this alone. I promise you!"

"Leave what alone?" I asked.

He squeezed his eyes shut as he gently held his ruined leg. No answer, and time was running out.

"Sorry about your German friends." I gestured toward their bodies with the pistol, hazarding a guess based on the make of the Mauser pistol.

"They weren't my bloody friends. You've got to get me some help," he begged.

"Sure I do, pal," I said. "Sure I do." Germans, I thought. The men on the *Mauritania* were probably Germans too. Great. Goddamn Germans. Gavin and his old friends in Germany. Berlin, that's what Sarah said. Perfect. England and now Germany. That was just perfect.

Despite my numbed eardrums, I began to hear sounds down the corridor. I'd run out of time, and I had a decision to make.

I stood and pried a second German pistol from the dead hand holding it. I put the Colt and one of the German pistols in my bag. Time to go. With my suitcase in hand, I moved to the window and pulled it open. My room was on the second floor, the first floor if you are a local. It looked like a hell of a drop. I pushed my bag through the window and dropped it to the alley below. I turned back to the man on the floor.

"By the way, did they tell you my name?" I asked.

"John Griffin, you bloody Yank," he answered. If the police questioned him, he'd tell them.

"Wrong fucking answer, mate," I said. I lifted the Mauser I still held in my hand and shot him through the forehead. The pistol's report was almost a surprise to me. I tossed the pistol on the bed where one of the Germans lay sprawled.

I could feel my stitches pull as I hung from the window and dropped, but the fall was not as bad as it looked. It seemed funny now that, when I had checked in, I'd been annoyed that my window only had an alley view. Good thing I'd been too lazy to complain.

Following in Mitchell's footsteps, I turned down the dim alley toward Charing Cross Station. I'd need to find Mitchell before he tried to find me at the Savoy. I'd leave my bag at the station. Like it or not, I had no choice but to visit Weybridge again.

I wiped my hand across my face, and it came away bloody. The first thing I needed to do was clean up. I thought of the man in my room. His surprised and then pleading eyes sought some human connection with mine. They found none. No remorse. Just like the war. Just another Bosche even if he did speak the King's own.

He shouldn't have known my name.

---

At precisely 0624, I caught the train from Charing Cross to Waterloo and from there through to Farnborough. It would be awkward finding Mitchell if he was staying at the Ship Inn, but my chances of being recognized in Surrey were less than being detained and questioned in London where three dead bodies decorated my room. I was sure that the Armistice hadn't changed attitudes toward Germans so much that the authorities wouldn't take great interest in finding out what they could about the two dead ones at the Savoy. Not to mention the dead Englishman.

The conductor had to wake me at Farnborough. From there, I managed to get a ride with a fellow passenger who lived not far from Weybridge. His son had come to Farnborough with a wagon to pick him up. I lay down in the back of the wagon and again fell into a restless sleep. They woke me at their turn.

"Weybridge is just down that road," the father said, pointing. I climbed off the back of the wagon and thanked him. He clucked the horse forward. As I started down the road, I heard, "Good luck, Yank." I was leaving a trail as obvious as Broadway, but I had no choice. I'd find Mitchell, make new rendezvous plans, and then skedaddle and find some place quiet to hide and heal.

The afternoon sun was warm as I hiked across the fields surrounding the hamlet. I didn't want to go into Weybridge if I could help it. I decided to try to find Mitchell at Sarah's house. I was glad I'd been to the house before. My memory of that visit allowed me to avoid walking through Weybridge. Instead, I crossed the river north of the town and approached from her back garden. I moved very carefully. I stayed to the shade of the bushes bordering her house, and I looked into the kitchen. I can be very patient, and I was patient now. My only hope was that Mitchell would return here before he left. It was almost certainly the first place he stopped when he arrived, and it would be the last place he checked before he left. He would want to know if Sarah had come back.

I pushed my way through the bushes to find a concealed spot to watch both the front and the back of the house. I found a good place at the foot of a large oak. I sat with my back against the tree, and with a little neck craning, I could see the approaches to both doors, if not the doors themselves.

Four hours later, I saw the dusty figure of Mitchell, umbrella in hand, approach Sarah's front door. I heard him knock on the door. I edged around closer to the path and waited in case he had been followed. No one appeared, and I stepped onto the front path and called to him.

"Will!" I called softly.

"Hey, John," he said, looking completely unsurprised. "Didn't think I'd find you here. Couldn't stay away, could ya? She must be a real beaut…"

"No, you fool. I had no choice. They found me at the Savoy."

Mitchell raised an eyebrow, turned, and rapped once more on the door and looked back at me.

"She's not here, is she?" he asked, realizing that I must have been waiting for some time.

"No," I answered. "No one's here. We need to talk. I think it's time to let Armistan know what's happened."

"Gotta report to the ole CO huh?" Mitchell could be a very irritating man.

"I've killed three more men. Things are not right."

Now I'd surprised him.

"My God, Griffin, there are only so many damn people in this country." He seemed genuinely worried about the English population. "You can't just kill every person you happen to take a disliking to, honestly."

"Look." I tugged on his sleeve and glanced back toward the road. "I told Sarah I was staying at the Savoy. She must have told them. Two of them were Germans." I pulled the Mauser from my belt. "See?"

Mitchell took the pistol, turned it over, and handed it back. Finally he started to look worried. "Where in the hotel? Did you go to the police?"

I looked back toward the road again and said, "Come on. Let's go sit at the back of the cottage. We'll know if she comes home, and we're less likely to be seen."

Mitchell followed me back to Sarah's garden, where we found two weathered wooden benches. He sat staring out at the garden.

"This morning, they came to my room. Two Germans and an Englishman. Londoner, I think. They kicked in the door and started shooting. I was lucky I was already awake. It was a goddamn gunfight. They knew my name."

"I've seen you do some amazing things, but to come out of a room with three other men all shooting at you..." Mitchell shook his head in amazement. "That's... You are one lucky son of a bitch. You don't look so good though."

I ignored that. "I don't think anyone saw me, but I can't go back to the hotel. It doesn't matter what name I registered under. They'll recognize me." I didn't want to tell Mitchell the rest of it, but I had to tell him something. "I can't be questioned by the English."

He started to speak, and I held up my hand. "Listen. I can't be recognized here. It wouldn't be good."

"Why? I mean, aside from killing five men, what the hell could be worse?"

"I just can't talk to the English authorities. I just can't." Mitchell was a good friend. He wouldn't press me if I didn't want to be pressed, and he believed that, whatever my reason was, it had to be good.

85

"Well," he said, "I've talked to Sarah's neighbors. Yesterday looks like she left. Packed her bags and had them brought to the station. I kept hoping she'd come back today, but she's gone. Meets you on a Tuesday, and she disappears on Wednesday. You're a charming devil." He tried a smile. Because he was my friend, I forced a laugh.

He stood. "John, my friend, one question: Is it worth killing to keep you out of the bobbies' hands?"

I thought back to the dead Englishman in my room. "It is for me, but it shouldn't be for you."

He reached a hand down to help me off the bench. "If it is for you, it is for me," he said simply.

THIS COMMENT WAS A REMINDER OF WHY I LOVED MITCHELL. His friendship was not fashioned of some false bravado that would vanish with the first crackle of rifle fire. For six hellish months, from Belleau Wood to the Meuse, he'd proved to be not just a great friend and my best friend but really my only friend. I had deliberately abandoned my English friendships in 1916. By fleeing, I accepted that I would no longer be the person I'd planned to be, that I had wanted so desperately to be. I would have no professional career, no beautiful English wife, no future as I had contemplated it. The violent epiphany provided by the Western Front had purged me of my prewar fantasies, leaving only the basic, and in my case, base, desire to survive.

But the desire to live lasted only until I came home. Upon my return, I had time to reflect on all I had lost: my future and my honor. Without either one, my self-loathing drove away all considerations except a desire for some sort of absolution and perhaps death. Mitchell had seen my wartime recklessness first-hand. He had seen my indifference to survival. When out of the front lines or on leave, he had seen the trouble I would get into, but he ignored the darkness within me. Instead, he persisted in talking about the future as in "after the war." He was undeterred by my adamant refusal to discuss the future. He simply included me in his. He forced me to think beyond the war and beyond myself.

"John," he'd say, "after the war, we need to go to New York City. I know places there that can make your blood run cold or hot, just like hotel tap water," or "John, you need to meet my cousin. Now, she's not real smart, but she's ugly," and despite myself, I'd laugh. Whether the world he promised was real or not didn't matter. He made me think beyond the violence, the fear, and the horror.

I had often toyed with the idea of telling Mitchell about the cowardice that led me to enlist in the Corps. Had I done so, it is almost certain he would have mocked my arrogance at assuming that my presence in the English trenches even mattered. He would have rolled his eyes at the thought that I could have changed the fate of my mates with men like Haig in command. In all these things, he would be right, but I would never give him the chance to say them—because I had grown to value him too much. My irrational fear of his unlikely rebuke kept me silent.

Although generally invincible to shellfire, shortly after leaving me at the aid station during the battle of the Meuse, Mitchell was wounded. A few small shell fragments in his legs were enough to get him sent home before much of the rest of the regiment returned. Like me, in war, he was always strangely lucky. He managed to avoid being stationed in Germany. Hell, as far as I knew, some of the Second Division was still in Germany.

In the brief months following my return home, we had stayed in touch using short letters and penny postcards. I think he had grown to consider me his older, somewhat unbalanced, brother. I learned from our communications that soon after his return, while he was still convalescing, his dad had convinced him to go to medical school. Knowing I was from Texas and likely to end up back there, Mitchell decided he would go to school down in Galveston. He had just about convinced me to reapply to Rice for the fall term when Armistan found me. In finding me, Armistan had provided me an unparalleled opportunity to avoid confronting my unwanted future. It didn't matter that Mitchell was the one promising me a future. More than any real desire for the money or the action, I think Mitchell's real motivation in accompanying me to England was to protect me from myself. He knew my mind very well indeed.

By that evening, we were back in London, installed at a new hotel in a grimy neighborhood on the south side of the Thames. In the morning, we decided to send a cable to Armistan. He needed to know that his worries were justified. I felt like a fool for doubting a father's intuition.

IN THE MORNING, WE FOUND A POST OFFICE WITH A TELEGRAPH, and with our heads together, Mitchell and I composed a short but ominous message:

*"G and P remain missing Stop Fear the worst Stop S found but lost Stop Follow to Continent Stop Await instructions Stop JG"*

Despite using Armistan's money, I remained too cheap to buy any punctuation in the message. We struggled over whether to mention the attacks, but my terror of being recognized overcame my desire to inform Armistan. We didn't mention Germany for essentially the same reason. It was all too likely that any such reference would force the man keying the message to report it to the authorities.

We presented the terse message to the telegraph clerk.

"How long for replies?" I asked.

"Day or two, usually," he answered. "But it depends. Where are you sending this to?"

"New York City," I said.

"Shouldn't be long then, should it?" he said.

We decided to change hotels. I agreed to spend some of Armistan's money that I saved on a cheaper telegram on a nicer quality of lodging. Mitchell chuckled at the fact that I pinched pennies on the cable but was willing to splurge on a hotel. He suggested staying at a place called Claridge's. He had read about it somewhere, and he insisted that it was pricey enough to prevent unwelcome visitors. Personally, I would have thought the Savoy charged enough to keep Heinies from kicking in my door at four in the morning. I wrote out our address for the reply, and we left.

## 9

## Quarry Riddles

After sending the telegram, we moved into Claridge's near Regent's Park and settled in to wait for the reply. Well, at least I settled in. Mitchell wandered through London, learning its nooks and crannies. Inevitably, each evening, he would return to the hotel, meeting me in the bar, anxious to share new information about the city.

I, on the other hand, was becoming moody and increasingly anxious. Since the attack at the Savoy, I was convinced it was just a matter of time before I was recognized. I avoided leaving the hotel. I slept, read the newspaper, and tried to recuperate. I convinced myself, probably truthfully, that my body needed the rest.

That rest came to an end with a response to our message to Armistan, and the answer was not by telegram. Instead, it came one evening in the form of an interrupted drink. I was sitting at the Claridge's bar, with my back to the room, staring bleakly into the dregs of my beer. A working-class drink, a beer, and it matched my thoughts. For sitting in this London hotel, I found that I could not but think of my English war. With my memory all too eager to provide its own color motion picture with sound, my gaze turned sightless, and I remembered.

*In the trenches, the boredom often seems like the worst part. Because with inactivity comes the opportunity to dwell on the prospects of survival. The weather, so often cold and wet, makes every moment, waking or sleeping, a torment. Every physical sense and mental condition are simply taxed beyond endurance. Only my devotion to the men around me keeps me at my post. These men are closer than any family could be, yet I have very little in common with any of them. It doesn't matter, for I find that riding on a carousel of misery and fear with my messmates is enough.*

*We are to attack shortly before dawn—a first personal bloody test. I'd been at the front for three months, taking part in the ordinary rotation to the front lines, to reserve and to rest. I endured the shelling and snipers. I went into no-man's-land to help mend the wire. But I didn't take part in any formal assault on the German trenches. This morning, the fledgling dawn cannot compete with the maelstrom of artillery fire scouring the German lines. The impact of the shells is numbing even at a distance. This awesome display of support is some small comfort to those men more optimistic than I.*

*With whistles and hoarse cries ending our anxious shifting, we claw our way numbly onto the broken and scarred killing floor. As if trained from birth, unquestioning, our line stumbles forward. My senses are incapable of comprehending the events of which I am a part. I feel like I am one step behind where I'm supposed to be—forever unable to catch up.*

*To my left, two nameless shadows fall, in death synchronized with each other and with the malignant rhythm of the machine-gun fire that fells them. One collapses like a pen-killed steer, no sound at all, just a sudden, nerveless deflation. The second, no longer nameless, is sweet Evelyn's brother, Bert. He jerks backward and upward as the bullets shred him nearly in half. I stumble and fall too—slipping on some unknown savior—another victim writhing and squirming on the churned earth. The Maxim fire passes over me. For a fleeting instant, I think about helping Bert, but the instant is gone and I am up and moving again. Racing with the others toward the dim smoking shadows ahead.*

*Later, curled into the earth, our breath rasping in our throats, we realize that all the officers are gone. Bert is already a shadowy memory. The absence of officers doesn't matter because, after only a short pause, we move forward toward the line of voracious fire that is our goal, only to die on the uncut wire before it.*

"Excuse me."

A voice behind me pulled me back to Claridge's and the long marble bar.

My pulse pounded, and I was convinced the dreaded and expected moment of recognition was at hand. Ready to flee, I turned on my barstool.

"Mr. Griffin?"

When I saw who stood before me, I began to relax. I had not been recognized after all. At least not recognized by one of my former comrades labeling me a coward and shirker.

For before me, dressed in a stylish dark suit and looking a bit tired but every bit the freshly barbered and shaved English gentleman, stood Gavin Kingsbury. He held a ridiculous straw boater hat in one hand, and his expression was contrite.

I drained my pint and stood. "Yes," I answered.

"Gavin Kingsbury," he said as he offered his hand. "I trust you are John Griffin?"

"Yes," I said again. "Mr. Kingsbury, it's a pleasure to finally meet you. I suppose you know I've been looking for you." We shook hands.

"Yes, I recently learned of your search for me. It is a pleasure to meet you," he answered. "Quite convenient that you are staying at Claridge's as well."

"Quite," I said, but I was sure he didn't catch my irony. For some reason, I was unsurprised that I was staying at the very same hotel as the man I had been hunting.

"Drink?" I asked.

"Scotch with soda," he answered.

I ordered his drink and a second pint and turned back to face him.

"I learned from my father-in-law that he had hired you to find me," he continued, "and I thought it only right that I find you and apologize in person for the trouble I have put you through."

"No trouble, Mr. Kingsbury. I'm getting paid to stay at Claridge's. You'd actually be doing me a favor if you'd stay gone."

Gavin laughed. "I'm sure I would be, but I've been dreadfully irresponsible, haven't I?" he asked rhetorically. "Over dinner, if you would allow me, I would like to explain my absence and, I hope, set your mind at ease as I have already done with good old Harry's."

"Well, now that you are here, magically appeared from your honeymoon no less, why don't you give a little preview?" I suggested.

"A fair request, sir. But if you'll allow me, I will answer it over dinner. It's the least I can do. Is your associate, Mr. Mitchell, about? I would like to invite him as well."

"He should be here any minute," I answered. "Mr. Armistan must have given you a full briefing if you know that Will is here as well."

"Indeed," Kingsbury answered cryptically.

Our drinks arrived.

"Why don't we take a table?" I handed him his drink as we moved to one of the empty tables in the bar. "Will Mrs. Kingsbury be dining with us?" I asked innocently.

He smiled as we sat. "No, no, unfortunately not. She stayed in Paris. We went over to Paris on the spur of the moment. And Paris simply is the most romantic city in the world. It's quite the place to be now that the war is over. Sadly, Patricia gets seasick, and so she didn't want to recross the Channel if she didn't have to. We agreed that her time would be better spent in Paris than here attending to Daddy's business."

He said that last sarcastically, inviting me to join the joke about *Daddy*. I didn't smile.

I remembered my conversation with the steward on the *Mauritania*. It was odd that the helpful steward, whom I'd tipped handsomely, hadn't seen fit to mention that one of the bridge-playing, cocktail-sipping women he had served had problems with seasickness. Somehow I trusted my Geordie steward more than Gavin Kingsbury.

"Well, that's too bad. Will your sister be able to join us?" I asked in jest.

Gavin nodded. "Yes, as a matter of fact, she specifically asked if she could dine with us. She's not one to miss a good feed." He chuckled. "She's up from her home in the country. She seemed quite keen to see you again actually."

"I'm not sure whether that's good news or bad news," I said sincerely.

"Really?" He appeared genuinely surprised. "I would think it can only be good news. I mean, after all, she really is a very beautiful woman. Now, I know she can be a bit of a shrew, but I understand from her that you got on quite well when you stopped by, looking for me."

"Well, that reassures me then," I answered.

"Do you know Mr. Reynolds? Morgan is Mr. Armistan's special assistant. He recently arrived from New York City. He'll be joining us too. He's staying here as well."

I remembered Armistan's assistant, of course. He seemed extremely connected to his prospects in New York, but Armistan did warn me that Reynolds might appear if Gavin and Patricia were found. I wondered if the two would agree to be bundled home from their honeymoon as Armistan planned.

"Together, I think we will be able to explain the confusion that resulted in your trip," Gavin stated. "There was a bit of the left hand not knowing what the right hand was doing, I'm afraid. As much my fault as anyone's."

I nodded as I watched Mitchell cross the bar to our table.

I stood, and Gavin stood with me.

"Mr. Kingsbury, I'd like to introduce my associate, William Mitchell."

Mitchell's eyebrows rose. Whether at my use of the word *associate* or at the fact that I'd just introduced him to our quarry, I was unsure.

He shook Gavin's hand, and I watched him take in the smudges under the eyes, the expensive suit, and the polished shoes.

"Nice to meet you, Mr. Kingsbury," Mitchell said, wearing his best poker face.

"Over dinner, Mr. Kingsbury and Mr. Armistan's assistant, Mr. Reynolds, are going to fill us in on where Mr. Kingsbury has been," I explained to Mitchell. "Sarah Willoughby will be joining us."

"Really? Well, this should be a helluva dinner then," he said, looking Kingsbury in the eye.

Kingsbury looked undisturbed by the obscenity or the scrutiny.

He was a very cool cucumber, was Mr. Kingsbury.

"Mr. Reynolds and my sister will arrive shortly," Gavin said. "Why don't we go into the dining room? We can take our table." Gavin stood and brushed a nonexistent speck from his jacket.

I looked at Mitchell, who remained sprawled in his overstuffed leather chair, looking very much like a house cat whose prey remained just out of reach. I cocked my head in silent invitation.

"Absolutely, Mr. Kingsbury," answered Will. "Let's go grab our table."

Together, we rose and followed Kingsbury from the bar.

It was already clear that Mitchell didn't care for Gavin Kingsbury. Since I didn't much like him either, this fact didn't particularly bother me.

"I hope we won't have to wait for everyone else to arrive for you to fill us in on your travels," I said as we moved toward the dining room.

"Of course not, my dear fellow." Kingsbury laughed. He signaled to the maître d', who greeted Kingsbury by name and showed us immediately to a relatively private table.

I turned to Mitchell. "Clever of you to choose a hotel where the restaurant maître d' knows Mr. Kingsbury by name."

Mitchell shrugged. "Dumb luck, I guess."

"Yes," said Kingsbury, misunderstanding our exchange. "I've always enjoyed Claridge's."

"Do you enjoy the Savoy as well?" I asked innocently.

"Patricia likes it, but I can't stand the place, too many foreigners." He stopped, embarrassed by his honesty when he was speaking to foreigners. "I mean the French, really, they can be so bloody arrogant, can't they?" he finished lamely.

"That's the truth," Mitchell and I said in unison.

Kingsbury laughed. He finished his drink and signaled for another.

"So," I said to Mitchell, "Mr. Kingsbury tells me Mrs. Kingsbury, Patricia, is staying in Paris."

"Yes, with some friends," Gavin added.

"Really, on your honeymoon?" chimed in Mitchell. "They must be good friends."

"Quite good," said Kingsbury.

"I imagine," quipped Mitchell.

Kingsbury's description of his new wife did not match what his sister had told me about Patricia's predilection for expensive haunts. Kingsbury leaned back and sipped his newly arrived drink.

"Friends from before the war?" I asked.

"Yes, we'd shared some of the same interests and became friends. They absolutely adore Patricia. It is so nice to have one's friends and one's wife get on, isn't it?"

"I suppose it's better than them not," I said. "Where in Paris are you staying?"

"Do you know Paris, Mr. Griffin?"

I shook my head.

"Well, they live in the 7th Arrondissement. To me, it is the heart of the city."

"It's nice that Mrs. Kingsbury can stay with friends and enjoy the town," said Mitchell.

Kingsbury nodded. "Yes, we're very lucky to have such good friends who managed to survive the damn war. Sadly, I lost many of my old friends: English, French, and German."

Neither Mitchell nor I responded, and over Kingsbury's shoulder, I watched Sarah Willoughby enter on Reynolds's arm. Sarah caught sight of us and directed Reynolds toward the table. I rose, as did Mitchell and Kingsbury.

"Mrs. Willoughby," I said as they approached, "a pleasure to see you again."

"Mr. Griffin." Sarah nodded.

Reynolds raised an eyebrow, and I turned to him. "Mr. Reynolds, I see you were required to leave New York City after all."

"Mr. Armistan did mention he would send me once things reached a critical juncture."

"Yes, as I recall, he did say something like that." I laughed, thinking about Armistan's promise to have Patricia and Gavin bundled back to New York at the hands of Morgan Reynolds.

"I hope you've come prepared for the work," I said as we shook hands.

"I have indeed," Reynolds answered, involuntarily glancing at Kingsbury.

"Well, it seems like everyone here works for Mr. Armistan except for Mrs. Willoughby, of course." I turned to Sarah. "Or do you work for Harry now too?"

"I think you know quite well that I don't, Mr. Griffin."

"I gestured toward Mitchell. "I'd like to introduce you to my associate, Mr. William Mitchell. He, like everyone else except you, works for Mr. Armistan."

"Just temporary employment, I have a feeling," said Mitchell, bowing slightly. "After all I've heard about you, ma'am, it's a pleasure to meet you."

Sarah smiled at Mitchell's courtesy.

Reynolds pulled out a chair for Sarah, and we reseated ourselves around the table. I sat next to Sarah. Unlike many women in the dining room, she did not seem enamored with the new use of cosmetics, and whether through skillful application or lack of use, her face, though apparently unpainted, remained beautiful.

"Sarah, when did you leave Weybridge for London?" I asked, her first name slipping out. "I'd hoped to say goodbye, but I missed you before you left." I wanted to understand whether she had staked me out for the now-dead assassins, but I wasn't optimistic I would learn the truth.

She took a sip of her drink, considering her answer. "I left the evening of our dinner, John. One of the locals came by with a note from Gavin, and I had to leave in a rush. I'm sorry I didn't get a chance to tell you, but I knew Gavin wanted to see me and would be in a hurry to get back to France. I didn't want to disturb you that evening," she explained, making it clear she believed I needed rest after my beating in her garden. "And I did tell you I wouldn't help you find Gavin."

Her delivery and demeanor were so damn believable it was hard to accept she'd left me alone to be slaughtered by her houseguests. "Well, no harm," I said. "I've found your brother, or he has found me. And it is good to see you again."

"Well, Mr. Kingsbury, I have got to admit, a good mystery catches my interest. Mind tellin' us how you and Mr. Armistan managed to lose each other?" Mitchell jumped in with his folksy style.

Kingsbury glanced at Reynolds and then began speaking to me. A curious thing to do, considering I was not the one Kingsbury had to convince. I wanted nothing more than to believe everything was hunky-dory and to leave Europe on the next damn boat, but Mitchell had his blood up. He was focused. He hated to be manipulated. Having been manipulated by the general staffs of several nations, Mitchell had no patience for it now. But then Gavin didn't know Mitch. I suspected he would learn of his mistake soon enough.

"Well, frankly, it is a bit embarrassing, if expected," Gavin said, swirling his scotch.

He looked at Reynolds as if to include him in the audience for this admission. I watched Reynolds for any jealousy he might show toward Kingsbury. If Reynolds felt any, he kept it well hidden.

"We'd just been married," he continued, "and Tricia is a beautiful woman. I simply lost track of both time and my business obligations. Before I knew it, I was in Paris with my bride. After a few days, well, I finally realized that I'd let Harry down." He glanced at Reynolds. "That's when I contacted Harry and told him I was coming back to London straightaway. He was a bit angry but also understanding. He told me he'd hired some Americans to find me, and he mentioned you and Mr. Mitchell. He did say you had told him that we'd probably just run off somewhere unexpected, Mr. Griffin. How right you were." He smiled ruefully. "Understandable or not, Harry did make it quite clear that it was up to me to meet you and convey my apologies. I am so glad I found you. I can't tell you how embarrassed I am."

During his monologue, I studied both Sarah and Gavin. I watched Gavin because I wanted to know if he was lying. I studied Sarah because she was beautiful, and even though I thought she had tried to have me killed, my incredible attraction to her remained. She returned my gaze without a shred of guilt and with a lingering hint of the warmth I'd felt at her cottage.

Gavin seemed sincere, and Sarah seemed to believe him. I looked over at Mitchell. He clearly did not believe Gavin, but since Kingsbury had already discarded Mitchell as unimportant, he didn't seem to notice.

"Well, it's good that your diligent search for us worked. Have you had a chance to take care of your business for Mr. Armistan?" Mitchell asked innocently.

Gavin gave Mitchell a sharp look, then cut his eyes to Reynolds. I got the impression he was seeking either permission or help with his answer.

"Not to discuss Mr. Armistan's private matters, but my efforts here have been successful as Mr. Reynolds will attest."

Reynolds nodded.

"Well, that's good news," Mitchell said blandly.

The waiter, who had been hovering, finally got our attention, and we ordered more drinks.

"So you see, gentlemen, that's the story of my travels. Not too mysterious, but slightly embarrassing. Now, Mr. Griffin, I must admit, as a big brother, I am curious how you got on with my sister."

Although Sarah smiled as he spoke, she seemed uncomfortable with his brotherly possessiveness.

"I'd gone out to her cottage in Weybridge to find you," I said, nodding toward him, "and despite my desire to find her big brother, who she was certain didn't want to be found, and despite my intrusive questions, she was kind enough to invite me to dinner."

Sarah's face was unreadable as I spoke, and I had no way of knowing how much she had told her brother. While it was possible, even likely, that he knew all about my stay and the aborted assassination attempts, it would have been ungentlemanly to mention sleeping at her home. For some reason, despite my conviction that she tried to kill me, I still very much wanted Sarah Willoughby to think me a gentleman.

"I certainly didn't expect to see her here tonight." I laughed at the improbability of Sarah being in London. "But then again, I didn't expect to see you," I said, looking at Kingsbury. "I must admit I'm pleased you came into town, Mrs. Willoughby. I wanted to thank you again for your hospitality."

"A hospitality most likely learned of necessity during the war," interjected Reynolds with a chuckle.

I wondered at Reynolds's implication, but neither Sarah, Gavin, nor Mitchell seemed bothered. Mitchell's lack of reaction was probably because he felt that Sarah deserved whatever she got. Gavin, on the other hand, simply knew his sister too well to think that she required any defending.

"Sarah's always been kind to strangers," was his only comment.

In my mind, his words and tone had the effect of comparing me to a stray dog. Not an inappropriate comparison, really.

Sarah smiled and looked me in the eye. I found myself responding to her smile.

"Well, Mrs. Willoughby, Sarah, if I may," said Reynolds, "I envy Mr. Griffin. Had I known you had a soft spot for uninvited strangers, I would have tried to visit you as well." He wore a smarmy grin as he finished his clumsy compliment. At least, I wanted to think Sarah found his compliment clumsy and his smile smarmy.

I recalled Sarah's opinion of those who worked for Armistan and hoped that Reynolds's efforts to ingratiate himself with her were wasted.

"Perhaps you should have, Mr. Reynolds, but I did meet you at Patricia and Gavin's wedding. And I found that you're not nearly as interesting as Mr. Griffin. I certainly mean no offense in saying so," Sarah finished, clearly giving offense.

I suspected Reynolds found me about as interesting as a hobo.

"Well, you can't consider the wedding," Reynolds noted. "I mean, after all, Harry had you all to himself, and I can be an interesting fellow if one takes the time."

"But one would have to *take* the time, Mr. Reynolds," said Sarah.

"But I *am* taking the time, Sarah, and I certainly wish you would," insisted Reynolds.

Mitchell chuckled, which earned him a glare from Reynolds.

"Well, Mr. Kingsbury, I'm certainly sorry I won't get to meet your wife sooner rather than later," I said as Mitchell offered a conciliatory cigarette to Reynolds and then Kingsbury and Sarah.

To my surprise, not only did Reynolds and Kingsbury accept, but Sarah did as well. She stretched her long neck toward the match Mitchell cupped in his hands and inhaled like a sailor. It surprised me to see her smoke the same way it surprised me during the war to see colored boys dressed up like American soldiers. Not that colored fellows couldn't fight. I boxed with a few, and I knew they could fight. It was just that I didn't expect to see them all lined up and disciplined and acting like soldiers. And I didn't expect Sarah to smoke like a man. It didn't offend me; I just didn't expect to see an English lady smoke. The war had changed a lot. When colored boys can fight just like white boys, and ladies smoke, well, the world's not the same. I suppose it shouldn't be after the hell of the past four years.

"I'm afraid you won't get to meet her at all, Mr. Griffin," said Kingsbury, answering my comment about Patricia. "Once I've finished Mr. Armistan's business here, I will be going back to Paris to meet Patricia, and we will be traveling on to Italy as originally planned."

"Well, it seems a shame for us not to meet her after coming all this way and even more of a shame not to see some of the sights," I continued. "I've always wanted to see Italy. I've already seen plenty of France."

"I'm afraid Mr. Armistan was quite clear about you both returning to New York City for payment," interjected Reynolds. "He wants to thank you personally for your efforts."

"Really?" Mitchell said, jumping in. "Hey, that's just great." Through the smoke, I looked him in the eye, and I remained silent. "John told him that this was a wild-goose chase."

I turned to Reynolds. "When did Mr. Armistan decide he could call off the dogs?" I gestured at Mitchell with my chin and implicitly included myself.

"Once he received Gavin's telegram, he knew he was back to

business as usual. There have been some developments since Gavin and Patricia left New York, and we decided it might be worthwhile for me to discuss them with Gavin in person," he answered with his fake smile. "Of course, none of this is really your concern. After all, you've found Gavin, and Mr. Armistan does expect you to return to New York City."

I snorted my disbelief at both his use of *we* and his suggestion that any developments other than the disappearance of the briefcase, Gavin, and Patricia mattered. I thought of the good men who had died while this slick-haired, overconfident prick was alive and drinking expensive scotch, and I felt my patience evaporate.

"Really?" I said. "Business as usual... despite the fact that you still haven't seen Patricia and..." I looked under the table. "I don't see the briefcase Harry asked me to recover. Curious that it's back to business as usual despite accomplishing nothing at all."

I waited for Reynolds to start to speak so I could interrupt him.

"Look Griffin...," he said, his face turning red.

"Mr. Reynolds," I said, talking over him, "you may not know it, because apparently Mr. Armistan didn't see fit to tell you, but it wasn't part of the job to find Mr. Kingsbury and then take his word about his wife's safety. I was also instructed to return Mr. Armistan's briefcase." I looked over at Gavin. "I don't suppose that the briefcase has turned up, has it?"

"Delivered it to the city this morning," he answered, ignoring Reynolds's scowl.

"Then all that's left is for Mr. Armistan to verify that. And he'll also need to confirm that he wants us to go home without seeing Mrs. Kingsbury," I stated.

Neither Kingsbury nor Reynolds looked happy with this pronouncement. Sarah, on the other hand, looked strangely pleased.

Both men started speaking at once.

"Maybe we weren't clear...," said Reynolds.

"Well, you certainly are the right man to find someone...," Kingsbury began.

I held up my hand. "I wasn't finished," I said sharply. "Reynolds, Armistan didn't think you important enough to this assignment to include you. You remember that? My recollection is that your role only begins once Mr. and Mrs. Kingsbury have been found. And I don't see Mrs. Kingsbury anywhere. I find it difficult to fit you into my chain of command. And Mr. Kingsbury, let's be honest. You disappeared with the man's daughter and some sort of work papers, and you've reappeared with neither one. I'd be doing a god-awful job of completing the assignment if, as soon as you tell me to vamoose, I do. So, until Armistan tells me to quit and go home, I'm staying."

Reynolds tried to interrupt, but I continued. "Now if Mr. Armistan sends me a telegram ordering me home, that might be enough. Another possibility is that Mrs. Kingsbury walks through that door"—I nodded toward the restaurant entrance— "and tells me she's fine. Then maybe, maybe I'll go home. I'd like nothing better than to go home. But not on these terms. Sorry, gents."

Gavin raised his hands in a placating gesture, perhaps to calm Reynolds as much as me. "I'm sure we can get Armistan to instruct you as you require, Mr. Griffin. I should have realized my word would not be enough."

"My apologies, Mr. Kingsbury, but Mr. Armistan didn't hire me to take anyone's word for the safety of his daughter," I said, looking at Reynolds as I spoke.

"Gavin please. Call me Gavin. And I completely understand," Kingsbury answered. "It seems he couldn't have found a better man for the job."

After a rather uncomfortable dinner, made more unpleasant by Sarah departing afterward on Reynolds's arm, I followed Mitchell up to his room. We needed to talk. From what I gleaned during the conversation at dinner, we agreed about our course of action, but I wanted to impress upon him that we could be throwing away fifteen thousand dollars. I knew I wasn't doing that lightly, and I wanted to make sure he wasn't either.

"Well, what do you think," I asked.

"I think Sarah Willoughby is a very attractive woman who is very attracted to you. I also think she has far too many qualities in common with a black widow for my taste, but then we're not talking about me."

"Dammit, Mitchell, we're not talking about Sarah either. We're talking about what to do about Gavin turning up all of a sudden. We're talking about whether Patricia's okay! And we're talking about fifteen thousand dollars!"

"What's to talk about? Gavin says she's okay; Reynolds doesn't really care if she's okay. And Sarah, her friend, didn't say anything about her at all. Which means, of course, that you want to find her and make sure she's okay. So that's what we'll do." He watched me, smiling. "If I'm wrong about what you want to do, and you don't want to find her and make sure she's okay, well, then we're going to have a longer discussion 'cause that's what *I'm* going to do."

Ah, the bulldog Mitchell had appeared.

"I don't think we're going to have to have a longer talk. What if Armistan really does tell us we're done and to return to New York?" I asked.

"If we are not in London to get the telegram, it's a little hard for him to tell us to do anything, isn't it," Mitchell said.

I nodded. "What did he say to me again? *Hurry, time is of the essence.* Well, that's my excuse. We couldn't stay here woolgathering. Time is of the essence. You know Armistan might be angry. He may not pay us," I finished.

"So what! We don't need his damn money," he said sharply. "I came along for free chow, a free room, the possibility of some excitement, and your good company. And he's already given us plenty of money for that. I don't need any extra blood money. Hell, this is the perfect excuse to avoid having to face civilian life. My friend, I've been itching for action ever since the Meuse. I hate to say it, but I may not be cut out to be a doctor. Hell, I may not be cut out to be much of anything, but don't tell my dad."

I patted him on the shoulder and chuckled.

"And to think I thought you came along to keep me out of trouble," I said.

"Hell, John, I can't keep you out of trouble. I can only get you out of it. So how do we play this?" he asked.

"Well, we send a telegram to Armistan, telling him what's happened, and explain our plan. We make it sound reasonable. We pack our bags tonight and leave at first light. We'll take a train down to Southampton where we can catch a ship for France. I've got to admit, I'm as worried about Reynolds as I am Gavin. There's just something not right there. And he just looks like a mean son of a bitch."

Mitchell nodded. "Yeah, and you sure didn't butter him up by telling him to his face that he's nothing but the hired help. Especially since he thinks he's the high muckety-muck of muckety-mucks."

I shrugged with a laugh. "I didn't like the way he talked to Sarah."

"No shit. I don't guess you would," he said knowingly.

"Well, whether because of Reynolds or Gavin, we know we need a head start to find Tricia and to keep her from vanishing again," I said. "And I think we're just going to have to take Gavin's word about that damned briefcase. There's just nothing I can do to prove he didn't deliver it anyway... unless you want to torture Gavin."

"Don't tempt me," said Mitchell. "What about Sarah?"

I shrugged. "She's a strange gal, but she's gotten under my skin. I'll just have to worry about her after we find Patricia."

Mitchell nodded.

We agreed that I would come down to Mitchell's room in the early morning.

On the walk back to my room, I felt a weight lift from my heart at the thought of departing, and that night, for the first time since landing in England, I was able to relax when I finally stretched out on my bed. I was leaving England. Hallelujah!

---

A SOFT YET INSISTENT TAPPING ON MY DOOR WOKE ME. QUICKLY and quietly I threw off the sheets covering me and slipped the Colt off the nightstand. The memory of the Savoy was all too fresh in my mind. Terrified that the door would suddenly burst inward, with one hand, I clumsily but quickly pulled on my clothes, relying on my suspenders to hold my unbuttoned trousers over my unbuttoned shirt. The tapping continued.

I was busily hunting for my shoes in the dark when I heard a hushed call from the other side of the door.

"John, hurry, let me in."

"Sarah?"

Now angry, I unlocked the door. Sarah, still dressed for dinner, put her hand on my chest, pushed me out of her way, and slipped into my room. I looked up and down the hallway, confirming that it was empty.

"Sarah, you scared the bejesus out of me. What the hell are you doing here? It's not proper. What would your brother think?" I asked in a rush, unintentionally sounding both anxious and staid. I was extremely conscious of my unfastened shirt and pants. Without waiting for her answer, I closed the door and put the pistol on the nightstand. I then awkwardly turned my back to her and set about buttoning my clothes as quickly as I could.

Sarah stepped close behind me and pulled me around to face her. She placed her hands over mine, stopping their fumbling efforts at buttoning my shirt. I looked down at her hands and then into her eyes, which promised exactly what my heart desired. My heart began to hammer in my chest at the nearness of her. I could feel the warmth radiate from her body. I took a deep and audible breath to try to control myself.

"What are you doing?" I whispered.

"I wanted to see you," she said, looking up at me.

"Why?" I asked.

"John, now that you've found Gavin, I didn't know when you'd be going back to New York, and I have to go home tomorrow... to tie up some loose ends. I wanted to see you before I left." She stopped as if uncertain how to say what she wanted to say. She smiled shyly as she pushed her arms through my half-buttoned shirt. Tracing the puckered scarring along my ribs, she pulled herself close, fitting her soft, flexuous form firmly against mine and hiding her face against my chest. She held me tight.

With my heart racing, I could think of nothing to say, so I put my arms around her and marveled at her presence.

After a moment, Sarah spoke again. "I want to see you again, Mr. Griffin," she said formally. "I know this isn't proper to say, but all our lives have been turned upside down, and I'm afraid I'm not proper anymore, and I don't care to be. John, I was afraid you would leave and I would never see you again, and I didn't want that to happen. Not when I've found someone that I care to see." She lifted her mouth to mine.

The pressure in my chest threatened to explode. I kissed her hard as I crushed her body against mine. All gentlemanly and rational thoughts disappeared with her kiss.

After a time, I gently pulled myself away from her. I needed to think, and I also wanted to confirm that Sarah, the beautiful English woman I'd become infatuated with, really was in my room, in my arms, and within my reach.

"Sarah," I said, shaking my head at her presence in my room. "Until I came to England and met you, I didn't think that God had any particular vendetta against me, but... now... now I'm positive he's hell-bent on destroying me—in every possible way. Look, we need to talk. I need to understand some things. I need..."

She kissed me under the chin and on my neck. "Welcome to Armageddon, Mr. Griffin," she murmured softly into my neck, and my moment of resolve evaporated as she dragged her nails down my naked back.

I knew, intellectually, that I should have stopped her and insisted on answers about the men in her house and her brother's initial disappearance. But stopping her was simply not possible. Stopping me wasn't possible. I wanted her so badly that there was no room for any other thought. Yes, I wanted her physically. But emotionally, she gave me something I had entirely forgotten existed. Not since 1915 had any real hope for the future entered my mind. Instead, my life had spiraled steadily downward like an airplane shot down over no-man's-land. I lived in the depths and the mud of the Valley of Death, and it had seemed like there would be no return. Not just a return from the front alive. I mean that I stopped believing in a return to light and joy and love. I never thought I would care to live again.

But with this enigmatic, dangerous woman in my arms, I did care. I cared very much. With my heart in my throat, I cared to live and breathe and wrap myself around her.

I kissed her, tasting wine, cigarettes, and something that was uniquely her own. I smelled her hair and body, and I was dangerously close to falling in love. I forgot the gunmen at her home, the three dead men in my room at the Savoy, and the lies she and her brother had told. I immersed myself in Sarah and Sarah alone. I forgot Mitchell and Patricia and Armistan and my own shame, guilt, fear, and despair. No regrets. I would have no regrets. And, as our clothes fell away, I had none.

---

I AWOKE LATER WHILE SHE WAS QUIETLY DRESSING. I DIDN'T MOVE. Instead, I lay on my back with my eyes half-closed and enjoyed watching her slim form move about the room as she donned last night's clothes.

I wanted to call her back to me and to curl against her, but something stopped me. In part, I just wanted to watch her graceful movements, but at the core of my silence, despite my unchecked infatuation with her, was the knowledge that I couldn't trust her. I needed to know what she would do and why she had come to me. Mitchell was right. Despite her beauty and allure and despite my uncontrollable need for her, she did have too much in common with a black widow spider.

As she finished fastening her dress, she raised her eyes to look at me. I wondered if she would steal out of the room, but instead, she came to me and leaned over me, placing her hand on my chest.

And just before she kissed me, she said, "I know you're awake, John."

I smiled through our kiss.

"After home, what will you do?" I asked.

She sat on the side of the bed next to me.

"Once my business at the cottage is done, I may just visit New York to see you," she answered. In the dim light of the room, I tried to read her expression. "But first I think I may have to chaperone Gavin and Patricia a bit more. Gavin worries that having to do Harry's business on the honeymoon is going to make Tricia unhappy, and he asked if I'd go along to keep her company when needed." She shrugged. "So, I suppose for the next few weeks, I'll be traveling the Continent with them."

This plan was not what I'd hoped to hear. I wanted her as far from Gavin as she could be. I wanted her innocent and uninvolved with the plots of Gavin, Reynolds, Armistan, or the various killers I'd encountered. Clearly, that was not to be.

I looked into her guileless eyes and concentrated on the warmth of her hip touching mine, the curve of her neck, and my unquenchable need for her, and in that instant, I decided that what was to happen in the morning or in a week of mornings was too remote to consider. For now, I would cherish this moment and revel in it. I pulled her down to me and kissed her as I fumbled with the fastenings on her dress. I could feel her smile.

AFTER SARAH LEFT, THE ROOM SEEMED EMPTIER THAN BEFORE SHE had knocked on my door. Only her scent lingered: a rich, heady fragrance that seemed to confirm the link between us. We had not talked any more. She believed I would return to New York, and I did not tell her any different. I knew I was going in search of Patricia, but now this duty became more attractive because of the possibility of seeing Sarah during the hunt. The circumstances of the contact didn't matter. I hungered for Sarah, and in desiring her, I found that my commitment to solving the dangerous riddles posed by her and her brother was redoubled.

I was in deep, deep trouble.

I wanted answers to the riddles, not because they would help me complete my job for Armistan. I wanted them because they were a key, perhaps *the* key to Sarah. I was in trouble that there was no good way out of. And I had no intention of talking to Doc Mitchell about a cure.

# 10

### Back to the Front

"Will," I called softly as I tapped on his hotel room door. "Will, let's go, open up."

I had my bag in my hand and scanned the hallway as I waited for Mitchell.

He opened the door and stepped out of his room. "Five in the morning. Kinda makes me feel homesick for the navy," he said insincerely as he followed me toward the stairwell.

We checked out quickly and walked toward Knightsbridge. We wanted to get away from the hotel, and then we planned on a cab back to Charing Cross, and from there, a train to the coast for a ferry to France.

"How'd you sleep," he asked innocently.

I turned to look at him. "You've been watching my room?" I asked accusingly.

"Didn't need to. I know that look."

"What the hell are you talking about?"

"Your look. That smug, self-satisfied look of a leatherneck who just got lucky. That no-sleep, bleary-eyed, guilty look. Other than that, hell, Griff, I'm not talking about a thing." He laughed.

I felt an irrational surge of anger, which was more the product of my predicament with Sarah than anything Mitchell had said. I took a deep breath. Mitchell, knowing both how to get my goat and when not to get it, kept silent.

"I think it is fair to say I've got a serious problem on my hands. How much do you want to know?" I asked, keeping my eyes straight ahead as we walked.

"Damn, John, you just told me everything I need to know. I'm not going to lecture you. I just hope the gal really is worth all the trouble you're in for. All the trouble *we're* in for. I like her, and she's a lady. I just hope she isn't really trying to kill you, 'cause I'm not sure how my momma would feel if her favorite son killed an English lady, or vice versa, for that matter. That sort of thing is such a spoiler at Thanksgiving."

I had to smile. "You're not your mother's favorite," I said with certainty.

After Mitchell's little speech, I felt better. He understood me and wouldn't judge me—at least not on this. I just hoped that my infatuation wouldn't get him killed.

"Don't expect me to think straight where Sarah is concerned. I just can't do it," I said. "And you need to know that. My judgment's shot, and I have a feeling she's hip-deep in this whole shebang."

Mitchell shook his head. "Tell me something I don't know. Your decisions weren't ever any good. Hell, boy, I still remember you at Blanc Mont, charging that damn machine-gun nest." He chuckled. "Everybody else lying as low as they could get, all of us praying to God we wouldn't get hit, seventy-sevens going off like popcorn popping, and you just standing up and charging, bayonet fixed, shooting from the hip, screaming God only knows what. I couldn't hear a goddamn thing it was so damn loud... Now that was damn near the stupidest thing I've ever seen. Beautiful, don't misunderstand me, but damn that was stupid." He paused meaningfully. "Although falling for a woman who's already sent five guys to kill you, now that"—he looked at me out of the corner of his eye—"that would be even stupider."

I shook my head and kept walking.

"That's why you brought me," Mitchell said, warming to his topic. "You needed someone levelheaded. Someone sensible. Someone smart." He looked over at me, nodding his head in agreement with himself. "You needed someone you could count on. Someone just a little tougher and a little braver than you... that and you needed somebody who could out drink you. Otherwise, you'd never get home at night." He clapped me on the shoulder. "Let's face it, buddy, you needed the navy." With that, Mitchell began to hum "Anchors Aweigh."

It was going to be a long trip to Paris.

---

THE WEATHER IN PARIS WAS COLD AND WET. IT WAS NOT THE weather I'd hoped for, but it matched my mood. I thought about Sarah constantly, and worse than that, Mitchell seemed to know it. Whenever I would start to daydream about her, I would hear Mitchell humming "Anchors Aweigh."

When I wasn't thinking about Sarah, I worried about Tricia, and I prayed we would find her and that she would indeed be all right. I continued to consider myself a fool for ever doubting Armistan's intuition.

I was not confident that our lead on Gavin would last. Even if we did find Patricia, I didn't see how we could do so quickly. Kingsbury had claimed that his bride was staying with his friends in Paris. Having grown up with two sisters and having had some contact with the opposite sex, I found his claim nearly impossible to believe. No woman of Patricia's class would allow herself to be a houseguest on her honeymoon. I imagined that Tricia would be none too happy with Gavin if he even suggested leaving her with his friends in Paris. Trusting more to instinct and Sarah's description of Patricia, we decided that once we settled in, we would canvass the larger hotels to see if we could find Patricia.

Mitchell had claimed that he knew several outstanding hotels in Paris, but after our experience in London, I argued—and he agreed, despite some grumbling—that we would find a small pensione hotel in a part of town that would not be frequented by a man of Kingsbury's class. Although our natural inclination, being young and fresh out of the service, was to gravitate toward a younger, racier and, perhaps, rougher part of town where the digs were cheap but the saloons comfortable, we agreed to look for a quieter middle-class neighborhood.

We asked a ticket collector at the Gare du Nord train station for such a neighborhood.

"No, no." He laughed. "*Vous êtes jeunes et forts. Il faut rester à Montmartre,*" he insisted. "*Beaucoup de femmes, eh, beaucoup de belles jeunes filles.*"[1] He finished with a lecherous gleam in his eye. Discarding his well-meant and obviously sincere advice, we ended up in what we hoped was a staid bourgeois neighborhood called Montparnasse.

During the taxi ride to Montparnasse, we found that with the Armistice signed but no permanent peace in place, Paris was, in Mitchell's words, "suffering from a tragic case of schizophrenia." Mitchell tended to take his medical knowledge more seriously than he took other things. After reading the work of some German doctor, he insisted that he was something of an authority on mental disorders. In his opinion, Paris had a doozy.

"Honestly, Griff," he said, "Paris and Parisians have lost contact with reality; they've deluded themselves into ignoring the real world. Paris is delusional. They think that the war really is over."

"The war is really over," I said, stating the obvious.

He shook his head. "Not you too. You know that no war's over till you destroy or at least defeat the enemy's armies in the field and take their capital. In 1870, after Sedan, the Germans marched into Paris. Sparta took Athens. In the War of 1812, the Brits took Washington, but they didn't destroy our army. See? Hell, why do you think the War of Northern Aggression never ended? The Yankees never took Richmond, so the war never ended. Just ask my granddad. We should have gone to Berlin. Of course, if Messiers Wilson, Clemenceau, and George had insisted on that, you and I'd be dead. So maybe it's good they chose not to insist after all."

I shook my head. "For Christ's sake, where do you get your tortured view of the world? The Germans, after getting a whipping, agreed to the Armistice. Hell, marines are occupying parts of Germany. What are you talking about?"

"Wait and see, John, wait and see," he said, shaking his head.

Although Mitchell was clearly wrong about the war's end, I learned that he did have a point about Paris and the Parisians. On the one hand, the city seemed somber, as if she had finally had time to calculate her incalculable losses. On the other hand, especially at night, the bars and cabarets were crowded. People were out on the town; I was just not sure if they were celebrating or in mourning.

In checking the hotels, rather than splitting up to cover more ground, we decided to be safe and work together. Since I spoke the best French, I would go to the front desk and ask if my friends Gavin Kingsbury and his lovely wife had checked in. When the inevitable *no* would come, I would leave, and Mitchell, who had entered the lobby after me, would linger, seeking to determine if my questions had aroused any interest. The first day, we spent hours hoofing it from expensive hotel to expensive hotel. We had absolutely no success. The second day followed the same luckless pattern, and quickly, as creatures of military habit, both good and bad, we fell into a cycle of rising early, having breakfast at café La Closerie des Lilas, searching until 1700h, and returning to "our" neighborhood and the La Closerie terrace in the evening, footsore and ready for a drink.

In part, we had chosen Montparnasse because the

Metropolitan "Vavin" underground train station allowed us access to the rest of the city. But it didn't take us long to determine that we had stumbled upon a bohemian enclave made up of many different nationalities, professions, and avant-garde attitudes. It seemed that most of the café patrons we spoke with fancied themselves to be artists of some ilk or another. It also seemed that very few were Parisians.

It was blind luck that put us on Patricia's trail.

We had had a particularly grueling day, and we had decided to call it quits earlier than usual. We were still a few blocks from our home café, and by tacit agreement, we stopped at a café called Le Dôme. The café had inviting tables set along the sidewalk, and we just didn't want to walk anymore. It seemed our plan to find Patricia by scouring the hotels had failed. As had become my habit, I bought *Le Monde* and was skimming the paper in the ridiculously futile hope that it might contain some news of home and the Senators. Eventually I gave up and began reading Mitchell the news. Today I settled on news about the upcoming negotiations with the Germans for a final peace treaty. Mitchell was sipping his first absinthe of the evening. Although absinthe had been outlawed in France in 1915, it seemed that Parisians didn't agree with that bit of legislation. It gave me a ray of hope for the States and the impending implementation of Prohibition. Of course, the waiter was discreet and the glass opaque.

"The Germans will shortly send their delegation here," I said to Mitchell, beginning to loosely translate the news as I had for the past two evenings.

"Really," he grunted. "I suppose they have no choice. Should have gone to Berlin. Then they'd know who won the war. But we'd likely be dead."

"The Allies are keeping 'em waiting…," I continued, ignoring him, but I was interrupted by a voice behind me.

"Sorry, I couldn't help overhearing. Are you Americans?" a young female voice asked with a French accent.

I turned and looked over my shoulder. Sitting at the next table were two pretty young women. The one who had spoken glanced at me and looked back at Mitchell. She had short, dark hair, dark eyes, and a small, expressive mouth with ruby lips. She was very young with a feline air about her. In the dying daylight, I could see Mitchell's green eyes light up.

"Why, yes, ma'am, we certainly are. And I must say, I have heard some charming accents from California to New York City, but none so charming as yours," he said.

Both young women smiled at Mitchell. They seemed flattered by Mitchell's attention, but he was a good-looking cuss, so I suppose they would be. He could charm a snake out of its skin when he wanted to. It was lucky that they had caught us early in the evening before the absinthe and wine started to erase the charm and more snake than snake charmer appeared. He had a weakness for La Fée Verte,[2] a weakness I certainly didn't share. The shit would burn your brain to ash, both literally and figuratively. I just hoped he'd manage his dosage tonight. He usually did.

"I heard your friend reading the news, and I was surprised. Surprised hearing an American voice I didn't recognize. I thought I knew all the Americans who live in Montparnasse, but you two are new," said the second woman, a girl really. She couldn't have been more than twenty or twenty-one.

"Yes, we are—both American and new," Mitchell said as I nodded.

I stood and offered my hand to the nearest girl, the American, who was a slim, brown-haired girl with the strong facial planes and features of a Jewess. In contrast, her accented friend was purely French, from her plucked eyebrows down to her rounded ankles.

"John Griffin," I said, introducing myself to the Jewess. She took my fingers in her small hand.

"Rachel Eisen," she said. "I'm an American too," she added unnecessarily.

Mitchell had also stood. "William Mitchell, ladies," he said as he bowed to each of them.

They both nodded back.

"My name is Kiki, Kiki Prin,"[3] said the original speaker in her accented French.

"Kiki's a native," Rachel explained, "and quite a talented one at that."

"Mind if we join you?" Mitchell asked.

"Not at all. It'd be good to hear some news from home," Rachel said as we pulled our chairs around. "What brings you to Paris?" Rachel looked at the scar on my face.

It was at that moment that Mitchell had a stroke of genius.

"We're actually looking for a friend, but this is a darn big town if you don't know where to look," he said.

"Really? Well, what's his name?" Kiki asked.

"Not actually a *he*," I said.

Looking disappointed, Kiki turned back to Mitchell.

"We're looking for Patricia Armistan, although I guess it's Trish Kingsbury now. She just got married. She's really more of a friend of a friend, but we were told to look her up," Mitchell said, smiling at Kiki. Kiki immediately brightened at this information. Whether because she knew Patricia or because she was glad Patricia was married and not a good friend of Mitchell's was unclear to me.

"I know Tricia," Rachel said with surprise. "What a small world."

I resisted the urge to look at Mitchell. "Really?" I said. "How 'bout that? You haven't seen her recently, have you? We ran into her new husband in London, and he mentioned that she was staying with friends here in Paris."

Rachel laughed. "I haven't seen her recently. But I wouldn't leave Tricia alone in Paris if I were her new husband. I know she is part of the American artist crowd here. They're sort of avant-garde in their attitudes." She glanced at Kiki, who smiled and looked at Mitchell, who smiled back.

"I just don't know who she'd stay with," Rachel continued. "Actually, if you come here later, lots of Americans frequent Le Dôme in the evening." Rachel glanced at Kiki. "You might be able to find her then or at least get an idea where she might be. But if you do come back, you need to watch yourselves. It can get a little rough if you're not careful."

Mitchell chuckled, which made me smile.

"Rachel, we're never careful," he said, leaning forward to pat me on the shoulder, a devilish gleam in his eye.

Kiki laughed and clapped her hands.

"Look at old Griffin here," he said. "Does he look like a fella who knows how to be careful?"

All four of us laughed. Mitchell could even charm the ladies using my beat-up kisser.

"We will definitely plan on coming back here tonight," Kiki exclaimed.

"That would be swell," Mitchell said, "but I have a feeling John and I will just stay here till then. Drinks?" he suggested.

Kiki and Rachel exchanged looks, and using the telepathy that only females of the species have, reached an unspoken agreement.

"Of course," Kiki said as Rachel nodded.

Mitchell managed to corral the waiter.

"How many Americans are there in this neighborhood?" I asked.

"Well, I don't know for sure, but I can just say that there are a bunch who come out of the woodwork at night," Rachel said.

"And it's not just Americans," Kiki explained. "You have all sorts of nationalities in this bohemian little corner of Paris."

"And all sorts of lifestyles," Rachel added.

Mitchell made a show of rubbing his hands together. "Now this is the Paris I'd hoped to see," he said, looking at Kiki. Both women laughed.

"Are you an artist, William?" Kiki asked.

"Of a sort," he said with a wink. "I specialize in conventional and oriental healing arts."

"Oh God," I groaned. "Here we go."

"Truly?" Kiki asked Mitchell.

"Please don't get him started," I begged.

"Why ever not," said Rachel. "But you do look a little young to be an ancient oriental healer, William."

"Ahh, ladies, that is part of my secret. Take Griffin here. He's actually a ninety-nine-year-old man. With my healing arts, I keep him looking young. Well, as young as possible... considering the material I have to work with."

We laughed.

"No, what he means is, I feel like a ninety-nine-year-old man, and he's kept me alive," I said truthfully.

"Can you make me look seventeen again?" Kiki asked.

"Mademoiselle, you already look seventeen," Mitchell said gallantly.

"You are shameless," she answered, slapping his arm.

"What about you, John? Are you a doctor like William?" Kiki asked.

"Other than being a guinea pig for Will's oriental hocus pocus, I think it's fair to say I'm on a paid vacation to Europe, but I don't know how long the paid part of the vacation will last. Do you live here now, or are you on an extended visit?" I asked, wanting to change the subject.

"Oh, we live here, at least for the time being," Kiki answered. "Rachel's an artist, a writer, and painter, although she denies it, and I am an artist as well, but I don't deny it. I am a singer and dancer. Madeline, who should be here in a bit, is our good friend..."

"Who gets money from home more consistently than I do," finished Rachel.

"Kiki, are you from Paris originally?" I asked.

"No, no. Burgundy, but it was inevitable that I come here."

"But what made you come to Paris during the war?" Mitchell wondered.

"Well, the war is over now, isn't it?" Kiki said. "And Paris is the most liberated and liberating place in the world. Why wouldn't a girl who wants a little adventure come here?"

"Amen," said Mitchell.

"But don't get Mitch started on the end of the war," I said with a wink at Mitchell.

"I came over to help the YMCA and just never went back," Rachel said, ignoring my jibe at Mitchell. "It's already been quite an adventure."

Rachel waved to someone over my shoulder, and I turned and watched a third young woman weave her way gracefully through the tables toward us.

"My friend, Madeline Moore," Rachel said by way of explanation.

"Madeline," Rachel said when she arrived at our table. "I'd like to present William Mitchell and John Griffin. Two Americans as far from home as we are but probably missing it more."

Madeline smiled at us both. "Pleased to meet you," she said. She was tall with the open face and fair hair and skin I associated with women from the Midwest. She was a pretty girl, and she looked like she smiled easily. I found myself liking her for no reason other than her smile.

"Madeline worked with me at the YMCA, sharing the YMCA adventure. With the Armistice, we both decided to come to Paris," Rachel said.

"I sure wasn't ready to go back to Chicago," Madeline said.

"Or New York," Rachel declared.

Will chuckled. "Yeah, we came over with the YMCA and had an adventure too," he said. "The 'Why did I join the Marine Corps?' adventure."

All three girls laughed. Kiki, who didn't seem to understand, laughed just because she enjoyed laughing. Mitchell's kidding seemed to break the ice that we hadn't even known was there.

"I knew it," said Rachel, slapping Mitch on the leg. "I could tell we could trust you guys right off. I just knew you'd been in the war. You know, it's hard to trust anybody who wasn't."

"Hell," I said, "it's hard to trust anybody who was."

They laughed.

We drank for a little longer, and then Kiki, after explaining that she had to prepare for a show she was doing at a nearby cabaret, left with a nod at me and a peck on the cheek for Will.

It was then that we got our first real lead on Patricia Kingsbury when Rachel mentioned that she had seen Patricia.

"It was just in passing," Rachel said. "She was at one of Kiki's shows, a cabaret a couple of nights ago. We only spoke for a moment. To say hello really. I didn't know any of the people she was with, but I want to say one of them was a Russian, maybe a composer or something. I'm not sure where she's staying. Sorry I didn't tell you sooner."

"Well, you've told us now," said Mitchell.

"Rachel's a regular Mata Hari," interjected Madeline, who clinked her glass against each of ours.

"I suppose I am," said Rachel. "Salut!"

"Salut!" we chorused and drank.

"Nude dancing and all?" I asked, referring to Mata Hari's checkered career from before the war.

"No!" said Rachel sternly over Madeline's laughter.

"Do y'all think it's worth going to that cabaret tonight?" Mitchell asked.

"Doesn't he have just the cutest accent, Maddy?" Rachel said.

Mitchell laughed.

"He sho nuff does." Madeline poorly mimicked a Southern accent and then answered Mitchell's question. "Sure, it'd be good to go see Kiki's show anyway. Even if Patricia isn't there, the show's worth seeing. Do you speak French? It's best if you can understand her lyrics."

"*Un petit peu*,"[4] I answered.

"I understand it better than I speak it, that's for damn sure," Mitchell said.

After another half hour of drinking and telling lies to peals of laughter from the girls, we were convinced we could all speak French fluently, and we decided to walk over to the cabaret where Kiki was to perform. We paid and stumbled out of Le Dôme arm in arm with our young escorts. Again, using their female telepathy, Rachel took Mitchell's arm, and Madeline took mine. I wondered how the distribution would have worked if Kiki had still been with us.

The club was extremely crowded, and we had to wind our way to the bar where only the girls managed to claim seats. They seemed to know many of the other patrons, and to my surprise, many of them were Americans. I mentioned this to Madeline, and she nodded.

"I was surprised, too, when I first settled here," she said. "And the most surprising thing is that many of them have been here since before the war." She pointed out a few writers or artists that seemed to impress her, but I quickly forgot their names.

Kiki was not yet on stage. Instead, there were four dancers singing and high kicking to the delight of the clapping crowd. Out of the corner of my eye, I saw Madeline wave at someone near the stage. A man stood and signaled her over to his table. She grabbed my hand, and we threaded our way between the small round tables and the many patrons surrounding them. Mitchell and Rachel followed closely on our heels.

"Horace Merchant," Madeline said, kissing the still-standing man on the cheek. "This is John Griffin and Will Mitchell. Formerly of the US Marines and currently exceptional drinking partners."

"Navy, Maddy. I was navy, a corpsman," Mitchell said.

We shook hands.

"I'm a cousin from across the pond, English, I'm afraid," Merchant said. "A Lieutenant in the Royal Welsh Fusiliers during the scrap." He spoke in a crisp, public school accent I knew so well from my time in England.

"A heck of a scrap. I expect you've seen hell for the past four years. I'm sure you're glad to be out of it. I know I am, and I was in it for an eyeblink compared to you folks," I lied.

"None of it a cakewalk," he said, dismissing the war as the past and of no interest. He gestured with his thumb to a young man next to him.

"This is Walt Disney.[5] He drives ambulances, draws cartoons, and studies art."

Disney had a quick smile. He shook hands with us.

"Pull up some chairs," Merchant insisted. "They keep some in the hall downstairs by the bog."

"Bring extras, boys, you never know who else will show up," called Madeline as we pushed through the crowd. Together, we brought up six chairs and squeezed around two tables.

"*Trois bouteilles de vin rouge, s'il vous plaît,*"[6] Merchant called to the harried waiter bustling between the tight tables. "No Father Pinard or rum swill here. Just honest French red, gentlemen."

We loosened our ties but kept our jackets on for the time being.

"So, Madeline, would these gents know Tricia?" I nodded at Merchant and Disney. Before Madeline could answer, Merchant jumped in.

"Armistan?" said Merchant. "We certainly do, don't we, Walt? She's hard to miss and might have caught young Walter here's attention."

Disney blushed but admitted that he had seen Tricia. "I saw her a few days ago, but she was with a crowd I didn't know and frankly didn't like. Swiss, I think. They were clubby and had no time for a youngster like me."

Disney's answer made me like him. I didn't really appreciate Merchant's embarrassing him in front of the ladies, but I appreciated the lead.

"Where was this?" I asked. Mitchell leaned in to hear Disney's answer.

"Joey's club on the rue de Caumartin," he answered. "I was there to see Eugene and the band he's with and ran into Tricia."

"Y'all live in a tight little community here," Mitchell quipped. "Joey and Eugene. It sounds like a small town."

Disney laughed. "Joe Zelli[7] set up a dancing club and brought Eugene, Eugene Bullard,[8] in to play with the band. I think he manages part of it for Joe too. Both good guys, but I wouldn't lend Joe money," Walt said with a smile.

"I have to agree with that," Merchant added.

"I don't think Eugene will be playing tonight, but the club is worth a visit. It's supposed to be members only, but I'm pretty sure we can get Joe to let us in," said Rachel. "We'll have to buy a membership for those who don't have one."

We all agreed to visit Zelli's club once Kiki finished her act. The evening began to blur as we waited for Kiki to come on, and when she finally did, the applause and lewd shouts from the tables around us should have warned me. Before the war, I suppose I would have been scandalized by Kiki's provocative burlesque performance, but it seemed to fit the Paris around us. Mitchell was certainly taken in by her flashes of flesh, and her singing wasn't half-bad. After her performance, Kiki returned from backstage and joined us at the tables, working her way between Mitchell and Disney, which amused me. We had one more drink with her and then decided it was time to go to Zelli's club north of the river.

When we got to the club, the girls twittered like birds at the doorman in French. Rachel pried twenty francs from me for Mitchell's and my club "membership." With a glower at the men, the doorman bowed the ladies into the club, and we followed.

Rag music, dancing bodies, and smoke filled the room.

We pushed our way deeper into the club toward the bar. It was a bottle club, and we were required to order a bottle of what- ever liquor we wanted. The girls left us no choice, and we ordered two bottles of champagne. We carried the bottles as we orbited around the tables, eventually grabbing one where we could place our glasses as the girls dragged us out onto the dance floor. I wasn't much of a dancer, but I managed to shuffle Madeline around the floor without too much embarrassment. Mitchell swung Kiki through the crowded floor with grace and confidence. Somehow Disney had outmaneuvered Merchant for a dance with Rachel, and I was pleased for him. As I circled the floor with Madeline in my arms, Merchant would pop into view through the dancing figures. He nursed his drink and smoked, exhibiting an admirable calm at being "pipped" by the Americans.

We drank, danced, and laughed, and eventually Merchant got in a dance or two, but we made no progress at all toward finding Patricia Armistan. Not that Mitchell was particularly thinking about her. His attention was fully on Kiki.

I met a lot of expatriate Americans whose names I couldn't remember, but none of those I asked had any leads on Patricia, and most didn't know her. We failed but not for want of commitment to enjoying Zelli's club. When we finally stumbled out with the girls holding their heels as they leaned on each other, only a few hours were left before dawn.

THE NEXT MORNING, I LEFT THE HOTEL WITHOUT WAKING Mitchell and crossed the street to the café. I didn't wake him for two reasons. First, judging by the amount I watched him drink and considering the way I felt, he'd feel crappy too. Second, I didn't really want to know who he ended up bringing back to his room. It was a certainty in my mind that he'd had company.

The day was bright and the sky clear. The fresh smell of spring almost made me forget my pounding head.

"*Une carafe d'eau et un café, s'il vous plaît*,"[9] I ordered when the waiter wandered up. I had gotten the train schedules in and out of Paris. I wanted to have a sense of when and where the trains to the French ports, to Germany, and to Italy arrived and left from. The train was the most likely way Patricia, and for that matter, Gavin and Reynolds, would travel.

I drank most of the water when it arrived. Then I tried to develop a plan for finding Tricia in the bohemian Paris into which we had fallen.

There seemed to be no use in canvassing the hotels any longer. The best bet would be to immerse ourselves as quickly as possible and as deeply as possible into the community in Montparnasse. I was certain Gavin and Reynolds were now in Paris. It was likely I was simply grasping at straws, hoping to turn up Patricia after their arrival. It all really depended on whether she was acting independently, as her visit to Kiki's cabaret show seemed to indicate. Assuming that Rachel was correct and Tricia really had visited the cabaret.

I thought about Rachel. A pretty girl. Probably from a good Jewish family. Instead of staying at home, finding the right husband, she was playing the bohemian in Paris. Madeline too. It was hard to understand them but easier to understand the French singer, Kiki. I think Kiki was interested in two things: having a good time and being able to eat a meal every once in a while. She struck me as a survivor with a practical, simple view of life.

If I had to guess, she was the girl in Mitchell's room.

It appeared that at least a small part of the American crowd in Paris accepted us as belonging. The acceptance started with Rachel and Madeline. Just by being seen with them gave us a mantle of credibility the two of us alone lacked. Of course, Mitchell's charming idiosyncrasies didn't hurt. It certainly wasn't because of my warm and engaging ways. People wanted to trust Mitchell with his stage actor's looks and his doctor's manner. I didn't blame them. After all, I trusted him too.

To my surprise, Mitchell stumbled out of the hotel front door and crossed over to the café.

"You're looking a hell of a lot more spry than I would have thought possible, Will," I said.

"What? You mean because I'm moving," he said, signaling the waiter. He reached over, took my glass of water, and finished it before the waiter arrived.

"You can have your own glass," I said as he set my empty glass back in front of me.

He ignored me. "God, that was one doozy of a night," he said after he ordered.

"Well, unless you can think of a better way to find Patricia, I think we're going to have to continue having nights like that. I'm sure Gavin's already here, and we'll have to rely on a little luck to find Patricia," I said.

He leaned over and put his head in his hands. After a moment, he looked up. "Okay, let me make sure I got this. You want me to go out every night, drinking vin blanc, vin rouge, champagne, and absinthe, seducing these very seducible young women until we find Patricia? Hell, I hope we don't ever find her."

"Is seducible even a word?" I asked. "If it will take away the incentive to find her, I didn't say anything about seducing anyone."

"Some things just kinda happen naturally. I mean, it might come in handy, knowing these ladies well," Mitchell said.

I chuckled. "I'll bet. Well, I suppose we can at least continue to explore this ville a little during the day. Never know what we'll find. We'll cover more ground if we go separately."

I stood. I needed to walk. To work out some of the booze. Mitchell pretended to look hurt.

"Probably so," he said. "But keep an eye out for Reynolds and Kingsbury. If you see either one of them, you need to take cover and head back here."

"Unless I see them here," I said jokingly.

"Yeah, there is that possibility. See you back here at around 1700?" he asked.

"On the dot," I confirmed.

I decided to walk toward the river. The general rule, in any town or city, especially a European one, is to walk downhill to find the river. Not only will you reach water, but you will, usually, find the center of town. Paris, while bigger, is no exception to this rule. It just has a long, serpentine center.

One of the joys of Paris, perhaps more than any other city, even New York, is the richness of smells that accompany and sometimes assault the pedestrian. Whether it is the smell of fresh-baked baguettes or the stench of urine wafting from an open alleyway, there is always something to smell. Despite myself, I started to feel good. My headache was ebbing, and Sarah Willoughby snuck back into my thoughts. Daydreaming about Sarah was fine because I didn't think I'd stumble across Patricia, Reynolds, or Kingsbury on my stroll.

I walked through a large park with women pushing small children in prams and old men sitting on benches, smoking cigarettes, talking with young men who were missing limbs and smoking cigarettes. Beyond the park, I walked by what I thought was the Odeon Theater. By stretching my legs, it didn't take me long to reach the Seine, and Notre Dame came into view.

I crossed the river and found a small café off a square. I was far from what had become our usual haunts and was confident I wouldn't see any of my new acquaintances.

I wanted some time alone.

*"Espresso, s'il vous plaît."*[10] I ordered from the white-jacketed, heavily mustachioed waiter. A dignified, well-groomed, and well-grown cavalryman's mustache, I thought.

I leaned back in the wicker café chair. Turning my face to the sun, I took off my hat, closed my eyes, and let the heat soak through my eyelids. There is no feeling quite so wonderful as the caressing warmth of the sun. Especially after one has known the merciless cold and soaking wet I had known. Adding to my physical comfort was the thought of Sarah Willoughby, and a sense of well-being threatened to blossom.

But the feel of the sun and the thought of Sarah did not warm me in equal measure. Physical warmth could not compare with the warmth generated by the possibility of falling in love again. Seven months ago, if you'd told me that I'd be in Paris, enjoying this warmth both inside and out, I would have called you a damned liar. A self-satisfied sense stirred just under my heart. I tried to quash it as soon as I recognized it for what it was, but I was afraid I'd already jinxed my recent good fortune.

I believed life moved like a child's swing. Swinging from highs to lows and back again. I relished the feeling of my swing going up, while at the same time, I dreaded the inevitable trip back down. Being superstitious, as was anyone who'd survived the war, I felt a need to slow the upward rush, because the longer it lasted, the longer it would take to start the certain drop back down.

But I had learned long ago not to worry about what I couldn't control. No point in worrying about Sarah. We either had a future or we didn't. She wasn't here, and while it was nice to remember the time we spent together, it was silly and downright dangerous to ruminate over our possibilities or our future. Good or bad. Hell, anything was possible.

During the war, I'd found the best method of controlling my fear was to deliberately do everything I could to rein in my imagination. If you don't contemplate the possibility of the high-explosive shell smashing your dugout and you into atoms, it doesn't mean the shell is less likely to strike, but it does make maintaining control—when one should be gibbering like an organ grinder's monkey—much easier. If you don't imagine it, you can control your fear. The trouble lay in trying not to imagine.

Now, I decided, in what was likely a vain effort to undo the jinx I'd put on myself by feeling good, I needed to limit my thinking about Sarah. If you can't control it, you don't think about it, I told myself. These words had become my personal motto. I would focus on the job. Think about the job. Think about things I could control.

I could try to control the amount of time it took us to find Patricia, but I could sense that our time was running out. It seemed like the only option was to focus on the Paris nightlife and hope for some good luck. Since I was generally lucky, I expected this desperate strategy to pay off.

In any event, Mitchell was right. There were worse things than spending time every evening with Rachel, Madeline, and Kiki. Especially if they kept me from thinking about Sarah.

# 11

## A New Job

That night our search for Patricia came to an end.

Mitchell had made a triple date at Le Dôme with the two American girls and the French singer. I'd walked over to Le Dôme with him, but once there, I had decided to leave Mitchell to his harem. I again made the rounds of the various cafés, clubs, and cabarets that Rachel and Madeline had recommended we frequent to find Patricia. I promised to return in a few hours.

When I got back to Le Dôme, Mitchell and the three young ladies were laughing, drinking, and smoking cigarettes, which was the same thing they had been doing when I left them. They had moved out onto the terrace where they shared a table tucked away in the corner. Mitchell, facing the entry to the terrace, waved me over. It was clear that all four of them had been drinking since I left, and although Mitchell was still funny and charming, he had reached that dangerous point where his charm could evaporate in an instant.

"John, Kiki insists we should give up our quest to find Patrician. Ha!" Mitchell laughed. "Patricia," he said, correcting himself.

Rachel and Madeline giggled wildly, and Kiki smiled.

"Well, I suppose she is something of a patrician," he said, looking at the American girls.

I pulled a chair around next to Madeline so I could watch the terrace.

"She insists we should call it quits, abandon Tricia, revel in Paris," he continued.

I looked from Mitchell to Kiki to the American girls. "You already are," I said.

Kiki aimed her feline smile at me and took a drag off her cigarette.

"But you're not," said Mitchell with a wink at Rachel and Madeline.

"Well, I suppose we could just stay here and tell Armistan that we're still looking," I offered.

But Mitchell was no longer listening. Peering through the halo of smoke around him, his eyes were locked on someone beyond our table. I felt my heart begin to beat faster, and I followed his gaze. Near the entrance to the terrace, Morgan Reynolds stood talking to a shabbily dressed man.

I turned to Mitchell.

The girls could already sense the change in him.

He ground out his cigarette in the ashtray.

"I think we need to talk with Mr. Reynolds," Mitchell said, pushing back his chair.

"Outside," I said.

Mitchell nodded, never taking his eyes off Reynolds.

"What is it?" asked Rachel, putting her hand on Mitchell's arm.

"It's business, honey. We'll be back as quick as we can. Buy us another round." He tossed a wad of francs onto the table.

I worked my way around the outside of the terrace to get between Reynolds and the exit. Mitchell waited briefly, then approached Reynolds directly. Our unspoken plan, such as it was, was to drag Reynolds outside and beat the truth out of him. We needed to find Gavin and find out what the hell he was doing. You couldn't really expect a better plan from men who had been ordered to execute frontal assaults into entrenched machine guns.

As we neared, Reynolds, who appeared to be agitated, shifted, jostling a dark, bearded man standing just behind him. The man snapped an unheard comment over his shoulder at Reynolds. Reynolds flushed and, turning, said something back. Before Mitchell and I could get any closer, the man spun toward Reynolds, grabbed him under the jaw, and slammed his head into the wall behind them. From where I was, I could hear the *thonk* of his skull striking the surface.

To Reynolds's credit, he didn't fall. His knees buckled, but he caught himself against the wall. His hat fell to the floor. The dark, bearded man stepped back, balling his fists and giving Reynolds room to stand. The café crowd formed an instant circle no different from those schoolyard rings of my youth. I felt an urge to begin the chant: "fight, fight, fight." Up until now, we had managed to steer clear of the fights that seemed to occur all too frequently at Le Dôme.

I hurried forward. If there was a way to avoid a brawl with a bar full of drunks and still end up with Reynolds in any condition to talk, I hoped inspiration would strike before I covered the fifteen feet separating me from Reynolds.

Mitchell got to Reynolds first, and whether it was some evil inspiration or the absinthe taking over, he instantly became the center of attention.

"There you are, you son of a bitch," Mitchell said as he pushed Reynolds hard back into the wall behind him. "Getting a little of what you deserve."

He turned to the bearded man.

"*Il, ahh, il me doit le, l'argent,*"[1] Mitchell said in horrible broken French by way of explanation. He bent and picked up Reynolds's hat and smacked the dazed New Yorker in the head with it. "*Bâtard!*"[2] he said to Reynolds.

"I don't give a damn if he owes you money," the swarthy man said in English. "He owes me an apology."

Mitchell turned to him. "American?"

The bearded man nodded.

"Well, son," drawled Mitchell, "I'm sure he does owe you an apology, but I need to talk with him. And I can't do that if you beat him senseless, can I?"

The man grinned a mean, crooked grin, and my heart fell.

"Listen, cracker," answered the bearded American. "I'm going to get that apology, and if I have to come through you to get it, I will."

Mitchell's eyes narrowed.

"Crap," I said under my breath.

I moved next to Reynolds, who had regained some of his self-possession. I grabbed his arm behind the elbow and squeezed just enough to get his attention.

"Unless you want that fella to knock your pretty teeth down your throat, you'd better apologize," I hissed in his ear.

Reynolds turned to me. Recognition lit his eyes, and he tried to jerk his arm away. At the same time, a fist exploded off the side of my head, knocking me into Reynolds and both of us to the ground.

At that point all hell broke loose.

Anger surged through me. As I landed on top of Reynolds. I tried to drive my knee into his belly to keep him from getting away. He squirmed to the side and clawed at my face. I head-butted him once directly on his nose, which burst, splashing blood all over the both of us. He covered his face with his hands, and kneeling over him, I hit him as hard as I could just below the vee of his ribs. He struggled to breathe. I turned, looking for the man who hit me and instead found a hard boot in the ribs. I was knocked off Reynolds. Together, we lay gasping for air.

Reynolds's shabbily dressed associate was standing over me with a snarl on his face. He reared back to kick me again, and I hammered my forearm across the side of his supporting leg. I heard a pop, and he fell to the floor next to me, gnashing his teeth in agony. He was writhing so close to me that I could smell his rotten breath and see his blackened teeth. I drove my fingers into his eyes.

I rolled away from his thrashing form and pulled myself to my feet. At least I could breathe again.

Mitchell had knocked down the bearded American and was in the process of knocking down a second man. He had a small cut over his right eye, which surprised me. He usually escaped such brawls without a scratch. Other fights had broken out in the bar and on the terrace. I didn't know if they had any connection to Reynolds.

I turned back toward Reynolds just in time to catch sight of him stumbling out of the café into the street. I ran after him and caught him as he started to cross to the shadows of a nearby alley. I pushed him from behind, knocking him to the paving stones. As he started to rise, I grabbed his oiled hair and kneed him in the face. He screamed, so I must have hit his nose again. He stopped resisting, and I dragged him into the alley.

"Time to talk, Mr. Reynolds," I said.

"Go to hell, Griffin," he spat out.

I slapped him with the thick part of my palm.

Mitchell turned in to the alley. "John, don't hurt your hand smacking him around. Let me have a little chat with him."

I leaned into Reynolds, holding him tightly by his lapels. "If you're gonna talk, I'd do it now. You don't want my buddy here to work on you. Really, you don't," I said sincerely.

Reynolds struggled to break free, and Mitchell stepped in close to him. He poked Reynolds in the throat, and Reynolds stopped struggling and started gagging.

"Where is Patricia?" I asked.

Reynolds began struggling again.

Mitchell pressed Reynolds against the alley wall and pushed his middle knuckle into the junction between Reynolds's head and neck. Reynolds let out a strangled scream.

"Where's Patricia?" I asked.

"Gone," he sobbed.

I shook my head. "Where were they staying in Paris?"

"Rue de Babylone," he answered.

"What number?" I whispered.

He remained mute.

Mitchell jabbed him again.

He screamed and bucked.

"Number?"

"Twenty-eight."

"Now," I said softly. "Where were they going?"

He shook his head and began crying.

"Where?" I asked patiently.

"Italy."

"Really?" I was enjoying myself. I looked at Mitchell, and he grinned back. It looked like both of us craved the sort of action Armistan's little adventure was providing. For us, the veneer of civilization remained very thin indeed.

"What station did they leave from?"

"Gare de Lyon," he answered.

"No," I said. "No, Mr. Reynolds, I think you're lying. Trains to Italy leave from Gare d'Austerlitz."[3]

Again, Mitchell stabbed his knuckle deep into Reynolds's neck. And again, Reynolds thrashed and screamed.

Despite the cool night, he was drenched in sweat, and he was pale and sobbing.

A passing couple peered into the alley.

"*Sortez d'ici!*"[4] Mitchell hissed. His accent was now impeccable. They hurried off.

Slowly Reynolds recovered enough to respond. "Switzerland and then Germany." He gasped. "I swear to God."

I smiled. Of course, I'd no idea where trains for Italy departed Paris. Given that Lyon was on the way to Italy, I suspected that Reynolds had guessed right. But he didn't know he was right, so his guess did him no good.

"Where in Switzerland?" I asked.

"Geneva," he answered. "Near the lake. On Utrecht Platz." Mitchell had broken him.

"And in Germany?"

"Berlin."

"Address?" I asked curtly.

"It's on Wandersee Strasse. I don't know the address."

"Reynolds, what the hell is Gavin up to?"

Whether because of his awkward position or to get away, Reynolds squirmed under Mitchell's weight. Mitchell tapped his broken nose with the tip of his middle finger.

"Stop," he admonished softly.

Reynolds let out a choked scream.

"Do you remember the question, Morgan?" I asked.

After a moment, Reynolds was able to answer.

"He works for Mr. Armistan. Mr. Armistan tells him where to go."

"Did Armistan tell Kingsbury to kidnap Patricia?" I asked.

"No, no," he answered. "Patricia never was missing. It was Gavin we wanted, and we've already found him. Just like we told you at Claridge's. The search really is over." He was almost begging to be believed.

"Then where is she?" I asked.

"She's with Gavin," he said, trying not to show his frustration with my stupid question.

I toyed with the idea of asking more questions about his business relationship with Armistan, but I kept thinking about the man he was speaking with in the café. If I could avoid it, I didn't want any more trouble tonight.

"We're almost done, Morgan, I promise," I told him. "Who was the shabby-looking Frenchman you were talking to in the bar?"

He hesitated, and Mitchell started to reach for him.

"No. Please. It was Bertrand. He works for my father. He was to follow Gavin. To make sure he's delivering on what Harry Armistan has promised his investors."

"And what's that?" I demanded.

"Profits, of course."

I reached into his jacket and took out his wallet.

Reynolds looked up at me. "So, you're a thief as well as an animal. I'll find you, Griffin, and don't think that Armistan won't help me," he threatened weakly.

Again, Mitchell pressed his knuckle into Reynolds. His eyes rolled back in his head, and he mouthed a muffled mewing.

I leaned close to his face, and he shrank back. I could see real terror in his eyes.

"Just hope I'm not a murderer," I said softly.

I took out his folded passport, his money, and threw the wallet against his head. He tried to move his arm to protect his face but failed. Mitchell must have paralyzed the arm.

We left the alley.

I glanced over at Mitchell as we walked. "How do you feel about Germany?" I asked.

He looked back at me and gave me a grim smile. "Real bad," he answered.

"We're going to have to visit rue de Babylone just to make sure they've really gone," I said.

"And if they've really gone, we need to get moving," answered Mitchell.

"Yeah, if," I answered. "There are no more trains tonight."

Mitchell smiled tiredly. "I sure do hope they haven't left. Paris is starting to grow on me. No wonder all the boys in our outfit wanted to get leave to Paris. This town is crazy." He put his arm around my shoulders. "Let's head back to Le Dôme, and I'll buy you a quick drink. We can go to Babylone, and we can catch a train tomorrow," he suggested.

"We're already in Babylon," I said, joking. "We'll just be going to a different part. By the way," I added as we neared the café, "let's try to avoid a fight with any other Yanks if we can. If we find my feisty little Frenchman, that's one thing, but Blackbeard and his friends…"

"Hey, it was the Yankee who started it," Mitchell insisted. "I just did what I had to do."

Unnoticed, we stepped back into the café. We spotted the American and his two bruised and slightly bloodied friends. Reynolds's French associate was nowhere to be seen.

As I should have known he would, Mitchell walked straight to the American's table. I could feel my heart begin to pump a little harder.

"Excuse me, gents," Mitchell said politely.

The three men stood so quickly that two of their chairs fell over.

"Whoa," Mitchell said, holding his palms out. "I came over to apologize."

I counted out some of Reynolds's francs and tapped Mitchell on the arm with them.

He took the money and held it out to the bearded American.

"The guy who bumped you said he's sorry. Real sorry. He wanted to buy you fellas a drink or two."

The American scowled for a moment, then he reached out, took the money, and smiled. "Apology accepted," he rasped, "by me anyway." He held the money up to his friends. *"Des excuses par le vin, peut-être?"*[5]

The men smiled.

*"D'accord,"*[6] one answered, shrugging and looking at us with less suspicion.

The bearded American hesitated, and then he offered his hand to Mitchell. "Name's Shed Bean," he said.

"Will Mitchell."

"John Griffin," I said as we shook.

"It's been a pleasure... of sorts," he added, rubbing his jaw.

We both smiled.

"Of sorts," Mitchell agreed.

"Drink?" Bean asked.

I shook my head. "Maybe later. We've got a little business to finish."

Bean smiled, looking out to the terrace. "Yeah, I'd want to get back to that business too," he said.

We walked out to the terrace. Rachel, Madeline, and Kiki stared wide-eyed at us as we sat.

"Nice bar," Mitchell said to Kiki.

She smiled, and I could sense their knees touch under the table.

Madeline touched the side of my head where I'd been punched. Her fingers were gentle and cool.

"Kiki's right," she said, returning to our prefight conversation. "You both should stick with us. You're way too unrefined for Patricia Armistan," she said.

"Of that, I have no doubt." I cradled my wine in my hands.

"There's no real way to know if Reynolds was being straight about Gavin and Patricia already being gone," I said to Mitchell.

Mitchell shook his head. "No, he told us what he thought was true. That I promise."

The girls had leaned close to share our mystery.

"Maybe he doesn't know where Trish is," suggested Rachel. "It's not like Patricia to hang around waiting for anyone."

"Maybe not." I finished my wine. "Well, hell," I said, "I might as well go check the address he gave us. I won't be able to relax till I do. If no one's there, we'll go back by in the morning."

Mitchell glanced at Kiki and shrugged.

"Hold on a minute," Rachel said. "You are looking for Patricia Armistan, right?" she asked smugly.

Mitchell and I both looked at her.

"Yes." I nodded.

She smiled. "Well, she's just over there speaking to the poor man William knocked down." She pointed toward the terrace entrance.

As we watched, Shed Bean gestured toward us, and Patricia Kingsbury turned and looked directly at us. When I saw her, I felt both disappointed and relieved. Disappointed because our job was over and relieved because, well, our job was over.

Patricia walked toward us. She was every bit as beautiful as the picture Armistan had given me. Bean remained standing, watching her as she left his table. I glanced at Mitchell, and I could see that he was captivated. Next to him, Kiki pursed the lips of her small mouth in disapproval. Judging by Mitchell's expression, I could understand why.

Patricia was small, just as her father was small. And, like her father, she carried herself with a confidence that belied her stature while declaring her social class.

Mitchell and I stood to greet her.

"Excuse me," she said as she approached. "I've been told that you are Americans." She looked at Mitchell and then me. "I'm looking for a particular American. A soldier. John Griffin."

I kept my face impassive. Far too much remained unexplained for me to dance a jig at Patricia's appearance.

"I'm Griffin," I said.

Despite her confident carriage and her haughty manner, I could sense her relief at my answer.

"I've been looking for you." She looked up at me with interest. "You've been quite hard to find."

I raised an eyebrow at her statement. "That's a coincidence," I said, "because I've been looking for you too."

She ignored my statement. "I want to hire you," she said bluntly.

I tried to remain expressionless. "I already have a job. For your father." I didn't bother to explain that with her appearance, my job, such as it was, was essentially complete.

"No. I think you will find that my father has fired you," she responded confidently.

"Easy come, easy go. I was ready to head home anyway," I answered.

"I have another job for you. Here, in Europe."

"Lady, aren't you on your honeymoon?" Mitchell interjected.

She turned to Mitchell. "We've not been introduced," she said, offering her hand.

I could sense the electrical charge pass between them when they shook hands.

"We need to speak privately," she said to me. She turned to Rachel. "Please don't be offended, Rachel," she said to the Jewish girl. "It's life or death that I talk to Mr. Griffin."

"Of course it is," said Rachel sweetly. She stood. "Mr. Griffin and Mr. Mitchell will be able to find us across the street at La Rotonde."

The other women stood. Kiki turned to Mitchell and gave him a very possessive kiss, which embarrassed me if not him. Together, we watched the three women leave. Without hesitation, Patricia took the seat Kiki had vacated.

"I understand that my father hired you to find me. Well, you found me, but it wasn't me he wanted found. Gavin brought back what he really wanted. Now he wants all complications out of the way. That includes you. In any event, you ignored his express instructions to return to the United States. He won't pay you the rest of your fee."

"We got no instructions," I answered lamely. "Unless you consider those delivered by Morgan Reynolds hand in hand with your husband. We could hardly be expected to believe Reynolds or your husband."

She ignored my jab at Gavin and continued. "Yes, but you left London before my father could confirm what Reynolds told you. Sorry, but as I said, my father won't pay you. He will not tolerate disobedience. He sent Morgan Reynolds with your new instructions. As he told you he might. In his mind, that will be enough to label you as disloyal."

"How do you know all this, Mrs. Kingsbury?" I asked. "I don't care if your father pays us or not. And what exactly did Gavin bring back?" I thought about mentioning the valise expressly but decided not to play that card.

"I will pay you," she said, ignoring both my questions.

"What could you possibly want us to do for you?" I asked.

"Find my husband and bring him back to the United States," she said flatly.

"Oh my God," groaned Mitchell.

I shook my head in disbelief.

Indifferent to her status or her beauty, I was sick of being used by the Armistans.

"Lady," I said brusquely, "why in hell would we want to find your yellow, supercilious prig of a husband?"

My rudeness didn't ruffle her.

"Because he intends to foil the Armistice," she said.

Neither Mitchell nor I spoke. We waited. Her declaration was so horrific and so absurd that there was nothing we could say. We could only wait for her explanation. She took our silence for disbelief, which, I suppose, it was.

"I'm telling the truth," she insisted. And she certainly seemed to be.

"How exactly does your husband plan on foiling the Armistice?" I asked, repeating her claim back to her.

"I don't exactly know, but I do know that my father is part of the plan. They're in it together."

I remembered her father's sincerity. He had seemed to be telling the truth too. He acted like a worried father, but was he more worried about the missing valise or his missing daughter?

I signaled the waiter. It was long past time for another drink.

Mitchell and I exchanged looks. The continuation of the war was too appalling to contemplate. Just as her father did, Patricia Kingsbury knew how to manipulate men. She had said the one thing that was guaranteed to get our attention.

"That makes no sense, Mrs. Kingsbury. Your father hired me to find you. He would know I wouldn't allow anything to prevent the peace treaty. He wouldn't throw me in the middle of this mess if he wanted the war to continue."

"Gavin was tasked to deliver to bankers in the city of London certain bearer bonds issued by various companies in which my father and his associates have investments," she explained. "These bonds were intended to do two things: first, fund the effort to thwart the Armistice and prevent any treaty; and second, to invest in various armament firms now with their prices depressed as a result of the peace talks. My father's plan is to buy low and sell high once the war restarts. My father panicked when Gavin didn't deliver the bonds to the bankers in the city. I'm sure he thought Gavin ran off with his money. It wouldn't surprise me if *Daddy*"—she used the title as an insult—"thought I was to blame for diverting Gavin."

Bearer bonds, I thought. That confirmed what Reynolds had told me in New York. It also explained what the money would be used for. Reynolds had cleverly left out the intention to start World War Two.

"But Gavin did deliver the bonds, and that's why your father no longer needed me searching," I concluded for her. "So you never were the object of my search."

"Exactly," Patricia confirmed. "Once the funds were delivered, my father believed the plan was still going forward, and he didn't need you to find me, or more importantly, Gavin. He needs Gavin to use his contacts and my father's funds to restart the war."

"Why not go to the French authorities if you believe this?" Mitchell asked.

"It's too ridiculous to believe, isn't it?" she answered. "And I don't want my husband arrested. But really, how can one single man prevent the peace?"

"You have an answer, of course," I prompted.

She nodded. "My husband is not alone. Gavin is a Bolshevik. You must know that there are Bolsheviks throughout Europe. By continuing the war, he hopes to bring the revolution to Germany, France, and even Great Britain. Because of the war, people are desperately unhappy, starving, angry. Gavin is convinced that revolution, like the one in Russia, is the only real guarantee to prevent another pointless war. He's willing to continue this one if it will bring about the revolution now," she said sincerely.

"Ah, the 'you've got to break a few eggs' theory of preventing future wars," I said. "After all, you've already got a perfectly good war, why go to the trouble of waiting for another one when this one could bring about a European Bolshevik revolution?"

"I know it sounds horrible and ridiculous at the same time," Patricia said. "Sometimes history needs a push, I believe Mr. Lenin said. Gavin intends to give it a push."

"Don't the Bolshies have to win in Russia first?" asked Mitchell. "There's no way Britain and France are going to let them win in Russia."

She didn't answer.

I thought about the men on the *Mauritania* and the men in Weybridge and in London.

"What about the sister?" I couldn't help but ask.

"You mean Sarah. I don't know," she said honestly. "She was a Fabian,[7] and she lost her husband in the war. She might see this as a way to prevent others from enduring the same tragedy she suffered. She loved her husband very much, you know. In any event, she'll support Gavin."

Irrationally, I couldn't help but feel a twinge of jealousy at the mention of Sarah's love for the late Captain Willoughby.

"Speaking of which," Mitchell said, "why aren't you helping Gavin? Surely you had some idea of this before you married him?"

"My marriage was arranged by my father," she said tersely. "I did know Gavin hated the war, and in fact, that made me start to care about him in a way that I hadn't before. He wants to prevent future wars, but I just can't allow him to interfere with the Armistice. It's too dangerous. He could be hurt, and even though I'm here asking mercenaries to find him, I have grown to love him in my own way."

Mitchell raised an eyebrow at her disparaging reference to us as mercenaries. I shrugged and rolled my hands in a silent gesture of indifference.

She continued. "I had friends who died in the war too. I hated the war. But the way to stop war isn't to continue this one. More men will die, and while my father might make money off its continuation, I can't stomach the thought. And I'll never be a Bolshevik. I suppose I'm too much my father's daughter to ever be a Red."

"And yet your father wants to start a Bolshevik revolution," I said.

"No," she declared. "He doesn't think the Bolsheviks can win and certainly doesn't want them to. He just wants to restart the war for the profits it will bring."

"Lady, your dad is a real peach," Mitchell said.

She studied him for a moment and gave a slight, rueful smile. "Isn't he though?"

I nodded, thinking of the information Morgan Reynolds had shared. Gavin's job was to deliver profits to Armistan's investors. His method of delivering those profits was to restart a war.

"Well," I said, watching Mitchell out of the corner of my eye, "maybe Gavin has it right, Mrs. Kingsbury. Maybe the Armistice is a waste of effort. I've actually heard people say the war isn't really over anyway. Educated people."

Both Mitchell and Patricia shook their heads at my statement.

"Sure, I said the war wasn't over, but I never said that the killing hadn't stopped," Mitchell said to correct me. "I don't know about you, Griffin, but I need a break from assembly line killing."

"I wouldn't know about a break. As you may recall, Gavin and Sarah's friends, who are apparently Bolsheviks, have had their sights on me since London, and I haven't gotten any break from killing at all," I said more harshly than I intended.

"What on earth are you talking about?" Tricia asked.

"Well, you see, Mrs. Kingsbury, since arriving in England looking for you," I said pointedly, "I followed up on the only lead I had: your sister-in-law. And since meeting her, I have been beaten, stabbed, and shot at. In addition, I have had the distinct pleasure of killing not one or two but five men. But since they were probably part of your large but secret army of passionate, dedicated Bolsheviks, I'm sure it's okay with you. In fact, can I get payment for the work I've already done?" I finished angrily.

"But your sister-in-law is a very beautiful and kind woman," Mitchell said, "who has been a pleasure to meet, and I'm sure the men Griffin killed were Gavin's friends, not Sarah's." His comment, made without any sarcastic emphasis, washed away my anger. He understood exactly my feelings for Sarah Willoughby.

"Yes, she is beautiful and kind and a dear friend, and I'm sure she doesn't really understand Gavin's plans," she said, somewhat confused by Mitchell's statement. "I'm sorry for what my husband's put you through, Mr. Griffin. But that is all the more reason for you to help me find him. You know how serious he is."

I turned to Mitchell as if to ask his opinion. Patricia watched us in silence.

He hesitated, then answered, "In for a penny, in for a pound. I'm not really ready to go home anyway, Griffin. I know you may think you are, but you're really not either. The trouble has been that we haven't ever known what was going on. Well, now we do."

"Mrs. Kingsbury, you want us to bring your husband back to the United States, but you and I both know he won't want to go," I declared. "And it appears that he or his friends have tried to kill me and will try to kill me again. Are you sure you want me to find him? I won't guarantee not to hurt him. Hell, I won't guarantee not to kill him."

Patricia remained undeterred by my threat. "My father is an extremely good judge of character, Mr. Griffin. If he hired you, you were the right man to find my husband and me, and you're still the right man to save Gavin from himself. I'll take my chances."

Her faith in her father's judgment was not misplaced. Her error was in concluding that, if I was the right person to find Gavin and her when her father thought they were together, then I must be the right person to find Gavin when he was alone.

Armistan had convinced me to search for Gavin using Patricia as bait. He knew I took the job only because of the pretty girl, just as General Neville had promised I would. Hunting for a man who was both a Bolshevik and a threat to the current peace was an entirely different prospect. To keep the peace, I might have to kill Gavin. Harry Armistan was a good judge of people, but his daughter was not. I saw no reason to educate her.

"Okay," I said. "We'll help you find Gavin. We'll even try to get him home. Dead or alive," I finished ominously.

Patricia proceeded to explain her understanding of Gavin's plans. "I last saw Gavin here in Paris just a few days ago. He was going to London to see the two of you. He had telegraphed my father and told him of his plans. My father sent the family lapdog, Morgan Reynolds, to make sure the bonds were indeed delivered and the two of you sent home."

"So you haven't seen Gavin since then?" I asked. "He should have already returned to Paris."

"No. I haven't seen him," Patricia confirmed.

"Reynolds seems to think he's going to Germany," Mitchell chimed in.

"I'm sure Gavin wants him to think that, but the treaty won't be prevented in Germany. It will be ruined here in Paris," she said with conviction.

"Now that is probably the first thing you've said that makes sense, Patricia," I noted darkly. "As I said, we'll help you find Gavin. And we'll be looking here."

## 12

_____

**Babylon**

S atisfied with extracting our commitment to her cause, Patricia said her farewells and left. She set a breakfast meeting with us for nine o'clock in two days' time at Les Deux Magots,[1] a well-known café on boulevard Saint-Germain. I was certain she would expect a report on our progress toward finding her wayward husband, but I was not optimistic about that task. Mitchell offered to see her home, but she insisted she needed no escort. When she stood to go, I walked with her from the terrace. I left her in the bar and turned toward the head. I stepped down the short hallway for just a moment. When I came back out, she was not in the bar. I looked discreetly through the door of the café just in time to see a man help Patricia into the back seat of an expensive motorcar. Standing in the shadows of the doorway, I watched her companion climb into the car after her. Patricia was not as alone as she wanted us to think.

Once back in the bar, I saw Mitchell coming in from the terrace. He had Shed Bean with him. The two of them were laughing at something Mitchell had said. It didn't surprise me that Mitchell had charmed him. Having lost out on escorting

Patricia Armistan to her hotel, Mitchell insisted on going to La Rotonde to find Kiki and the American girls. Bean was more than happy to go with him.

I had lost my taste for carousing and decided to go back to the hotel. The conversation with Patricia had put me in a foul mood, which the red wine had only made worse. There was no point in inflicting my poor company on Mitchell or the girls.

But Mitchell and Bean wouldn't let me leave without having a quick drink. I agreed.

We forced our way through the crowd and pressed up against the bar.

"*Trois absinthes*,"[2] I ordered without consulting either man.

"Oh crap," I heard Mitchell whisper under his breath.

"What?" I demanded. "If poor Shed here is gonna go out with you and the girls, I want to see you properly primed," I said, half joking.

"It's not me I'm worried about," Mitchell assured me.

"I'll be fine, and I'm sure Shed will be too," I answered. "Where are you from in the States, Shed?" I asked Bean.

"Wisconsin, but I moved to Chicago before the war. My fiancée is…" He hesitated and then continued. "Was from there. Her dad was a cop, promised to get me on the force, but the war came." He stopped. I had intended an innocent question, but from his reaction, I'd struck a nerve. "Sorry," he continued. "Annie, my fiancée, she got the flu. She passed away over Christmas while I was still here in the army."

"Shit, I'm sorry, Shed. I didn't know."

"Course not. How could you? Anyway, I just decided I'd never go home. Nothing there for me with her gone."

The bartender arrived and discreetly placed the three drinks on the bar in front of us. Mitchell slapped Shed on the shoulder and handed him a drink.

"I'm sorry too, Shed, but I'm glad you're here." He picked up a drink and raised it, saying, "To Annie."

I picked up my drink, and Shed and I both echoed Mitchell. "To Annie."

I could see tears welling up in Bean's eyes, but I ignored them. I tossed back my drink and signaled the waiter for three more.

We had two more absinthes, which were two more than I needed. We left the club together, but I insisted on going back to the hotel. Mitchell could tell that I was no fit company and allowed me to leave.

Once back in my room, I paced, thinking only of Sarah and her insane brother. He had to be insane. What sane man would want to prolong the war? Of course, he hadn't endured the war, and he had no real understanding of the horror he intended to perpetuate.

Sarah had told me she was loyal—at the same time she acknowledged that she was a disappointment as an English matron. The memories of the evening at her cottage and our night at Claridge's made me smile. And they made me sad. I could see no common ground on which to build my romantic fantasy. I was a fool.

I decided to walk by the address on the rue de Babylone. There was no point in dwelling on Sarah. I would find her brother. That was the most I could hope to do now.

I pulled the heavy Colt from my bag, checked its load, pushed it under my belt at the small of my back, and left the room. Once out of the hotel, I turned north toward the river and rue de Babylone. The night was dark in a way I hadn't noticed as I returned to the hotel. It felt menacing. It was the same menace that hung in the night air before a trench raid: the promise of death, in the dark, alone. I wondered if this foreboding was the product of my own dismay at learning of Gavin's plan and Sarah's participation in it. As outrageous as the plan had sounded, I believed Patricia Armistan had told us the truth.

But how could they hope to thwart a peace that all of Europe and the world desired? I suppose they could assassinate delegates to the conference, but I couldn't fathom what that would accomplish. There was an endless supply of diplomats and functionaries.

As I walked, it began to rain, more a mist than a shower, and the water beaded on my jacket. The cobblestones in the street became slick against the smooth leather of my shoe soles. I arbitrarily decided to turn left onto rue de Babylone and searched for a number to tell me the direction of 28. The buildings were three- and four-floor apartments with intermittent limestone rock walls running along the street and separating the sidewalk from the inner courtyards of the apartments.

As I walked, I reviewed the conversation with Reynolds in the alley. Why would Reynolds believe that both Gavin and Patricia had left for Switzerland? Judging by the dinner at Claridge's, the two men had seemed close. He should have known whether Gavin intended to stay in Paris to disrupt the peace talks, but after Mitchell's attentions, I had no doubt he was telling us the truth.

Number 17. An imposing six-story residence. My steps echoed off the pavement of the deserted street. Number 19. I was moving in the right direction. Few lights shone in the windows of the apartments above.

I wondered how many American soldiers remained in France and Germany. Surely there were more than a million. If the war restarted, how could Germany hope to stand against such numbers?

Number 29.

I turned to look back at the last house I passed. It had no number, was three stories high, and had no lights in the windows. As with the other houses on the block, where they were not flush against the sidewalk, a wall about eight feet high blocked me from the inner courtyard leading to the building. I walked back along the wall and looked again for a number but could find none. A heavy wooden door in the wall promised entry if I could just get through it. The door was painted wood. Solid. I gently tested the latch. Noiselessly it slid out of its catch, and with barely a whisper, the gate swung inward. An unexpected invitation. I stood motionless, staring through the open gate toward the darkened building. It was separate from the buildings around it. Different. A house more than an apartment building. The rain began in earnest. The sound would make it hard for me to hear anyone moving along the wall or through the yard should I decide to go to the house. The rain would also make it hard for anyone to hear me.

Good sense told me to find Mitchell. I didn't need to investigate the house tonight. But I stepped through the gate anyway and pulled it closed behind me. The hair on my arms and neck prickled, and my heart beat faster in my chest. Good. It was good that I was afraid. My body was preparing for action. Maybe I wasn't ready to die after all.

I followed the curving walk to the tall wooden front door. Only the weak light of the distant gas lamp down the street eased the darkness around me, but I didn't look back toward it. I wanted to preserve what night vision I had. I moved close to the door, opened my mouth slightly, and listened. I breathed softly, hoping to hear any movement from inside, but the rain interfered. I tried the door. It was locked. I let out a breath I didn't know I was holding.

I told myself that I had done enough for the night. But instead of walking back out the gate, I stepped off the path and began to work my way to the rear of the house, carefully placing one foot after the other. The night deepened as I moved away from the street.

I considered pulling out the pistol, but I decided that I didn't want to shoot some innocent Parisian coming to chase off a prowler. Reluctantly I left the Colt stuck under my belt, hidden by my sodden jacket.

As I edged my way along the side of the house, I came to a set of heavy wooden doors set into the ground. The coal chute for the house furnace. I felt around the double doors. No lock. I began to regret my decision to come to the house alone. I shrugged. No point in worrying about it now. I could leave, but I knew I wouldn't. Since I wasn't going to leave, there was no point in delaying. It was time to go into the house.

Moving as quietly as I could, I pulled open one of the cellar doors. It came up smoothly and with barely a sound. I stared down into the blackness. I glanced around me and squatted to enter the cellar. The coal grit stuck on my hands as I scuttled crabwise, feet first down the coal chute, braking my slide with my shoes and palms. No pile of coal bricks lay at the bottom. Instead, the chute ended on a hard, cold, stone floor. I stood and turned my back on the open cellar door and the overcast sky outside. I waited, knowing my eyes would eventually adjust to the stygian shadows into which I had come.

Despite the coolness of the cellar, I began to sweat. Slowly my eyes picked out shapes from the darkness. I tried not to stare at them as they developed, for if I did, I knew that they would disappear back into the uniform blackness. I'd learned in the war to use my peripheral vision to try to see shapes in the dark. It worked now. I could discern what appeared to be the stairs from the cellar up into the house. Carefully I crossed to their base and started upward. Every few steps, I paused, listening for any noises from above. Other than my tense breathing and the creak of my wet leather shoes, I heard nothing.

At the top of the steps, I found a small wooden door. There was no handle, so I pushed it with my fingertips. It moved outward slightly and caught. It was locked from inside the house. Stupidly, I had not considered this possibility. The cellar doors were open, so of course the door into the house was locked.

By feel, I examined the door again. Using a talent learned from defying my older siblings, who, when I became too irritating, would lock me in a handy closet that hooked from the outside, I opened my pocketknife and slid the open blade upward between the door and the doorframe. Just below shoulder level, the blade caught. Holding the contact with the blade, I hooked my nails on an edge of the door face and pulled the door toward me while I jiggled the knife blade. The hook popped free, and the door opened.

I stepped through.

A glow coming through a small window showed I was standing in a short hallway. The light looked like it was coming from the kitchen.

As I moved down the hallway, I stayed near the wall and away from the center of the hardwood floors. I passed a room, but I couldn't discern any shapes in the darkness. I came to a second doorway and made out some shapes inside. It looked to be a large dining room. Four heavy tables were pushed against the walls. On the tables, despite the dark, I saw neatly arranged rows of rifle barrels reflecting the meager light.

I stepped closer. From the nearest table, I picked up a US Winchester 12-gauge shotgun, the same type of gun that was issued infrequently after Soissons or maybe Saint Mihiel, I couldn't remember. I put the shotgun down. Even in the dark, the two efficient and deadly Browning Automatic Rifles and several 1903 Springfield rifles were identifiable. On the next table were open crates holding German Mauser 98s, two with optics, and the terrifying Bergman MP 18 machine pistols. On the third table lay a Lewis gun and a dozen Enfield rifles. On the fourth and final table were two awkward-looking Chauchats with their half-moon magazines and a handful of Lebel rifles and Browning FN pistols. On the floor between the last two tables stood a wicked-looking Vickers machine gun and a German MG08 Maxim gun. I looked in the crates stacked against the walls opposite the tables. Grenades.

There was an arsenal in the room. An arsenal of weapons of all the major combatants in the war.

Under the tables were uniforms, helmets, and web gear. In the dark, I couldn't make out the color, but I had a queasy feeling that if I could see better, the uniforms would be gray, khaki, or horizon blue. German, American, British, and French uniforms.

Distinctive German, French, and English helmets stood neatly stacked on the floor, confirming my suspicions.

This was not a good development. Patricia Kingsbury's claims didn't seem so absurd when enough weapons to start a second world war were sitting in the dining room of number 28 rue de Babylone.

It was time to get out and find Mitchell. Hell, it was time to contact the French authorities.

Silently I stepped toward the hallway.

Before reaching the doorway, I heard a deep, long, low growl.

There was a dog in the house!

"Son of a bitch," I heard myself say in terror.

I backed into the dining room.

Clicking nails rushed along the wood floors in the hallway.

I had nowhere to run. The Colt was stuck under my belt and wet jacket. I'd never get it out in time. My eyes came to rest on the shotgun on the first table.

The dog rounded the corner.

I swept up the shotgun barrel first and swung it like Ruth had swung at the Yankees' pitches. In that instant, an enraged blur of black dog was on me. I swung hard, twisting my torso and concentrating on the dog's head as it came at my throat. With a loud crack, the butt of the shotgun caught the animal just below the ear. The dog spun by me and slammed into the tables. As it tried to find its balance, I stepped close and rose onto my toes, bringing the shotgun up and over my head. I could feel my face contort in the same savage snarl as the dog's. With all my weight, I swung the shotgun down using the same motion I learned splitting logs at my grandparents' house.

The gunstock struck across the crown of the dog's head. I raised the gun again, but the dog had stopped moving. I couldn't tell if it was dead, and I had no intention of finding out.

My heart was hammering in my chest.

I dropped the shotgun and pulled out the Colt, jacking a bullet into the chamber as I brought it out in front of me.

Now I didn't care who was in the house. I was going to kill anything or anyone I came across.

The kitchen would have a door to the outside. There was no way I was going back into the cellar. No dog was going to catch me by the ass as I scrambled up that damned coal chute.

I hurried to the kitchen. Between an enormous double-sided sink and a big wooden icebox was the door. To the left, another doorway led deeper into the house. The kitchen door was made of thick, dark wood with three small windows across its top. I looked down the hall toward the dining room. No dog. I peered out through one of the door windows into the yard. It was raining harder. Nothing moved in the garden.

I set my hand on the heavy iron bolt.

From behind me came the metallic click of a hammer being cocked.

I didn't turn from the window. I froze. They would wait to shoot until I started to turn. Goddamn Heinies. Did I really want to die? Here was the answer to the question: I didn't want to, but I sure as hell would!

I started to smile the same flared nostril, teeth bared, maniacal grin I'd felt on my face a hundred times before. Every time I'd faced the guns. Every time death cuddled close. Those goddamn machine guns couldn't hit me. Did they really think anything less could? They'd better be damn quick.

"John?" a voice said from the doorway.

The grin left my face, and my traitor heart soared.

"John, is that you?"

Sarah.

Sarah Willoughby. Sarah Kingsbury. Sister to Gavin. Keeper of the arsenal in the dining room. I should have known. Nothing is ever easy.

They hit me after all. It just wasn't with a bullet.

I dropped my head against the door, and my gun fell to my side.

"Sarah," I said hoarsely.

If she heard the disappointment and sadness in my voice, she gave no sign of it.

"John, I need you to drop your gun on the floor. Please."

I saw no point in arguing. I wasn't going to shoot her. As gently as I could, I let the pistol fall to floor.

Behind me, Sarah moved toward the hallway.

"John, what happened to Coco?"

"Coco?" I snorted. "The dog?"

"Yes."

"In the dining room with your flatware," I said sarcastically.

"Lead me there please."

I turned.

In the light from the street, I could just see her. Even though she had clearly come from her bed and her hair was tousled from sleeping, she remained every bit as beautiful as I remembered. She was wrapped in a long, thin robe, and in her hand, she held a big revolver aimed at the center of my chest.

"This is romantic," I said flatly.

"Go into the dining room," she commanded.

I found myself hoping she wasn't fond of the dog. This already promised to end badly.

"John, I told you to go home. I told you I would come to you there. But you didn't go home. You shouldn't have come here."

"Sarah, what the hell are you doing here?" I asked in frustration. I began to wonder if she really would shoot me.

"I told you I was loyal," she said. As if her loyalty was all the explanation her presence needed.

"Is Gavin about?" I wondered aloud.

"No. If he were, you'd be dead," she said with certainty.

I must admit that I took offense at her assumption that her brother would be able to kill me, but I didn't think it was the appropriate time for me to point out my doubts.

We entered the dining room. The dog, a large rottweiler, had rolled around itself just where it had fallen. It reminded me of a dead spider with its legs curled in, looking smaller in death than it had in life. But I had found that all creatures look smaller in death. Including men.

With her pistol, Sarah indicated that I should move away from the dog.

"Sit on the floor against the wall over there." She pointed to the wall away from the weapons. She waited patiently as I took my time getting comfortable against the wall.

"Cross your legs," she ordered.

I hesitated, not liking the length of time it would take me to stand if she decided to kill me, but I did as she commanded.

Once my legs were crossed, she picked up the shotgun from where I'd dropped it. She laid the revolver on the table near the door. She checked to see if the shotgun was loaded. She had no trouble working the pump action. Again, I marveled at her grace and strength.

"Don't tell me it's actually loaded," I said from my seat on the floor.

She nodded.

"I'm afraid so. It might have saved you a bit of a scare if you'd known," she finished with a sad smile.

"Might have."

She squatted down in front of the dog. With no more warning than the click of the safety, she braced the shotgun against her shoulder, pointed it at the dog's battered skull, and fired. The unexpected blast of the shotgun made me jump. The dog's head dissolved into an unrecognizable pulp. The recoil rocked Sarah back on her heels. She stood, flexing her wrist, and dropped the gun. She turned toward me. Slowly, giving her a chance to reclaim her pistol, I stood. She made no move toward the table.

"That'll wake the neighbors," I said through ringing ears.

"There are no neighbors. Most of the apartments around us are empty. Husbands and sons dead. Wives and daughters turned out. Equally lost," she explained.

"Sarah, what the hell are you doing here," I asked. "You can't really be part of this. It's insane. Tragic. It's evil, Sarah."

"John, you must leave. They'll be back at any moment. I'll tell them I killed the dog because she turned on me. They'll believe that. She really didn't like women much."

"Who?" I asked.

"Coco," she answered, "the dog."

"I don't mean the damn dog. I mean who will be back!" I nearly shouted.

"Gavin, his men, what does it matter. You must go!" she hissed.

I moved toward her. Drawn against my will and indifferent to the pistol on the table, the smell of cordite in the air, or the flecks of blood on her cheeks and forehead, I reached out to her and pulled her to me. I kissed her fiercely, and she didn't pull away.

"John, you must go. Now."

"What is going on? What are you doing?" I asked softly.

"I know you won't understand. Can't understand. Gavin sees an opportunity to truly end all wars now. But for that to happen, governments must fall. These sham republics. All dancing to the tune of men like Armistan. Led by evil, self-serving men who claim to be patriots. Clemenceau, David Lloyd George. They want to keep their empires, and in doing so, they will bring an even greater war. Even Wilson. He's too weak to resist the old powers. The Russians have the right of it."

She spoke passionately. Perhaps trying to convince herself as much as me.

"Sarah, millions more will die if there is no peace. Certainly Gavin. Certainly me. And almost just as certainly Tricia and you. Even if Gavin disrupts the peace, the French will find him. They'll find you. They will execute you, and the whole country will cheer. No one wants the war to continue."

She pushed away from me and straightened. "As I said, you can't understand."

I heard sound of a door opening and voices toward the front of the house. Sarah grabbed me by the hand and dragged me toward the kitchen.

162

"You must go," she whispered, pulling on my arm. "Out the back. John, please don't interfere."

I shrugged off her hand and stooped to pick up my pistol from where I'd dropped it.

"I won't let Gavin restart the war," I said coldly. "I suggest you kill me now, because I'm not going to let that happen." I met her eyes unflinchingly. "I'm not," I promised with certainty. She dropped her eyes and turned toward the sound of the voices, like a soldier turning toward the sound of the guns.

I pulled open the heavy kitchen door, turned, and ran into the rain. No shots followed me across the yard. I stayed to the shadows as I worked my way back to the hotel.

I had to see Mitchell and tell him what I'd found.

As I hurried, I could feel the alcohol and long nights dragging at me. I was confused and hurt by Sarah's presence here and by her consent to assist in a deed so monstrous that it beggared the imagination. It didn't matter that the plan, no matter how well supported, was doomed to fail. What plan could restart a war that no one wanted to continue? I also knew with an iron certainty that I would do whatever it took to stop Gavin and his scheme. I hoped that Sarah would stay clear. But I knew she wouldn't, and I was afraid of what I would be forced to do if she sided with her brother and his Bolshevik friends.

Part of me wanted to go to the French authorities, but I knew if I did, it would doom Sarah. I could not doom her. I could sail home. Far from France and Sarah. But what would become of her? She needed my help. I couldn't tuck tail and run from this.

My emotional shell, created by terror and hardened by killing and death, was useless as a defense to my yearning for her. I was in a bad way. I was like a turtle flipped on its back, spinning without control and fearful of what would come next—a spike through the guts or a tip back onto my feet. She trapped me and made me vulnerable. *Go home*, she'd said. How could I go home when she was on a road to be hanged?

Damn her!

Mitchell would know what to do.

As I turned off rue de Babylone, I increased my pace. No one followed. It appeared she had kept her word. Loyal she was... loyal even to me.

Ironically, it appeared that helping Patricia would also help save Sarah. It looked like we still had a job.

# 13

------

## Bring the Help

When I got to the hotel, it was very early morning, and there was no answer at Mitchell's door. I decided not to pound until it opened. I was exhausted and Mitchell likely occupied. Better for me to rest for a few hours.

My sleep was unsettled but better than nothing. When the sky outside my window was bright enough to promise the morning and not the dawn, I dressed and dragged myself across the street for a strong coffee and a vicarious smoke—given that all the French patrons at the café were smoking. I was drinking my third espresso and no closer to a plan to thwart Gavin when Mitchell stepped out of the hotel into the sunlight with Kiki on his arm. After a quick kiss, the French girl turned down the street, and Mitchell crossed to the café.

"Good morning, sunshine," Mitchell quipped. "How was your evening? I'd hoped you would have changed your mind about coming out last night once you got back to the hotel."

"I went to the house on rue de Babylone. It's Gavin and the Reds' hideout. No doubt. Sarah was there," I reported.

"Well, hell! That explains your long face and the bags under your eyes. You okay?" he asked.

"I'm lost, Will, and I need your advice." I proceeded to detail what I'd found: the dog, the guns, Sarah, and the Bolshevik plan, according to Sarah at least.

"So let me get this straight," Mitchell summarized. "You think you love this girl, and you're afraid you'll have to kill her brother, maybe her, or at best, be responsible for turning her in to the Frogs, who then kill him and probably her."

"Goddamn it, what I said was Gavin and the Reds are planning to start World War Two," I growled.

"Well, now, that's what your words said, but your miserable ole face looks as sad as the great Earle Williams when he finds poor Louise dead in the train crash.[1] So what you're really saying is you're screwed and can't find a solution to being in love with a Commie, who has a brother who's a Red. See, I understood you perfectly."

"But my problems aren't the problem."

"But of course they are, my friend," Mitchell said smugly. "The only way to solve your problem is to solve the war problem. But if we solve the war problem without solving your problem, then we've failed, because a whole bunch of folks'll be dead, one of whom I think you love."

Mitchell's logic made me pause. He was right. I was so focused on the horror of a continuing war that I was willing to sacrifice Gavin, his Commie buddies, and Sarah to stop it, and that result was simply unacceptable. There had to be a way to prevent whatever they planned without getting everyone killed, but to do that, we had to know what they planned.

"All right. We don't know their scheme, but we know where their tools are to carry it out: 28 rue de Babylone. We destroy their tools. We delay them. The challenge will be delaying them without killing Sarah and her brother," I said.

"You sure about Gavin?" Mitchell asked. "I mean, I could kill him by mistake."

"I like your thinking, but if we kill Gavin, *accidentally* or not, two bad things happen. First, Sarah will hate me, and my problem is not solved; and second, Tricia will hate us, and she won't pay us."

"Both true, at first, but I have a lot of confidence in my ability to bring Tricia around. Comforting the grieving widow and all," Mitchell said with a smile. "I really would make it look like an accident. And I don't care if we get paid anyway."

"You're torturing me on purpose, Mitchell. Just stop. We can't kill Gavin. All we really have to do is delay him until the final treaty is signed. How much longer can that take? Everybody and their dog have been here since January drafting the damn thing."

"Everybody but the Germans. They weren't invited to the party. They've only just arrived in Paris. That makes me suspect they're going to be served a big pile of shit and not given the opportunity to complain."

"There is no way that will happen with Wilson leading the negotiations. He's going to want it to be fair so he can start his League of Nations off right. Folks love him."

"I don't know, Griffin. I've been talking to Kiki. Sure, the Froggies loved him at first, but he's a cold fish. He hasn't really visited the battlefields. He took one trip out and never got out of the car. Kiki says the French don't like that he doesn't value their sacrifice. Ignoring, of course, that they are just as responsible for their sacrifice as the Germans, the Russians, or the Serbs. It's been in the papers," he said, returning to his original point. "Wilson has no respect for the dead or the cost. For a really smart guy, he's not really very smart. I think he's used up all that love at first sight without really accomplishing much. It doesn't help that the French love Clemenceau.[2] Especially since the assassination attempt, stupid anarchist bastard." Mitchell chuckled as he referred to Clemenceau's would-be assassin. "Clemenceau is really the leader of the negotiations now."

Mitchell's words made me shift my focus from Sarah and Gavin to the news of the world.

In February, before I'd even heard of Harry Armistan or Sarah Willoughby, an anarchist, who was probably in cahoots with the damn Bolsheviks, had tried to kill Clemenceau, the French prime minister. He'd shot at his car, at point-blank range, seven or eight times and only managed to hit Clemenceau once. Clemenceau survived, and the French now adored him. Le Tigre they called him. The Tiger. The problem was that Clemenceau wanted to cut out Germany's heart and eat it. Any treaty drafted by him would be beyond draconian. Not the recipe for a happy, stable Germany, and Berlin had already seen Bolshevik riots. Not that the French cared about that.

"Maybe the reason it is taking so long to draft the damn thing is because Wilson is battling Clemenceau and the Brits to make it fair," I suggested.

"Hah! That's a good one, Jack," Mitchell scoffed. "It's taking so long because the world is broken. Whole countries don't exist anymore and new ones do. And the damn Brits, French, and Italians want to split up the whole thing like kids dividing up a bag of pogey-bait.[3] They all want to grow their empires and keep the Krauts under their thumbs. I think Wilson is in way over his head. He's like a new preacher thinkin' he can prove himself handling snakes that he ain't got any sense of how to handle. He's gonna get bit. And worse, he's gonna let our allies profit from our dead marines, sailors, and soldiers. It's bullshit, but unsurprising bullshit."

"Any treaty is better than no treaty," I responded. "We can't control the high muckety-mucks. Maybe raping Germany is the right thing to do. The militaristic bastards. Maybe growing these empires will bring stability and peace. And the world needs peace. We can't let Gavin interfere with that."

Mitchell slowly nodded. "I know. I'm just afraid that the peace we get is not the one we want, the one we need, or one that will last."

"You may be right, but we can only control what we can control. And we can't control the Limey, Frog, or Wop diplomats," I said, throwing the grasping Italians into the mix. "We just gotta hope Wilson can work it out. But all this political talk has given me time to come up with the start of a plan."

"What do we know? We know Gavin and his Bolshie buddies want to keep any treaty from ending the war," I said, answering my own question. "We know they would like to restart the war. We know that they are willing to kill, well, willing to kill me at least, to make this happen. We know that they have international support—German, English, probably French, and maybe American. We know they have a base of operations at rue de Babylone, and they probably have plenty of money, which very likely comes from my buddy Harry Armistan. And we know they have an arsenal of German weapons and allied weapons, including American ones." My fingers drummed the table as I considered the problem. "What have I forgotten?"

"We know the German delegation recently arrived," added Mitchell. "We know we have a spy of sorts in their operation, Sarah, but we don't know how reliable she is. We know we can probably get some local information from my girl, Kiki. Sadly, we also know we can't kill Gavin, or your problem won't be solved. Then again, Tricia would be a grievin' widow, which ain't bad." He smiled.

"So," I said, ignoring his quip, "our objectives must be indirect. First objective: prevent anything that disrupts the treaty negotiations. Second objective: get Gavin back to Tricia safe and sound, after which he is welcome to drop dead. Third: try to keep from getting killed or killing Sarah."

"I'd say the order of priorities for the objectives is one, three and then two," clarified Mitchell.

"Agreed."

The waiter returned to clear our cups. We ordered two more.

"So, what's your plan?" Mitchell asked.

"We burn the house at rue de Babylone. To the ground. We have to hope that without their weapons, they can't do whatever they're planning. We should try to make sure the house is empty, which means I doubt we can do it at night. It may have to be during the day."

"And I'm not positive," noted Mitchell, "but I'm pretty sure arson is a crime here in France."

"Yep, probably."

The coffees came, and Mitchell and I put our heads together to plan our visit to rue de Babylone. Thank God the dog was dead.

## 14

---

### A Boxer and His Fleas

Mitchell insisted on asking Kiki about the neighborhood where the house was located, which meant waiting until the evening. He assured me she would be asleep until past noon and the best time to catch her was at the club before she performed. He also thought it would be worthwhile to share what we knew with the American girls.

I chafed at the delay, but I remained certain that Gavin and his comrades wouldn't act until the German delegation arrived. In the meantime, I sketched the layout of the house on rue de Babylone as best I could remember it. In addition to the floor plan, or as much as I knew or guessed, I included the yard and the streets surrounding it.

The weather was fine, and I could tell Mitchell was bored as he set aside *L'Humanité*. He had bought both *Le Temps* and *L'Humanité* at a nearby newspaper kiosk along with some truly vile French cigarettes. His French had improved in just the few days we had been in Paris, and he no longer needed my basic translations. While I drew, he had riffled through both newspapers looking for information about the German delegation or the signing of the treaty while chain-smoking the filterless French fags.

"Smoking those evil things is going to kill you faster than the phosgene is going to kill me."

"You're probably right, but they're just so good." He laughed in an explosion of smoke. "I'm not finding anything new on the Germans," he continued. "The negotiations are ongoing and complicated. If I understand it right, the *Times* is optimistic and *L'Humanité* is not," he explained.

"We've got a few hours before lunch and a few more hours after that before we can share any of this with the girls. Let's take a walk," I proposed. "We can pick up some supplies. Also, I wouldn't mind strolling past the house again."

Mitchell stood. "Probably a terrible idea, but let's go. Hats on and low as we go, Johnny."

---

WE DECIDED TO DO THE SHOPPING FIRST, OUR THINKING BEING that if we carried packages, we'd look more local and less like two peeping Toms as we walked past the house on rue de Babylone. After much asking and getting lost a few times, we found an *amurerie*, a fancy gun store on rue de Richelieu. The old gent running it sold us some gun-cleaning supplies and was perfectly happy to take our money. We also found a hardware store and got a short crowbar, bolt cutters, and some wire. I bought a few heavy nails as well. We then circled back toward rue de Babylone, walking the block around the house but finding no other obvious entrances. It appeared that the various apartments were built against each other, and only number 28 stood unattached in its surrounding, overgrown garden. We would have to overcome the complexities of French architecture once we were inside the house.

After our recce, we stopped for lunch at a café a short walk from our hotel. We sat and waited patiently for the waiter, who would arrive eventually. We were in no hurry. We wouldn't meet the girls at Le Dôme for another three hours.

"I'm worried about the fire spreading," I said to Mitchell in a hushed voice. "The buildings are packed in tight, and if we really want to destroy their supplies, we're going to have to burn it down completely."

"Buildings get destroyed in war, Griffin. Civilian casualties happen in war. You're going to have to accept that until we put a halt to Gavin's plan, you're in a war again. I know you don't like it. I don't like it, but it's just the way it is," Mitchell assured me.

"That's fair, but maybe we could get someone to alert the Paris Fire Brigade. We'd have to synchronize the timing. Too soon, they keep the building from burning, too late and half of Paris goes up," I said.

"The French firemen are good," Mitchell noted. "Kiki told me the Pompiers did a fine job controlling the fires caused by Big Bertha's shelling of the city. You don't want to give them too much time. It would help if we brought some gasoline or something to really get the flames going before anyone shows up."

The waiter sauntered up, and we each ordered beers and duck foie gras and toast.

"I have no desire to carry gas cans across Paris. The gendarmes may be few and far between, but they're not that few," I said.

"Well, we can't exactly build a fire that will quickly destroy that house without some help."

I snapped my fingers. "I've got it, my friend," I said with a smile. "We get us six or so bottles of absinthe, and we use that to get the fire going."

Mitchell looked horrified. "Oh my God. You will not waste perfectly good absinthe on a house fire. I forbid it," Mitchell cried. "Plus it's no different from gasoline. It's still illegal!"

"I am afraid that there are casualties in war. And a few bottles of absinthe are a small price to pay. I'm sure the coppers would forgive two Americans for drinking a little absinthe."

Mitchell looked shaken, but the waiter arrived with the two beers, and he moved on from contemplating the horror of burning absinthe.

"If we want their help, I think we need to level with the girls about what we think is happening and what we intend to do about it," I said. "We need to ferret out as much information as we can before we head back to the house on Babylone."

"Agreed, but I don't think we need to be leveling with Patricia Kingsbury, if you're including her in your grouping of 'girls.'"

"I'd hardly do that. I'd either say she's our 'boss' or a 'woman,' who, I have to say, Mr. Mitchell, is a woman way out of your league."

"Oh, I doubt that, sir, but I agree, we don't need to share our plans with her," he responded.

Our food arrived, and as we ate, we discussed the possible complications of attacking and burning the house. Unfortunately, we devised no clever strategies for accomplishing the task without risking ourselves, the occupants, or the neighbors. Nevertheless, we agreed to move ahead and hope for the best.

I stood, tossed a handful of francs on the table, and gathered up our packages. "Let's head back to the hotel for a couple of hours. I could use a nap."

"Now that's the ticket," Mitchell said with a smile.

A few hours later, feeling more rested and less agitated, I met Mitchell in the lobby for the walk over to Le Dôme. The afternoon crowd was thin. With the fine weather, we took a table on the street. Not long after we arrived, Rachel and Madeline appeared, arm in arm, looking quite attractive in the afternoon light.

We stood.

"Good afternoon, ladies. We just got here ourselves and haven't ordered. Wine, beer, coffee?" I asked as we seated them.

"A noisette[1] for me," Rachel answered.

"And me," Madeline said. "Spending time with you gentlemen tends to lead to long evenings." She smiled.

"Tonight may be no different, girls," Mitchell said. "John has some information about Gavin, and we need your help. You're gonna think he's crazy, but, well… John, just tell 'em."

I told them about the house on rue de Babylone and the guns. I left out the dog and my meeting with Sarah. No one likes a dog killer or a sucker in love. I ignored Mitchell's shaking head, and I told them what Tricia had revealed about Gavin's plans to sabotage the treaty and restart the war. When I finished, they were quiet, both slowly taking drags from their cigarettes, their eyes cutting from each other to Mitchell and finally to me.

"So what are you going to do about this?" Madeline asked, looking me in the eye. I liked that she assumed we were going to do something, and I liked that she assumed that I had a plan. Yes, I was besotted with Sarah, but Madeline was an attractive girl, and I was always a fool for a pretty face.

Mitchell looked at me. "Tell them."

"We're going to burn the house down with the weapons inside. Without the weapons, whatever they're planning can't work. If we delay them long enough, the negotiations will finish and a treaty will be in place," I said.

"Just the two of you?" Rachel asked, putting her hand on Mitchell's arm. "It sounds like there must be fifteen or twenty of these anarchists for that many guns."

"We're not planning on fighting them, sweetheart," Mitchell answered with a smile. "Just burning down their house."

"Rachel's right though," Madeline said. "If there are men at the house when you go, you'll need help if you don't want to end up in a gunfight, and you could still end up in a gunfight."

Rachel looked at Madeline, and they seemed to reach some sort of agreement.

"Eugene would help," Madeline stated. "I am sure he would."

"Eugene?" I asked.

"Remember, Horace and Walt mentioned him the other night," Madeline said. "He works at Joey Zelli's club. He leads the band and helps manage the club. He just wasn't there the night we went. He used to be a boxer. He could help if you don't want to have to kill anyone."

"Boxer?" Mitchell asked, always intrigued by any martial art.

"Yes, boxer, airplane fighter pilot, and a budding musician," Rachel added.

"I'm startin' to get jealous," Mitchell said, joking.

"We should go back to their club tonight. We can pick up Kiki when she's done dancing, and then go to Joey's," Rachel suggested.

"Definitely looks like another long night, boys," Madeline said, waving at the waiter. "Another noisette, Rachel?"

"Hell no," Rachel answered. "Time to start the drinking! We got a war to stop."

We laughed as much to ease the tension as at her humor.

"Amen, sister," whispered Mitchell, catching my eye. "Amen."

---

THAT NIGHT, AFTER KIKI FINISHED HER PERFORMANCE, WE ALL piled into a couple of taxis to go back to Zelli's club on Caumartin. The girls drunkenly still insisted that we absolutely needed to recruit Eugene Bullard.

Rue de Caumartin was a narrow street north of the Seine. We could hear the rapid beat of the jazz music even before our taxi stopped. A crowd on the sidewalk swayed slowly out of time with the music.

"That is Jacques and his band playing," Kiki explained excitedly. She clutched Mitchell's arm tightly as if Tricia Kingsbury was nearby, threatening to steal him.

"Jacques?" I asked.

"Eugene." Madeline looped her arm through mine in a parody of Kiki, earning herself a glare from the French girl. "The French call him Jacques. He speaks better French than me," she noted, which was a compliment, considering that her French sounded flawless to my ear.

We pushed our way to the entrance of the club and paid the maître d' for another "license" to enter and for a table. Learning from our last visit, I also added thirty francs of Armistan's money, and the maître d' quickly summoned a doorman, who bulled his way through the crowd and rousted two couples from near the packed dance floor. He aggressively held the newly vacated chairs for the ladies, and I dug some of Armistan's francs from my pocket and tipped him as well.

"That's Jacques playing the drums," Kiki volunteered as we sat.

Four men dressed in dinner jackets were on stage, all black. The drums were set up center stage, between the various horns, and the drummer was hammering out a frenetic beat on his kit.

"Eugene's colored?" I asked, stating the obvious, assuming Kiki identified Bullard accurately.

"Of course," Rachel stated. "You don't think a white man could play the drums like that, do you?"

"Good point," Mitchell noted.

We ordered a bottle of champagne for the ladies and a bottle of whiskey for Mitchell and me.

"He speaks French wonderfully," Rachel echoed Madeline's earlier comment, "and some German as well. He really is a modern renaissance man. And boys, I know you're marines and all…"

"Navy," said Mitchell in his case.

"But Gene is a real live hero of France," she continued. "I mean, he was in the Foreign Legion and fought at Verdun. He won the Croix de Guerre and the Médaille Militaire. He's a hero, the real McCoy. So make sure you treat him with respect."

It was clear that Rachel was worried that we would embarrass her and the other girls by bringing our prejudices to the club. I should have expected it, and my comment about his color didn't help. I suppose I should have told her not to worry. On the inside, all men look the same. I'd seen enough insides to know. Bullard could be green for all I cared. I caught Mitchell's eye, and he shrugged. I wasn't sure how this was going to work out. The girls were certain that Bullard could help. I was not, but not because he was a negro. He was a drummer, for Christ's sake. He might have won the Croix de Guerre, but a medal didn't make the man. Granted, to win a medal like the Croix de Guerre as a black man couldn't have been easy, and I knew there was no way he could have won such a medal fighting for the Americans. In the war, I'd learned not to judge a book by its cover, but we'd just have to see what a rag drummer could offer that we couldn't do on our own.

Kiki was waving wildly at Bullard. He dipped his head in acknowledgment and kept working his kit, sweat gleaming on his forehead. His face was expressive, alive as he played. He clearly enjoyed the freedom the jazz music gave him.

The song wound down and, with it, the set. The dancers hooted at the band and begged them to continue, but Bullard smiled, showing bright white teeth, and shook his head.

"*Nous reviendrons. Bientôt,*"[2] Bullard promised in a deep hoarse voice. He pulled out a handkerchief and wiped down his face.

Kiki waved again, and Bullard stood and moved toward our table with a slight hitch in his walk, shaking hands and kissing cheeks on his way. Almost like a damn politician. Despite the limp, he was light on his feet, and it didn't surprise me that he boxed. He was probably pretty good at it too.

Mitchell and I stood to greet him.

"*Salut ma belle, comment vas-tu?*"[3] Bullard asked Kiki, who stood to receive his exuberant hug and a kiss.

"*Trés bien.*" She smiled.

"Ladies," he said, greeting Rachel and then Madeline with "la bise," brushing cheeks with them both, and turned to us.

"Gene Bullard," he said by means of introduction. "Or Jacques, if you're French." He extended his hand to me. "You gentlemen must be the new Americans I've heard so much about. Bar fights and carousing till all hours. You will fit perfectly in my Paris." He smiled. "I just hope you didn't bring too much of Dixie with you, unless you've got Dixie Kid hiding somewhere under the table."

Darky or no, Bullard was a handsome man with high cheekbones and a direct gaze. I'd heard of Dixie Kid. He was a boxer who'd been a fine fighter in his own right. Bullard was clever putting the "dixie" reference directly on the table for Mitchell and me to consider.

"John Griffin," I said, shaking his hand. His eyes strayed briefly to the scar across the side of my face, but he seemed unimpressed. He had been more than a pilot. He'd been in the trenches. "I think the war shelled most of the Dixie out of me, Mr. Bullard, but I'd be a liar if I said I didn't have some. Still, you'll find no hoods in my bags. I've discovered that all men look the same on the inside."

Bullard smiled and said under his breath, *"Tout le sang qui coule est rouge."*[4]

I nodded and turned to Mitchell, who reached across me, shook Bullard's hand, and introduced himself.

"It's a big city. I'm surprised you've heard about us," Mitchell said.

"The American community in Paris is like the small town in Georgia where I grew up, Mr. Mitchell. With small-town gossips. It's a racy small town but still a small town for all its glitter."

Mitchell laughed and nodded. "That makes a lot of sense. It seems like we've met more Americans than French. And call me Will."

With Mitchell's invitation to use his first name, I could see Bullard relax slightly. The girls couldn't know how we would react to Bullard, and neither could Bullard.

I pulled a chair from a nearby table, ignoring the table's occupants, who were perched on a single chair, wrapped in a kiss. "Please join us."

Bullard sat and waved at a waiter for a glass. The club was loud, and the likelihood of being overheard was slim. I glanced at the girls, trying to determine how to start the conversation. How do you tell a man that you just met the worst possible news without sounding insane, getting punched, or getting laughed at?

Before I could begin, Rachel spoke.

"Gene, you know Gavin Kingsbury?"

"I do. Has a pretty girlfriend he found in the States while he was avoiding the war. Bolshevik. Nice dresser and wonderful manners. Balding, but you'd hardly notice," he added with a glimmer of humor in his eyes.

"That's the man," Rachel confirmed. "He's now married to that pretty girl, and John and Will have learned something from her that is truly terrifying."

Bullard cocked his head, as if he'd heard a shell fired and was judging where it would fall. He didn't speak. He waited. I liked that.

Rachel looked at me, passing the baton.

"I hope you're not a Bolshevik, or I'm about to make a terrible mistake."

"Hah! Do I look like a Bolshevik?" he said, pointing to himself. "I'm running a bar and playing drums in the most decadent city on earth. A city that pretty much runs on liquor and money. Not to mention, I'm a black man, not a red."

I smiled briefly, shook my head, and leaned forward in my seat.

"Mr. Bullard, Will and I were hired by Patricia Armistan's father to find her after she went missing on her honeymoon. It turns out she wasn't missing. Now Gavin, her new husband, is. This might sound crazy because it is crazy. But Gavin, with help from a bunch of his Bolshevik friends from Germany, England, and France, is planning to restart the war. Somehow, and I don't know how, he wants to upend the treaty negotiations. He hopes that by restarting the fighting between the Allies and Germans, total chaos will come to France. And with this chaos, he thinks the Bolshevik revolution will spread here and to Germany and England."

Despite the doubt I saw in Bullard's eyes, he said, "Well, folks are already rioting in Berlin, from what I hear."

"They are," I agreed. "And it wouldn't be too hard to bring

riots to France. Both Kingsbury's wife and his sister have told me Gavin plans to restart the war. But Mr. Bullard, more important than what they have told me is what I've seen."

I studied Bullard to be certain that I had his attention. I did.

I continued, "We got a lead from an associate of Patricia Armistan that Gavin might be staying at a place on rue de Babylone. I went there to do a little reconnaissance. To see if Gavin or any of his red friends were there."

I had deliberately left out the events in Weybridge or London. I'd just met the man, and detailing all that information would complicate what had become a straightforward story. Not to mention my admitting to murder attempts and murder might scare him off.

"I've seen Mr. Kingsbury about," Bullard said indifferently.

"I went to the house and went in," I continued. "Broke in, really. It is filled with weapons. German, French, British, American. A Maxim gun, Mausers, Lewis guns, Chauchats, BARs, rifles. Uniforms too. Bolsheviks are using the house. I know this because Kingsbury's sister told me that's who was using the house. She was there." I could feel Madeline and Rachel frown as they heard about Sarah's presence for the first time. "She's part of this. So is Kingsbury. I'm telling you this because the girls are convinced you can help." I nodded toward Kiki. "I hope they're right. I don't know what you can do, but I do know what Will and I are going to do." I looked at Mitchell. "We're going back to that house, and we're going to burn it to the ground. Without the weapons, whatever they're planning will be harder for them to accomplish."

I had spoken with passion, and my audience waited for me to finish. I pressed on.

"Mr. Bullard, I don't want to hurt anyone or kill anyone, but I'm not gonna let Gavin Kingsbury and his Bolshevik friends restart the war."

I stopped. I hadn't realized how much this mattered to me. I looked over the faces at the table. No one else spoke. It seemed to matter to them too. All eyes were on Bullard.

He knocked a cigarette from his pack and offered it around the table. After lighting up for the ladies and himself, he took a long drag and exhaled as he considered my words.

"Don't burn the house. Blow it up. If done right, it's less likely to damage the surrounding buildings. More likely to destroy the weapons before any fire could. When do you want to do this?" he asked.

I gave a relieved laugh. The others leaned back in their chairs with smiles on their faces.

"Mr. Bullard, that's a damn good idea." I raised my glass to him. "We'll jump off as soon as we can work out the details and get the explosives. I don't know when the house will be empty, so we'll have to figure that out."

"Please. Call me Gene."

"And you can call me John."

"Okay, John, leave the explosives to me. The house too. I'll have *mes petites puces*[5] watch the house. They'll figure out when its empty," Bullard promised.

"*Puces?*" I asked, looking from Bullard to Kiki.

"Yeah, sorry," Bullard said. "Lots of widows and orphans now. War tends to make them. I pay them to bring me information. Really information just like this. I call them my fleas because they're everywhere. They also tip Joey and me off if the flics show an unhealthy interest in the club. The flics are like coppers anywhere. They need watching and feeding."

Bullard finished his drink and stood.

"One more set and I'm done," he said. "Stick around. This is a bottle club, so keep ordering bottles and you can keep your table. Enjoy yourselves. Joey and I can use your money. But John, don't enjoy yourself so much that you can't talk. When I'm done, I want to know more about the house and about Kingsbury's sister. There're some things I don't understand, and I think maybe just you and me should talk through them. Will that work for you?"

Bullard was a sharp man. He was asking if I was willing to answer hard questions from a black man. A fair question. I'd never had a negro question me about anything because it wasn't their place to be questioning me. But it seemed like we needed Monsieur Bullard. Without the buffer of Mitchell or the girls, he could dig into the gaps in my story. I was going to have to tell him all of it. The dead men, even the dead dog. I didn't like being in a position where he could judge my actions. Tough shit, I told myself. Stopping the war was more important than my ego. I was beginning to accept that it was indeed possible for Bullard, a black man, to be a pilot, a jazz musician, and a businessman who spoke three languages, all in one package.

Also, what I said or the way I said it must have piqued his interest in Sarah. I was certain that he smelled something fishy about my relationship with her. Colored or not, I appreciated both his perception and his discretion. I preferred to speak with him alone where matters of Sarah were concerned. It seemed like the girls had made a sound choice directing us to Bullard. I needed to make the most of him.

I nodded. "Sure, Gene. I'll be here when you're done."

His look as he left told me he could read every thought that had just run through my head.

The club got even more crowded, hot, and smoky. Mitchell and the girls danced. I took a turn or two, but I didn't have the heart or the rhythm for it. Well after midnight, Bullard's last set wound down in a wild hammering of horns and drums and frenzied whoops from the band and the crowd. Mitchell and Kiki worked their way back to the table arm in arm. Madeline had a dazed-looking Walt Disney in tow, and Rachel had found a bleary-eyed Shed Bean.

She looked at me when she reached the table. "What?" she asked at my raised eyebrows. "We know he can fight."

"Indeed he can," I answered, looking at Bean. "Good to see you again, Shed."

Bean didn't bother to speak, or perhaps couldn't. He merely gave me a sloppy salute and stood swaying next to Rachel.

Bullard worked his way through an admiring and now more drunken crowd to the table. Mitchell glanced at me, and I nodded. He turned to Kiki, whispered something in her ear, provoking a smile, and then threw his arm around Bean's shoulders.

"Let's see if we can't find one final club open, big fella," he said, leading Bean and the three ladies toward the exit.

I stayed in my seat, holding my unfinished whiskey. Bullard threw himself in a chair across from me.

"What'd you think of the music, John?" he asked.

"I think I may be turning into my father, Gene. I can't say I like it, but it may be that I just don't have the ear for it yet. I know Mitch and the girls like it a lot."

"Well. Maybe it'll grow on you if you're around here long enough." He waved at a waiter, motioning for a glass. "On my way over, I saw the look you gave Mitchell. Y'all didn't need any words at all. How long were you in combat together?"

I smiled. "Yeah, we find it easy to read each other. We were together for five months, give or take. Some of the time I was wounded, or he was," I said.

"Jeez, a drop in the bucket," he lamented. "I started the war with the French Foreign Legion in '14. Meuse, Somme, Verdun. Hell, I even got a few medals. I also got a hole in my thigh and most of my teeth are fake, but I got to learn to fly, so who's complaining?"

I thought about telling him I'd served with the British, but I refrained. The fewer who knew that the better, and he'd either help us or not based on what I said now, not what I'd done three years ago. And I'd judge him from what I saw, not what he or the girls told me.

He watched me for a moment, and I let him.

"Tell me what you didn't tell me in front of the others. In front of the girls. How ugly is this going to get?" he demanded.

Right to the point our Gene Bullard.

"With no sugarcoating?" I asked.

"No sugarcoating."

"I've been on this job for about a month. In the beginning, I went to the sister's house outside of London. Two men attacked me while she was there. They ran off but not before they knifed me." I pushed up my sleeve to show him the new pink scar. "The one on my leg is not as pretty, so pardon me if I don't show it. That same night, I stayed at the sister's house, in part, because I was cut up, but also I wanted to see if she had more information. In the middle of the night, she left, and two men broke into her home. I killed them before they could kill me, and on the way back to London, I dumped their bodies."

Bullard didn't bat an eye at my story.

"After I got back to London, three men came to my hotel room in the early morning," I continued. "They didn't knock. Instead, they kicked in the door and shot to death a perfectly good mattress. I'm afraid they're napoo[6] too. The sister knew I was staying at the hotel, but I'd signed in under another name."

At this, Bullard couldn't resist commenting.

"You're a goddamn Wyatt Earp, John."

I ignored him and continued.

"I did speak with one of them before he died. He was English but confirmed his partners were German."

"How d'you convince him to tell you that?" Bullard asked.

"He was in pain and needed help." He gave me a hard look, and I quickly moved on to prevent more questions about London.

"Then, here in Paris, when I went to the Bolsheviks' house on rue de Babylone, there was a guard dog. A vicious, giant beast named Coco. She's dead too."

Bullard laughed out loud. "You killed a dog named Coco. You best not tell any of the ladies that." He chuckled.

"The sister was in the house too. Her brother is a fanatic, and he has the support of other fanatics, and she's completely loyal to him. She was very clear about that, but she did let me get away. That's a long way of answering your question, Gene. This is already very ugly, and I'm sure it will get uglier."

"What about this sister?" he asked.

I waited for him to explain. I was not going to volunteer anything about my feelings for Sarah.

"And you. The sister and you? You must have something for her or with her. I want to know what. And don't try to con me. Sounds like she's a big part of this, and you've fallen for her. I need to know how far."

I wondered what it was in my mention of Sarah earlier that made him question my relationship with her. My stomach churned at the thought of sharing my personal life with this man, but I saw no option.

"All right, but no jokes. I don't have the patience," I said. "We have a mutual attraction. It's pretty damn strong. I can't help myself, and I don't think she can either. Despite this mug, she cares about me." I shrugged, knowing exactly how pathetic and desperate that sounded. "At least I think she does. She could be blowing smoke up my ass." I finished, smiling for no other reason than to try to convince Gene Bullard that I wasn't some girl's patsy.

He nodded. "What if it comes down to a choice between saving her or stopping a war? What will you choose?" He stared at me with his penetrating dark eyes, demanding the truth.

"Gene, I'm not a good man. If she stands in our way, I'll kill her myself," I said as sincerely as I could.

Bullard nodded. "Good," he said. He seemed to believe me, but I wasn't sure I did.

With my love life laid to rest, Bullard explained with clarity what he would ask his people to do.

"We'll try to get into the house. It's not likely we will, but we'll try a delivery. It's not that I don't believe you, but I'd like to have someone else see these weapons. We'll have eyes on the house day and night. One full day and night only though. I can't have folks hanging around not working for too long. I'll get them over there tonight.

"I have to tell you Griffin," he continued, "I don't think there will be a time when no one is in the house, and since I don't think my people will get a look inside, I have to take your word that what you say is in there is actually in there. I don't know you, but I'm trusting Kiki's judgment of you."

"Bullard, I wish I'd made it up, but the weapons and equipment were in that house last night. I'm worried that Gavin and his people might move them. The sister might have told them I was there. I told you she's loyal to him. And she'll have to explain the dead dog, which might scare them. The longer we wait, the more likely it is they move the weapons." I stopped. In explaining the urgency to Bullard, I reached a judgment I didn't like at all. "We should go as soon as we can. Today, if possible."

"It's gonna take time to get the explosives and get my people in place," Bullard objected. "Ten o'clock tonight is probably the soonest we could be ready."

"Okay, but a lot can happen in the next twenty hours. If we don't go tonight, we might lose the weapons. We can't take that risk."

I could see that Bullard didn't like my conclusion. I was beginning to understand that Gene was a planner who wanted all his ducks in a row before he committed himself.

"We won't have complete information, but we wouldn't have that anyway, and we can't wait another day," I said, pushing him.

"I don't like it, John, but I think you may be right. We'll watch the house for the rest of the day today and go in tonight. I'll let Joey know I won't be at the club tonight. Four of us will have to be enough. I won't have time to get more men," he finished.

"Four?" I asked.

"We'll bring Shed too," he said. "He's reliable and he'd want to come. He already knows anyway."

I didn't comment. If Bullard believed Bean was reliable, I would have to trust him. I did know Bean was good in a bar fight, but I wasn't expecting a bar fight.

"You said you can get the explosives," I confirmed.

"Yeah, you let me worry about those," he said. "I've got connections for what we'll need, and I've worked with explosives before, tunneling during the war."

I didn't question him. Tunneling was a brutal, horrific job, and it was not something I had done.

"Gene, if there are folks in the house and they try to stop us, there's gonna be a hell of a lot of shooting, judging by all the weapons I saw. It'll be loud and very messy," I said as a warning. I wanted him to understand that he was going back into combat.

He laughed. "I guarantee it is going to be loud and messy. I'd just like to make sure that we are out of the house before things blow up, so to speak."

We outlined our entry into the house and where we would set the charges. Once inside, Shed would watch Bullard and the outside of the house while Bullard wired the demolitions. Mitchell and I would clear the house of people as Bullard worked. With the details hammered out, we agreed to meet at the hotel at eleven o'clock that evening with all our gear in hand.

I stood. After a brief hesitation, I offered my hand. He looked at it and at me and then took it.

"Till tonight," I said.

"Till tonight."

Dawn was only a few hours away, and I was keenly aware that I was meeting Tricia Armistan for breakfast. I suppose she'd want to know how I planned to save her husband from himself. She didn't need to know about the details for the house on rue de Babylone. God help him if he was inside when we got there.

# 15

---

## A Bon Bonfire

I woke early and collected Mitchell for our meeting with Patricia. The weather remained clear as we strolled north toward the river. Despite the early hour, Mitchell seemed to be in a fine mood, twirling his umbrella with great dexterity. He actually began to whistle a tune that sounded like it might have been one of Bullard's rag music numbers.

"What has you so chipper?" I asked.

"Well, three things, really," he answered. "I have just left the arms of a loving woman, I am on my way to meet a beautiful woman, and I suspect that we'll be in action soon. So, altogether, it's an excellent combination of factors."

"You are also leaving out the possibility of getting killed or horribly maimed," I said.

"Nope. If someone's gettin' killed, it's you, Griff. You're the fella who's been courting death ever since I met him. Make sure you leave me your Colt. I do love that gun."

I laughed, beginning to share Mitchell's mood.

As we walked, I briefed him on the plan for the evening that Bullard and I had worked out. He didn't argue with the need to go immediately. He could see the risk of waiting as well as we could.

"What do we tell Tricia about this?" he asked. "I don't really want to lie to her. I mean, I barely know her, and I don't want to start off our relationship with a lie."

"I'll tell you what. Let me do the talking, and that means I'll do the lying, and I don't really care what that means for my relationship with Mrs. Kingsbury."

"Well, I am certainly glad we don't have to argue over who gets the girl," he said seriously.

"She is married."

"I am an optimist, Griffin. You know that."

Indeed I did.

We reached the café a few minutes before our nine-o'clock meeting and took a table on the east side, off the main street. We sat with our backs to the café, looking out on the Saint-Germain church and up the boulevard Saint-Germain.

Before the waiter came to take our order, a beautiful four-door automobile pulled up in front of the café. Patricia Kingsbury stepped out of the back seat before her chauffeur could dismount to let her down. It was probably the motorcar Patricia had used the evening at Le Dôme, but I couldn't be sure.

She carried a man's valise. Outlined by the clear morning light, Patricia was more beautiful than when we had first seen her. I resented her beauty and felt my hostility at her manipulation return.

I could hear the air leave Mitchell's lungs when he saw her.

"The day just gets better," he whispered under his breath.

We stood as she glided toward us.

"Good morning, Mrs. Kingsbury. You remember my associate Mr. Mitchell."

"I do. Good morning, and please call me Tricia," she answered.

"William," Mitchell said quickly.

"John," I said.

Mitchell held her chair as she sat, and I signaled the waiter, who had previously ignored us. With Patricia's arrival, he was now intensely interested in serving us.

We ordered coffees and pastries.

"That's a lovely automobile, Tricia," I said as the auto pulled away.

"Yes, it's our family town car in Paris. It is a Hispano-Suiza, built in 1916.[1] It will soon be time to get a new one, but it is very comfortable. Do you drive, John?" she asked.

"Poorly, Tricia, but I do enjoy it and hope to get more practice," I said.

"Then I shall make a point of getting you time to drive the Hispano. And you, William?"

"No, Tricia," answered Mitchell, testing the sound of her name on his lips. "I don't drive yet. I mean to learn. I do ride horses, but I haven't had the chance since getting back from the war."

"We share that joy, William. Perhaps we could find some time to ride here in Paris." Without waiting for his response, she turned to me, her socialite veneer dropping away.

"What have you done about finding Gavin and preventing his delusional plan?" she demanded.

While Will Mitchell was enamored with Tricia Armistan, I found her to be too much like her father for my taste. It's one thing for a man to be pushy, but coming from this tiny woman, it rubbed me wrong.

"Mrs. Kingsbury," I said, ignoring her Christian name in light of her tone, "we may have agreed to help you, but we did not agree yet on specifics of payment, per diem, or information. We are not your servants. If we don't come to an arrangement first, perhaps you can find others, more subservient than I, to rescue your insane husband. So, while you may want a report, which I can provide, I'd like confirmation of payment, which I hope you can provide, and a clear understanding of our relationship."

Out of the corner of my eye, I could see Mitchell frown, but I kept my focus on Patricia.

After a brief hesitation, she laughed. "Please, you really must call me Tricia, and I apologize. I am my father's daughter, and sometimes I bark more than I should. And I admit I have come to expect men to dance to my tune, given how I look," she said without embarrassment.

I could see Mitchell nodding in agreement.

"You are a beautiful woman," I said, acknowledging the obvious. "But helping you will be complicated and dangerous, and as I think I made clear the other night, I really don't like your husband."

"I completely understand, John," she said, glancing at Mitchell to make sure she continued to command his attention. She did. He could no more turn away from her than a mouse from a cobra. She opened the valise, showing me its contents. It was filled with stacks of money: francs, dollars, pounds, from what I could see. She closed the bag and leaned down to place it next to my chair. I couldn't help but join Mitchell in admiring her form as she did so.

"Your pay. All up front. No delays, but no per diem," she continued. "Now for information, let's start with what you've found, and then I'll share what information I have."

I was certain she would limit what she told us based on what she thought we needed to know. She also understood that she would have to share enough information to gain our trust. Actually, to gain my trust. Mitchell was already her slave.

"Fair," I started. "Gavin and his associates have a house here in town. I've been there. It is filled with military weapons, uniforms, and gear. It appears he intends to use this equipment for exactly the purpose you described. To stop any treaty finalizing the end to the war."

As I spoke, her eyes grew large, and she caught herself raising her hand to cover her mouth in horror. Her hand dropped to her cup.

"I see," she said. "So, it really is true, not some fabulous nightmare. Where is the house? What will you do? How can you get Gavin clear without the French finding out?"

"At present, you don't need to know where the house is," I answered. "It's dangerous to go near it, and I don't want you to try to confront Gavin. I'm sorry, but I also won't tell you exactly what we intend to do, but be assured, we are working to delay any plans the Bolsheviks may have. We are trying to do this in a way that will not jeopardize your husband, which isn't easy. If we can delay their plan, we hope this will give us time to find Gavin and bring him to you. That's what we'll need your information for. Where will he go, and what will he do if we derail his plans?"

She pursed her lips, clearly not liking my refusal to tell her the location of the house or our plan. After a moment, she nodded.

"What will you do about the weapons?" she asked, ignoring my questions.

"We'll destroy the house," Mitchell said.

So much for not telling her our plan.

"But you let us worry about that," I added. "That's why you've hired us. But what do you think Gavin will do if the equipment is gone?" I asked once more.

"He won't give up. He'll try again," she concluded.

"Would he contact your father or Morgan Reynolds?" I asked.

"No. He needed my father's money, not his advice," she answered. "And Reynolds is my father's flunky. Not Gavin's."

"Well, Reynolds is here. We had dinner with him and Gavin in London, and we saw him in a café here in Paris. He may be your father's man, but he's doing something with Gavin too," I told her.

"Don't worry about Morgan," she said dismissively. "I can control him."

"So what will Gavin do without the weapons?" I asked again.

"He'll find more. If he has the men to use them, and it sounds like he does, he'll just get more guns. There is no shortage in France. He has sufficient funds. He has access to all my wealth now because of our marriage." I thought I detected a hint of resentment in her voice. "He'll either buy them or bribe his way to getting more. It will take time though, and I agree that while he's waiting for more weapons, you might capture him," she said approvingly.

"Maybe," I said. "Where are you staying? We're going to need to contact you, and once we have Gavin, we're going to need you to talk sense into him. He won't listen to us. For him, we're thugs and mercenaries." I threw back at her the label she had used at Le Dôme.

"I'm sorry I called you that," she said. "I'm afraid and alone, and I took it out on you." She turned to Mitchell as she said the last. "Hôtel de Vendôme on Place Vendôme. Send word to me there, and I will come."

"So, not staying with friends of your husband?" I muttered. She either didn't hear me or chose to ignore me.

"But even if I can convince Gavin to leave Europe, I will need your help escorting him to a port where we can get transatlantic passage. I have some resources here but none as qualified as the two of you."

I could sense Mitchell preening at her compliment.

"I will check on the steamship schedules, but the sooner we get him out of France the better," she finished.

"It may be that we have to truss him up and put him in a steamer trunk. Do you understand that?" I asked.

"Just get him to me," she said. "Please."

Patricia finished her coffee, and as if by some magic, her automobile appeared on Saint-Germain. It was exactly half past the hour.

"William, please call on me this afternoon, at two, and we'll go riding," she said as she rose.

We both stood and watched her walk to the Hispano where her chauffeur handed her into the back seat.

"Christ! She is her father's daughter but in a most attractive chassis," I said. "Mitchell, you've got to make sure she doesn't wrap you around her little finger any more than she already has."

"I would argue that I don't know what you're talking about, but, well, I know exactly what you're talking about. I will try to keep my admiration in check."

"Try to figure out what she knows about Reynolds," I continued. "I don't believe for a second that he's not part of this whole mess. And see if you can figure out who else is in her entourage. We know she's at least got a damn chauffeur. Make sure you're back at the hotel by seven. We've got to be ready to go when Bullard arrives. And keep in mind that there can be more than one black widow in Paris. I'd hate for you to get gobbled up."

"Oh, I wouldn't mind that at all," Mitchell said with a smile. "But I'll be home by 1900, ma."

---

A KNOCK ON MY DOOR AT SEVEN P.M. WOKE ME FROM THE armchair in my room where I had dozed. Light still shone through my window, and it wouldn't be dark for another hour or so. I opened the door and found Mitchell standing before me with his kit bag over his shoulder, grinning like a monkey.

"How was the riding?" I asked, already knowing the answer from his face.

"Fine."

"Glad to hear it."

I decided not to ask him anything else, certain that he would shortly explode with the details of his time with Patricia.

I gestured toward my bed where I'd laid out my weapons and gear.

"No long guns. We should cross the yard quick, and then we'll be in the house, and pistols should be fine. And if we meet resistance in the garden, we need to get the hell out of there anyway," I explained.

Mitchell glanced at the bed, dropped his bag at its foot, and walked over to the window, looking down on the street. I could see the smile still on his face.

"She really is too good for Kingsbury," he blurted out. "Really, she is."

"Well, I suppose we need to talk about your afternoon before we talk about preventing a second world war. Obviously, it's much more important."

He ignored me and continued.

"Her father wanted the match. And it probably didn't hurt that Gavin is handsome, aristocratic, and pursued her while all us joes were out of the country, fighting the damn war!" he declared. "But her father forced it."

"Did she tell you all that, or did you make that up in your fevered dreams?" I asked dryly.

"Goddamn it, Griffin, I'm serious. I think, with time, she could fall for me."

"She's married. And maybe I think she could fall for you too, but is now the time to chase her? We're trying to stop a war while trying to save her husband from himself, which will be damn hard even without you mooning over his wife."

"My point exactly. I don't think we'll save him. He's an amateur playing in the big leagues. He'll find a way to get himself killed."

I decided there was no arguing with him, and I understood his view, given my relationship with Sarah.

"What did she tell you about Reynolds?" I asked.

"Nothing at first. She told me about her mom, who passed a few years ago, and I told her about growing up as a navy brat. We laughed a lot. She seems lonely. As for Reynolds, there's something there. I asked if he was close to her father and her. She was coy. She repeated the lackey story, but it's clear he's here to be the eyes and the ears for her dad, and I think she's in contact with him. She didn't say it, but I got the impression that Reynolds works for her too. Wouldn't surprise me if he's keen on her. She came to us because she didn't think he could find and control Gavin, but anything else she needs, I think Reynolds would either do it or coordinate it."

"She's probably right about controlling Gavin, not that we will be able to either. And I don't like that Reynolds may be working with her. Do you think he knows she's hired us? After our little tête-à-tête with him in the alley, he'll do everything he can to make us miserable, and he's a lying snake," I concluded.

"Griff, if Reynolds is working for her, she controls him. I guarantee that. And I doubt he told her about our discussion in the alley. I know I wouldn't tell a gal I'm keen on that I got slapped around in an alley."

"Then we'll just have to be careful what we tell her. We'll have to assume that she'll share it with Reynolds," I said sternly.

"Oh, I agree, Johnny," he answered, his smile back. "Just 'cause I'm smitten doesn't mean I'm some simp who can't see her for what she is."

We cleaned our weapons, stowed the gear, mentally reviewed the raid, and waited.

At 2300, a sharp tap on the door announced Bullard and Bean. Like us, both men wore dark clothes, their gear in bags in their hands.

I invited them in and poured whiskeys for the four of us.

"To peace," I said, raising my glass.

"To peace," they answered.

We toasted, tossing back the drinks.

"I'll run through the plan. Save your questions until the end. Interrupt with any corrections," I said.

I began to brief the team on what Gene and I had decided earlier at his club. I laid before each of them my hand-drawn diagrams and a detailed map of the garden and the house.

"I'll cross the garden first since I've been there," I explained. "Bean, Mitchell, and Bullard follow, in that order. Got it?"

The men nodded.

"I'll open the front door, whether with force or otherwise. Shed, you enter and go to the right, and I'll follow and go left," I said, looking at Bean. "Mitchell, you go straight through, but stay within ten paces of the door. My recollection is that the dining room with the weapons is on the left side of the house, and we'll move immediately to the weapons." I turned back to Bean. "Shed, keep an eye on the rooms on the right side so there are no surprises. I think there's probably a salon or sitting room on that side that connects to the dining room through a hallway farther back in the house. Gene, follow us into the entry and close the door, but don't latch it. We may be in a hurry to leave. Once we've found the weapons and gear, Gene, you set the demolitions and fuses, and Shed, you cover him. Mitchell and I will move together through the house, first the downstairs and then the upstairs. We need to make sure we aren't going to blow up anyone by mistake. If we find anyone, we'll either wire them up and drag them out, or if they resist too much, kill them." I stopped and looked at the men. "Any problems with this or any questions?"

"Any reason you have me going in last?" Bullard asked in an even tone.

"Gene, no offense is meant, but you need to stay in back for two reasons: first, you've got a bum leg, and second, if someone has to take a bullet, I don't want it to be our explosives expert," I answered. There were three reasons for him to go last, but I only told him two of them even though he guessed the third. Croix de Guerre or not, he was still a black man.

"What have I missed?" I asked. "Anything else?"

The three men shook their heads, understanding the gravity of the task. I hoped Sarah wasn't in the house. I knew that subduing her and dragging her out would create problems with her later, but if it had to be done, I would do it.

"I spoke with my fleas before coming here," Bullard said. "They saw four men leave the house"—he looked down at his watch—"forty-five minutes ago, and no one has entered the house during that time. My team on watch is expecting us, and when we get to the house, they'll tell us if anything has changed."

We left the hotel to find a black automobile parked in front with Disney sitting in the driver's seat, smoking a fag.

"Gentlemen," Disney said.

"I borrowed the auto from Zelli," Bullard explained. "Walt got wind of what we're up to, and seeing as how he's a driver, it seemed natural to bring him."

"Our mission security is shit," Mitchell said, shaking his head.

I appreciated that we didn't have to carry our weapons and gear across Paris. I was sure Bullard had thought of his leg when arranging the car, but I agreed with Mitchell that too many folks knew what we were up to.

I pulled open my bag, dug out Armistan's Webley, and handed it butt first to Disney. "Drive by the house and stop a few yards down the street. I'll tell you where. That doesn't have a safety," I said, nodding at the pistol. "There's no bullet under the hammer, so it only has five. Keep the car running and have the pistol under your leg. Don't smoke. Anyone coming could see the glow. And keep your eyes moving. Walt, these folks could show up while you're out front, and they mean business. If that happens, drive off, and when you're clear, toot the horn and fire twice into the air. Do not come into the yard. Got it?"

"No worries, Griffin. I'll stay sharp and be careful," Disney answered with suppressed excitement.

I nodded. Another young man eager to prove himself in the face of death. I just hoped he wouldn't die.

"Let's load up," I said.

Bean climbed into the back seat, and Bullard slid into the front, next to Disney. Both men pulled identical Browning FN 1900 pistols from their bags. They checked the loads, and each man pushed extra magazines into their jacket pockets. Bean also had a short double-barreled shotgun. He left his empty bag on the floor of the automobile. Bullard kept his bag close on the floor between his feet.

"The explosives?" I asked.

He nodded.

Mitchell had brought his own Colt 1911 and the 9mm broomhandle Mauser I'd acquired from my would-be murderers in London. I loaded my Colt and pushed it behind my belt in the small of my back. I put three extra magazines in my left coat pocket and the nails and wire in my other pocket, handed the bolt cutters to Mitchell, and hefted the jimmy bar in my left hand.

"The key," I said to Mitchell with a fierce smile.

He grinned back.

I climbed into the back seat and moved close to Shed to leave some room for Mitchell.

Mitchell walked to the front of the car and gave it a crank. The engine caught, and he jumped onto the running board next to me as Disney eased away from the hotel.

The drive wasn't long, and Disney was an excellent driver. There were no cars and only one or two drays on the roads along the way, but a few couples were still out walking, despite the late hour.

Disney followed my instructions to the letter. Rue de Baby-lone was empty. I pointed out the house, and he coasted past number 28 with the car out of gear and stopped just past the property. The four of us climbed out of the car, and I moved immediately to the gate.

A small boy stepped from a doorway across the street, spoke briefly with Bullard, and disappeared again.

"No change in their numbers," Bullard told me.

I nodded. Just as the first time I'd been here, the gate was unlocked. I eased up the latch and stepped through.

The yard was dark and quiet. Tonight I had no intention of creeping around. I moved straight to the front door of the house. I heard the crunch of gravel as the three men moved behind me. When I tried the door, it was locked. Bean crowded up behind me, ready to go. Quickly, but carefully, I pushed the crowbar into the doorjamb between the latch and the lock and wrenched it toward me. The frame splintered, but the door didn't open. I pushed the jimmy into the gap I'd created, wrenched one more time, and the door swung open.

Bean shouldered by me going right, and I went left where I could see the shadowed dining room. I pulled the Colt from behind my belt and pulled back the slide as I stepped toward the dining room.

As I moved deeper into the house, I heard the distinctive ratcheting sound of a heavy bolt being drawn back.

"Ambush!" My shout was drowned out by the heavy, stunning fire of a machine gun. The muzzle blast lit the entryway in flashing yellow light. Four, then five, rapid blasts.

Shed reeled back toward the door as splinters, plaster, and blood showered across in the entry.

"Chauchat!" Mitchell yelled.

Bean was down.

I scrambled into the dining room, past the stacked weapons, to get out of the line of fire. I could see the shadow of a second ambusher moving along the dining room wall. I fired as I moved forward. My muzzle flash showed a man with a second Chauchat. My bullet must have hit the weapon, forcing him to stumble back. He was trying to regain his balance. My next bullet punched him high in the chest.

Five more rapid machine-gun blasts lit the house. The Chauchat firing into the hallway must be cutting Mitchell and Bullard to ribbons.

I ran through the dining room, past the downed man, and fired once more into his body.

The machine gun continued firing. Twenty rounds in a Chauchat magazine. If I didn't hurry, we'd all be dead. I didn't want to think about Shed.

I came out of the dining room and rushed across the hall. The machine gunner was firing from the next room, the grand salon. If there were more than two men, I was likely dead.

Five fast pops from the front door confirmed that Mitchell was still alive and fighting. He was emptying the Mauser to keep the ambushers' heads down.

A quick peek around the corner into the room showed two

men behind stacked furniture, one aiming a rifle at the front door of the house, and a second fitting a new clip to the Chauchat. The rifleman saw me, shifted his aim, and fired. A blast shattered the doorframe by my head. Crap! Not a rifle, a shotgun!

I had four rounds left and no time. I fired twice—fast, the noise deafening—and rolled into the room.

The shotgunner ducked with my shots and rose to track me. I fired once more, knocking him back.

The machine gunner had finished reloading and swung his heavy weapon toward me. I fired and missed, moving at an angle away from his aim. My pistol was empty, and I had no time to reload. I cursed myself for not topping off the Colt's magazine before coming into the house. I was a dead man.

The gunner began firing before his weapon could bear, but it didn't matter. Even though I kept moving, crawling, as furniture and glassware shattered around me, I would be shredded when his traverse caught up to me.

The boom of Mitchell's Colt stopped the hammering of the Chauchat. He fired a second time. Mitchell leaned in the doorway, his pistol pointing at the now-dead machine gunner.

I raised my hands and called out, "Mitchell, it's me."

I could feel blood dripping down my face from the splinters and glass maelstrom created by the Chauchat. Goddamn French vases. I reloaded my pistol. The smell of cordite hung in the air.

"Shed?" I asked.

"He's gone," came Mitchell's muffled answer.

"Disney's fired two shots!" Bullard shouted. I heard his voice as if through cotton wool. The gunfire in the enclosed space had partially deafened me.

I hurried into the entry hall. Bean's body was sprawled against the front wall with his head at an angle. He'd been hit twice, once in the neck and once in the chest. Either would have been fatal. He'd died quickly. I looked out the front door to see men coming through the front gate. We would be trapped unless we did something fast.

I shut the front door and, using the jimmy as a hammer, wedged the door shut with the nails I'd brought. It was a messy unworkmanlike job with nails in the wooden floor and doorframe, but it would hold for a time. Before I had even finished, the door shivered from the kicks of more attackers.

I turned away from the door and saw Bullard in the dining room, carefully placing his charges across the four tables stacked with weapons. Something about the tables caught my attention, but I couldn't put my finger on what.

Mitchell crouched by Bean's body.

I could tell from the look on his face, the same look I had seen on his face across so many French fields, that he was ready to pull Bean's body onto his shoulders to carry him out.

"Doc, we can't get Shed out of here. We can't," I repeated. "We won't get clear."

Mitchell looked up at me.

"Help me move him into the dining room," I said. Reluctantly, Mitchell helped me move Bean's body.

Bullard looked up from his work and shook his head sadly. "Shit. He was a good man. Well, we'll make this damn house his Viking pyre. Help me place the charges, Mitchell." He handed two wired explosive blocks to Mitchell. "Under that table."

I could now hear shouts from the front, and the kicks to the door redoubled. I was filled with guilt and anger. Shed was dead because of my half-assed plan. The damn Bolsheviks had us trapped.

"I'm firing," I warned Bullard and Mitchell. Both men nodded. I walked to the entryway and emptied the .45 through the door.

The kicking stopped and wailing cries of the wounded on the other side of the door started. I moved back to the dining room just as the bullets began to slam into and through the front door. Fortunately, there was no machine-gun fire, which meant the ambush had been set up for inside the house. The men coming from the outside were just here to mop up the mess. I reloaded the Colt. We'd have no time to check the house for innocents. I prayed Sarah was not here.

Mitchell was pulling weapons from the table. He had separated out a Browning Automatic Rifle and a musette bag of magazines for me. He checked the load on a Winchester trench gun for himself.

Christmas in spring.

I found a second musette bag and filled it with shells for the shotgun and boxes of rounds for the .45.

"I'm done," Bullard declared. "The fuse is set for two minutes. There'll be a secondary explosion when this ammunition goes. We need to be out of the yard and at least behind the front wall."

"Do you want the Chauchat?" I asked Bullard, gesturing toward the bodies in the sitting room.

"Hell, no! I'll stick with my FN and these grenades." He held up his pistol and a bag of grenades he'd found on the table.

"Light her off, Gene. And I may need to borrow a grenade." I turned toward the back of the house. "Follow me."

I quickly retraced the path I'd taken when I'd first come to the house, back to the kitchen and the cellar steps. We'd have to go up the coal chute and hope the Bolsheviks didn't have it covered.

I could hear shouts from the rear of the house. They were coming in through the garden.

I pulled open the cellar door and pushed Mitchell and Bullard through. Carefully I pulled the door closed. I wouldn't have time to try to hook the latch. I just hoped in their hurry to clear the house, our hunters would miss the cellar—for ninety seconds at least.

By the time I got down the narrow stairs, Mitchell was already up the coal chute and peeking through the cracked cellar door. He was looking toward the front of the house.

"No time to be shy, Will. Toss them both open and let's get going. Gene, stay between us."

Before I was done speaking, Mitchell had thrown open both

doors to the coal chute and scrambled outside. Despite his bum leg, Bullard quickly followed. I pulled myself up the chute and raced after them.

Bullard threw a grenade high and far. It landed between the front of the house and the gate. It didn't explode but instead burst into a pillar of smoke that grew as we ran toward it.

"Brilliant, Gene!" I shouted.

Mitchell raised the trench gun and fired three rapid shots into the front entryway of the house to deter any Reds inside from coming outside.

I didn't bother to fire but ran like hell toward the gate. Mitchell pushed Bullard through the gate, turned and fired past me at the side of the house where men were emerging.

I stumbled by him and fell with my back to the stone wall. An instant later, Mitchell joined me. As he did, the night turned to day. I felt the immense pressure of the detonation of Bullard's charges in my chest accompanied by the stunning sound of the explosion. A second blast followed, and shattered bricks, wood, and dust rained down. So much for being more surgical than a house fire, I thought.

I looked over the wall and saw the glow of flames in the sagging house. Bodies lay in the garden, some moving, others not. Innumerable smaller explosions and pops followed as the ammunition in the house cooked off.

Down rue de Babylone, I saw headlights approaching through the dust. I put the Browning to my shoulder, fearing the worst, but the driver was waving wildly as he swerved through the dust and bricks in the street.

It was Disney. Thank God! He'd come back.

The three of us clambered into the car.

"Go, Walt!" I shouted as he looked toward the gate, hoping for Bean to appear.

"Go now! Shed isn't coming."

Disney didn't hesitate. He jammed the automobile into gear, and we bounced down the road. The neighbors along rue de

Babylone were starting to peer out their doors and windows at the now-blazing house.

I took a deep breath. "Gene, did the explosives do the job on those guns?"

"They won't be using what was in the house. I'm sure of it," Bullard confirmed.

I nodded. "Good." We'd accomplished the mission, but my gut twisted with guilt. I'd lost Shed.

"They knew we were coming," I said, stating the obvious.

Mitchell leaned forward and put his hand on my shoulder. "Griff," he said, "there was nothing else you could have done. We had to destroy those weapons."

"He's right, John," Bullard agreed. "And Shed knew that too."

I nodded once more. Thoughts of the violence and Shed were jumbled together in my mind. I couldn't shake the feeling I'd missed something obvious in the house. It bothered me, but I wouldn't figure it out tonight. Tonight I would mourn.

"Walt, take us to my flat," Bullard commanded. "We can't pull up to the hotel armed to the teeth and covered with dust." He glanced at me. "And bleeding. Every flic in Paris will be on to us."

With Bullard's directions, Disney drove to his building, pulled the car through the carriage gate, and parked in the interior yard. The three of us followed Bullard up two flights of stairs, and he showed us into a well-furnished apartment. I was surprised but didn't have the energy to comment.

"Sit." He directed us into the salon. He moved to his liquor cabinet and poured amber whiskey into glass tumblers.

The four of us sat quietly, nursing our drinks, still in shock from the violence of the evening.

"He told us he didn't have anything to go home to. He wanted to stay here. That true?" I asked.

Bullard and Disney both nodded their heads.

"Nobody close that I know of. Maybe some family in Milwaukee," Disney answered. "We'll need to tell the girls."

As we finished our whiskeys, Mitchell and I disassembled the shotgun and rifle, putting the pieces into a large travel trunk Bullard donated. Disney returned the Webley, which I put into the trunk as well. Bullard promised to have it sent to our rooms the next day.

Mitchell looked at the small cuts on my face and scalp and pronounced me fit for duty. We then took turns washing up in Gene's bathroom.

Gene poured a second round. We sat quietly for a time, each of us nursing his own thoughts.

I looked at my watch. Only twelve thirty in the morning. It seemed like it should be much later.

I stood to leave.

"Gene, thanks. I can see why you're a goddamn French war hero," I said, shaking his hand. "I'm sorry about Shed. I hope we made a difference."

"I wasn't sure I believed you, John," he replied. "But when we went through the front door... Well, I sure as hell believe you now. I'm real sorry about Shed too, but we did the right thing. Let me know what you want to do next. I don't think this is the end of it."

"I'm sure it's not, Gene. I'll keep you in the know. Let's catch up this evening before your show. Can Walt return Joey's car later today? I'd feel better if he wasn't driving around tonight."

"Sure," Bullard answered. "It'll be fine in the courtyard."

Mitchell and Disney shook his hand, and the three of us walked woodenly down the apartment stairs and out into the street.

## 16

---

### Clever Plans

I slept poorly. Nightmares. But I did not dream of being discovered by my former mates. This sleep was plagued by the ubiquitous, indescribable terrors of the front that so many men shared. Collapsed trenches, suffocating gas, crushing artillery, machine guns. Ordinary nightmares. Nightmares the violence of the night's work had triggered. I woke early.

In my troubled sleep, I had figured out what bothered me about the house and the weapons, and I needed to see Patricia. She was a complication I wanted to resolve before we faced the bigger problem of the Bolshevik scheme. I didn't want to bring Mitchell because I didn't think I would get the outcome I needed with him along.

When we first met her, I had thought Tricia Armistan was a poor judge of men. In choosing me to save her husband, I had concluded that she didn't understand me or what motivated me. I was wrong. Like her father, she was an excellent judge of men and their motivation. She understood that I was a womanizing romantic and I would chase to the ends of the earth to save a pretty face, even a manipulating one. And I had two to save: her and Sarah. She also correctly deduced that I would not go out of my way to save her husband.

In fact, I was convinced she hoped I would murder him.

While she couldn't understand the details of my antipathy toward Gavin, her intuition correctly told her I was the perfect tool to effect his demise. Of course, our conversation on the subject didn't hurt. She would also be conscious that he was aristocratic, supremely confident, and handsome. All attributes she could reasonably expect would not endear him to me. She didn't know my hostility sprang in no small part from my conviction that he was a much braver man than I.

I wanted to think him a coward for refusing to fight, but in my heart, I knew the courage it would have taken to resist the fanatical fervor of 1914. I hadn't resisted. Hell, I didn't have the intelligence to see the sham for which I was volunteering to fight. Then, when I had the chance, I ran. I wanted him dead because he was a better man. Despicable of me, yes, but I didn't see any point in lying to myself.

Of course, he was also a traitor to his country and an insane fanatic, but I could understand how the ostracism he had endured could have driven him to such a place. I couldn't accept that he was bringing his sister to ruin with him. This added to my willingness to put a bullet in his head.

My hope for this unplanned morning meeting with Patricia Armistan was to reach a clear, unequivocal understanding as to what she truly wanted. The simplest answer would be she wanted Gavin dead. This was what my heart told me she wanted. A dead husband. While we were already on a collision course with Gavin's lethal scheme, she couldn't know that he would die. By hiring us, as a beautiful, worried wife, she ensured we remained in play. As Mitchell said, Gavin was an amateur, likely to get himself killed, but we were a wonderful backup plan. If she wanted him dead, I could then allow this to happen or do it myself, ideally in a way that wouldn't implicate me, while saving Sarah. It would simplify our planning. It was also much easier to kill a man than rescue him.

If, on the other hand, she really did want him packed into a steamer trunk safely and securely on his way back to New York City, then I had a problem. A beautiful woman was asking me to help her, and that I could not resist. That damning attribute was what had prompted General Neville to recommend me to Harry Armistan in the first place. I had a pathetic weakness for women in need. I wouldn't be allowed to kill Gavin or even ignore him. I would have to try to save him. His survival would become part of rescuing the girl.

I dressed, packed the valise of money Patricia had given us, and tucked the Colt behind my belt.

I had a quick coffee at the café across from the hotel and walked to the Hôtel de Vendôme. It was still early, but I was sure that Patricia would see me.

As I walked, I stoked my anger against the Armistans. Against their class, their privilege, their indifference to sacrifice, and their assumption of service by others. It was important for Patricia Armistan to feel that anger so she'd believe what I would tell her.

I gave my name at the front desk, and after a quick call to her room, the concierge summoned a bellman to take me to her suite on the second floor.

The bellman tapped on the door to announce me, gently opened the door on her call of "enter," ushered me in, and shut the door behind me.

"John, what brings you here at this hour? Is there news? Where's William?"

She stood in the sitting room of her enormous suite, wrapped in a silk dressing gown, fully aware that the sunlight from the windows behind her outlined her figure. I could feel a rage building.

"There's news," I said flatly.

"What happened? Is Gavin safe?" she asked with a tremor in her voice. Either she really was an artist, or she was sincere.

"We tried to find Gavin last night. We tried to prevent his insane plan. He ambushed us. Killed one of the men with us."

"William?" she asked.

"No, but it could have been." I let my anger bleed through. I didn't tell her that we were successful in destroying the weapons because I wanted her to believe stopping Gavin was still urgent. And I was certain she wasn't being honest with me.

I threw the valise at her feet.

"Here's your money back. I won't protect your husband, Mrs. Kingsbury. If I can find him, I'll kill him."

"No. Please." She picked up the bag. "Please, I need your help. I can't save Gavin alone. I beg you. Please." She cradled the valise to her chest like a baby.

"Get Reynolds to help you. He's here. He's smitten with you. Hell, you probably won't even have to pay him."

"He can't stop Gavin," she insisted. "He doesn't have the strength. Please, John, please." She started to cry, making no effort to hide her face or wipe away the tears. She wanted me to see them. "I know what Gavin has done is horrific, but I can't help but love him. Please help me."

I turned away from her as if in disgust.

"Lady, just stop," I said over my shoulder as I moved toward the door. "Don't you really just want Gavin dead? Really?" I turned back to her. "Isn't that what you want?"

"No! God, no!" she exclaimed. "I don't know why you'd say that. I've told you the truth. I want Gavin safe. I've tried to find him, but until he accomplishes his goals, he doesn't want me close because he thinks I could be hurt. I'll find him myself. Better that than for you to hunt him down thinking I want him dead."

"Mrs. Kingsbury, I know I look like a stray mutt, but don't assume I have the brain of one. You're manipulating William, showing interest where there should be none, and you've invited me into your room while you're still in your nightgown, yet your face is painted, and you look like a peach. I'm telling you: you don't need to manipulate me. I know that's what you Armistans do. All I'm asking for is a little honesty. I took your job and agreed to find Gavin, but don't you think it would be simpler if you were just straight with me and told me what you really want? If you want Gavin dead, that's fine by me."

"Please," she said, starting to tear up again, "I just want Gavin safe. I don't know why you think so poorly of me, Mr. Griffin, but I'm telling you the truth."

I had failed. She was either sincere in her claims about wanting to save her husband or she preferred to have him die without having to expressly ask for that result. If the latter, I was sure that she was annoyed that I was so obtuse and déclassé as to speak openly about murdering her husband. Well, I was not accustomed to unspoken, hinted-at orders.

It looked like Mitchell and I would have to try to save Gavin while stopping another goddamn world war. Perhaps I could get something positive from this meeting.

"Fine," I said. "I'll find Gavin. I'll stop his plot. If I can, I'll capture him, but I'll leave him where I find him. If you want to know where he is, you'd better be close or send someone with me. I won't risk William or myself to save Gavin. You will have to get your daddy's servants in Europe to bundle him onto some steamship and smuggle him to America."

She took no offense. "I'll come with you myself. Just tell me where and when. Please just find him. Stop him from doing anything else terrible."

I studied her face, her blue eyes brimming with unshed tears.

"I'll need more money. Bribes work better than strong-arming folks, and with the mess Gavin's made, we'll need to bribe a lot of folks," I said. I neglected to mention that much of the mess had been created by Eugene's artful use of explosives in the 7th Arrondissement. "And I'll need Mr. Reynolds to coordinate logistics directly with you and me."

"I've already given you sufficient funds," she said, the teary wife giving way to the business mogul's daughter. "And what makes you think I can get Reynolds to help?"

"You'll get me another five thousand dollars, or William and I don't help you. And you'll get Reynolds because he's here and works for your family. You'll need someone to arrange the logistics of getting Gavin out of the country. He can do that. And since I don't trust him, I'd like him under your thumb, and I'd like it to be clear to him that he is under your thumb."

She was quiet for a moment, keeping most of the calculation from her eyes.

"Two thousand, and I'll speak with Mr. Reynolds."

"Come to the Le Dôme café at two this afternoon with Reynolds," I said. "We will agree on a way to communicate our progress to you. You need to make it clear to him that he must help me, and that in helping me, he is helping you. Reynolds and I do not get along. I do not like him, and he does not like me, but he must help me if you are to have any hope of saving Gavin. Do you understand?"

Patricia Kingsbury nodded. "Please just bring me Gavin back safely," she said softly. She held out the valise.

I took it and opened the door to her suite. I turned back to see that she had moved, and she was once again framed by the light of the windows. She really was a breathtakingly beautiful woman.

I shook my head. We remained her pawns.

"You should be careful what you wish for, Patricia."

I turned and left.

I had failed in uncomplicating our mission. While Reynolds would be out from the shadows, purportedly helping us, I had not shaken Patricia's claims about wanting to save her husband. I didn't believe that she wanted to protect Gavin, but I had no solid support for my suspicions. She manipulated men automatically, without thought, and it could be that my view was my involuntary hostile response to her knee-jerk manipulation of me as a man.

There was no point in dwelling on my failure. I had succeeded in getting more help through Patricia and her connections, and I had squeezed more money from her, which gave me some small comfort that she might be telling the truth about wanting to protect Gavin.

I turned my thoughts to the bigger problem. When I first had gone to the house on rue de Babylone, the weapons in the house had included both allied weapons and German weapons. When we returned to destroy the house, the truly dangerous German weapons were gone. Only a few of the bolt-action Mauser 98s remained, stacked on one table. The Maxim gun, sniper rifles, and the modern Bergman machine pistols I had seen on my first visit were not there, I was sure of it. I didn't know about the uniforms. We didn't check the entire house because we didn't have the time, but there would have been no point in Gavin and his revolutionaries moving the uniforms from the dining room to another room in the house. No, they had moved the most dangerous of German weapons and German uniforms to another location.

If Gavin had planned the Bolshevik response because of the dead guard dog, even with the explanation Sarah had promised to give, he was cleverer than I believed he was. The planning logic was sound: if the Bolshevik ambush of any intruders succeeded, their plans are uninterrupted, and they continue to have access to the cache of allied weapons. If the ambush fails and the weapons are taken or destroyed, their enemies likely don't realize that the deadliest German weapons were moved. With the ambush and the mop-up assault from the street, any intruders would be under attack the entire time they were at the house. They would have had no time to catalog the weapons. And this is exactly what had happened. We'd had no chance to really examine the weapons or search the house. It was a clever, well-executed plan. I found it hard to believe that Gavin had developed it.

Unfortunately, I didn't have any idea what to do next. It seemed everyone had clever plans but me. I would need to update Mitchell and relay to him, in favorable terms, my meeting with Patricia. Once in the know, he would have suggestions on how to use Patricia's resources. I was sure Eugene would have some ideas as well.

<hr />

I RETURNED TO THE HOTEL AND GOT A FEW MORE HOURS OF SLEEP. I woke to a rapping on my door and found Mitchell outside, looking grim.

"We need to talk to Patricia," he declared before my door was completely open. "These folks mean business. If Gavin is really part of this, there is no way we can keep him alive and get him back to the States."

I pulled the door open and gestured him into my room.

"I agree, but it doesn't matter," I said. "I saw Patricia this morning, early. I was angry about Shed, and I wanted to get some things straight." I described my visit to Patricia completely. I left nothing out. Maybe I was groggy from just waking, or maybe I just didn't want to lie to Mitchell.

"You accused her of wanting to murder her husband?" he asked, shocked.

"Yes, I did. All the information we have tells me we can't save him. Her job for us is a farce. She's a smart gal, so that led me to logically conclude she just wants him dead but is too refined to say so. I think she sees us as some wild and uncontrollable gunmen. Perfect for murder and mayhem in Paris."

"She's got that right," he declared.

"Exactly. With us around and disliking him, she should reasonably expect us to kill him. 'Cause we might. It doesn't help that she's buttering you up. If she loves her husband so much, she shouldn't be doing that." I finished aware that I sounded like a prude.

"Jeez, Griffin. What? Do you want to put her in a chastity belt and lock her in a tower? This is the twentieth century. A woman can go out without a chaperone and talk to a man without you breaking out in hives. Honestly!"

"You can pretend you don't know what I'm talking about. Maybe you can ignore that she's making eyes at you because you're so damn irresistible, but you can't pretend that her job for us adds up. It just doesn't. But it doesn't matter. I pressed her, and she stuck with her 'I love Gavin' story. We've got to find Gavin, keep him alive, get him to her or Reynolds. And we must do that while keeping the Bolsheviks from succeeding in disrupting the peace talks. That's the mission. She could be lying about wanting Gavin back, but it doesn't matter."

Mitchell started to laugh. "Well, that's disappointing to hear," he said through his chuckles. "I thought I'd made a real impression on her."

"You might have. Just not enough for her to admit she wants us to kill her husband."

"I don't think she does, John. I think she likes me well enough, but unlike you, I believe her. She's got a good heart and wants to save her worthless husband. It makes me like her more."

"Well, shit!" I said with conviction.

# 17

## Bait in the Trap

We arrived at Le Dôme early and sat on the terrace. I had thought about checking to see if Gene was available to join us but decided not to bother him. We could fill him in later, and I liked having him as our ace in the hole that neither Reynolds nor Patricia knew about.

I saw Patricia's Hispano-Suiza pull up to the curb. I gestured with my chin, and Mitchell turned to watch her arrival.

Reynolds stepped out of the car and turned back to offer Patricia his hand. As she left the motorcar, she gave Reynolds a small smile that annoyed me and I'm sure made Mitchell's blood boil. I did take some satisfaction from the tape covering Reynolds's nose and his two black eyes.

Reynolds turned toward the café, and he caught sight of us watching him. He hesitated slightly, then offered his arm to Patricia. With his arrogance firmly back in place and his employer, or his employer's daughter, on his arm, he arrived at our table.

We both stood for Patricia.

"Patricia." Mitchell leaned forward to brush her cheek with his.

I nodded and made no other effort to greet her. Instead, I watched Reynolds's narrowed eyes glare at Mitchell and dart to me.

"I understand that you gentlemen have met Morgan," Patricia said.

Mitchell matched Reynolds's stare.

"Yes, we've met. It's a pleasure to see you again, Morgan," I said, greeting Reynolds with a smile.

He grunted.

"I came across this," I said, reaching into my jacket pocket and handing him his passport. A peace offering of sorts. I kept the money I'd taken and ignored the question in Patricia's eyes.

The waiter arrived as if drawn by a magnet named Patricia Kingsbury, and we ordered.

I looked to Patricia to confirm our agreement in front of Reynolds and Mitchell.

"I understand from John that Gavin's plans have taken a dangerous—no, a deadly—turn," she said firmly. "We need to apply all our resources to stopping him safely. We all understand this?" She looked to Reynolds and Mitchell for agreement.

"Yes," they answered in unison.

She then turned to me. I nodded.

"John, tell us what you need in addition to this." She gestured to Reynolds, who placed a lady's small travel bag on the café table.

I put the bag in my lap and opened it. Stacks of dollars filled the bag. I closed it and put it by my chair.

"Good," I said as I turned to Reynolds. "We'll need you to arrange discreet passage back to the States for"—I looked at Patricia—"three people?"

"Five," she said. "We will be bringing Sarah back with us, and my driver."

I was surprised and tried not to show it. And not by the addition of the driver.

"Fine," I continued. "It can't be fancy. Spare rooms on a cargo freighter out of Le Havre are better than rooms on a passenger liner from Brest. Make the arrangements for departure in ten days' time. Don't make it sooner because we might not have him. A little more is okay. You understand?" I was acting like we had a plan because I had no choice. If we didn't have Gavin within two weeks, I had a terrible feeling that whatever the Bolsheviks planned to do would have happened by then.

Reynolds nodded. It was clear that Patricia had laid solid groundwork for his present obedience.

The waiter returned with our order: a café au lait for Patricia, a whiskey for Reynolds, and two draft beers for Mitch and me.

"Now, if we get Gavin, we will need to move quickly," I continued. "So, Reynolds, we will need a discreet flat or house where we can keep him until the ship sails. I'd suggest it be in whatever port the ship is leaving from. We'll take him there directly. By car would be best. We'll need to borrow your Hispano for that, Patricia."

"Of course." She nodded.

"If we can take him straight on to the ship, all the better, but we can't depend on that," I said. "It would be a good idea to have a strong sedative to keep him quiet." I looked at Patricia. "You know he won't come easily."

"I know that's a possibility. We will take the necessary steps to control him," she said with certainty.

I saw Mitchell rock back slightly at her cold-blooded statement. Good. Mitchell needed to understand that under the pretty packaging, she was just as bloody-minded as Haig, Foch, or General Fucking Pershing.

"One last thing. Patricia, we need to get ahold of you day or night, which means you have to stay at your hotel. You can't wander off and see the sights or visit friends or drink in the nightclubs. You need to be in the hotel where we can find you."

Patricia took a sip of her coffee and watched me over the rim of her cup. "I have a better idea, John." She put down her cup. "I'll move to your hotel and stay near you. Day and night," she added, smiling.

"I think that's a mistake. You can't stay with Griffin," Reynolds interjected protectively and angrily.

"Morgan," Patricia said sharply. "You will remain at the Vendôme and coordinate from there."

As much as I hated agreeing with Reynolds, I did not want Patricia dogging our steps. She would get in the way, endanger us, and possibly get killed.

"Patricia, Reynolds is right. We were ambushed last night. Four trained, veteran men, and one of us still died. We can't protect you," I said.

"Nevertheless, I will be with you," she declared defiantly. "This is not a discussion. You have made clear your requirements, which I have met. And now I have made clear mine, which you will meet."

Mitchell shook his head. As much as he was attracted to Patricia, he knew exactly how hard our job would be shackled to a civilian. And a woman. This was an appalling idea, but I wasn't going to argue anymore. Gavin needed to be stopped, and she was funding our effort to stop him.

"Well, I'm glad you paid us up front," I said. "Can you shoot?"

"A shotgun. Bird hunting."

"Fine," I said. "Let me be clear, Patricia. We work for you, but when we're in the field, you will do what I tell you, when I tell you. You will not hesitate. You will just do what you are told. If you can't do that, I will tie you up and leave you in your hotel room. That way I'll know where to find you. Understood?"

"Yes, sir," she said with sarcasm.

"And when we're working, don't expect us to carry your bags and open your doors. You must be able to fend for yourself."

"I understand," she promised.

"Walk to the Hôtel de Vendôme, pack your shit, and walk

back here. Don't bring your car. Walk. And have Reynolds go buy some trousers that'll fit you. When we go hunting Bolsheviks, you're going to want to be wearing pants so you can piss 'em."

Patricia grimaced. Mitchell barked out a laugh.

"I can see why you were a successful soldier," she said, not intending that as a compliment.

"I wasn't a soldier," I said. "I was a marine."

"Damn right he was," Mitchell interjected with a grin.

Reynolds walked to the Hispano, glancing at Patricia wistfully as she began her trek back to the Hôtel de Vendôme on foot.

"Another beer?" I asked Mitchell. For some unaccountable reason, my mood had improved. I still felt guilty about Shed, but being short with Patricia had cheered me up.

"I'd love one," Mitchell said. "You know this is a terrible idea having Patricia join us."

"Yup."

"I do appreciate you getting me more time with her though," he added.

"She could end up dead, Will."

"She could, but hell, so could I."

As I ordered the beers, he leaned back, lit a cigarette, and crossed his legs, the picture of relaxation.

This mission could end disastrously, but I was feeling pretty relaxed too.

Patricia returned two hours later, looking somewhat disheveled from her walk to the Vendôme and back. To her credit, she carried one bag of manageable size.

I waved at the waiter, who also noticed Patricia's arrival.

"*Une pression, s'il vous plaît,*"[1] I ordered.

Patricia sat. Her face was flushed, but she met my eye with her head up, too proud to comment.

The waiter promptly brought the draft beer.

"Welcome to the party, Patricia. The beer's for you."

We finished our drinks in silence and walked back to our hotel with Patricia carrying her bag. It was tough on Mitchell.

From the corner of my eye, I could see him glancing at me, then watching her struggling with her bag. He knew why I wanted her to carry it, but it was still hard for him. Harder for her though, and that was the point. If she was coming with us, she had to carry her weight if she was to survive.

The desk clerk gave her a room on the floor above ours, and she went directly to her room. I was glad she was on the floor above. It would be marginally easier to protect her and keep an eye on her. I was worried that having Patricia with us would risk Gavin's learning of our plans, whether through her directly or through Reynolds, but there was nothing I could do about it. I supposed that Patricia and I would just have to work on being honest with each other. I smiled to myself at the thought of that unlikely possibility.

We planned to meet again for dinner, and after dinner, we'd hunt up Gene before he started playing. With time to kill, I disassembled the Browning Automatic Rifle and cleaned it meticulously. Since I was in the mood, I recleaned the Colt and the Mauser pistol. The Mauser was new to me, and breaking it down and reassembling it took some time. For practice, I did it three times, getting faster each time. The work of my hands left my mind free to calculate and plan. By the time I slid the Mauser's magazine floor plate home for the third time, I knew what we would do.

Secrecy could be a problem, but I already knew that would be the case with any plan involving Patricia. Also, I wasn't sure if Patricia would agree. She would be key. And she would have to commit to helping us. If she didn't, the plan wouldn't work. Finally, if Reynolds was secretly working for Gavin, we'd be dead. No plan is perfect.

We met in the small hotel lobby to wait for a taxi to take us across the river to a restaurant Patricia recommended. Once again very much the financial magnate's daughter, she made sure that our hotel concierge had telephoned ahead to ensure that we had a table. Despite the relatively small bag she carried to the hotel, she managed to look modern and stylish as we waited in the cramped lobby. I was impressed but refused to show it. However, Mitchell was very happy to compliment her.

Patricia's restaurant of choice was L'Escargot de Montorgueil, a restaurant about a twenty-minute walk from Joey Zelli's club. She insisted on ordering. If Patricia had hoped we'd balk at escargot, she was disappointed. In the service, we'd eaten food that was nearly inedible. We didn't bat an eye at the garlic, parsley, and butter-soaked snails, French bread, and a crisp French white wine. The meal was delicious, and, surprisingly, the company was good. I enjoyed myself. Mitchell was charming; Patricia was beautiful and even more charming. I found myself wishing that Sarah was with us.

As if she could read my mind, Patricia blurted out, "Oh, John, I do wish you could spend time with Sarah when we are free from this terrible business." Her cheeks were flushed with wine, and she still had a smile on her face from Mitchell's last story. "She has a sharp wit, which you likely endured when you met her. Since her husband, James, died, she doesn't like military men. I am sure she treated you poorly when you spoke. But she really is the dearest creature."

"Actually, after a rocky start, she was quite pleasant," I said noncommittally. I ignored Mitchell's smile, and I don't think Patricia noticed it.

"And she does not like my father. Or really anyone who works for him. In part, I am sure this is because Daddy invests in the arms business, and Sarah hates war. But I am sure the two of you would get along famously," she concluded, returning to her original thought.

"I'm sure we would. I hope we get the chance."

"I will hold you to that, Mr. Griffin," she said formally.

"Me too," Mitchell agreed, and Patricia favored him with a smile.

Shortly after this awkward pact, we finished our coffees and I paid for dinner with Patricia's money. The evening was fine, and we agreed to walk to the club. Patricia placed herself between Mitchell and me, linking her arms through ours. It was a sweet gesture, inconsistent with my view of her as a socialite scion of a financier. I liked her better for it, but I warned myself not to make too much of it or her. Despite the French white wine loosening her social restraints, she remained her father's daughter.

Perhaps because of the early hour or because the next day was a working day for most Parisians, Zelli's club was quieter than it was on our previous visits. We found Eugene alone at a table not far from the stage. As we approached, he waved the waiter over and stood to greet Patricia.

"Patricia, this is Gene Bullard, boxer, war hero, drummer, and club manager," I said. "Gene, Patricia Kingsbury is a New York treasure and our employer."

They shook hands in a thoroughly modern fashion. Tricia did not seem fazed in the least by Bullard's race. I chalked it up to her bohemian, New York lifestyle, and I did appreciate it.

The waiter interrupted the introductions. We ordered a bottle of white wine Bullard recommended, and I got right to the heart of the matter.

"Patricia, Eugene took part in our raid on the Bolshevik house where your husband and his associates stored their weapons," I started. "We were successful in destroying some of the weapons." Both Mitchell and Bullard looked at me sharply upon hearing that only some of the weapons had been destroyed. "Gene has connections here, and if he's willing, I'd like him to be part of our plan to remove—*safely* remove—Gavin from his continued plotting."

Patricia glanced at Bullard and nodded. His face remained impassive as he quietly smoked, waiting for me to reveal the plan.

"Even with Gene's help, we won't find Gavin without incredible luck, and by then it could be too late." I turned to Bullard. "Patricia thinks that Gavin won't give up even though we destroyed most of those guns. She thinks he'll acquire more. He's got the money since he controls much of her fortune, and he has the continued desire. Did I get that right, Patricia?" I didn't want to speak for her. I needed Gene to hear her view of things in her owns words, and I wanted to hear them too.

"Yes, that's right. Gavin won't give up. He's stubborn, and when he believes in something, he will stop at nothing to see it through," she said. "He'll continue whatever the task. I learned this about him early in our relationship."

"So, while we've delayed whatever their mission is, we haven't prevented it. We need to capture Gavin to do that," I concluded.

"That's assuming he's the leader," Bullard commented.

"That's a fair point, but we have no reason to believe he's not. He's the link between the English, French, and Germans. He likely has connections with the Russians too. If someone else is in charge, we can't begin to guess who it would be," I said.

"It's Gavin. I'm sure of it," Patricia insisted. "He has my money and the will to act."

Bullard nodded but didn't comment.

"So how do we capture him?" Mitchell asked.

All three watched me, waiting.

"We bait a trap. We bait it with Patricia. She's the cheese!"

"What does that mean?" Mitchell asked. I could see his desire to protect her might be more of an obstacle than I expected.

"Listen. Gavin loves Patricia. He adores her. He knows she's here looking for him. Yes?" I looked to Patricia for confirmation.

"Yes," she said. "He's promised that once his business is done, he'll meet me in Italy, but he refuses to see me until he's finished."

"So we have to convince him that you have been abducted. By white Russians or German nationalists. It doesn't matter. We convince him that you've been taken and the only way to rescue you is to ransom you. This way we get as much of Gavin's revolution money as we possibly can, and we capture Gavin when we exchange Patricia for the money."

"I will not lie to Gavin," Patricia said sharply.

So much for our pleasant evening interlude, I thought. "You will if you don't want him dead or rotting in a French prison."

"He would never trust me again. Our marriage would be ruined. I can't lie to him."

"Patricia, you just said that you think he'll continue to try to restart the war until he succeeds, that he won't give up. He will end up dead. I have no other plan. Unless you can think of another way to find him and bring him to us, you have no choice."

"I will not..." She stopped speaking. Mitchell had laid his hand on her arm.

"Trish," he said gently, "John is right. We must grift him into coming to us. We can't hunt him. Even if we found him, he could get the jump on us and hurt us. We have to catch him safely. To do that, you need to help us convince him you've been taken."

"And you'll have to make sure Reynolds toes the line," I added.

Bullard spoke for the first time. "Hiding in ambush beats the hell out of walking into one, and if we can convince him that you're in danger and he needs to come alone to get you, everyone is safer. I like it."

"It won't work," she said.

She was desperately looking for arguments to get out of tricking her new husband. I didn't blame her.

"Why would Germans or Russians want money?" she continued. "That will make him suspicious. Bolshevik, nationalist, white, red, aren't interested in money. Crazy isn't interested in money. It wouldn't occur to them to ask for it. They'd just kill me to hurt him. A demand for a ransom won't make sense to him, and I think he'll see through the lie. He may even see my hand behind it."

Her words stopped me. She was right. I was thinking like a small-time crook. Fanatical German nationalists or white Russians wouldn't want money for her return. They'd want to stop the Bolshevik plan just like we did.

"You're right," I said. Mitchell and Bullard looked at me sharply. I was sure they could still hear the Chauchat blasts echoing in their ears. They liked a plan where we got to do the ambushing. So did I.

"And you're wrong," I continued. I suddenly understood exactly what we had to do to draw Gavin out.

"We don't ask for money; we ask for an exchange. Gavin for Tricia," I said with certainty. And I *was* certain. I knew exactly how Gavin would react to this demand. He would react in the same way I did when I returned to the States in 1916. The difference was that he was a genuinely brave man and people believed him a coward. On the other hand, I was a coward, who people believed to be a brave man. I had enlisted in the Marine Corps because my guilt was eating me alive. Better to die appearing to be brave. Gavin would exchange himself for Patricia to prove himself brave to others. Brave to her. I was sure of it. I was sure that Gavin was still as affected by his war experience as I was by mine.

"He would never do that!" Patricia nearly shouted.

I looked around at the other tables to make sure no one paid us any attention.

"Sorry," she said, "but he would never give himself up for me. He loves me, but it's not in his nature."

"You're wrong, Patricia. In this, I think I know your husband better than you do. When I met with Sarah, she told me how Gavin was treated when the war started. She described him as resolute and noble. She said everyone thought he was a coward. It sounds like even you think of him as intelligent and confident, but you don't think of him as brave. Trust me when I say this: your husband has plenty of courage. He just chose not to fight in a war he thought was wrong. But that doesn't mean he's a coward. And it doesn't mean that the opinion of everyone he cares about doesn't matter to him. He thinks everyone believes he's a coward. I don't care how confident a man may be, that has got to make a mark. He will want to atone for his past even though he believes he was right. We give him that chance. I think he knows that you don't believe he would sacrifice himself for

227

you. He won't be able to resist sacrificing himself. He will have to. We make it look like you've been abducted by German nationalists who suspect him of Bolshevik plotting. The only lie in this story is that you've been abducted."

"I could take her," Mitchell said with a smile. "Then there'd be no lies."

Patricia glanced at him but didn't smile. She was thinking, and I think she was worried. Rightly so. When Gavin learned that she had helped trick him, it could ruin their young marriage.

"Patricia?" I waited for her answer.

She looked from me to Mitchell and back. "Tell me what you want me to do."

"We write a ransom note in German," I said. "He speaks German. Yes?"

She nodded.

"Gene, we'll need you for that part. Patricia, you tell Reynolds to spread the word through your European contacts that you've disappeared. Hell, he should even tell your dad. We need to make sure word gets to Gavin. Whoever we use to pass information to him will be in danger. I suggest that we have Reynolds do it."

Patricia looked at me sharply.

"Not because I don't like him," I insisted. "But because he is a natural conduit and Gavin and his allies will see him as just that. They will be hunting for the kidnappers. We use that. It is even possible that your dad will hire us to find you again." I nodded to Mitchell. "And we'll have to let him."

"What do we do once he gets word that she's missing?" Eugene asked.

"Before that, we need to find a place that looks right for an exchange. We must assume that while he's willing to sacrifice himself, it doesn't mean his Red buddies are willing to let him do it. Gene, we'll need your help finding a good location."

"We should hide Patricia, Griff," Mitchell said. "Out of town where we won't be seen by accident. But she needs to be in touch with us and Reynolds." He turned to Bullard. "She'll need a tele-phone or at least access to one."

"Agreed." I turned to Bullard also. "Gene, how quickly do you think you could find us a place? It has to be done discreetly. Folks can't know it's associated with Patricia or any of us, at least until we're ready."

"I'll work on it after I leave the club tonight. People see us talking now, but you wanting to have a drink with me is natural enough. I mean, I am famous." He smiled.

"You are that," I agreed. "And Gene, I think the fact that you are meeting with Patricia and us now will get back to Gavin and his people. Famous or not, they'll want to know what you spoke to Patricia about. And what you spoke to us about. It wouldn't surprise me if he sends people to talk to me or Mitchell too."

"That's fine, John," he said calmly. "If they ask, I'll tell them the truth. That I'm famous and that Patricia is looking for Gavin. She came to me because the two of you brought her. You'd met me a few days ago through Kiki. You two thought my connections in town might help you find Gavin. I told you I'd keep an eye out for him but made no promises. I'll also tell them that I didn't much like the two of you. You're both crackers who didn't see much value in a nigger like me, despite asking for my help. I'll leave them with the impression that I wasn't gonna help ignorant peckerwoods like you two. How's that sound?"

Mitchell and I looked at each other and smiled at the truthful ring of it.

"A little too much like it comes from the heart, Eugene," I said, shaking my head.

"Don't worry, boys." He laughed. "That's what they expect to hear, so they'll hear it. You just need to be ready with the same story when they come to you. I'm going to tell them where you're staying."

"They'll learn that Patricia was staying there too," Mitchell said.

"Yes, and that's where she'll disappear from." I looked at Patricia, and she nodded. "We just tell them the truth, and if Gavin is with them, we make a judgment about whether we can take him safely. You okay with that?"

"Yes. But please make sure it is safe if you try to capture him. And Gene, get me a nice place to hide out."

Bullard nodded. "I'll come by your hotel tomorrow midmorning to tell y'all the arrangements. I'll try to make them cozy."

With our plans in place, we left the club and went back to the hotel, the three of us trooping up to my room. I poured us each a whiskey without asking.

"Tomorrow I'll do a little shopping before I disappear," Patricia said. "I'll need clothes because I'll have to leave what I brought here. And I'll order some for delivery here so it will look like I expected to return. William, you will come with me on my shopping trip."

"My pleasure, Trish."

"While the two of you are shopping, I'll think of a way to sneak you out of here, Patricia."

"One more thing," Patricia said. "I'll need a gun."

She could see the reluctance on my face.

"I'll be alone wherever I go," she said matter-of-factly. "If the Bolsheviks find me and Gavin is not with them, I don't want them to decide to simplify their lives by killing me. I'd prefer that not happen."

Without consulting Mitchell, I went to Bullard's trunk, which had arrived earlier in the day. I opened it and retrieved the Webley that I had loaned Disney. I checked the load, again leaving the chamber under the hammer empty, and handed it to Patricia.

"I wish I had something smaller, but I don't. You point and pull the trigger. Use two hands. After you've pulled the trigger five times, you run away." I wasn't sure five rounds would keep the Reds from killing her, but if the gun made her feel better, she could have it.

"We'll stay put through the day, and then we'll join you," Mitchell told Patricia. He turned to me. "We'll have to have a story about where we're going."

"Italy. Based on Reynolds's information," I said. "And Patricia" —I nodded to Bullard's trunk—"that's your way out of here."

With the promise of being stuffed into a trunk the next day, Patricia said her good-nights and went up to her room to pack. Mitchell left shortly after. I wasn't sure if he was going to his room or hers, and I wasn't going to ask.

I was worried about our plan. While I was certain that Gavin would willingly sacrifice himself to save Patricia, I was not certain that we could convince him she had really been kidnapped by German nationalists. Also, we didn't know how important Gavin was to the Bolsheviks' plans. We were assuming he led them, but he could be just a figurehead or rich tagalong, dabbling in revolution. In any case, if we could remove Gavin from the picture, it would make confronting the Bolsheviks easier. We wouldn't have to be careful or pull any punches. We could just kill them all.

# 18

## Chaos in the Sticks

Late the next morning, I was sitting inside the café across from our hotel, waiting for Bullard, when Mitchell and Patricia Kingsbury left the hotel. I stepped outside to wave them into the warmth of the bar, but despite the brisk, overcast day, they were in a hurry and didn't stay for coffee. Patricia was hell-bent on getting her shopping in. Before leaving me, she explained that she had called Reynolds to her room earlier and briefed him on his role as conduit for the demand letter to Gavin. She insisted that she explained to Reynolds the importance of his messaging to Gavin and his associates. I didn't press her for details. She was perfectly capable of briefing Mr. Morgan Reynolds without my advice. Also, from the way she looked at Mitchell, I could tell that she was more interested in spending time with him than talking to me.

They waved goodbye and left arm in arm, looking very much like newlyweds.

A few minutes later, Eugene arrived at the hotel. Again, I went outside and called him across to the café to join me at my table.

"I've found a place," he said with no preamble. "It's out in the sticks. In Garches, outside of Paris."

I signaled for the waiter, who finished wiping down a nearby table and went into the kitchen. I have a way with people.

"No promises on when you'll get to order, Gene. Sorry."

"Didn't you hear me?" he asked.

"I heard you, but I figured you would tell me where Garches is, why you chose it, and how we'll get there. I'm more interested in your progress on the German note for Reynolds."

"It's done," he said smugly. "It says simply: 'We have your wife. If you want her to live, you will come to 20 rue de Kronstadt, Garches, at 2000, eight p.m. on Wednesday. Alone. If you don't come or don't come alone, she dies.' It is signed by Hauptmann Müller, Deutsche Freikorps."

"Well, that's certainly blunt enough to be from a Kraut," I muttered. "Can one of your fleas deliver it to Reynolds? According to Patricia, he's expecting it. She gave him his orders this morning."

The waiter arrived. Bullard ordered and waited for the waiter to leave before answering.

"Yes, as soon as we are done here, I'll have it delivered to Reynolds at the Vendôme anonymously."

"Perfect. Okay. Tell me about Garches, starting with how to spell it."

Bullard laughed. "G-a-r-c-h-e-s," he said. "The *E* and the *S* are silent. It's west of Paris, about nine klicks from here. The house is on a cul de sac. I arranged for two houses. The house where y'all will be holed up is number 18. The house where the exchange will take place is number 20. They connect through their yards, but you can't really tell from the street. I've got an autocab on standby that will pick up Patricia this afternoon at 1400. I'll have another cab take you and Mitchell to Garches this evening. The cab will stay with you until we arrive with the second motorcar. How are you getting her out of the hotel and to the house with no one knowing?"

233

"I'll be sending your trunk to Garches. With her in it."

"I can't imagine that's gonna be popular with Mrs. Kingsbury." He chuckled.

"Nope." I pulled a stack of francs from my jacket pocket, put them under my newspaper, and pushed both across the table to Bullard.

"For your expenses. It's on Patricia Kingsbury," I said.

He pocketed the francs, tucked the paper under his arm, and tipped his hat.

"I'm not playing tonight, but I'll be at the club anyway. Drop by and let me know if Gavin's been in touch." He sauntered out of the café into the cold May morning.

His coffee arrived a few minutes later. Well, I could always use another coffee.

As I left the café, I thought about visiting the house on rue de Babylone. On reflection, I decided that was just plain stupid. Between the explosion and the burned, twisted weapons, I was certain the French authorities would be interested in the place. With my hands stuffed in my overcoat pockets and my hat pulled low, I walked along boulevard Raspail, which intersected with rue de Babylone. It had started to drizzle. As I passed rue de Babylone, I could see that the street to the west was blocked and policemen scurried about. I put my head down and turned east, away from the house.

I had nothing to do until we packed Patricia off, and I was bored. And so I walked. The chill started to penetrate, and I found myself on boulevard Saint-Germain looking across the street at Les Deux Magots. I had no desire to go back there. I suspected other Americans besides Patricia might frequent the café, and I was not in the mood for conversation. I saw another café just down the street, Café de Flore. A café of flora on a miserable day. Excellent. I crossed the street and pushed through the door.

Sometimes, as my grandfather used to say, it is better to be lucky than good.

Sitting in a padded booth with his back to the windows was Mr. Gavin Kingsbury himself. I felt a surge of anger at the sight of him, remembering Shed's shattered body. I took a deep breath. Perhaps a simple conversation could get Kingsbury on a boat home without anyone dying.

He sat next to a well-dressed older woman with dark eyes and still darker hair. Across from him sat a smaller middle-aged man with dark, thinning hair who was speaking Spanish with great animation.

I removed my hat and looked directly at Kingsbury as I passed his table. He looked up with surprise and paled when he recognized me. I didn't stop but instead moved deeper into the café. I heard the woman ask, "*Estás bien*, Gavin?"[1]

Although the café was crowded because of the chilly weather, I found a table at the back wall. It was cramped. On one side sat two Asians who were arguing in what sounded like Chinese, and on the other sat a somber fat man with a magnificent mustache who was reading a newspaper.

With my back to a mirrored wall, I could see Kingsbury speaking to his Spanish friends. He appeared to be saying his goodbyes, and he glanced in my direction. I saw no point in trying to summon one of the waiters who glided through the room. I was sure when Kingsbury reached my table, a waiter would show up. I found myself regretting that I didn't have my pistol, which I'd left in the bottom of my suitcase. Not because I wanted to shoot Gavin here in the café but because if I'd had it with me, I had the option.

I watched him work his way through the crowded tables toward me.

"Mr. Griffin, John," he said with excessive enthusiasm, "it is good to see you."

I stood and shook his offered hand. I couldn't bring myself to smile.

"Except I thought you'd be back in New York by now reporting to Mr. Armistan on your successes," he continued.

"Gavin, I don't know you well, but I do have some respect for you. So let's agree that we won't lie to each other more than is absolutely necessary during this conversation. Agreed?"

Fatso next to me looked up at my sharp tone. The Asians just kept jabbering away. Kingsbury's mouth dropped open slightly, and after a moment, he began to chuckle.

"Agreed," he promised.

"Will and I don't work for Harry Armistan anymore. You were pretty clear that he wouldn't pay us if we didn't head back to New York, and I couldn't see us heading back to New York without finding Patricia."

"I did warn you," he said with just a hint of smug "I told you so" in his voice.

Again, I saw Shed's body in my mind's eye.

"Gavin…" I needed to be careful. "We found Patricia. Actually, she found us."

Kingsbury went very still.

"She hired us," I said.

"What?" he exclaimed, loud enough to get the Chinamen to look up from their conversation.

I waited for him to calm down before I continued. He nodded, understanding my hesitation.

"Please explain, John."

"Patricia is worried about you. She thinks you are dabbling in postwar politics, getting cozy with Reds. She is convinced you're going to get hurt, and she has asked Will and me to find you so she can speak with you. She desperately wants you to go back to the States."

"I can't do that," he said firmly. "For two reasons. First, I am working for Armistan, and second, the work is too important to leave it now. Even for Patricia." Kingsbury's demeanor changed from that of a supercilious aristocrat to a man entrusted with a sacred mission.

"Gavin, listen to me," I said earnestly. "I can bring you to Patricia today. You can meet her, talk this through. It's what

236

couples do. If you are in bed with the Reds, the French authorities will find out. They will hunt you down. You owe Patricia at least a meeting, don't you?" I said the last almost pleading. I hated the way I sounded. But I couldn't help but think of Sarah trapped in her brother's dream of a dictatorship of the proletariat.[2] I wanted to save her.

"Griffin, I know you think me a coward for not fighting in the *Great War*," he said sarcastically. "But all these peace negotiations will do is perpetuate a world where the rich remain in power, manipulating the poor and the weak. Where countries with empires control lands and peoples who don't have the armies to prevent it. I know you can't see this, but Bolshevism is the only answer to the disease that caused the war. I wouldn't fight in your war, but I will fight in this one. It is worth dying for. That is the work I do, and I can't give that up for Patricia, or anyone."

"Jesus Christ! Gavin. Really, *the work you do*? You can't begin to understand the work you do. Have you seen the work of death, Gavin? That work is measured in the death of friends. Of loved ones. You're going to get yourself killed too. Probably by people you think are your friends. The least you can do before reaching this wholly deserved end is meet with your wife. Won't you meet with her?" I asked.

"I can't," he answered. "I am an imperfect man, and she is a very persuasive woman. She might convince me to change course."

"What about Harry? I find it hard to believe he wants a world ruled by the workers."

"Harry is a stooge. He wants to sell the weapons he makes to the English, the French, and the Germans. I was delivering contract proposals and bonds to solicitors in the city. Arms contracts. Working for him gives me the freedom and the money to pursue the greater purpose. I know you think I was a scrimshanker for not fighting, but I did what was right, and I am doing what is right now."

"Gavin, I don't think you're a coward. But I do think you are a fool. You may be right that the old men who caused the war will continue to rule, but you will not succeed in preventing it. Instead, you will be caught and killed. And I am afraid your sister will be too," I concluded. I couldn't keep myself from adding the last. She had remained in my thoughts.

"Sarah should not be here. I know that. But she feels guilty about the war, and she's still mourning her dead. You should take her back to England. I'd pay you."

I laughed out loud at the offer. I couldn't help myself. How twisted this all had become! Fortunately, the waiter arrived and forced me to control my mirth.

"Gavin, please order a drink and quit talking nonsense," I said with a smile.

"*Un vin rouge,*" he said without looking at the waiter. "I'm serious. I think she trusts you. She would go with you."

"*Deux vins rouges, merci,*" I told the waiter. I looked back at Gavin.

"She will not leave you. She still feels horrible about how she treated you during the war, and that guilt will keep her by your side. She told me this that night I had dinner at her home. She's loyal. Even to death, she will stay by you. And you know this. You may not be a coward, but you are a selfish bastard." I sneered the last, some of my disgust for him leaking through.

He dropped his eyes.

"I don't want her here, Griffin, I swear it. I had wanted her to keep Tricia company, but now, with Tricia on her own mission to rescue me from myself, I don't want her with Trish either. I just don't know how to get her to leave."

"Why don't *you* take her to England?" I said, thinking how clever I was. "You could get her home, and then if you want to get yourself killed, you can come back and do that all by yourself."

"I can't," he said with regret.

"Bullshit. You won't," I answered.

"I can't leave now. The timing is too delicate, and I've had setbacks in the work. I must stay. I am sorry, Griffin. I really am.

I know what this may cost me and Patricia and Sarah, but after all the death of the past four years, we can't miss this opportunity," he said sincerely.

"What are you doing?" I asked. I wanted to hear it from his mouth.

"I'm sorry, but I can't tell you. You wouldn't understand."

"I hope it is worth your sister's life," I said brutally. I stood and pulled my coat from under the fat man, who had shifted onto it. "I'll tell Patricia we spoke and that you refused to meet her. She'll be heartbroken."

"I'm sorry. Truly," Kingsbury said.

The waiter arrived with our drinks.

"What about your wine?" Kingsbury asked.

"You drink it. Think of it as an early start on your last supper."

---

I WAITED IMPATIENTLY AT THE HOTEL FOR PATRICIA AND MITCHELL to return. When they finally did, I heard their voices as they came down the hall. I couldn't understand the words, but the tone was light and happy. A knock on my door brought me to my feet, and I let them into my room.

"What's the matter, Griff?" Mitchell asked.

Patricia looked from Mitchell back to me. I could see concern growing on her face, mirroring the worry on Mitchell's.

"I found Gavin. By accident. At a café. I tried to convince him to meet you, Patricia. He refused. He doesn't want to risk you changing his mind. He didn't admit what he is doing, but he did admit that the timing is critical. He won't go back to the States without a fight. I told him he was risking his life and Sarah's. He made it clear that he's willing to sacrifice Sarah if he has to." I shook my head in dismay. "Tricia, I'm sorry, but he has become a fanatic. It's like he's got religion."

"Like a goddamn Baptist preacher," Mitchell added with disgust.

"Then our plan is still on," Patricia said, undaunted. "We'll grab him and take him back to New York. But now you have an additional task, John. Once we leave for New York, you find Sarah and escort her home. Do you understand? His fervor changes nothing."

"You're the boss," I said with only a hint of sarcasm. I looked at my watch. Gene's motorcar would be at the hotel in an hour.

"Time for you to get ready, Patricia." I nodded at the trunk pushed in the corner of my room. "I'll toss a pillow and a blanket in there for you, and you might leave them for Gavin when you're done with your trip."

Mitchell laughed. Patricia did not.

The taxicab arrived on time for the trunk as promised, and we sent Patricia off to Garches. Mitchell had fussed around her like a mother hen, padding the trunk carefully with blankets and pillows, leaving her a small bottle of water, and knocking holes with my nails and pry bar to keep her from suffocating. Ridiculous stuff, really. I shook my head and left them alone to say their goodbyes.

Reynolds would have the demand note by now. Patricia had instructed him to actively leave word for Gavin with their various friends, acquaintances, and business associates. It was just a question of when news of Patricia's abduction would reach Gavin.

Not knowing what the next few days would bring, Mitchell and I decided to visit Le Dôme. We hoped to see the girls there. We had not seen them since Shed died. None of us had known him long, but I was sure they would mourn his loss. I knew I did. I still felt responsible. It seemed more tragic somehow to have survived the damned war only to be machine-gunned down in a Parisian foyer. I wasn't sure what I would say to them. I was sure that we would finish the evening visiting with Eugene at his club. At some point either tonight or tomorrow, Gavin would contact us. Then things would start to move.

Remembering my wish for the Colt during my conversation

with Gavin, I pushed the pistol behind my belt in the small of my back. Giving free rein to my paranoia, I put an extra magazine in my jacket pocket.

I met Mitchell in the lobby. He came down the steps, buttoning his coat, with his umbrella hooked on his arm. The rain that had threatened all day was now coming down in earnest.

"Gun?" I asked quietly.

"*Bien sûr*,"[3] he answered. "Not that I'd need one."

"He'll contact us tonight," I said with certainty.

"God willing. I'm ready to get the field clear so that we can take another crack at those damn Reds," Mitchell said with passion.

The crowd at Le Dôme was sparse, maybe because of the weather. Madeline sat alone at a table toward the back. Smart girl. We'd catch our deaths sitting near the door. The damn Spanish flu might be winding down, but only an idiot would sit near drafty doors.

"Boys." Madeline greeted us as we arrived at her table, offering her cheek for us to kiss. She looked tired with circles under her eyes not hidden by cosmetics.

"You heard about Shed?" I asked.

She looked up at me sharply. "Yes. Walt came by and told us."

"You okay, Maddy?"

"Sure, I'm a tough girl," she said, knocking a cigarette from the pack on the table to prove it.

"You alone?" Mitchell asked.

"Rachel's in the ladies'. We just got here."

Given the small crowd, a waiter appeared quickly and took our drink orders. Madeline ordered two French 75s, one for her and one for Rachel.

"Kiki won't be out tonight though," she explained.

"That's okay. Not sure she wants to see me anyway," Mitchell said. "Patricia has… complicated our relationship."

Madeline rolled her eyes. "There's nothing complicated about it. You're a man. You're interested in another pretty woman. What's complicated?"

That prompted me to laugh.

"It feels complicated if you're inside the triangle," Mitchell said with pain in his voice.

I could see Rachel leaving the loo, and I stood to give Mitchell some cover from the fire he was taking from Madeline.

"Hi, Rachel." I greeted her with a kiss on the cheek.

"John." She favored me with a sad smile.

"Hello, Rachel," Mitchell said.

She ignored him and sat down next to me.

"We may be leaving town, and we wanted to make sure you heard about Shed," I explained despite the sudden chill.

"How thoughtful of you," Rachel answered.

"Rachel, stop it," Madeline chided her. "Don't be mean to Griffin just because William dropped poor Kiki like a hot potato for a New York socialite."

Mitchell, to his credit, refused to run from a fight, even one he could not win.

"Ladies, you are both right. I did pay more attention to Patricia than I should have. And I don't want to make excuses, but"—he held up his hand as both women started to interrupt him—"you know Kiki better than I do. You've got to believe I was a bit of Yankee fun, and it was coming to an end. The mistake I made was being the one to end it. That, and I should have been clear that it was ending."

After some hesitation, both girls nodded. "Exactly," they said in unison.

"I am sorry," he said sincerely.

The waiter brought the drinks. With Mitchell's apology to their absent friend accomplished, the interruption allowed the girls to move on to other matters.

"What happened in the house on rue de Babylone? What happened to Shed?" Rachel demanded. She asked us both but looked at me.

"Ladies, you've seen a lot during your work for the YMCA, so I'll tell you straight. We went to the house we told you about. We were ambushed. It's my fault. We weren't careful enough going in. Shed was killed right away."

"That is such a crock of shit story, Griffin!" Mitchell said. "The house was a trap. They had two machine guns hidden. They were waiting for us. No way to avoid them if we wanted to destroy those guns. And there were a bunch of guns. Griffin saved Eugene and me. Shed was killed with the first shots. Gene blew the place up." He raised his eyes to mine. "We had to leave Shed's body."

Madeline leaned across the table and put her hand on my arm. "I am so sorry, John. Walt said it was bad, but he hadn't been inside. The French are saying it was an explosion from coal dust, but the police have been asking a lot of questions."

"Yeah, well, there was an explosion all right. Gene saw to that," I said.

"So what happens next? With the weapons gone, it's done, right?" Rachel asked.

"Maybe not. I may not like Gavin, but he's not a quitter. I actually saw him today. He made clear that he's got a plan, and he's going to see it through come hell or high water."

"You should have killed him," Rachel said fiercely.

"No. We've got to find him again and tell him he's got a bigger problem," Mitchell said. He hesitated as if ashamed to speak. "Patricia's missing."

Mitchell, always the better storyteller, explained our fairy tale about Patricia's disappearance. We'd leave it to Reynolds to add the German militarist angle as the story got out.

"She could have just gotten tired of Paris and her absent husband and gone home," Rachel said, her tone acidic.

"Maybe," I answered, "but if I were her husband, a *maybe* wouldn't satisfy me. We need to make sure he knows. So spread the word around if you could. It might divert him from his dingbat scheme."

"Or free him entirely to start the war again," added Rachel.

"Oh Lord, Rachel," William declared, waving at the passing waiter. "Let's get you another drink before that dark cloud over your head rains on all of us."

"Don't tell me you haven't thought of it," Rachel said with a smile. She was apparently remembering that she liked Will Mitchell.

"He may be more of a revolutionary than a romantic," Madeline said. "And Patricia really doesn't seem like she'd inspire men to feats of romantic derring-do, no matter how beautiful she is. She's a bit of a cold fish."

I glanced at Mitchell. He met my eye and looked away. He would be inspired, I thought.

We shared a drink with the girls and invited them to Zelli's. They declined, preferring to sit quietly in the uncrowded café, enduring the drumfire of one French 75 after another. If we hadn't needed to speak with Bullard, I wouldn't have minded staying with them.

As we stood to leave, two men came in from the street, hats low, their faces in shadow. They stood in the entryway with their right hands in their right coat pockets. Rain dripped from their shoulders as they scanned the café. They divided the room between them as they surveyed the patrons. I could tell when they saw us because they spoke briefly. I suspected that they were hard men who had seen war. I was glad for the Colt even though I didn't think they were here to kill us. They started through the café, clearing each corner and doorway like they were on a trench raid.

"Mitch," I said, "take a seat next to Maddy." Without comment, Mitchell removed the coat he'd just put on and sat with his back to the wall, his coat in his lap. I could tell from his eyes when he saw the two men making their way toward us. I was sure that under his coat the broomhandle pistol was tracking the approaching men.

I remained standing and moved slightly to the side to stay out of Mitchell's line of fire. I could tell that the lead man noticed. The one following was not focused on us but on the rest of the room.

When they arrived at the table, it was clear that they had been involved in some sort of accident. Both had cuts on their faces, and I could see that the right eye of the man nearest us was completely bloodshot from ruptured blood vessels. Almost as if he'd been too close to an explosion. I kept my hands at my sides and waited.

"John Griffin," the man with the red eye said. It was a statement, not a question, said with a slight accent, Russian, perhaps. Of course, given the Red connection, I could be imagining things. It was clear that he spoke English well enough.

"What can I do for you?" I asked.

"I am an associate of Mr. Kingsbury. He is seeking his wife. He has asked me to inquire of you where she might be."

Yup, Russian.

"I find that hard to believe," I said. "I saw him just a few hours ago and offered to take him to her and he refused."

"Yes, well, he now wishes to see her," the man answered. "Where is she?"

"Who are you?" I asked, cocking my head at the question.

"I told you, I am an associate of Mr. Kingsbury."

"That's not helpful," I answered. "You see, I too am an associate of Mr. Kingsbury. And I know that if Gavin wanted to see his wife, he'd be here himself. I don't know you, and I'm not speaking to you about another man's wife, especially one who is also a client." I finished my statement sanctimoniously. I wanted to spin the story of her disappearance, but I was worried that if I made it too easy for them, Gavin would be suspicious.

"It would be easier for all of us if you would answer our questions now. It would prevent any inconvenience or misunderstandings." He eased his hand halfway out of his coat pocket so I could see the butt of a gun.

I made a show of looking from his eyes to his gun and back. I swallowed and tried to let some fear bleed through. Of course, with the puckered scars deforming my face, there was a risk I might just look angry, so I also made a calming gesture with my hands.

"Hey, look, we don't want any trouble." I needed to convince him that I was afraid of him and his gun. He needed to believe my story. "We've been looking for Patricia Kingsbury for weeks and only just found her," I continued. "And now we've lost her again."

"Lost her?"

"Yeah, I went to the hotel to tell her that Gavin wouldn't see her, but she wasn't there. It was strange. She was supposed to be waiting to hear from me. But she was gone. We were hoping to find her out at a café. That's why we're here, asking around," I finished.

He watched me quietly for a moment, and then a look of disgust flashed across his face. I saw in his eyes that he thought us incompetent drunks more interested in a party than duty. I suppose he was partly right.

"So you came here to search for her." It wasn't a question. The Russian looked from the pretty girls to the drinks and back to me. "I see," he said. "Thank you for your time."

He turned and made his way to the exit with his buddy trailing in his wake.

I took off my coat and sat again. "One more drink?" I asked the table.

---

WE LEFT THE GIRLS AND WENT DIRECTLY TO RUE CAUMARTIN to see Bullard. As with Le Dôme, the club wasn't busy. Gene sat at a table with Disney, Horace Merchant, and two men we didn't know: one black and one white.

Bullard waved a waiter over as he made introductions.

"John, Will, please meet Charles Nungesser[4], a friend of mine from my flying days with the Escadrille, who despite his

246

German-sounding name, has killed more Germans than most Frenchmen. And this is Henry Johnson.[5] He's been recuperating from wounds, and I'm just showing him a little hospitality before he goes back to the States to muster out."

To the waiter he said, "*Deux bouteilles de Sancerre frais.*"

Nungesser, the Frenchman, had rugged good looks and a ready smile. He raised his glass in greeting.

The negro, Johnson, stood and offered me his hand. He looked wary, whether of us or the club wasn't clear. His head was shaved bald, and I could see pink, newly healed scar tissue on his scalp. I hesitated, but Bullard was growing on me, and I didn't want to embarrass him. When I took Johnson's hand, it felt frail, like he'd been convalescing for a long time.

"A pleasure, gentlemen," I said, looking at Johnson and then Nungesser. I wasn't sure I was comfortable sitting at a table, sharing a drink with one black man, much less two, but I was still coming to terms with Parisian culture. When in Rome, I supposed.

Mitchell didn't seem bothered at all.

"Horace, Walt, good to see you again."

"Hello, John," Merchant said. "Gene told us about Shed and what you found. He's been recruiting. Is he telling us fairy tales?" He said the last with a smile to take out some of the sting, but it was clear that he was having trouble accepting Bullard's version of events. He wanted my confirmation.

"Horace, while I know Gene is a skilled entertainer—he drums rag music, after all—he doesn't make up stories. He's telling you the truth," I said.

Bullard nodded at my unequivocal support.

The waiter returned with the wine and poured a glass for each of us.

"Damn!" Merchant swore. "That Kingsbury isn't just a coward. He's a real danger."

Disney nodded. Nungesser tossed back his original drink and picked up his wine for a sip.

"We're going to pack him off to the States with his wife. At least, that's the plan," I said, turning to Gene. "Gavin's been in touch. He sent two Russians looking for his wife. They found us at Le Dôme. We told them that Patricia has disappeared. I think they believed us."

"Russians?" he asked.

"Only one spoke, but he spoke with a foreign accent. Not French." Mitchell looked at Nungesser. "No offense, Charles," Mitchell apologized, using the French pronunciation of Charles that Bullard had used in introducing Nungesser. "He sounded Russian to me too."

"*Aucune prise*,"[6] Nungesser said.

"So the ball is rolling," Bullard said. He turned to Nungesser and Johnson. "What do you think, gentlemen? Will you help? I can't promise you won't get killed."

Nungesser pursed his lips. "Absolutely," he said in his smooth French accent. "Will I get to meet Madame Kingsbury? I understand she is very beautiful."

"Oh, she's beautiful all right," Mitchell said.

"Just ask Walt," Merchant added. "He can draw a picture of her beauty with his words, and his pencil for that matter." Merchant laughed.

Nungesser nodded.

"Henry?" Bullard asked Johnson. "I know you've just recovered, but we could use another steady man."

I agreed we could use another steady man, but I wasn't sure Johnson was steady.

He was slower to respond than Nungesser. After a moment, he nodded. "Sure, Eugene," he said in a low voice. "I'll help out."

"Horace?" Gene asked.

"If you are certain you need me," he said, hesitating to commit. "I did have other plans."

"Really, Horace? Plans more important than preventing a war?" I asked.

He looked from me to Eugene and answered, "Fine, my

Yankee friend. I can't have Britain's many-colored allies standing together in the fight and not have England represented, can I?" Merchant said, smiling at his own humor. "And since you're including native infantry"—he nodded at Johnson and Bullard— "you'll need a British officer."

I shook my head. Merchant rubbed me wrong. It wasn't just his colored joke. I thought him a bully. I didn't like him belittling Eugene or Disney. I'd seen Bullard in action, and even with a bum leg, he could handle himself. And Disney was plenty brave, if young.

I turned to Bullard. "Can we get enough weapons?"

Bullard ignored Merchant's mild slur as he had likely done from similar men for a lifetime.

"Yes. They'll be French: FNs and Lebels. Let's hope we won't need to use them."

"Let's hope, Gene, but we can't be surprised like we were at the Babylone house," I said. I drank down my glass of wine. "I'm going to the hotel to gear up, and then I'm going out to the house."

"I'm coming with you," Mitchell said. He stood, leaving his wine untouched.

"We'll probably have to wait all night and all of tomorrow," I told the group. "I want to be in place well before Gavin shows up."

"We'll finish here and be out there as soon as we're fitted out, John," Bullard assured me.

"Thanks. And Gene, everybody stays with you. Shed got killed because the Reds knew we were coming. So this time y'all stay together. Understood, gentlemen? Everybody stays with Gene until you get to the house, and no talking to anybody outside this group. And no offense intended, gentlemen, but only Gene knows where we're going, and it's got to stay that way. Stick together."

I looked at each man in turn to judge their understanding of my demand.

Nungesser shrugged and nodded.

Disney softly answered, "Sure."

Merchant looked like he wanted to argue, but instead, said "Fine."

Johnson smiled and explained, "Of course. I was gonna stick with Eugene anyway."

It was still early enough for the Metro to take us back to Montmartre. Gene had assured us that a motorcar would be waiting at the hotel to transport us to Garches, and it was. On the way to my room, I snuck into the pensione's kitchen and stole a stale baguette and some cheese. We packed quickly, bringing only small carryalls. We didn't expect to be at the house more than a few nights. We wrapped the still-dismantled shotgun and automatic rifle parts in sheets and covered them with our overcoats as we left the lobby for the automobile. We didn't speak on the way. Not because we didn't trust the driver. He likely couldn't speak English. We both were too wrapped up in our own thoughts of Shed, rue de Babylone, the war, and for me, Sarah.

---

ON ENTERING GARCHES, THE MAIN ROAD RAN PARALLEL TO THE train tracks. We drove west for a short time, and the driver turned north onto rue de Kronstadt. The street forked, and he pulled right into an apparent dead end. He stopped by an unmarked gate. A house loomed large above us, three floors just off the road but surrounded by a low stone wall with tall, pointed iron spikes topping it. The enameled white number 18 on a blue background was affixed to the gate. The image of the rue de Babylone house flashed through my mind.

"*Ici*," the driver said, gesturing with his chin.

"Merci."

We took our gear and walked to the gate. It was not latched. Fear crept into my heart as I stepped through the gate toward the red painted front door. A red door. An ugly omen.

The house was not so grand as the one on rue de Babylone, but it still reminded me of that house. It was hard not to crouch down as I moved, remembering the shocking violence of our welcome there. Mitchell cleverly kept himself behind me.

I rapped my knuckles on the wood and softly said, "Patricia." There was no answer. I tried the door, and it opened without a sound.

In the dim light from the street, I could see Patricia standing at the foot of the stairs just inside the doorway. She held the Webley pointed at my head in two very steady hands.

"Hello, Patricia. Mind if we come in?" I asked, surprised at the nonchalance in my voice.

"Thank God! Yes. Is William with you?"

Mitchell stepped into the doorway, and she took a half step toward him. She stopped herself and turned to lead us deeper into the house. The open trunk was pushed against a wall where Bullard's men had left it after freeing Patricia. The bedding and pillows remained inside.

We followed Patricia down a hallway, passing a sitting room and another set of stairs upward into the dark. She took us to a small kitchen, where a percolating coffeepot boiled on the stove.

"All the comforts of home," Mitchell said, smiling at her.

"Gavin has been in contact," I told her. "He sent two men to question us at Le Dôme. We dropped the news that you were missing. He should show up as the ransom letter demands."

"Good," she said, her hands busy laying out the cups and saucers next to the stove top. "I haven't been to the other house yet. I didn't want to go alone."

"Don't blame you," said Mitchell with an encouraging smile.

"They'll recce the other house sometime tonight or tomorrow before Gavin is supposed to turn up. I'll be spending the night there," I said. "If we can discourage them enough, Gavin should play it straight and just knock on the front door. In case they don't, Bullard has recruited some more men. They'll be a big help if Gavin doesn't come alone."

"What?" Patricia exclaimed. "Why would you let more men get involved?"

"Patricia, the more the better," I said. "If they come in force, Gavin could take you, and then you'll be stuck in the middle of whatever he is planning. And he won't be on his way to New York and safety."

"It's fine, Patricia," Mitchell assured her, backing me up. "They will be here, not at the other house, and they will only get involved if we end up in a gunfight."

I didn't like this concession but didn't feel like arguing.

She looked at Mitchell and seemed to accept his assurances, but it was clear she didn't want more people to know her family's dirty laundry.

She took the percolator from the stove and carefully poured three cups of black coffee. I was mildly impressed with her domestic skills.

"Tonight, Mitch will stay here with you," I told her as I watched her work. "Bullard and the others should be here before daylight."

"I'm afraid there's no milk or sugar," she explained. She set the coffee in front of me, almost as a peace offering. I didn't like the nerves she was showing. It seemed out of character. But she had been trapped in a trunk and alone most of the day. That would rattle anyone.

I drank the coffee as I reassembled the automatic rifle. Mitchell did the same with the shotgun.

"I'm going to check out the house," I told them. Realizing that if I wanted to discourage Gavin's Bolsheviks quietly, I would need different weapons. I pulled a knife from the block on the kitchen counter.

"Mitch, I don't plan on shooting anyone, so I'll leave the Browning with you. If you hear gunfire, stay put and wait for Bullard and daylight before you check out the house. Okay?"

"Sure. Be careful," Mitchell said as I left.

I cut through the side yard of the house to the wall adjoining number 20. There was a low gate in the stone fence between the two houses. I moved quickly through an overgrown garden and went up the steps to the back door of the house. It opened silently. The layout was similar to number 18 with the kitchen at the back of the house. I wanted any visitors to come in through the kitchen only, so I went immediately to the front door and made sure it was locked.

I worked my way through each room on the ground floor and found no other doors to the outside. Remembering how I got into 28 rue de Babylone, I made sure the bolt on the cellar door was also locked.

The house was empty of furniture, but I found some scrap electrical wire kicked into a corner. I coiled it and put it in my jacket pocket.

I let myself out the back door and found a gap in the bushes that would hide me in the dark. Before daylight came, I might have to move, but for now, I was confident no searchers would see me if they came through the garden.

I settled in to wait.

*I stand on the fire step, peering through a gap in the parapet. It is dark, but the sun will be rising soon. There is just a hint of gray on the horizon when I look east. I don't have to turn my head much to see it, but I am very careful when I do. I wear my helmet low over my eyes to lessen their reflection. The parapet's sodden sandbags, held up by wooden planks, shield me, but I move my head very slowly. Smoothly. A sniper has been active to our front. I'm tired, wet, and cold, but I bite the inside of my cheeks to stay alert. I am also afraid. I am always afraid. The Germans have been raiding the trench line to the west, and I expect they will move to our line at some point. I've been on sentry duty for nearly two hours. Almost time for us to stand to. Then some tea and sleep, if I can.*

*I sense a shadowed movement. I shift my stance to use my peripheral vision to pick up the shadow better and realize I've made a mistake. I moved too quickly.*

*I remember nothing more of the trench.*

*I learn later that the sniper's bullet came through the sandbag and wood next to my head, splintering both the bullet and the planks. Pieces of lead and wood struck my helmet and my face, driving my head into other side of the parapet wall, fracturing my skull.*

*I also learn that I cannot see. I am horrified by the blind future that promises nothing but darkness, yet I am relieved. At least I have a future.*

A shadow moved at the front of the yard, and I abandoned my memories. A second shadow followed it. Only two men. I tracked them by focusing just ahead of them, their forms clear at the edges of my vision. I didn't move at all.

Only two men. Good. They quietly climbed the back stairs and entered 20 rue de Kronstadt. They would search the house, find nothing, and one would hide while the other would report back to Gavin. I would have a problem if they decided to search the garden, but I didn't think they would. They might have fought in the war, but even if they had, they would think in terms of strongpoints and fortified positions. The house was the strongpoint. They would not imagine that Germans who fought from strongpoints for much of the war would use anything else as cover.

I waited.

The back door opened, and a figure slipped out. He moved quickly across the garden and out the front gate, secure in the knowledge that the house was empty except for his friend, who was currently looking for a good place to set up his ambush once Patricia was in the house.

As I rose from the bushes, I kept watch for the departed man, but he was gone. I moved to the bottom of the back stairs and took the knife from my belt. It had not been the longest in the wood block at only five inches, but I didn't need longer. I stopped thinking about what I was about to do and focused on what I was doing. The back door was unlocked. I wanted to catch the watcher by surprise. I hoped he would think I was his buddy returning for some reason. I needed him to hesitate.

Fear threatened to paralyze me. I forced myself to focus on my actions in the moment: moving up the stairs and easing into the house. I listened. Light footsteps came down the hall away from the front of the house, back toward the kitchen where I stood. There was no cover. When he came through the kitchen doorway, he would see me.

The steps were almost on me, and I slipped forward to meet him.

He came through the door, and I was on him. He was fast. He blocked the low punch of my knife with his hand, pushing it away. I managed a grip on his throat with my left hand and stabbed low again. He couldn't block this thrust, and I felt the knife pass through the resistance of his jacket and then the muscles of his abdomen. He exhaled sharply. I punched the knife twice more up and under his ribs. The blade broke as I twisted it with the last thrust. I pushed him away, and he fell back into the wall, slipping down into a sitting position. His bleeding hand waving weakly, trying to plug the tears in his body.

He looked up at me, and the light left his eyes. Red Eye, from Le Dôme.

I locked the back door and searched the body. He had one FN pistol with extra magazines and a small Ruby .32 caliber automatic. I put the pistols in my coat pockets. I considered what to do with the body. Just dead meat now. Action and not thought, I told myself. I grabbed the feet and dragged the body on its back to the coal cellar door. This kept most of the blood off the floor from what I could tell in the dark. I unlocked the door and pulled the legs partway down the stairs. I climbed back over the legs and picked up the shoulders and shoved the corpse down the stairs. It tumbled headfirst part of the way down and stopped. Good enough. I shut and locked the cellar. I searched the remainder of the house as fast and thoroughly as possible. In the front room, I found a bag with some food: meat, cheese, bread, which Red Eye had brought to see him through the long wait ahead of him. He had no wait now.

Forget Red Eye, I told myself.

Gavin would believe he had a man inside the house where the exchange would happen. He would enter secure in the thought that he could surprise the kidnappers. He'd have more people nearby, who would come once the shooting started.

I needed to warn Mitchell. We could trap them as they came into the yard. Gavin would be in the house, safe from the ambush.

For the first time, I believed we might succeed in saving Gavin from himself.

I crossed to the other house and tapped on the back door. Shadows moved behind the windows, and after a few seconds, Mitchell cracked the door to let me into the kitchen. Patricia was standing behind him, the Webley in her hand.

"That was quick," Mitchell said. "Change of plan?"

"Yes," I answered. "They've already made their reconnaissance. Two men. They checked out the house. One left to report back to Gavin, and the other stayed to hide. I think their plan was for the man in the house to ambush us as Gavin entered. Gavin could then rescue Patricia and leave with the support of whoever else he is bringing."

Mitchell narrowed his eyes. "That *was* their plan?"

"The man in the house is dead," I said bluntly. "We need to set up an ambush just outside the house for Gavin's friends. We can keep Gavin away from the ambush. Keep him alive. Kill his Red friends in the yard, but you have to go tell Gene and get him here and set up quietly. And we'll need his motorcar nearby to get out of this neighborhood once we're done."

"What happened to the man in the house?" Patricia asked.

I turned to Patricia. Her eyes were wide, and she looked pale in the dim light, the heavy gun still hanging from her hand.

I took the two pistols from my coat. I put the FN on the table and offered her the small Ruby automatic.

"It's lighter," I said in answer to her question. When she looked down at the pistol, she could see the sticky blood on my hand. She took a deep breath and nodded. She put the Webley on the table and took the smaller Spanish-made pistol.

"I'll tell Gene and get back here as quick as I can," Mitchell said.

"Patricia and I will wait in the other house. I don't want to run the risk that anyone else gets in. Mitchell, be careful, and bring someone back with you. Make sure everyone moves with a buddy from now on."

"I got it, Griff. You take care of Patricia." With that, he was gone.

Patricia and I collected the pillows and blankets from the trunk, locked the house, and crossed to 20 rue de Kronstadt.

Once inside, we made ourselves as comfortable as possible by spreading the blankets and pillows into makeshift beds on the floor in the front room. I confirmed that all the doors were locked. I also told Patricia to stay out of the cellar.

She didn't ask why.

By the time we finished our domestic arrangements and I made sure all possible entrances were secure, it was late enough for us to try to get some sleep. I was sure I would only doze, which I was used to from my time with the English in the trenches. My current accommodations were downright palatial compared to what I'd had at the front.

I burrowed down into the blankets and tried to relax. In the quiet, with just the sound of Patricia's soft breathing, I told myself not to think. *Don't think. Don't think about Red Eye or Coco or the men in London. Or Shed. Or Red Eye's cold body just a few feet away. Think about Sarah, instead.* But as I thought about Sarah, I started to worry. Would she come with Gavin? Would she be outside? How cruel would it be for us to save Gavin while killing Sarah? *Don't think about Sarah,* I told myself.

"John, tell me about William," Patricia demanded softly, rescuing me from my fears. Her head was turned toward me, resting on her arm. Her hair, which fell across her face, seemed to glow in the room's darkness.

"Why do you want to know about Will? You're a married woman."

"I don't want to fight with you. I know you don't like me. Or trust me. And you're right. I am married, but I have never met a man like William. Or you for that matter. And I am lying here in the dark, terrified of what may happen tomorrow, thinking only horrible thoughts. I don't want to think those thoughts. I want to think about something that makes me smile and gives me pleasure, and that happens to be William right now. It is selfish, but I am scared. And I know you're not sleeping. I can feel how worried you are. So let's talk about William. He makes me smile, and I know you love him. Let's focus on someone who makes us both happy. I'd talk about Sarah, Gavin's sister, whom I love, but you don't know her as I do, so it wouldn't be the same for you."

I snorted at her last comment. *If only you knew,* I thought.

"She might be the perfect person for us to talk about then," I said, ignoring her acknowledgment of my distrust. "You can tell me only the very good things about her, and I will fantasize about them," I said, joking. "But first I'll tell you about Will. He told you his dad was in the navy?" I asked, knowing the answer.

"Yes. And that he traveled a lot when he was young. Some of it sounded so fantastic, and he told his stories so that they sounded like, well, stories," she explained.

"That's William Mitchell. It's hard to know exactly what is true, but I tend to believe most of his stories are. And I base that just on what I've seen of him," I said.

"Tell me what you've seen, John."

And I did. I didn't dwell on the horror of the war that Mitchell and I had fought together, but I did tell her of his bravery, his humor, and his compassion. She listened intently to it all.

"You know, Patricia," I said, concluding my abbreviated history of Will Mitchell's life, "this will sound obvious, but given any two friends, one will always have a bigger heart than the other. Be a better person. Not more successful, just better. Between me and Mitch, he's the better person. He's got the bigger heart. He's generous, caring. Not to say he can't be ferocious, but the difference between us is that Will came out of the war with more compassion, not less. His heart is huge. He cares. He cares in a way I never have and never could. A braver, more decent man you will never meet. Having him as my friend reminds me that people can be good. Not all people, but some. And that's not something I am inclined to believe. It is important for me that he's around. I need you to know that. He is important."

I stopped speaking.

She was quiet for a long time.

"I understand, John. I don't plan to hurt him." After an awkward silence, she asked, "How do you think you turned out after the war? William thinks you're brave and decent too."

"He's wrong. But don't tell him. I didn't really come out at all. I am now only fit for war. I am good at it. When I was home, I missed it even though I've always been terrified of it. Now that I'm here, I am terrified, but I belong here. Some men probably shouldn't have survived. I suspect that I am one of them."

"I am sorry. I'm glad you survived." She sounded sincere. "Which is selfish, I will admit. You are very capable. And that is a comfort. The way you describe William describes how I feel about Sarah. She is my rock. Without her, there are many times when I would have been lost. I knew her before the war. I met her through James, her husband. He went to University with Gavin. She and I became fast friends immediately. But she has more faith in people than I. Like William, she sees the good. I look for the bad. She is the perfect counterweight for me. I love her." She put her other hand under her cheek and continued. "If we survive this, I will make a point of ensuring that you spend some time with Sarah. You'll find that she has the same effect on you that William does. She has been my lifeline through very tough times. I think you two may be a match."

I didn't comment. I couldn't imagine any tough times that this beautiful, rich, spoiled girl might have had. A broken heel. Rain after the hairdresser. I almost wanted to snarl. But if she thought well of me, that could only help me with Sarah. My sarcastic bitterness went unvoiced. Because I, too, looked for the worst in people, and I was a selfish prick. I would use Patricia as she was using me.

"James's death broke her," she continued. "When she came to New York, she was a shadow of herself. But she put all that aside to help me. She stayed with me. I have a difficult relationship with my father, and she helped deflect some of that."

I remembered Sarah's dislike of Armistan and the reason for it.

"I did get the impression that she didn't much like your father," I said.

"She hates him, and so do I," Patricia said fiercely.

Her emotion surprised me. I was curious to know more, but I knew better than to delve into family squabbles, so I held my peace. She'd tell me if she wanted to.

"With any luck, he will die," she whispered, so softly I wasn't sure she had spoken.

With our conversation spent, we both pretended to sleep as we waited for Mitchell and the others to arrive.

Mitchell and the other men came in the early-morning hours. They opened the wrought iron gate to the yard of number 18, and Disney backed in the motorcar so it was out of sight. Remarkably, Patricia slept through Mitchell's light tap on the back door.

I crossed to number 18 and arranged the men for the planned ambush. Merchant and Johnson, both former infantrymen, along with Mitchell, were positioned by the wall in the yard of number 18. There, they had a view of both the front and back door of number 20. They scraped out shallow trenches beneath the overgrown hedges so that their shoulders were level with the top of the low stone wall. I wanted them placed when Gavin arrived at the house. I was worried about Johnson. He seemed frail, but he worked alongside the others without complaint.[7] Merchant, on the other hand, bitched in a low voice as he worked. I could tell he was trying Mitchell's patience.

Bullard, Nungesser, and Disney would wait in number 18. We rigged a string between the wall and the house so that with a light tug the men in the house could be alerted to Gavin's arrival. If needed, Bullard would reinforce the men at the wall, and Nungesser and Disney would watch the street in case the Bolsheviks tried to work around our flank.

By the time the sun was fully up, everyone was in position. I felt bad for the men outside. It was cold, despite the month, and they would be stiff and miserable by this evening.

The day passed slowly. Patricia and I didn't talk much, our thoughts focused on the evening. Gavin wouldn't come alone. That would be too much to hope for.

---

Gavin arrived right on time. At a minute short of 2000, I could hear a motorcar drive up rue de Kronstadt and stop on the street.

An hour before, Patricia had started pacing the front room, stopping to look at the closed and shuttered windows without touching them, and pacing again. She was caged and waiting for action. I'd seen men in the war, reacting to an impending attack the same way. They couldn't sit still. They wanted to go over the top as soon as they could, to get the waiting over with. And many did get it over with. Forever.

When she heard the car, she stopped pacing.

"Go down the hallway into the shadow," I commanded. "I don't want him to see you. I don't expect him to come in shooting, but I'd hate for Gavin to kill his wife. And don't talk until we are sure he's unarmed. I don't want him to try to do anything heroic. Understood?"

"I understand, John." She held her Spanish pistol close to her side, but I couldn't read her expression in the shadows.

"And please don't shoot me," I said to ease the tension.

"Of course," she croaked. She was scared. She should be. I was too.

It was still daylight outside, although the light was quickly fading. The inside of the house was dim, and it would seem darker to someone coming from the outside. I had set the exchange time because I thought having light during any encounter would help us since we were hidden. After we had Gavin, I hoped the descending darkness would hide us.

I unlocked the front door and stepped back. I would be able to reach whoever entered, but they shouldn't be able to see me in the shadows. I took the Colt from the small of my back where I'd tucked it. I pulled back the slide, putting a round in the chamber and cocking the hammer, but I made sure the safety was on.

The gate to the street opened, and muffled steps came up to the front door. One person. Our visitor knocked. I didn't answer. Our guest tried the door and it swung slowly open. Gavin, alone, was silhouetted by the fading light. He had his right hand in his overcoat pocket.

"Take your hand out of your pocket. Slowly."

"Mr. Griffin? Is that you?" he said with a slight smile. "I didn't know you were now a German nationalist. What a surprise."

"Your hand, Gavin. I'd be happy to shoot you." I pushed the safety down on the Colt with my thumb for emphasis. At least, it emphasized my intention to me.

He took his hand from his pocket. He looked into the house, down the hall and up the stairs. He was waiting for the man he had left in the house, very likely expecting him to announce himself by shooting me in the back.

"Come in and shut the door," I told him.

"Haven't you gotten enough money from the Armistans?" he asked. "You've taken to kidnapping them?"

Despite his questions, he pushed the door shut without looking. I moved behind him and put the barrel of my pistol against the back of his head.

"Take your coat off. Very slowly. Let it fall to the floor."

He followed my instructions, his coat dropping with a muffled thump as the pistol in his pocket hit the floor. I pushed him between the shoulder blades, and he stumbled deeper into the house, toward Patricia. I bolted the front door.

I could hear other motorcars down the street.

"You didn't come alone," I said. "I'm disappointed. Maybe you don't love your wife quite as much as you claimed."

"Griffin, you really are a fool," he said half turning toward me. "You have no idea what you're doing or who you're dealing with. I am of no use to you. Give me Patricia and let us go."

"So you can continue using me as your whore and your bank roll?"

Gavin spun toward the voice. "Patricia," he said with relief. "You're safe." This last he said with a hint of surprise.

"We've come for you, Gavin," Patricia explained with a note of finality.

My patience with the happy couple was exhausted. When he stepped toward her, I kicked his feet out from under him.

He crashed to the floor, with me on his back.

"Enough," I barked.

I knelt on his back as he tried to rise. He started to struggle. I rapped him lightly on the head with the barrel of my pistol. "Stop."

Patricia stepped out of the shadows, and I could see her face. I couldn't understand her expression. She wept. I didn't like how this was going.

The cars were outside the gate, and men were shouting.

"Yuri!" Gavin shouted. "Yuri!" He was likely calling for Red Eye, and I decided to hit him harder. Bullets slammed into the front door, and I lay down on top of him instead.

Outside, a shotgun boomed, and the BAR began to fire. The firing escalated so fast that I couldn't keep track of who was shooting at whom. More rounds came into the house. Bullets smashed into the front door, and splinters flew. I rolled off

263

Gavin, fired a few rounds through the door, and tackled Patricia to the floor.

"Stay down," I shouted. I pushed her into a room off the hall and went back for Gavin, but he tried to fight me. I grabbed him by his suit jacket and swung him into the wall, stunning him. I dragged him into the room with Patricia. I leaned out into the hallway and fired again. Smoke and limestone dust filled the air as more rounds zipped down the hall, smacking into the stone walls inside.

The house door swung open, shattered by the volume of fire from the street. The men outside were shooting into the house, indifferent to Gavin or Patricia's presence. I quickly reloaded, and Patricia leaned past me and fired her little Ruby pistol down the hall.

The gunshots in the house were deafening.

Two men dove through the sagging front door, driven there by the fire from the yard. Mitchell and company must be giving them hell if they were willing to come in here, I thought.

I pushed Patricia back, steadied my aim, and emptied my pistol into them. I think Patricia fired past me at them as well, but by then, they were already shattered lumps in the entryway.

The shotgun boomed outside once more, and then it was quiet.

I turned back to Patricia. She was standing in the hallway, the pistol dangling in her hand. Her eyes were wide, and tears ran down her cheeks. She was looking at the unmoving figures of the dead men in the foyer.

"Check on Gavin," I said, reloading as I went to the front door to judge the situation outside.

I saw Mitchell and Johnson nudging the bodies in the yard with their toes, guns aimed at the now-still forms. Through the fence, I saw Bullard and Nungesser in the street, looking into the two motorcars. There were at least six bodies in the yard.

"Everyone okay?" I called to Mitchell.

"Pretty much," he answered. "Merchant got some scratches

from stone ricochets. I'm not sure the bastard even fired his gun, but other than him, everyone's fine. Disney's starting the car so we can get the hell out of here. How Tricia?"

"Scared."

"John," I heard Patricia call.

I turned back into the house.

"Oh no! John!" she cried.

I ran into the house. Mitchell pounded up the steps behind me. I found Patricia kneeling by Gavin.

He lay partly in the hallway. A bullet had taken him through the cheek. He was quite dead. The small leaking hole next to his perfect, aristocratic nose seemed too small to have brought an end to all this effort from all sides.

We left immediately. Bullard assured me that the house wasn't connected with him, and I didn't argue. I wanted to be away from rue de Kronstadt and away from Garches. We packed up everything we'd brought and bundled into Eugene's motorcar. Full dark had fallen, and we drove past the few neighbors brave enough to venture into the street to see what had happened. They were looking through the fence into the yard of number 20. Cries of alarm started as they recognized the mounds in the yard as bodies.

Disney drove with Bullard and Merchant crammed next to him. I leaned in the car with much of my weight on the running board. Merchant was next to me, shivering against my leg. His cheeks were wet. I couldn't fault him. Just when we thought the killing and the dying was done, we were right back at it. I felt bad for not liking him. I hadn't been fair. He was just like the rest of us. Scared and trying to hide it. I looked into the back seat. Patricia sat on Mitchell's lap between Johnson and Nungesser. Mitchell's arms were around her, holding her close to his chest. I couldn't be sure in the dark, but she looked like she was shivering, or sobbing.

I had no solace to offer her. I had failed in my promise to help her. I didn't care about Gavin. Shed was a much greater loss, but I believed her when she said she loved Kingsbury. I also believed that Sarah would be devastated, and I was worried about how Gavin's death would impact my relationship with her. I was, at least, consistent. Consistently selfish.

"Walt, take us to the Vendôme," Mitchell directed. He was right. There was no reason for Patricia to stay in our cheap hotel. She needed comfort even if just the comfort of expensive furnishings and soft sheets.

Disney nodded but didn't speak. No one spoke the entire drive. The reality of what had happened to Patricia was too immediate and horrible for conversation.

When we arrived at the Vendôme, Mitchell gave me a quick look. I nodded and said, "We'll speak in the morning. I'll be at the Closerie at nine o'clock. Come when you can. No hurry."

I watched him walk into the hotel, his arm around Patricia's bowed shoulders. He would sit with her or hold her, but he knew he could not fix what had happened. He was a navy corpsman again, doing what he could even though it wouldn't be enough.

Disney drove the rest of us to Gene's flat. As when we had lost Shed, we sat in the apartment, drinking whiskey, reliving the violence of the evening, all without saying a word.

It was past midnight when I stood and said, "I don't know if this is the end. I'll be in touch tonight. At the club?" The last was a question to Eugene.

"I'll be playing tonight."

"Gentlemen, thank you."

Their solemn nods followed me out the door.

# 19

---

### Reunited and United

I arrived at the Closerie des Lilas a little before nine in the morning. The weather was still chilly, and out the window of the café, the passing Parisians were wrapped in their winter clothes, mostly dark, somber colors. Men with thick mustaches and cloth caps hurried down the street, some with an empty sleeve tucked into their overcoat pocket. The women wore dark, threadbare shawls over the wide skirts of the previous decade. The people seemed tired. I suspected that I was tired, and I was seeing my weariness reflected in the people around me.

After spending time with Patricia, Kiki, and the girls, I had become used to more modern styles. One modern style that I did not appreciate was the boater hat that I saw one young man sporting as he strutted down the street. Seeing the boater made me think of Gavin. He wouldn't be wearing his boater again. His style and grace had departed this world along with his insanity.

I didn't know when to expect Doc Mitchell, but I had some serious thinking to do as I waited. I was sick of France. I wanted to leave but had nowhere better to go. Sarah was here. And Mitchell. I desperately wanted them both to have a happy ending to the chaos we were part of. And my instincts insisted that the chaos was not over.

Gavin could not have been leading the plot we uncovered. He wore a boater, for Christ's sake. I didn't see how it was possible that hardened French, German, or Russian war veterans and Bolshevik fanatics were following him. He wasn't that type of man. He was a thinker. His charisma came from his station in life, not what he had done or could inspire others to do. He instilled no belief or confidence. He might pay the bills, but he was not the leader. At most, he was the figurehead. Behind him, there would be someone the Bolsheviks respected. Someone who could inspire. I remembered reading in the *Times* about the Spartacist revolution in Berlin in January. Yes, it was led by intellectuals, but intellectuals who were also firebrands. Passionate. Charismatic. Liebknecht and Luxemburg. A man and a woman. They were dead, of course. The German military and the Freikorps suppressed the uprising, and the two were murdered. Charming, those Germans. Not that I blamed them for killing Bolsheviks. It seemed like I had done nothing else since returning to Europe.

My conclusion both worried and depressed me. It meant that Gavin's plot was not over and that it was not actually Gavin's plot at all. It also meant that while we could go to the French authorities, Sarah might still be exposed as part of it all. We would have to find a way to disentangle her from the bird's nest of this conspiracy before alerting the French.

Of course, it was extremely likely that the French already knew something was up and they were diligently hunting for Bolsheviks and the killers of Bolsheviks. We'd have to be careful. We needed to find Sarah. She needed to be away from this business. I was sure Patricia would be the key to finding her.

Mitchell arrived in a rush of frigid air, cheeks rosy from the cold. He sat across from me and waved at the waiter for a coffee. He had dark circles under his eyes from his long night, but he didn't look as miserable as I expected. In fact, he didn't look miserable at all. I watched him, waiting for him to speak.

"She's gonna be fine," he started. "She's tough. She's resting."

"I thought she was resting all night," I said with some bite in my tone.

He had the decency to look embarrassed.

"She needed comforting, Griffin. And it's complicated. Her relationship with Gavin is... was complicated. One thing led to another, and, well... we are really attracted to each other. No one planned anything. I didn't. Really. It just happened."

I didn't say anything. My Protestant sensibilities might be offended, but my twentieth-century reality told me not to judge him too harshly. Apparently my face showed only the bluenose disapproval of my upbringing.

"Come on, Griff, don't be like that."

"It's fine. I'm happy for you. I just don't trust her. She says she's in love with Gavin, and not two hours after he's dead, she falls into the sack with you?"

"Goddamn you, Griffin. You can be such a hypocritical prick. She was grieving and needed comfort. She loved Gavin, but not like that. I did what I thought was right!"

"Don't get sore, Mitch. I'm just being honest. I don't like it. I feel like we're being used, and I think she's doing the using."

"You're wrong," he said. He stood to leave, his face set in an angry scowl.

"Sit down. You may not like my view, but I will always be honest with you. And it isn't just about you or her. Gavin didn't have the brains or the know-how to organize and execute all the shit we've run into. From what I've seen of him, he couldn't plan his way to the head without help. Somebody with real ability wants to prevent the treaty. Somebody competent is leading the Bolsheviks. That's who we have to find. Your love life is just that. Yours. As my momma used to say when I was seeing a girl she didn't like, 'I don't have to live with her. You do.'"

He stared down at me for a moment, then sat.

The waiter brought his coffee, and he fussed over it, letting some of the tension ease.

"The only lead we have on the Bolshevik plan is Sarah," I continued. "We need Patricia to connect us with Sarah and hope that Sarah can lead us to the higher-up. That true leader is who we must find. That's who we have to kill."

"Sarah could be anywhere. I'm sure Patricia doesn't know where she is," he insisted.

"She doesn't have to know. I think Sarah will find her. Once Sarah learns Gavin was killed, she will have to go to Patricia. They're very close. She'll need comfort. Understanding." I should have stopped there, but I didn't. "Between the two of you, I'm sure she'll get all the comfort she can stand."

This time he did leave.

I wasn't worried that Mitchell wouldn't contact me when Sarah found Patricia. He would because he didn't want the war to continue. I was worried that he wouldn't forgive me for my parting words. I could do nothing about it now, and I wasn't sure I had it in me to apologize anyway.

I left the café. I wasn't ready to return to my empty hotel room to reflect on my predicament. I turned away from the hotel and walked. Motor buses, wagons, carriages, and motorcars rolled over the cobbled streets. On the corners, matrons and small, underfed children begged for a few coins. As my feet took me deeper into Montparnasse, the inhabitants of the street corners changed to younger women looking for work, horizontal or otherwise. Despite the clearing weather, the city depressed me. I toyed with the idea of getting good and drunk, but the thought of wandering through the city blotto depressed me even more.

To hell with Mitchell and Patricia. And Sarah too. Mitchell might not care about being used by her, but I did. It angered me.

Eventually I returned to the hotel. My walking hadn't helped me come up with any ideas at all. I would wait. That was all I could do. I cleaned the Colt, tucked it behind my belt, and went out to find the girls. I'd have some drinks with them and then go catch Eugene's show at the club. I wouldn't share Mitchell and Patricia's romance with Bullard or any of the others. That would be for the two of them to reveal.

I had a drink at both Le Dôme and La Rotonde, but I didn't see Kiki, Rachel, or Madeline. I took the Metro across the river and walked to the Zelli's club.

The place was full once again. Our expat crowd had cornered a table near the wall, and Disney and Merchant were chatting up Rachel and Madeline. I saw no sign of Kiki. Nungesser was at the table as well. He was facing one of the tables behind them, speaking to a very young-looking dark-haired girl. Henry Johnson sat at the end of the table. Although he was with the others, he was actually alone. He was not part of the laughing, drinking, white crowd. He was listening with great intensity to Eugene's band. I gave the girls each a kiss and pulled out a chair next to Johnson.

"Mind if I sit next to you, Henry?" I asked. I found his seriousness appealed to my mood. He was slow to answer. Perhaps that was my answer, but I pressed on.

"I wanted to thank you again for last night."

"Did it for Eugene," he answered briefly.

"Yeah, he's a good guy," I agreed.

In my life, I'd had few conversations with negros. Those conversations had been about horses or boxing, usually with black enlisted men on post or black servants at whatever club I might be visiting. This made sense because the colored folks I'd known were good with horses and good at boxing. I really didn't have anything else to talk to them about. We lived in different worlds that touched, at most, tangentially. And, if I were to be honest with myself, where our worlds touched it was never as equals. Because we weren't. Equals that is.

But just by their existence, Johnson and especially Bullard challenged the reality I'd grown up with. Two incredibly brave, thoughtful, intelligent, loyal men. This threw me. Fortunately, introspection was never my strong suit, and I was in Europe where few cared about the color of a person's skin. Instead, they cared about the school you went to and the amount of money in your pocket.

In an unpleasant flash of understanding, I realized that in all the ways that mattered to me now, my world and that of Bullard and Johnson overlapped entirely. They'd fought in the hideous war. They understood the loss, the terror, and the exhilaration that no civilian ever could. I now had much more in common with them than I did with the white folks who'd populated my youth. But I was uncomfortable interacting with Bullard and Johnson. I didn't know how. In the States, I knew how to act with a darky, and more importantly from my perspective, they knew how to act with me. In Paris, I wasn't sure what the rules were, but I knew they weren't the same as at home. I did know that I wanted to know more about Johnson. Because it might help me understand Bullard a little better. And damned if I didn't respect Bullard. This thought surprised me, so I disregarded it.

Johnson didn't speak again. He didn't look at me. He didn't give me a fake smile, trying to convince me that he was harmless. He ignored me. He seemed engrossed in Gene and his band.

"Henry, what do you see when you watch Eugene play?" I asked to break the ice. He looked at me and back at the band.

"I see opportunity and courage," he answered simply. I waited for more, but he was done. I thought about what he said. There was opportunity here. Opportunity that black men would never have in the United States. And courage. The courage to take the risk to seize the opportunity. I found myself agreeing.

A waiter passed by, and I ordered a bottle of whiskey and two glasses. I damned sure wasn't drinking champagne tonight. Between the dancing, twirling bodies, I watched Bullard and his band too. The whiskey came, and I poured two and pushed one over to Johnson. He nodded his thanks but didn't speak. Fair enough, I thought. I could sit and drink as the rag music and laughter washed over me.

We sat that way for a time, and I was surprised when Johnson said, "Eugene said you're from the South."

He was hard to hear in the din.

"Sorta. My father was in the army. I grew up on a lot of posts in the South."

"I'm originally from North Carolina. Didn't know much about the army. Now I know plenty. Don't much like it."

I chuckled. "Can't argue with that."

He leaned toward me to hear better. "I'm from New York now, but Paris, Paris is growing on me," he explained.

"I can't say the same," I answered. "I've met too many Reds here."

"Well, from what Gene tells me, you've killed most of 'em. And the Frenchies I meet don't care that I'm a negro. Hell, the French even gave me a medal. Croix de Guerre. In our army, some white boys wouldn't even share a trench with me."

"You gonna go home?" I asked.

"Was already supposed to. My Regiment, the 369th, the Harlem Hellfighters they called us, already had a victory parade in New York City,[1] but I was still recuperating with a French family outside of Paris when they went back. Don't think the army even knows where I am."

I nodded because some response seemed necessary.

"It's strange, my country sends me here, then gives me and my regiment to the French. Doesn't even have enough faith in us to have us fight alongside you white boys. I killed Germans. A bunch. Just like I was supposed to. With my hands and a Bolo trench knife." He looked down at his hands curled in his lap. "But who'd want a killer nigger back? I don't think the ole U S of A does," he said with a shake of his head, his brown eyes sad.

He was probably right, but I didn't say that out loud.

I did find that, in talking to Johnson, I understood Bullard better. Bullard had found in France the freedom that a colored man couldn't have in the States. Johnson was the evidence of that. He was an American honored by the French as a hero but

273

not by his own country. Bullard, even if originally an American, was revered by the French. In France, if you gave your blood for France, even if colored, you were a hero. In the States, if you were black and gave your blood, you were a nigger first and only.

I shook my head.

"Well, Henry, it won't mean much, but thank you. For what you did in the army and for what you did with us yesterday," I said seriously. "You're a good man. I mean it." And I did.

Bullard's set finished. He thanked the crowd and worked his way to our table. He gave Johnson a questioning look when he saw me sitting next to him but didn't comment. He pulled a chair around, sat down across from us, and the others huddled in.

"Well, John, what's the plan?" he asked me.

"We wait. We wait for Sarah to contact Patricia. They're close friends, and with Gavin dead, I think she'll want to see Patricia. She'll need a shoulder to cry on. So we wait. There's really nothing else for us to do. Every other lead we've had has gone cold."

"As in dead," I heard Merchant say. I met his eye and was surprised at the icy look he gave me. It was hard to argue with him, but I found myself disliking Merchant again.

Madeline punched him in the arm. "Jerk," she mouthed.

"Yeah," I answered with a laugh.

"And you think she will? Contact Patricia," Bullard clarified.

"I do. Her brother's dead. She was with him and the Bolsheviks. But I didn't get the impression that she knew the others well. Patricia is the only other person she knows here," I answered.

"If you're right," Rachel challenged.

"That's fair, Rachel. She may know other folks. She may have gone to school with Gavin's Red friends, but as far as I know, Patricia is all that's left."

"What do we do?" Nungesser asked. He had his arm around the shoulders of the dark-haired girl. No one had bothered to introduce us, and I wasn't going to make the effort.

274

"I'd keep doing what you're doing, Charles," I said, looking directly at the girl. "But if something comes up, I'd like to be able to call on y'all."

"Sure," Disney was quick to answer. "We can all stay in touch through Eugene." He hesitated and then asked, "How's Tricia doing?"

"Doc Mitchell is staying close, and I think she'll be okay," I told him cryptically.

My answers seemed to extinguish the interest in preparing for whatever came next. Eugene grabbed a glass, poured a drink from my bottle, and turned to talk with Johnson. Most of the others started dancing.

"Are you okay, John?" Madeline asked. She hadn't lost interest. She was a pretty girl, and I should have been interested too. I wasn't, and I couldn't explain why.

"I'm fine, Maddy."

"Okay, but you let me know if you need anything," she answered. She kissed my scarred cheek and walked out onto the dance floor to Disney, Nungesser, and his girl.

---

FOR THE NEXT SEVERAL DAYS, THERE WAS NO NEWS, AND I KEPT myself busy by reading the papers in the mornings, walking Paris in the afternoons, and listening to the gossip at the cafés and clubs in the evening. Both Kiki and Eugene were particularly helpful in keeping me updated about the treaty negotiations and the French authorities' investigations of the brutal shootings in Garches.

Their reports were clear that the negotiations among the Allies had finished, and the Germans, who had recently arrived in Paris, were presented with the treaty terms. Clemenceau had outmaneuvered Wilson. The resulting treaty offered to the Germans would radically weaken the country both militarily and economically and promised no real relief in the future. Germany would lose huge swaths of territory, millions in population, be required to pay reparations, and perhaps most galling of all, acknowledge responsibility and guilt for causing the war. France would succeed in achieving a peace that would create a shell of prewar Germany. Wilson would get his League of Nations in return for guaranteeing the security of Europe. It was not clear whether the Germans would agree. I was not sure I would agree to the terms Kiki and Bullard shared with me, but I had no desire to fight again in a European war, and so I hoped the Germans would agree. My understanding from the two of them was that the Germans, having just received the particulars of the demands, had a short period of time to respond.

As to the French police and their search for those responsible for the shootings in Montparnasse and Garches, Gene told me they had concluded that the same vicious criminal gangs were responsible for both shootouts. The authorities believed that gangs of Apaches were fighting for control of parts of Paris; however, they were surprised that Garches was an area of interest, much less fought over, by the gangs. Bullard assured me that there was no indication that the authorities thought that Bolsheviks or American tourists were shooting up the city.

Finally, the third day after our return from Garches, I got news of Sarah. That morning, the weather was clear and warmer than the previous days. I was sitting outside at the Closerie, enjoying the sun in my face and a cup of strong coffee in my hand. As had become my practice in Paris, I was also feeling sorry for myself. I was reviewing my current situation in life and had decided to apply a nearly scientific method to assessing it. That is, I was using the method of Miss Quartermouse, my old Sunday school teacher. I was creating a mental ledger of my life's blessing and its challenges. The idea was that at the end of the exercise, I would find that God had blessed me far more than I believed at the beginning of the process.

So, the positives... I had new friends who would back me through thick and thin, even two negros. I decided to count

Johnson as a friend, figuring no one would ever tell him. I'd recently met a beautiful, intelligent woman, who seemed to like me. She made life interesting again. I was young. I had a bunch of money, courtesy of the Armistan family, and guns to go with it.

And for life's challenges, there was no pausing to think here. These were easy. I had survived the war, but I wasn't sure I was fit for a peacetime world. I was on the outs with my best friend. Bolsheviks were planning to start World War Two. My girl was in cahoots with the Bolsheviks and possibly furthering their plan. I didn't know what the plan was, but I had managed to get her brother killed in a gunfight with these same Bolsheviks. Her best friend was a manipulating schemer who had caused me to be on the outs with my best friend. Oh, and part of my face looked like melted candle wax, and I would probably die before thirty because of phosgene in my lungs. But the last two challenges were old news, so I scratched them off my mental list.

I wondered if I had left anything out.

Patricia Kingsbury's Hispano-Suiza motorcar coasted to a stop in front of the Closerie, and Morgan Reynolds stepped out.

I had left something out. I had forgotten the challenge of Morgan Reynolds.

Thank you, God, for the challenges you provide to help me grow, I thought cynically.

Reynolds sauntered up to my table and, with a smirk, sat down across from me without being invited.

I tapped the table with my coffee spoon and waited for whatever he had come to tell me. He wanted to gloat, and I didn't want to spoil his fun.

"So," he began as he took a gold cigarette case from his suit pocket and made a show of taking out a cigarette and lighting it.

I sipped my coffee.

"Mrs. Kingsbury asked that I contact you. I was reluctant since all you've accomplished is getting her husband killed, but she insisted."

He looked at me, waiting for some response. I toyed with the idea of driving the little spoon into his right eye. I was pretty sure it wouldn't kill him. Instead, I said simply, "And?"

"She asks that you join her for lunch at the Hôtel de Vendôme. Sarah Willoughby is now staying at the hotel, and Mrs. Kingsbury believes you should meet with her. Of course, I don't see the point in continuing to involve you in the family business, given your failures, but again, Mrs. Kingsbury insisted."

So, Sarah did contact Patricia. I felt no satisfaction at guessing right.

"What time?" I asked.

"One o'clock."

"Thank you, Morgan," I said politely. "You may go."

Reynolds's disappointment at my indifferent response was obvious. I did promise myself a more enthusiastic response to Morgan Reynolds at some point in the future. I wondered how much he liked having Mitchell around Patricia. That must be hard for him to bear. I smiled at the thought.

After Reynolds left, I saw no reason to revisit my "blessings" list. It promised to change in the very near future. I went to my room, shaved, and put on a clean shirt with a tie. I would look my best even if I could never compare to the men Sarah was used to. I reminded myself to control my emotions. Mitchell was my guide as to what to avoid. I couldn't fall prey to my feelings for Sarah. I needed to understand exactly what the Bolsheviks planned. I needed the truth. I did not need my heart's promised fantasy.

At half past noon, I took a taxi to the Louvre. From there, I crossed the rue de Rivoli and walked down rue Saint-Honoré, following it to the Place Vendôme. The weather was still fine, if cool, and the walk was bracing. At the hotel, I presented myself to the concierge at the front desk and explained that I was there to see Patricia Kingsbury. He told me that I was expected and called a bellman to show me to the private dining room. He escorted me through the lobby and down a short hallway where I heard the high, tinkling laughter of women. We arrived at a private room. Patricia and Sarah were already seated at a round table, which was dressed in a pristine white tablecloth, crystal, and silver. I studied both women. Their blond hair and pale skin glowed, and their eyes were bright. In their stylish light dresses, they could have been sisters, one tall and lithe, one smaller and curvaceous. Both women were still smiling from their recent laughter. I saw no signs of grief or mourning. I was both relieved and disappointed. I found myself thinking less of Sarah for her smile. And I didn't even like her brother.

"Ladies," I said. "I am sorry for your loss."

A shadow passed over both their faces.

"As are we, John," Sarah answered. "Patricia and I were just remembering Gavin's humor. He could be so funny when he wanted to be."

"Sit, John, please," Patricia said, pointing to the third seat at the table. "Thank you for coming. I understand you have met Sarah."

I watched a look pass between them and was convinced that Sarah had shared the facts of our "relationship" with Patricia.

"Thank you for having me, and it is good to see you again, Sarah." I decided there was no point in calling her Mrs. Willoughby after seeing the look the two exchanged.

A waiter appeared and recharged the ladies' wineglasses with a white from the ice bucket between them. Without direction, he filled my glass as well.

"You're looking well, John, despite the terrible time Gavin and I have put you through. I wanted to apologize," Sarah said sincerely.

That surprised me, and it must have shown because Sarah smiled.

"You don't have anything to apologize for, Sarah," I said. "As you told me before, you're loyal. You were supporting your brother. He was mistaken in his beliefs, but I don't fault you for your support of him."

"That's generous of you, but"—she choked up slightly and

paused to regain her control—"I feel guilty. He was a good man in his way, but he was easily misled. And, by supporting him, I encouraged his dangerous dreams. I helped him kill himself." Tears filled her eyes.

"Nonsense!" Patricia said sternly. "You went along with him because you felt guilty about how he was treated in 1914 and after. He knew what he was doing, and as I've learned more about what his actions would have meant, I have trouble forgiving him."

Sarah reached across the table and squeezed Patricia's hand. "It's so good to be reunited. But enough about Gavin." Sarah brushed the tears from her eyes. "I have important news. I was at a house with some of Gavin's friends, Bolshevik friends, when I learned of the news of his death. There are only five of Gavin's supporters left. They were angry, convinced that the German Freikorps had killed Gavin and the others. I believed it as well. With the death of so many and their leader gone, they despaired about disrupting the final peace. In fact, when I left to come to Patricia, they had decided to focus on revolution through labor action and economic disruption. They're going home, wherever that may be. The plot involving the treaty is done. Abandoned."

Both women looked at me, waiting for a reaction.

I replayed in my head her phrase "their leader gone." I still couldn't believe Gavin was their leader, and because I didn't know how to react, I took a sip of wine and said, "Well, that's good news. What's for lunch?"

"John!" they both exclaimed.

"That's all you can say?" Patricia asked. "This means no more shooting. No more death." I could see her shudder as she likely remembered the gun battle where Gavin died.

"I understand that possibility, ladies," I said. "I do. And I'd like it to be true. But I am hungry, and I'm not sure I believe it."

"You think I'm lying?" Sarah asked.

Her question bothered me. That was not what I meant at all, but that was how she interpreted me.

"No, Sarah," I answered carefully. "I'm sure they did tell you they were giving up and going home. I just don't know that I believe it."

"Or you don't want to," she answered sharply.

"It is over, John. Surely you can accept that," Patricia added.

I remembered my conversation with Patricia in the house on rue de Kronstadt. I remembered telling her that I was only fit for war. It seemed she might have shared my bit of honesty with Sarah, and now both women would believe me a warmonger if I persisted in my skepticism. I didn't want that, and I wasn't skeptical out of any conscious desire to continue fighting. I just didn't believe Gavin was the leader of the scheme to sabotage the treaty.

I raised my hands in my defense.

"Please, ladies. I want it to be true as well. I just find it hard to believe that after so much effort and sacrifice, they are going to quit," I answered. "But it doesn't matter what I believe. If they're gone, they're gone."

"Exactly so!" Patricia said firmly. "It is time for all of us to move on. And I had made you a promise, Mr. Griffin. I understand from Sarah that you know each other better than you let on, but I still think the two of you should be the subject of my matchmaking efforts. Sarah is staying here at the Vendôme, and the two of you and William and I will make a point of enjoying Paris now that the war is done."

"Speaking of Will, where is he?" I asked.

"He thought it would be best if we had this conversation without him," answered Patricia. "I'm afraid he's still annoyed with you for not trusting me."

"Well, that's not likely to change in the near future, Patricia," I answered honestly. "But I'm perfectly happy to spend a few spring days in Paris with two beautiful, if devious, women." I finished by softening the truth with the truth, lumping Sarah in with Patricia.

Both women noticed but smiled anyway. It seemed that Gavin's death was a long time ago for everyone but me.

The next few days were exactly as Patricia promised. I spent them entirely with Sarah. I didn't go to La Rotonde or Le Dôme. I didn't see my American friends, Kiki or Bullard, whom I considered both American and French. I stayed with my personal Circe, beguiled yet willingly so. I saw little of Mitchell. Patricia seemed to think the less time he spent around me the better. I didn't mind. He had been cold when we spoke, and I had no mind to apologize. I still believed Patricia had used us, and despite my joy with Sarah, I believed she had used us as well.

We were having dinner in Sarah's suite in the Vendôme when the first cracks in the enchantment gripping me appeared. The hotel had delivered a feast to Sarah's room complete with linen and silver and including fine wine. We were half-dressed, ravenously hungry, and a little tipsy after making love and drinking champagne all afternoon. I was happy until a tap on her door announced the bellman. When I answered, he handed me a sealed note addressed to "S. Willoughby."

I carried it back to Sarah and held it out to her. Her long legs were curled under her, partly covered by a white hotel robe she wore. I found it hard to pull my eyes away.

"For you," I said.

"Put it on the table. I'll read it later."

I followed her instructions, but I did not forget the note. It was like a dash of cold water in the face of a drunk. I wanted Sarah, and I wanted to believe the Bolsheviks had given up. But I didn't believe it, and this message from the outside reminded me that I didn't believe. My failure to believe felt like a betrayal of Sarah, but my instincts refused to accept that the plotting died with Gavin.

The next morning, I woke with Sarah's head on my chest, her body curled against mine. She was breathing softly. I felt the warm glow of happiness. I was in love with her, no doubt, no ambiguity. I had not yet said the words to her, but I knew I loved her.

From the bed, I could see the table where I had placed Sarah's note. It was gone. Sometime during the evening, Sarah had read the note. Even if just an invitation to dinner, when unopened and unread, it was a meaningless puzzle piece. Now, with its vanishing, I was convinced that the Bolshevik plot continued and Sarah remained involved. If the conspirators were still active, more people would die while I fiddled in Paris. I sensed events unfolding outside the four walls of our room in the Vendôme. I could not sit by and do nothing.

I untangled myself from Sarah and the twisted bedsheets and quietly recovered my clothes. I was afraid she would wake and ask me what I was doing, where I was going. I would lie and tell her I wanted to collect some belongings from my pensione. I wondered if she had had the same kinds of worries when she left me in her house in Surrey. Likely not, since we had only the beginnings of a connection then. But she didn't wake, and I had no need to lie.

As I walked back to my hotel, I thought about the pieces of the plot that remained in place. We had not recovered the German uniforms and weapons. Sarah had said only five Bolsheviks remained. But even five men, united in purpose and will, with the right timing and right target, properly equipped and trained, could change history.

Suddenly I knew what the plotters intended. It should have been obvious from the start. I was not sure of the timing, but I knew it would be soon.

At the hotel, I packed my suitcase, but I reserved my room by paying for two weeks in advance. I might be away for a while, and I wanted a place to come back to if I could.

## 20

_____

**Chipped Cobbles**

With my bag heavy on my lap, I rode the streetcar west past the Eiffel Tower and across the river into the 16th Arrondissement. It was a well-to-do neighborhood and one I was unlikely to see any of my new friends frequent. I had the general sense of where the address I sought was located, but I didn't relish the idea of dragging my bag from door to door until I found it. I decided to ask for directions.

As soon as I got off the streetcar, I stopped at a corner news-paper kiosk and asked for the way to rue Franklin. I was in luck. Not only did the vendor know where the street was, he promised me it was just a short walk away. I thanked him and was soon turning down rue Franklin. On the right side of the street, a French policeman in his short cloak guarded what must be apart-ment house number eight. I crossed the street away from him and found myself next to a small, neat hotel. It was catty-corner to number eight and likely as close to the building as I would find. Across from the hotel was a tobacco shop and more apart-ments. This would do.

I went into the hotel and asked for a room with windows

overlooking the street but as far from the intersection of Franklin and rue de Vineuse as possible. Behind the front desk was a rail-thin matron who assured me she was also the hotel's owner. Madame Truchon explained to me how difficult it was to get good help with all the dead from the war, including both her sons, and from the Spanish flu, which took her second husband. I murmured my sympathies, and I signed the register as Morgan Reynolds. I handed her payment for one week in advance. She gave me the key for room twenty-one, which she assured me was at the far end of the hotel, away from the intersection. It was also on the second floor, she told me.

I climbed the three flights of stairs to the room, marveling once again that, for Europeans, one could equal zero and two could equal three. My room at the end of the hallway had two windows, and from them, I could see much of the far side of the street. The policeman on duty at number eight paced back and forth in front of the building. He appeared not so much diligent as bored. I stuck my head out one of the windows, and I could see the sidewalk below for nearly the length of the street. I was pleasantly surprised by my situation. I would watch the street, follow the news of the peace negotiations, and wait.

If I was wrong about the target, nothing would happen here. If I was right about the target but wrong about the location of the attack, I was wasting my time. But if I was right about both... Well, if I was right, all hell would break loose.

Because if the Bolsheviks assassinated Georges Clemenceau, Le Tigre, the Pére le Victoire, the Prime Minister of France at his home, the negotiations for peace would crumble. If they dressed as German soldiers and shot him down like a dog in the street, war would follow. He would be a martyr, and his death at the hands of Germany would have to be avenged. Lloyd George and Wilson would not be able to resist. The Bolshevik plot would succeed, and the war would resume.

I had no doubts about the target or the place for the attack. It fit too nicely with the facts I knew to be true. I didn't know if the

Bolsheviks had lied to Sarah or if Sarah had lied to me, but I was positive an attack on Clemenceau was imminent.

For the first few days in my new neighborhood, I mostly stayed in my room, trying to get a sense of Clemenceau's schedule. I learned that while his schedule varied, he usually left his apartments at ten o'clock sharp each morning. A black four-door motorcar would arrive at his apartment house. As the local church bells would chime the hour, he would come through one of the heavy wood double doors to his apartments, top hat firmly in place and cane in hand. He would greet the gendarme on duty at the door and climb into the back seat of the motorcar to be driven away at the pace of the traffic on the street, which is to say, slowly. Any morning, it would be a simple task to walk up to the car and shoot him as he sat in the back seat. I wondered at the failure of the assassin who'd try to kill him in February.

In the evening, Clemenceau would return any time between eight p.m. and midnight. His car invariably approached his apartment from the west, driving up the same side of the street as his apartments. With a little coordination, it would be a simple matter to shoot him dead as he stepped out of the car.

Neither of these simple plans made use of all the tools the Bolsheviks had at their disposal. And they would want to use all their tools: the uniforms, the machine gun, the automatic rifles, the grenades. The Reds would not kill Clemenceau cleanly. They needed a spectacle. And they had a Maxim machine gun, which was guaranteed to create a bloodbath. I needed to recognize the signs of these tools being deployed. So I stayed in my hotel room and watched the street in the mornings and the evenings. The rest of the day I explored the neighborhood, pretending to be a recuperating American soldier with poor but understandable French and money to burn.

Joseph, the owner of the tobacco shop across the street from the hotel, quickly became my most useful source for information. He was an immigrant to France from greater Syria, or what he called the Mount Lebanon Mustasarrif. I learned, in time, that he was from the city of Beirut and had left because his father's textile business had gone bankrupt late in the past century, something to do with a crash in silk prices. He was a talkative, likable grifter. He had been in France for nearly twenty-five years and a resident of rue Franklin for ten. He was excited about the Paris peace negotiations because he was certain that a new country of Lebanon would be formed, but he had no intention of leaving Paris to go there. He also had an encyclopedic memory for his neighbors' habits and idiosyncrasies.

From Joseph, I learned that Monsieur Clemenceau used to be a profligate womanizer who had slowed down his philandering in his old age. I also discovered that my landlady had been married and widowed twice, under suspicious circumstances, notwithstanding her blaming the Spanish flu for the demise of her second husband. I also learned that the banker down the street was having financial trouble. I asked Joseph how he knew that the banker was having money problems, and he said, "*Maintenant, il n'achète que des cigares bon marché.*"[1] Yes, smoking cheap cigars would be an important clue. A clever deduction by Joseph.

Ultimately I decided to risk recruiting him to my cause. I told him I was an agent of the American president, Woodrow Wilson. For this, I received an enthusiastic hug and kisses on both cheeks. I explained that I had been tasked with protecting our partner in the negotiations, Monsieur Clemenceau. This claim was supported by my terrible French and the scar on my face. I asked him if he would do a little quiet observation, which was, of course, "top secret." I also told him that the American government would be willing to pay for his help in US dollars. He tapped the side of his nose with a smile and agreed. I told him to pay close attention to anyone or anything that didn't belong on the street and to be on the lookout for anything suspicious. He promised me he would be most vigilant. I pushed a folded $100 bill into his hand, and his smile became a grin. I was sure that I had overpaid for his detective work.

Every day, I would circle the neighborhood, trying to get a

feel for its rhythm. Every evening, just before closing time, I would check in with Joseph. He would tell me the gossip of the day and describe any strangers on the street. He was extremely enthusiastic about his surveillance, and his reports were thorough. I suspected that he had recruited some family members to watch the street for him.

I didn't rely solely on Joseph. Despite Joseph's thinly concealed opinion that my landlady was a murderer, I also enlisted her as a watcher. Hers was the only hotel on the block, and it was possible that anyone stalking Clemenceau would let a room from her, just as I had. Madame Truchon was not so thorough as Joseph, but she did get great joy from reporting to me any new guests, particularly the "foreign" ones. I was excluded from her general dislike of foreigners, given my obvious wounds and that I was an American who both tried to speak French and, importantly, spent a lot of money.

After nearly a week with no evidence of Bolshevik activity, I started to be able to pick out newcomers to the street as I watched Clemenceau leave for work in the morning. A man and a woman walked down the street arm in arm one morning and then walked back up it not three minutes later. The next day, just the man, the same man, came down the street from the opposite direction. The third day, at 0955, a motor truck pulled past Clemenceau's house and stopped about fifty feet down the street. Canvas stretched over a frame covering the bed of the truck. The canvas flies to the back of the truck were tied shut. I watched carefully, but while the truck was parked, no one got in or out. When Clemenceau left home, his car drove past the truck. A minute later, the truck pulled away.

When I next spoke to Joseph, he identified the couple that I had seen as strangers to the neighborhood. He was excited that his efforts had born fruit. He was more excited when I questioned him about the truck. He had seen it too. Inside his shop was a small girl, who he told me was his brother's seven-year-old daughter and his favorite niece. He told me this in French, and the little girl smiled when she heard his declaration of devotion. He then explained that she had seen inside the truck.

" *Qu'as-tu vu dans le camion, petite?*"[2] I asked.

She glanced at her uncle and back at me. I don't think she was reassured when I smiled. Perhaps the tugging scar around my eye put her off. She stepped closer to her uncle.

"*Dis-lui*, Marie,"[3] Joseph said.

And she did.

"*J'ai vu deux hommes fumer. Ils ne parlaient pas. Ils se sont simplement assis là,*"[4] she said. "*Quand ils m'ont vu regarder, ils m'ont dit de partir. Ils étaient méchants.*"[5]

"*À quoi ressemblaient-ils?*"[6] I asked.

"*Vieux, mais pas aussi vieux que mon oncle,*" she answered. "*Vieux comme vous. Fatigués et tristes.*"[7]

Tired and sad, I thought to myself. Soldiers. Veterans of the war here on a mission to extend it.

"*Merci*, Marie, *merci beaucoup.*"

I left Joseph's shop with a lot on my mind. I bought a newspaper at the corner kiosk on rue Franklin and walked past the traffic circle to a small brasserie not far from my hotel. The weather was fair, and I took a table outside, periodically looking down rue Franklin to reassure myself that no black truck was parked near number eight. The waiter knew me from previous nights, and he had no expectation that I would patiently wait to order. He arrived with a draft beer, and I ordered the cassoulet for dinner.

From the newspaper, I learned that the negotiations were nearly complete. The Germans, after having received the draft treaty two weeks before, had made a counterproposal earlier in the week. The paper offered no details on the terms of the German counteroffer, but it was clear that the Germans would not accept the Allies' terms. They were negotiating for a better deal.

Isn't that what everyone does? As my mother used to say,

"Never take the first offer, Johnny, you can always get a better one." I supposed even Germans have mothers.

I was surprised to learn that the Allies were giving thoughtful consideration to the German proposal. The tone in the paper was outraged that some of the most onerous demands for territory, people, and reparations might be softened. I gleaned that the Germans also sought to rework the wording of the clause that placed the guilt for the war on Berlin. This, too, was under consideration by the Allies. Easing these terms would certainly make the treaty more palatable in Germany. Despite the jingo-istic tone in the newspaper, for the first time, I felt slightly opti-mistic that a lasting peace might be negotiated.

Then a cold fear washed over me. The Bolsheviks could not allow these negotiations to succeed. They could not take the chance that a fair treaty resulting in an acceptable peace was the outcome. They had to interfere immediately. Now. Tomorrow. In the morning. They had done their reconnaissance. They knew Clemenceau's habits. They couldn't let an even-handed treaty be signed.

I considered getting Mitchell and Eugene for support, but I decided against it. If I asked Mitchell, I would have to explain what I'd found, and he would blame me for finding proof that the girls were using us. Also, Sarah would find out that I didn't trust her. It was bad enough that I'd left her bed with no explanation. If I asked Gene, he would come, as would Disney, Johnson, and probably Nungesser and Merchant, but I kept thinking of Shed. I didn't want any more dead friends. If Sarah was right, there would only be five, maybe just four fighters, given that one of the five remaining must be a woman from what I had seen on the street. They would come in German uniforms, but they would be inside the truck with blankets over their shoulders until the moment of the attack. They would kill Clemenceau and likely everyone on the street in a magnificent slaughter. My stomach roiled at the thought of trying to prevent an assassination in the face of a Maxim gun and four men.

The next morning, I packed up. I stuffed the Colt behind my belt so that I could draw it with my right hand and pushed the Webley under my belt in front so that I could draw it with my left. I buttoned my coat and took my suitcase down to the front desk. I asked Madame Truchon to hold the bag for me, explaining that I would get it later in the morning. She offered to reimburse me the money I had paid for the week in advance, but I insisted that she keep it as a gift from the American government.

I also asked her to stay indoors until after half past ten that morning. She started to ask why, but I interrupted her and said, "Madame, *s'il vous plaît, faites ce que je demande. C'est pour votre propre bien.*"[8]

Few pedestrians were on the street when I crossed to the tobacco shop. I asked Joseph to stay off the street as well. He didn't argue, seeming to understand the grim look on my face. I gave him another $100 and thanked him on behalf of the Republic of France and the United States of America. He accepted the money gravely, and I heard his soft, "*Bonne chance,*" as I left the store.

Thirty minutes until 1000. The truck was not on the street. I walked past number eight, nodding at the policeman on duty. I noted that he had a pistol on his belt. I hoped that if he used it in the next few minutes, he didn't use it on me.

I crossed the street and walked around the triangular block of streets that held my hotel. I saw nothing suspicious. At 0950, I arrived back at the corner of rue Vineuse and rue Franklin. I looked up the street to number eight. A black truck was parked fifty feet up the road from Clemenceau's apartments. I was sure it was the same truck. From the exhaust fumes, I could tell it was still running. My heart beat faster. I took a deep breath through my nose and held it and then exhaled slowly. The assassination attempt was on.

I thought I saw a twitching of the canvas in the bed of the truck, but I could have imagined it. I unbuttoned my coat for easier access to the pistols. I looked back at the traffic circle and saw Clemenceau's limousine crossing the traffic to turn onto rue Franklin.

The door to Clemenceau's apartments opened. The great man stepped through the doors and onto the sidewalk. The door shut behind him. Clemenceau smiled a greeting at the policeman, who unwittingly stood between him and the truck. Down the street, the passenger door of the truck opened, and what appeared to be a German soldier stepped out.

The canvas flies covering the bed of the truck pulled back, and in the shadows, I saw men in uniforms and the silhouette of a Maxim gun.

And the Maxim began to fire. The horrible deep rattle of the machine gun echoed off the buildings' walls.

The policeman danced from the rounds striking him, his blood misting in the air. He spun back into Clemenceau, knocking the prime minister to the ground. I had already pulled the Webley from my belt, and I began to fire into the truck bed. I started to run toward the truck. Just fifty feet or so. Just a few seconds. I fired twice more. The Webley was empty. The passenger on the sidewalk turned toward me and raised a machine pistol. He held one of the new MP 18s that I'd recognized at rue de Babylone, I thought coldly. I brought the Colt up and put the front post sight on his German field gray uniform and fired. He started firing too. The cobbles between Clemenceau and me chipped from his misses as bullets walked between us. I fired again, and the passenger stumbled back into the truck door. My momentum slammed me into the back of the truck. I pushed the Colt into the bed and emptied it into the gray-clad bodies in the bed. From the corner of my eye, I watch a grenade spin from the front of the truck down the street. I dropped flat and dug another magazine from my pocket, reloading the Colt. At some point, I'd dropped the Webley.

The grenade exploded and people along the street started screaming.

From under the truck, I could see the driver's booted feet walking toward the back of the truck. He was firing the machine pistol at anything and everything. Empty shell casings dropped around his feet as he walked. Fortunately, until he cleared the back of the truck, he had no angle to shoot at me or Clemenceau. As he came around the end of the truck, I rolled onto my back and shot him twice in the chest. As the body fell, I realized that it wasn't a man at all. It was a woman. It was the same one I'd seen on the street walking arm in arm with her comrade past number eight.

The truck accelerated away from the curb. It raced down the street away from number eight, knocking carts and people out of its way. I stood and fired into the back of the truck until the slide locked back on the empty pistol.

Four or five dead in the street: pedestrians hit by the truck, the policeman, and the two Germans. Bolsheviks. They're Bolsheviks, I thought, correcting myself.

I looked back down the street toward the traffic circle. People were just stepping out from the buildings. I was wrong. There were many bodies down along the street. I didn't know what caused them, the Maxim fire or the grenade. Some were moving, but most were not. I could see people down to the end of the block and beyond. They were all lying well within the range of a Maxim gun.

I hurried over to Clemenceau, expecting him to be shattered by the machine gun. He was not. He was struggling to move out from under the body of the policeman. I gently moved the gendarme's body and helped Clemenceau to his feet.

"*Vous allez bien?*"[9] I asked.

He looked up at me with his strange Mongolian-like features, his bushy white mustache and brows twitching.

"I am fine," he answered calmly in English. "The blood is not mine."

He turned to the body of the policeman.

"*Je suis désolé*, Claude. *Quel gâchis*,"[10] he said to himself.

He turned back to me. "American?" he asked.

"Yes," I answered, sure that I was in way over my head.

"You saved me. Why are you here? With guns?"

His English was quite good.

"I have been tracking a Bolshevik plot to disrupt the peace negotiations. These"—I gestured at the bodies—"are Bolsheviks posing as Germans. They wanted to restart the war by murdering you, hoping the French would blame the Germans. They believed that a renewed war would start a revolution. I think they wanted to prevent the Allies from considering any German counterproposal." Of course, I was speculating, but it all made sense to me.

"Perhaps," he said. "But one enemy at a time." His face took on a calculating look. "You will come with me."

"Sure, but first let me pick up the guns."

"*Bien sûr.*"[11]

I saw Joseph and Madame Truchon on the sidewalk. I nodded to them both. Their eyes were wide as they saw Clemenceau step away from me to collect his hat and cane.

Joseph smiled and shouted "*Vive l'américain! Vive le* Yankee Doodle!"

More Parisians were in the street.

"*Vive le Tigre! Vive l'Amérique!*"

They shouted over the cries of the wounded.

Clemenceau raised his hat to the cheers.

I picked up the two MP 18s and found the Webley where I'd dropped it. I walked across the street and asked Madame Truchon if she would mind watching my bag for a little longer while I spoke with the prime minister. She agreed instantly and didn't comment as she watched me pack the two MP 18s and the Webley in my suitcase. I kept the Colt with me, which I hoped wouldn't be a problem for the French.

I recrossed the street and was greeted gruffly by arriving French policemen. They were angry. I thought they were angrier at the attempt on Clemenceau's life than at the dead and wounded in the street. Despite my assurances to Clemenceau that his attackers were Bolsheviks, the police clearly believed they were Germans.

They took me into Clemenceau's apartments and brought me to a wood-paneled meeting room with a rectangular table in the middle. The prime minister was conspicuously absent, and I began to worry about what I would tell the police. I still needed to protect Sarah even if she had lied to me, and I didn't want to be blamed for the deaths in Garches. I also didn't want to bring any attention to Eugene or the girls. I would play for time and delay. I would force them to find an English speaker.

They seated me in one of the chairs at the table. After nearly an hour, a heavyset man with white hair and a full salt-and-pepper beard came into the room. He wore a three-piece suit, pince-nez glasses jammed down on the bridge of his nose, and a scowl on his face. I wasn't sure whether it was for me or for the assassins.

"*Qui êtes-vous?*" he demanded.

I shook my head. "I'm sorry. I don't speak French well."

"Who are you?" he asked in English.

Damn. No delay at all.

"I'm John Griffin. US Marine. Working for the American government. More than that I can't tell you without the permission of the American delegation to the Paris peace talks," I said in my best professional voice. I smiled inwardly. They might decide to shoot me, but this sounded good.

"Why were you outside the prime minister's apartments?"

"As I said, I can't tell you more without permission of the American delegation. Speak to Colonel House."[12] I pulled his name from one of the newspaper articles I'd read. My recollection was that he was leading the American negotiators.

"You will tell me, or I will have my men beat you until you do," he answered. His dark shark's eyes told me that I would not be the first man he had had beaten, but I didn't think he would follow through on the threat. At least not yet. I was, after all, sitting in the prime minister's home. I figured they'd take me to a seedy police station basement for any beating. Also, I had my Colt .45 tucked behind my belt, and no one had bothered to search me, which meant they didn't think I was a threat.

"Look, I want to help you. I understand you are angry and upset, but I work for the US government. I can tell you that since the February attack on Prime Minister Clemenceau, our president has been worried for the prime minister's safety. I can say no more." Tell a lie often enough, with enough sincerity, and you will be believed. One down, another thousand to go.

I was gambling that Clemenceau had not spent much time briefing him on the attack. I would use his ignorance to my advantage if I could.

He studied me without speaking.

I studied him back, keeping all emotion from my face.

Finally, after losing our staring contest, he said, "I am Préfet Raux.[13] I will contact the American legation. If they do not verify your story, we will take you to the préfecture and speak more intimately."

"Excellent," I said with only a hint of sarcasm.

Raux opened the door and stepped into the hall where two armed policemen stood guard.

*"Procurez-lui un café et une cigarette. Il peut utilizer les toilettes, s'il en a besoin. Il ne doit pas partir avant mon retour. Compris?"*[14]

One of the policemen saluted and left. I assumed he was going to get my coffee and the cigarette I didn't want.

Raux turned back to me and said, "Thank you. For what you did for the prime minister. But if you lie to me, it will make no difference."

He left me alone with my thoughts of violence and death. And the promise of coffee.

After two hours, three coffees, and a trip to the head later, the door to the conference room opened. Préfet Raux reentered.

"You will come with me. I have spoken with the Americans. They wish to debrief you before briefing me. I have assured them that I will not question you further until they have debriefed you."

"Where are we going?" I asked.

"Hôtel de Crillon, the American headquarters for the negotiations. I am to take you to Colonel House," Raux answered. "I must warn you, monsieur, that they seemed surprised at your existence. It will not go well for you if they do not verify your story. This drive to Hôtel de Crillon is your last chance to be honest with me."

"I am not surprised," I assured him. "My orders were not well known." I decided to boldly stick with my story, and if I saw a credible chance to escape, I would take it. However, I wouldn't shoot any French policemen while I tried to get away.

We climbed into an automobile with a policeman driving, another policeman riding shotgun, and Raux and I in back. We drove along the river, and the drive to Hôtel de Crillon was disappointingly short. There was no opportunity to get away, and when we arrived at the hotel, the place was boiling with policemen and soldiers. As I climbed out of the motorcar, I saw armed American soldiers in front of the hotel. Unless I wanted to start a gun battle with my countrymen, I was going into Hôtel de Crillon, and I was going to meet Colonel House.

Raux and I entered the hotel. As we approached the neoclassical headquarters of the American delegation in France, I had the feeling that I was starting something I would later regret. The hotel's opulence struck me as we entered with its expanse of white marble and crystal chandeliers decorating the lobby. A young man met us, confirmed our identities, and immediately led us to a meeting room with a heavy, polished wood table and seating for at least twenty.

"I'll let the colonel know that you are here," he explained before shutting the two of us in the room. I looked at Raux, and he looked back without emotion. I got the impression that he didn't care what the result of this meeting was. He would be just as happy having me tortured or shaking my hand and patting me on the back. I supposed this was not a bad trait for a chief of police to have.

A tap on the door announced Colonel House.

Like Raux, he wore a three-piece suit as a uniform. He had a piercing look that indicated he took himself and his time seriously.

"Colonel House, this is the man that I told you about," Raux said.

"Thank you, Préfet Raux. I'd like to speak with him alone. I will brief you shortly." House delivered this request confidently with what I thought was a slight Texas drawl.

Raux, clearly unhappy about being excluded, hesitated, then left the room.

I decided to take the initiative. "John Griffin, sir. Thank you for seeing me." I didn't offer my hand. For some reason, it seemed presumptuous to do so.

House stared at me. I stared back. He had gray hair, dark eyebrows, and a white lampshade mustache. His eyes were closely set, and he had a weak chin that made me distrust him.

"Well, young man," he said. "I understand from Préfet Raux that you saved the prime minister's life. Thank you for that. If the Germans had killed him, the war would have resumed and thousands more would have died."

"They weren't Germans; they were Bolsheviks," I said.

"Bolsheviks? Really. Raux insisted that they were Germans. German uniforms, German weapons," House said.

"They were Bolsheviks," I said with confidence. "I think Clemenceau wishes they were Germans, but they weren't."

"Yes. That would make sense with what he wants. Why don't you tell me what happened and how you happen to be here?" House said.

Time for invention, I thought.

"I just got out of the service, sir," I started, knowing that a little respect goes a long way. "The Marine Corps. I'd come back to Paris because I wanted to see it. I never got here on leave, and since the war, I don't want to live with any regrets, and I regretted not experiencing Paris. I wanted to see what all the fuss was about," I continued, weaving in a small element of the truth. "At the cafés and cabarets, I got wind of a plot, by Bolsheviks, to try to kill Clemenceau, like that anarchist fella did in February. A lot of people don't like Clemenceau. Most folks feel like the war was for nothing and that it changed nothing."

"You heard this at the cafés?" House asked.

"Yes, sir. It's pretty bohemian, and folks are sympathetic to the Reds. Anyway, I got wind of a conspiracy but not the details. It was hard to believe at first. I thought it was just bar talk. But I got to thinking. There are a lot of Bolsheviks here. A lot of expats. If I were a Red, how would I start a revolution? It seemed obvious. I'd kill Clemenceau."

I watched him for his reaction, but he simply nodded for me to continue.

"So I thought about how I would kill the prime minister, if I were so inclined. I remembered the assassination attempt in February, so I thought I'd scope out the neighborhood where it happened. I took a room across the street from his house and just watched for anything suspicious. If it was a fairy tale, fine, I'd go back to drinking wine in the cabarets. But it wasn't a fairy tale. I got to know the neighborhood, and there were strangers studying the street. I'd seen the truck from today on his street before, and its presence made me suspicious. Since the prime minister leaves for work around the same time every day, I just waited outside to make sure nothing happened. Until today, when something did."

I paused for effect. "It happened so fast that my training took over, and I just acted without thinking."

"How'd you happen to have a gun?"

"Paris is a rough town, sir. I carry it everywhere."

"You from Texas?" House asked.

"My dad was in the army, and I spent a lot of time there."

"Lucky for the prime minister," House concluded.

"Yes, sir."

"Why'd you tell the French you were an American agent working for me?" House demanded.

"Well, that's simple, sir. Préfet Raux threatened to beat my story out of me. I didn't think he'd believe me no matter what I said, and I needed protection. I figured an American might at least hear me out before turning me over to a Frenchman for a beating. I remembered your name from the papers."

House preened a little at my mention of his name in the papers and said, "That's an amazing story, young fella. If it's true, you should get a medal."

"It's true, sir. All of it. One of the assassins was a woman. The German army doesn't use women. The Bolsheviks are happy to. It's true."

House considered the story and the situation. He thought for a moment, then seemed to make a decision. "I will claim you as our agent," he declared. "The French don't want to hear that it was Bolsheviks. They want it to be Germans. So it doesn't matter what you say about Reds. Stop talking about 'em."

"Sir?" I asked.

"We've had a tough negotiation. I should know. I've done most of it. I've done the best I could for my country and the world," House said. "For years, even before US involvement, I've been trying to negotiate an end to this useless war, but neither side would hear of it. I thought a peace without victory could satisfy all by satisfying none. I was wrong. Ultimately, the Germans pushed us too hard, and the United States ended up fighting too. But now that it's over, the French, they want their pound of flesh from the Germans, and they want American promises of defense. President Wilson has had difficulty understanding this, and he blames me for the current state of the negotiations. That's because he doesn't understand the French and their priorities. The Germans have made some counterproposals. At the president's insistence, I've been trying to get the French to consider them, but to say they are unwilling would be generous.

Now, with this attack, they will demand that we resume the war if the Germans don't sign the treaty as is."

"But, sir, it wasn't the Germans, and if they are forced to sign, any peace won't last."

"You don't understand the political realities. Neither does the president. It will be the treaty as proposed or continued war."

"Colonel, don't we have an obligation to argue for a peace that will mean something? Something for all the lives lost?" I asked, unable to hide the disgust in my voice.

House ignored me. "That we kept the prime minister alive will give us some leverage. I'll speak with Raux. You'll wait in the hall, and then you'll be released," he said, standing.

I stood as well. "Colonel?" I asked before turning toward the door. "Did you serve in the army?"

He looked at me, squinting his small eyes. "I never had the honor of serving in uniform, but I've earned my title through my political service to our country, young man."

I nodded. With his answer, he'd told me plenty. I opened the door and stepped into the hallway.

After his short talk with Raux, the colonel told me that I was free to go. As I left Hôtel de Crillon, the Americans ignored me, and the French police were all smiles and handshakes. Clemenceau had turned the attempt into exactly what the Bolsheviks had hoped the French would believe: an attack on France by Germans. Only his survival marred the outcome for the Bolsheviks, but it was perfect for the French. They would use the attack to force Germany to accept the treaty terms. I was disgusted and depressed. I had succeeded in stopping the plot to destroy the treaty, but I ensured that the treaty would be draconian.

## 21

### Regiments Revealed

By the time I returned to collect my case from Madame Truchon, it was past eight in the evening. She wanted me to remain, but I had no stomach to stay on rue Franklin for another moment. Eight civilians had died in the attack, and even Joseph hadn't known how many were wounded.

I looked for a motor cab to bring me back to Montparnasse, but all I could find was a horse cab. I was surprised at my disappointment. I had grown soft using the modern convenience of the motorcar. Sad.

I arrived back at my original pensione and got my key from the desk clerk. I unpacked quickly and sat on my bed, wondering what to do next. Find William or Sarah? Check in with Eugene? Lie down and sleep and hope the young woman wearing German field gray didn't haunt my dreams? I pulled the Colt from beneath my belt and looked at it. How many had I killed with it now? How many died in the back of the truck? I unloaded the gun and pushed it to the bottom of my suitcase.

I walked down the hall to Mitchell's door and knocked. No one answered. I tried the door. Locked. Likely he hadn't returned since we both went to the Vendôme. I considered walking to the Vendôme, but it felt too far away. I also wasn't sure that I wanted to see Sarah. Instead, I decided to visit Le Dôme. I would have a few drinks, then return to the hotel for a good sleep.

It was a nice night, and the walk wasn't long. I looked for a table outside and saw Kiki drinking with a man I didn't know. I caught her eye and nodded, but she didn't look like she wanted any interruptions. I went into the café and found a small table near the back. I was in no hurry for a drink. Just sitting with voices and music surrounding me seemed a balm for my nerves after the violence on rue Franklin. Eventually the waiter found me, and I ordered.

Two or three drinks later, Charles Nungesser came into the café with a young beauty on his arm. She was a different girl from the one I'd last seen him with. He saw me and waved. I liked Nungesser. He was living his life as hard and as fast as he could. He was going to get his money's worth. The table next to me was open, and Charles and his date came over.

I stood.

"Bonsoir, John," he said with a smile. "This is Claire. Her English is poor, but she is very pretty."

"Yes, she is," I answered, and to Claire I said, "*Enchanté*," because doing so made me feel sophisticated.

"Where have you been? Gene and the American cabal have been worried about you. The American girls should be here later."

"I've been working," I said in answer to his question.

"Did you hear about the attack on the prime minister today? Many killed and injured. Machine guns and explosions. It almost sounded like the Bolshevik plan, except, according to the authorities, this attack really was the Germans," Charles said, eyeing me closely.

"It was the Bolsheviks, Charles. I was there. They almost got him."

"Who," asked Claire. We both looked at her.

"Clemenceau," Charles answered and continued. "You were there? What did you do?"

"I stopped it."

Now Nungesser looked at me wide-eyed.

"How?" he exclaimed. "The reports said the Germans had a Maxim machine gun and that the French police and the local citizens overwhelmed them, but that many died."

"They got the 'many died' part right, Charles. I shot the attackers. Not all of them. At least one got away," I said succinctly.

"That I would like to have seen. *Mon Dieu.* You are like a Wild West show. Buffalo Bill, Annie Oakley! My uncle could not stop talking about their show when I was young. But you are real. Incredible. I should follow you. Excitement is always next to you." He said the last with admiration, which caused me to wonder about his sanity.

"Wild West show?" Claire inquired.

*"Oui, il est un vrai cow-boy vivant!"*[1]

*"C'est vrai?"*[2] she asked eagerly.

"No," I said. I needed to change the subject from my shooting a woman twice in the chest at point-blank range.

"Have you seen Mitchell or Eugene?" I asked.

"Yes. Last night at Gene's club I saw them both. I also got to meet the exceptional Mrs. Willoughby," Nungesser said with a glance to Claire to make sure she did not understand. Whatever he saw convinced him she did not. He continued. "She is remarkable. Grace, beauty, confidence. Remarkable. As remarkable as Mrs. Kingsbury. It is enough to make me glad I did not die in the war. Poor Capitaine Willoughby to leave such a beauty behind for glory."

"I'm not sure he died for glory," I said.

"Perhaps not, but the spectacular Mrs. Willoughby told me he was a Royal Welsh Fusilier, which must mean some glory," he said with a small salute. "The English and their regiments." He laughed. "I hear a bugle in my head every time I think of the English and their regiments."

The waiter took their orders and mine.

Nungesser's comment nagged at me. James Willoughby was a Welsh Fusilier. Why did that matter? I tried to work out why it should, but the wine and the company interfered with my thinking.

Nungesser and Claire were good companions. They would speak with each other, drink, and chat with me in between.

About an hour later, Madeline arrived and weaved her way to our table. She gave each of us kisses. She looked good, and I told her so. "You look beautiful, Madeline. To the nines," I said.

She looked at me questioningly.

"Perfect," I clarified. "You look perfect."

She gave me a smile that said more than "thank you."

"You'd better be careful, Mr. Griffin," she said. "I understand you're a taken man, but if you say things like that to a girl, she might just get the wrong idea."

"Just stating the facts," I said gallantly. "If Merchant or Disney see you, you'll have to beat them off with a stick."

She laughed. "Maybe Walt. With Horace, I think I'll be safe."

I looked at her questioningly.

"Oh, John, for a worldly seeming guy, you aren't very worldly," she said. "Walt has more to worry about from him than I do." She waved at the waiter, ordered a drink, and struck up a conversation in French with Claire.

I thought about her comment. Merchant had seemed interested enough in the girls to me, but I wasn't a good judge. Madeline wasn't just hinting; she was saying he was interested in men. That surprised me. I hadn't had a lot of contact with homosexuals, at least not ones who were open about it. But I was surprised that Merchant might be one. He seemed like a normal guy, but I guess that didn't mean much. If I'd given it any thought, I might have realized how common it was. Hell, the famous writer, Oscar Wilde, had been jailed for it. And ten or so years ago, the Kaiser's adjutant had had to resign over claims that he was one. I remembered my English friends making jokes about Wilhelm and his staff after the war started. So I shouldn't be shocked, but Merchant was a goddamn soldier. I mean, he'd been in the Royal Welsh Fusiliers.

Oh my God! He'd been in the Welsh Fusiliers. With James Willoughby. He must have known Willoughby. And through Willoughby, Sarah and Gavin.

I stood.

"Where's Merchant?" I demanded from Madeline.

"John, settle down," she said. "His preferences aren't any of your business."

"Goddamn it, Maddy, that's not why I need to talk to him. He must have known Gavin."

"John, what are you talking about? There's no reason he'd know Gavin," she declared.

I felt like I was about to boil over, but I sat down to steady myself. Nungesser and Claire leaned in to listen.

"Madeline, listen to me. Charles just told me that James Willoughby was in the same British regiment as Merchant. They were both officers in that regiment. From the beginning or, at least, near the beginning of the war. They must have known each other. I am sure Lieutenant Merchant knew Captain James Willoughby. And I'll bet he knew Sarah Willoughby and her brother Gavin."

"Oh my God!" she exclaimed. "But why wouldn't he tell us he knew Gavin? He could have helped us convince Gavin not to help the Bolsheviks."

"Unless he was one of the Bolsheviks," I said.

"*Merde!*" Nungesser spat.

"*Quoi?*" asked Claire.

"Holy moly, John! He could have been helping them all along. He must have arranged the ambush at the house on rue de Baby-lone. Shed. Shed may be dead because of him!" Madeline's anger was palpable.

"Maddy, the Bolsheviks tried to kill Clemenceau today."

"I thought that was Germans," she said. "That's what the evening papers say."

"I was there. It was the Bolsheviks dressed in German uniforms. Some of them got away. They might try again. I think Merchant is leading them."

I stood again.

"I need to find Will. If either of you see Horace, don't let him know we're onto him. He's dangerous. We need to be careful so nobody else gets hurt."

I left in a rush.

## 22

### Confederate-Blue Eyes

I went straight to the Vendôme. On my way, I recalled the conversation that I'd had with the Geordie steward on the *Mauritania*. He had described what he'd overheard Gavin discuss with the foreigners, but I'd ignored his information as too cryptic to help me. I was wrong. He was clear that Gavin and his associates hoped to find a "trader" on the Continent. But that wouldn't have been the word they used. They hoped to find "Merchant" on the Continent. Horace Merchant was their contact. The other names now made sense too. "Baby" was rue de Babylone, but the steward didn't understand the context and didn't hear the word correctly. It was the same with "Frank." Rue Franklin. Clemenceau's street. The steward heard the accented names, and he heard them as names of people. Not names of streets. He had told me everything, but I hadn't bothered to piece it all together.

It was already early morning when I arrived at the Vendôme, and the concierge hesitated to ring Patricia Armistan's room. One of Patricia's twenties overcame his reluctance. He connected me on the house phone, and I found myself speaking with her.

"John, where have you been?" she asked immediately with no sleep in her voice.

"Patricia, I need to speak with Will. Is he there?"

"No. He's out looking for you. We've been worried about you. You've heard about the German attack."

"I've heard about it. I need to come up and speak to you."

She hesitated but agreed I could come up.

When I arrived, the suite door was partly open, and Patricia was standing in the doorway. She let me into the suite and shut the door behind me.

"Patricia, is Sarah in her room?" I asked immediately.

"At this time of morning, I'm sure she is. She is hurt that you left, John. She loves you, you know."

That stopped my rush for a moment.

"I'm not sure why she would," I said. "And I'm not sure why I should care. She lied to us. To you too. She's been involved from the beginning, and she's known exactly what's been going on the whole time."

Patricia, poor patrician Patricia, couldn't believe her best friend would lie to her. I watched her work through the implications.

"What are you talking about?" she demanded.

"Sarah knew the Bolsheviks hadn't given up. The attack on Clemenceau this morning. That was the Bolsheviks. *They* tried to kill him."

"That can't be," Patricia declared. "The French authorities are saying it was German soldiers, and it's not clear whether they were rogue German soldiers or directed by Berlin," she finished.

"That's all bullshit made up by Clemenceau," I said sharply. "I saved the little bastard's life, and he makes up lies to pressure the English and the Americans into demanding the Germans accept the treaty unconditionally. And he'll get his way now. He couldn't have planned it better himself. He's Machiavelli in a top hat."

"Oh my God, you saved Clemenceau?" she asked.

I didn't understand her tone. She sounded like I had done something terrible, not that I disagreed after having met the man.

"Yes. I was there. At the attack. I've been watching Clemenceau's apartments since I left Sarah. The Bolsheviks were dressed as Germans when they struck. Just as we thought they might be."

"Oh, John, what have you done?"

"What? I told you. I stopped the plot, but some of them got away. I know who's leading them now. And Sarah's known all along."

She sank down onto the couch and started to sob.

"Patricia, what's the matter? What's going on?"

"John, I'm going to tell you a secret. Can you keep a secret?" she asked in almost a whisper.

I felt a cold hand grip my heart. Before I could answer, she took my silence as agreement.

"I tried to tell you in Garches. About my father, but you didn't seem to care. I can't tell William. I care for him, and he is very old-fashioned in his way. He is infatuated with me, but I don't know if he will love me if he knows the truth."

She was diverting me from my mission. I had to find Merchant, but I found myself irresistibly drawn by her hushed, confidential tone. She was promising me forbidden knowledge. Knowledge I was sure I didn't want, but knowledge, when still unknown, that I couldn't reject. I understood how Adam felt when Eve handed him the apple. I had to listen.

"As you know, my father is a wealthy man. He demands obedience in all things. He can appear to be loving, but he is not. With his horses, his dogs, and his family, he can play the jovial, loving family man. But obedience is expected and required. All are possessions for him to use as he sees fit. To promote his wealth, his station, his power. He used my mother. She was very beautiful. More beautiful than I. He beat her because she tried to resist his... demands. He broke her like he would his break horses. He used her in his business dealings. He would require her to seduce his competitors, then he would use the affair to blackmail them into deals that benefited him. He was careful in how he applied her. He was an artist. She killed herself shortly before the war. At the time, I didn't understand why. I didn't know any of this. But I began to learn."

"Patricia, I'm sorry. This is horrific. But…"

"I'm almost done, John. Just a little more please."

I had no choice but to nod.

"After the war broke out, he started grooming me to replace her. I thought he loved me. But he began asking me to entertain his associates. It was all very gradual. Carefully done. His demands became more extreme, and if I resisted, he would beat me just as he did my mother. By then Gavin Kingsbury was working for him. *Daddy*"—she spat out the title with such acidity that I cringed—"tried to ensnare Gavin by using me, but Gavin wasn't interested in me. He was interested in revolution and men."

"Men?" I said with shock. "Gavin liked men and you knew?"

"I knew. I'm a beautiful woman. I am used to men treating me in a certain way. Gavin did not. It was obvious."

"Does Sarah know?" I asked.

"We didn't speak of it when she came to New York after James died," Patricia answered. "We had other subjects to absorb us. When she arrived, everything changed for me. In her, I had a friend, an ally, a co-conspirator. She was rabidly opposed to the continuation of the war. She'd lost James, and she blamed the politicians, rightfully so. They all wanted victory when they all were at fault. She blamed the industrialists, the militarists, and the financiers for the slaughter. In short, she blamed my father and men like him. And quickly she began to blame her brother. He had worked so hard to enable my father's investments because with them came the promise of revolution."

She took a breath. "Then with the Armistice, they cut a deal, my father and my husband. Gavin would get me and the wealth that would come with me: a dowry, in the old-fashioned sense. Daddy would get all of Gavin's radical connections. They both thought they were manipulating the other. Gavin wanted revolution and needed the money to fund it, and my father had the money but not the means to create the chaos he wanted. He's made millions from this war, and he desperately wanted it to continue. A revolution fit the bill perfectly. Their interests were aligned."

I was captivated now. I needed to know the ending of Patricia's tale because it was important to the current plot and Sarah.

"And your and Sarah's interests? How did those align?" I asked.

"Closely, but not perfectly, I'm afraid," she answered. "She wants Clemenceau and Lloyd George dead, the Bolsheviks thwarted. Gavin disgusted her for what she sees as his betrayal of James and a lasting peace."

"And you?" I prompted.

"I want control. Control of my life. Of my fortune. But Gavin as my husband controlled it. I wanted it back. And I want my father dead."

"And Gavin? Did you want him dead?" She didn't need to speak. I saw the answer in her eyes.

"You made it so easy, John. Gavin had changed. He'd become a zealot. I couldn't love him even as a brother. I had intended to bring him back to the States. Really, I had. I would have divorced him using his perversion as my excuse, but in that house, with all the bullets and terror, I saw Gavin as my enemy. Just as my father is. He was using me. I was an object. He was trying to get to his feet to attack you, and I couldn't let him. He was just like my father. You were such a gentleman to give me that little pistol. It was providence. It barely moved in my hand when I shot him."

"Jesus Christ," I said, shaking my head. I tried to summon some anger or disgust, but so much had happened in the past hours that I couldn't manage it.

"Does William know?"

"Of course not. Will you tell him?"

"I should, Patricia. I really should. But I didn't like Gavin much anyway, and strangely, even though you're a coldhearted bitch, I like you. I'll leave it to you to tell William whatever you want. But if he asks, I won't lie for you," I said.

"Thank you for that."

"Do you think it's possible that Gavin and Horace Merchant were lovers?" I asked.

"What are you talking about?" she exclaimed.

"Merchant. That's why I came here. Merchant is the leader of the Bolsheviks, not Gavin. Gavin never was."

"That's utter nonsense," Patricia declared.

"Really, Patricia? You admit that you murdered Gavin, but you can't accept that Merchant might be the Bolsheviks' leader?"

"No! I mean, I really don't know what you're talking about."

"How well do you know Merchant?" I asked.

"I don't, and that's the point. If he were leading the Bolsheviks, he would know Gavin. And if he knew Gavin, I would know him," she said with certainty. "And if they were lovers, I would undoubtedly know."

"Okay, I'll accept you believe that, but they likely met before Gavin left for America. Probably through James and Sarah," I said. "James and Horace were in the same regiment. The Royal Welsh Fusiliers. It is nearly impossible that two officers in the same regiment wouldn't know each other. Especially after two or three years of war."

"Then Sarah must have known Horace as well," she said with surprise.

"I'm sure she did."

"She must have known about Gavin's proclivities too." She smiled. "She is such a clever girl. She would have known if Gavin and Merchant were lovers. She would also know that Gavin couldn't lead a band of Bolshevik assassins. She was using them both as her tools to get revenge on Clemenceau and Lloyd George."

"I'm sure you're right, but the problem is that if either one or both are killed by men dressed as German soldiers, the war will resume. Your father will win, and you and Sarah will lose. We need to find Merchant and stop the Bolshevik plot now," I said. "I know Sarah means the world to you, but I need your help convincing her to tell us where Merchant is. We need to find him. He will try again if he can, and if he succeeds, there will be no way to prevent a new start to the war."

Patricia stared back at me, thinking, and said, "Let's go speak to her now."

She led me to Sarah's room on the floor above.

As we neared Sarah's room, my heart started to race. I felt like I was going over the top for an attack. I was terrified and yet resigned to the need to see her.

Patricia tapped on the door.

There was no answer. She tried again. I put my ear to the door and heard nothing.

"Oh, what the hell," I said to myself and tried the door. It opened smoothly. I cursed myself for leaving the pistol in my suitcase.

"Wait here, Patricia," I said softly.

She nodded, her eyes large.

I eased the door open and looked into the darkened sitting area. A light was on in the bedroom.

I moved carefully past the couch and overstuffed chairs to the bedroom door. I could hear something soft. It sounded like bubbling. It would stop and start again. I peered around the edge of the bedroom door, and there, sprawled on the bed, was Horace Merchant. He watched me as I stepped into the room. His chest was tightly bound, but the dressing and the sheets around him were soaked with blood. The bubbling sound was Merchant trying to breathe. Next to his hand was a Lebel automatic pistol, but it was clear he didn't have the strength to raise it. He was dying.

"Fucking Yank," he whispered with a small shake of his head.

I didn't answer. I must have hit him when I fired into the truck. I checked the bathroom, but it was empty. When I turned back to the bed, Patricia was in the doorway with her hand over her mouth.

Merchant saw her too.

"Murdering bitch," he croaked out. "Did you know she killed Gavin?" Merchant asked me. "I went into the house to see him as you all were packing up to leave Garches. It was so clear what she'd done. My poor, lovely Gavin. Shot in the face by his fake wife while he was trying to impress me. I didn't think she'd kill him."

"Where's Sarah?" I asked him.

"You killed us all, Griffin," he said instead of answering. "Every bloody one of us. I was so shocked when I saw you. Running at us, firing that damn Webley. Every one of us in the back of the truck was hit. But you kept firing. I heard Jean-Claude's machine pistol and thought we might succeed. And the grenade, but then…" He labored for breath, the effort to speak clearly costing him. "Then I heard only Yvette shooting. I was sure she got you. I was so happy. Even though I knew you'd killed me. But you killed her too, poor girl. She just wanted to make the world a better place, and you took her from it. You've become an animal."

"And you killed Shed," I said. "Where's Sarah? We can get you help."

"There's no help for me. You hit me in the lung. I'm a dead man." He tried to move his hand toward the pistol on the bed, but the weight of his arm was too much. "I wish to God I could kill you, Patricia," he sobbed.

"Horace, please! What have you done with Sarah?" I begged.

He cracked a bloody smile. "Not a damn thing. She's gone to get one of the Mauser scoped rifles. She never cared about revolution. But she cares about killing Clemenceau. She wants her revenge for James. Poor James. Poor Gavin," he finished.

"Where? Where did she go?" I shouted.

His last breath left him, and his face went slack in death.

"Well, fuck!" I raged.

I turned to Patricia and grabbed her by her arms.

"You know her," I said desperately. "What will she do?"

I was sure I was hurting her, but she didn't struggle. She looked up at me calmly. "If she has the means, she will try to kill Clemenceau. She's come too far now. She won't give up. She is very loyal."

I remembered Sarah saying exactly that in her house in Weybridge. *I am very loyal,* she had said. But I had thought she was speaking of loyalty to her brother. She wasn't. She was speaking of loyalty to James, her dead husband. Loyal beyond death.

I couldn't go to Préfet Raux or to Colonel House. If I did, I would have to explain what I knew and the French police would be on the lookout for Sarah. In addition, I didn't want Raux to have the opportunity to make good on his promise to have me beaten. Somehow I still had to stop Sarah. If she succeeded in killing Clemenceau, his assassination would logically be blamed on the Germans after this morning's attack. The blood of nations would flow again, and she would certainly die. There was no way she could survive. The French were alerted now.

I could think of only one place where Sarah could hope to have a chance to kill Clemenceau. She would go to rue Franklin and look for a concealed place to take her shot at the prime minister. The French would be expecting another attempt. They would know that the attackers had access to all manner of weapons, and they didn't know that all the Bolsheviks were dead. Only Patricia and I knew that for certain.

I was sure it was Clemenceau that Sarah would seek. More than Lloyd George, it was Clemenceau who had demanded victory and not peace. She would go back to the 16th

Arrondissement where Merchant had made his attack. Sarah would be surgical. She had no desire to start a war. She only desired full payment for the last one. Rue Franklin was a long street. She would need a vantage point from which she could look down on Clemenceau's flat. She didn't want to be so close that the police would detect her.

With a rifle and an optical sight, she could be nearly half a mile from Clemenceau's front door. I recalled her telling me at her home in Surrey that she had been shooting both shotguns and rifles most of her life. But she wouldn't know the rifle and couldn't practice. She wouldn't use Madame Truchon's hotel, but I would have to check. Instead, I thought she would look at the buildings nearer the traffic circle leading into rue Franklin. She must. Her French was excellent, and as a woman, she would arouse no suspicion during her search for a blind from which to shoot.

However, the French were not idiots. They, too, would consider the building overlooking rue Franklin. Likely, they would have their own snipers on the rooftops. Lord knew they would have plenty of trained marksmen after more than four years of warfare.

I would have to find her before they did and before she took a shot. Then I would have to convince her to stop. To accept reality. To move on with life. I hoped that I could.

When I got to Madame Truchon's, it was half past eight. She was at the counter and beamed when she saw me. As I had for so many days before, I asked her if she had any new foreign guests. She did not. I thanked her and told her I was going to check the neighborhood, just as a precaution. She asked if she should remain inside until after ten thirty. I hesitated and said, "Oui, s'il vous plaît." She nodded as I left.

Sarah would know that the time to catch Clemenceau would be when he stepped out his front door around ten o'clock. She would have access to all the reconnaissance information that Merchant and the Bolsheviks had gathered.

I crossed the street and waved to the policeman on duty outside number eight. As I approached, he put his hand on his pistol. He had learned the hard lesson of his predecessor well.

"*Bonjour, je m'appelle*, Griffin. *Je suis l'Américain qui était ici hier. Avec le premier ministre.*"[1] I wanted to remind him that I'd saved the life of his boss's boss.

"*Bonjour,*" he said cautiously. He kept his hand on the butt of his pistol, and I kept my hands well away from my sides.

"*Que veux-tu?*"[2] he asked.

"Colonel House *reste inquiet pour la sécurité du premier ministre. Est-ce calme?*"[3]

"*Oui, tout est calme,*"[4] he assured me.

"*Bon, je vais faire un tour des environs. D'accord?*"[5] If I could find Sarah, I might need him to vouch for me as I bundled her to safety.

"*D'accord,*" he answered.

I walked around the block as I had the previous morning. There was nothing to see. No Sarah. Just the ordinary folks I'd seen before, excluding the Bolsheviks. I arrived back near Madame Truchon's at the traffic circle. There, I crossed the streets away from the prime minister's apartments. I tried to judge which building would have the best view of his front door. I concluded it was the building across the street from the brasserie where I had eaten so many meals. I looked up at the windows. It was a cool morning, yet one was open. It was on the third floor up from the street, and it faced the prime minister's front door. The view would be excellent from there.

I looked at my watch: 0950. I was running out of time. It had to be Sarah by that window. If it wasn't, it would be too late for me to find her.

I spied the entrance nearby just as a dark-garbed, elderly woman stepped out. I quickly walked over and tipped my hat.

"*Bonjour, madame.*"

She nodded and started down the street as the door began to

shut. I caught it quietly and slipped in. I doubt the old lady saw me, and I was too rushed to worry about it if she did.

Directly in front of the door, the stairwell circled upward. I took the stairs two at a time up the three flights. I left the stairwell for a short hallway with four doors. I chose the door that was, by my reckoning, the one closest to the traffic circle. I tried the door. It was locked.

I was out of time.

I stepped back, took a deep breath, and kicked just to the side of the doorknob. I heard something crack. I kicked again, and the door slammed open.

Sarah was in the middle of what must have been the sitting room of the apartment. She held a rifle aimed at my chest. It was a Mauser Gewehr 98 bolt-action rifle with an optical sight. If she shot me from where she stood, the bullet would go through me so fast that I would hear it ricochet in the hallway before I felt any pain.

She looked incredibly sad, but she wasn't crying. Her Confederate-blue eyes were steely and uncompromising.

"John, of course. I expected to see you sometime today," she said. "I got your calling card last night. So I knew it was just a matter of time until you returned to me."

"Horace Merchant?" I asked.

"Yes, a bloody, dying Horace Merchant. He was your calling card."

"Sarah, I am sorry I left you. I couldn't sit by when I was afraid the most terrible thing in the world was going to happen. I had to do something. And I didn't know how much you hated Clemenceau."

"I know. I was surprised you stayed with me as long as you did. Do you know that when I first met you, I was afraid you would ruin everything? All the planning. I could see it in your eyes. Your ferocity and stubbornness. But I liked you. You reminded me of an uncompromising, unforgiving version of James, and I missed James so. That's why I tried to warn you off.

The two men by the motorcar. But you were hurt, and I felt badly about that, so I brought you back into my home."

I nodded. "I'm very glad you did."

"But I knew it was a mistake," she continued. "So I ran away, and that left the way open for them to try to kill you. I'm sorry, but we had planned together so long, Patricia and me. I was afraid you would mess up our plot. Everything was in place."

"But why try to kill me, Sarah?" I asked. I needed to distract her as long as possible. Each second that passed might be the one that got Clemenceau safely into his limousine. I needed to delay her until he was gone. Then I would have time to speak with her. Time to convince her that she was on the wrong path.

"I didn't want you killed. That was Horace and Gavin. They found you at the Savoy because I told them you were staying there. I didn't think they would try to kill you in the hotel. They worked out your room through bribery and the fact that there was only one American with a scar like yours in the entire hotel. But that attack failed too."

"Not for want of trying."

"I know, John, and I'm sorry. And then I saw you at Claridge's. And I couldn't help myself. I hadn't cared for anyone since James, and there you were, so different from him and yet much the same, especially to the soldier James became. A soldier but broken inside and not even knowing it."

"You should have stayed with me," I said.

"But I ran instead. I still thought our plan could succeed. And I could still have you. So I came to Paris. To rue de Babylone. Horace and Gavin knew it was you who came to the house. Morgan had told them he'd been tortured for the address. They were livid that I did not kill you then. They took me to another apartment in the 7th Arrondissement, locked me there with Yvette to watch me, and set up the ambush at the house on rue de Babylone. I was wild with worry, but Yvette kept telling me that the sacrifice was necessary for the plan to succeed. For revolution to come. But neither Patricia nor I cared about revolution.

We wanted freedom from the past. For her, freedom from her father's perversity and my brother's control, and for me, freedom from sharing this earth with the butchers of James and so many like him. But you survived the ambush. And then the note about Patricia came from the Germans."

She reflected for a moment and smiled sadly.

"I didn't know the truth about the note. I didn't know it was you. I was worried for Patricia. Gavin and I, we thought it really was the Germans. And Gavin was eager to show he could be brave. He wanted to go rescue his wife. A wife he didn't love. He did it to impress Horace. Patroclus being brave for his Achilles. That's how he thought of Horace and himself. Horace learned of your scheme too late to warn Gavin, and he didn't know what Gavin planned until you told him Gavin was coming to trade himself for Patricia. He went along to protect Gavin if he could."

"Once Gavin was in the house, there was no protecting him," I said, thinking of Patricia and the small blue hole in Gavin's cheek.

"What do you mean?" As we'd been speaking, the gun barrel had strayed from my chest. Now she moved it back.

"Not me, Sarah. I didn't kill him. I didn't like him, but I didn't kill him."

"Who then?" Understanding dawned on her face and she dropped her eyes. "Patricia," she whispered. She looked back at me. "I should have known. I suppose I don't even blame her. So Patricia gets what she wanted, but I don't. I haven't gotten justice for James, for you, for all of us. Because of you, John, that hope is gone."

"I'm sorry, Sarah. I am, but please don't do this. James wouldn't want it."

She smiled. "And what about you, John? What do you want?"

Sarah, beautiful Sarah with the Confederate-blue eyes.

"I want you to be happy. With me. I want you, Sarah. I love you," I said with certainty.

"And I love you," she answered.

Through the open window, the church bells began to chime the hour.

Without hesitation, Sarah stepped to the window and raised the rifle to her shoulder. I jumped forward to pull her back, but I was too late. The windows and window frame exploded inward as bullets smashed into the room, flinging us both to the floor.

That is where the French police found me, cradling Sarah's shattered body against mine.

## 23

_____

**An Unaffiliated Agent**

I woke in a whitewashed hospital room. Three empty metal framed beds shared the room with mine. Each bed was made up with white sheets and gray woolen blankets. The sun poured into the room through tall arched windows. Whether it was morning or afternoon, I had no idea.

I woke because of the pain. My torso and right shoulder were wrapped in bandages. High on the right side of my chest and above my right hip burned with a pain I knew well. I'd been shot.

I remembered.

Sarah. The apartment at the end of rue Franklin. I remembered everything. I tried not to, but the fragmented pictures pressed me. The glass blowing in. The bullets striking Sarah. The wooden floor against my face. And Sarah, her blue eyes closed forever.

I squeezed my eyes shut as if I were recalling pictures outside my head. An ache began under my heart, and it expanded to knot my guts. I took a deep breath only to whimper. At the loss. Not the pain. My emotions threatened to overwhelm me. How had she become so important to me so quickly?

I took a slower, shallower breath. Get control, I told myself. Slowly I pushed my heartbreak back into a box in my head. I could do nothing now. I could have done nothing more then. My time with her was like found money: unexpected and a gift. The rest of my life I would spend paying for it. Get control. Don't think. Move forward.

I recited the empty phrases that brought me through the war, but they bounced around in my skull with no effect. Sarah's warmth, her passion, and her love were gone.

A sob broke free, and pain flared in my chest and side. The agony derailed my thoughts of Sarah. A rifle round through the chest is good for something.

Snipers on the roof of Clemenceau's apartments. They were waiting for another attempt on Clemenceau. Just by existing, he brought pain and death.

I heard the whisper of fabric swishing as someone approached my room. A nurse in a white uniform with a blue cap perched on her curly brown hair came into the room. When she saw that I was watching her, she put a sunny smile on her pleasant face.

"Good morning, Mr. Griffin. How are you feeling this morning?" An American. She appeared to be waiting for an honest answer.

"Fine." My voice croaked, and although I knew the answer, I couldn't help asking, "There was a woman," I rasped. "There was a woman with me. How is she?"

She shook her head. "You were brought here by the French in a great rush. You were alone. I'm sorry."

Her confirmation of my fears sucked the last of the hope out of me.

She saw the impact of her words and moved to distract me.

"Here," she said, pouring a glass of water from a carafe on a trolley behind my bed. I tried to take the glass with my left hand, but I didn't have the strength. She held the glass for me and allowed me a small sip.

"How long?" I asked.

"You came in yesterday." She understood the question without any clarification. "You'd been shot. You lost a lot of blood. You will be weak, but you're stable. You're very lucky, and our doctors are very good. They've had lots of practice."

Lucky. Yeah. So I've been told.

"What's your name?" I found short sentences were easiest.

"I'm Miss Clarke.[1] I and a few other girls will be taking care of you while you are here."

"Where is here?" I asked.

"Neuilly-sur-Seine, a little northwest of central Paris. Military Hospital No. 1. We're not far from the American Hospital of Paris, if that helps." She studied me, hoping to confirm my understanding. I didn't know where Neuilly was, and I certainly didn't know that there was an American hospital in Paris.

"Do you remember what happened?" she asked gently. She had decided I didn't understand.

"Some. I don't remember much after being shot." That was a lie. I remembered enough. I remembered holding Sarah's body, her chest soaked in her blood and mine. I remembered the French police.

"Well, that makes sense," Miss Clarke said cheerily. "You'd lost a lot of blood and likely passed out."

I didn't answer. I was done talking now. She had told me what I needed to know.

Miss Clarke hovered for a few seconds and then said, "Well, if you need anything, just ring." She picked up a small bell from the tray next to the bed and gave it a small shake. The thin jingle reminded me of Sarah and Patricia laughing as I joined them for lunch at the Hôtel de Vendôme. When was that, two weeks ago? Maybe less? Everything had changed.

I closed my eyes. After a time, I slept.

I woke to the sound of someone coming down the hall. The swish of thicker fabric and a heavier tread told me it was not the kind Miss Clarke. A man, if I had to guess. A policeman. Not that

I particularly cared. I thought about feigning sleep, but I couldn't be bothered.

Préfet Raux came into the room. As my ears had told me, he was alone.

"Bonjour, Monsieur Griffin." He greeted me with a smile that couldn't quite reach his predatory eyes. "I trust you are recovering well from your unfortunate wounds. Friendly fire. Isn't that what you Americans call it?" He watched me, unblinking.

"Bad luck, really, but that's what all friendly fire is," I answered. "And yes, I am recovering."

"Good. The doctors insist that you will be up and about in a few days."

"Easy for them to say."

He smiled.

I waited for him to continue. He wasn't visiting me because he liked me. He had a purpose for coming to Military Hospital No. 1, and since I couldn't guess what it might be, I would let him tell me instead of fishing for it.

He looked around the room, delaying his task. "I have spoken to Colonel House," he began. "I have reached an agreement with him."

He waited for me to speak. I remained silent.

He started again. "I have come for two reasons. First, on behalf of France, I thank you again. While we were more prepared for an assassin this time, we had not gotten so far as to discern the plan and the location of the attempt. You did, and your distraction of Mrs. Willoughby at the critical moment was…" He stumbled slightly, searching for the right word. "Helpful."

He continued. "Of course, we were unaware of your involvement, and thus, your unfortunate wounds. This brings me to my second point. We don't want to have such communication errors again. It would be best if you worked more directly with us. Colonel House has agreed to lend you to my office in much the

326

same way the United States Army lent certain regiments to the French army during the war."

I wasn't sure Raux knew or cared, but the only regiments permanently loaned to the French for the duration were Black regiments. House, on the other hand, was well aware of this fact. He was sending me a message. Fine. I didn't like the man, and I wasn't going to dance to his tune. Unfortunately, I had gotten myself into this predicament by claiming I worked for House, which meant that, in Raux's reasonable estimation, House had the ability to reassign me.

"Really?" I said. "What on earth could you want me to do for you? I may be well suited for charging machine guns, but I hope there will be less of that in the future. Anything else, I'll be almost useless. For several reasons, the most obvious being that I've got holes in me. Also, my French is appalling, and I'm a foreigner." I should have been less blunt, but my wounds were making me irritable, and the emotional part of my mind was still working through his claim that my distraction helped the French kill Sarah.

"It has come to my attention that, in your efforts to protect the prime minister, you have been indirectly aiding me, not just in thwarting the German assassination plot, but you have also assisted in cleaning up the Bolshevik problem in Paris."

Ah, now that was a worrying disclosure.

"Can you explain what you mean, monsieur?" I wanted him to say plainly what I feared he was getting at.

"You do not need to be coy, Monsieur Griffin. I am not condemning you or your actions, but while our investigation is still in its early stages, it appears that you may have been involved in the killings of a number of Bolsheviks here in Paris. Of course, this does not include the Germans involved in the shootings on rue Franklin."

"Germans, Préfet Raux?" I asked doubtfully.

"Yes, Mr. Griffin. Germans. And many Bolsheviks," he said firmly.

He suspected I was part of the events on rue de Babylone and in Garches, but he had no firm proof. He waited for me to comment, and when I didn't, he continued.

"Colonel House is impressed with your ability to sniff out these dangerous conspiracies. And so am I. He promised me you would be happy to work with us. I agree. I have no doubt you will be eager to help."

Now I couldn't help but react.

"And why is that, Préfet Raux?"

"Because, while your actions in our country were to the benefit of the Republic of France, it appears that you had a role in the deaths of several persons, some French, and likely blew up a house in the 7th Arrondissement. Also, my officers and agents have confirmed to me that others were possibly involved in these events. It would be a shame if Monsieur Bullard or Mademoiselle Prin were to come under the scrutiny of my office. Mr. Bullard, in particular, is a well-respected hero of France."

"What do you need from me?" I demanded.

"You will be my unacknowledged, unaffiliated agent to explore certain problems faced by the Republic."

I laughed, which sent a spasm of pain flaring across my chest. "Ouch! Goddamnit! Monsieur Préfet, that's hilarious, but please don't make me laugh. It hurts."

"I am serious, Monsieur Griffin, and Colonel House has agreed. You will do this," he said firmly.

His threats were real, and I couldn't expose Eugene and Kiki to the crushing weight of the French authorities when all the two of them had tried to do was help. He didn't know that his leverage was real. I would have to walk a careful line between outright refusal and becoming his puppet.

"Why should I care about a nigger and a whore, monsieur?" His upper lip curled in distaste as I continued. "But independent of them, if you pay me and agree that I will work for you only until the end of a specific, definable problem, perhaps we can come to an agreement. I will, of course, need to confirm all this with the colonel."

He examined me, not speaking, instead weighing my words and their sincerity.

"Come see me after you have seen the colonel," he said, standing. "We will confirm the details of your role then."

After Raux departed, I considered his statement about Sarah. In the past few years, I'd had plenty to feel guilty about, but I wouldn't feel guilty about her death. I had done all that I could to save her. Still, I was crushed by her loss. The thought of serving Clemenceau, however indirectly, sickened me. She would be appalled. I needed House to extricate me from the position I'd created for myself. I hoped I could convince him.

Raux's visit had tired me. I tried to sleep, but images of Sarah and the shattering windows flickered behind my eyelids. I wanted to curl up around the ache under my heart and die. Eventually I must have dozed.

I woke to yet another visitor. William Mitchell was standing at the foot of my bed, looking down at me.

"You're not very sharp, Griff," he said with a small smile. "I'd 'ave thought you'd hear me coming down the hallway."

I recalled my smart-ass remarks to him about Patricia and Sarah. I regretted what I'd said. I was angry at the time and disappointed, but he was my friend. He regretted the exchange as well. His comment and smile were an invitation for a reconciliation that I welcomed.

"No, I'm not," I answered. "I tend to drag in the mornings after I've been shot." I said the last with a smile and added, "It's good to see you, Will."

"I'm sorry about Sarah," he said. "And I'm sorry I didn't want to listen to your suspicions."

"There wasn't anything you could have done. I found her. I tried to stop her. But she was committed to finishing what she started. We could have had the whole Fifth Marines, and it wouldn't have made any difference." I stopped and took a deep breath to keep my composure.

He looked out the arched windows to give me time and then said, "Patricia didn't know what Sarah was going to do, John. She didn't know. I've pressed her. She wanted to get free of her dad. She wanted free of Gavin, but she didn't want to kill the prime minister."

"I know." He needed to hear me agree. And I did believe that Patricia didn't want to kill Clemenceau. She just wanted to get free of her father and Gavin. She certainly was free from Gavin. She'd made sure of that by putting a bullet in his head. Not that Mitchell knew that. The dowry that Harry Armistan had given Gavin Kingsbury upon his marriage to Patricia was now all hers with no strings or obligations to her perverted father. She was free, and Sarah was dead. But that wasn't Patricia's fault, and it wasn't Mitchell's. There was no point in railing against Patricia and her manipulations of us. Sarah's path had been set when her husband was killed in France. With singular, unvarying focus, she had worked toward the death of the French prime minister.

"How are you feeling?" Mitchell asked, hoping to move to safer ground with our reconciliation complete.

"Poorly. But I'll be fine. They're taking good care of me. Except they're not screening my visitors as well as I would like." He looked at me sharply, worried that I meant him. "Préfet Raux, the chief policeman in Paris, stopped by to tell me that I now work for the French."

"What the hell does that mean?" Mitchell demanded.

"You and I didn't get a chance to talk much after the attack in the street outside Clemenceau's apartments. After the attack, Raux interviewed me. I told him I was an American agent."

"You what?"

"Yeah, I know. Crackers, right? I told them I worked for Colonel House and the American delegation as an agent trying to protect Clemenceau. I had to tell them something. I'd just killed a couple of Reds in the middle of a Parisian street. Raux didn't believe me. Not that I blame him. He called the Americans and brought me to the Hôtel de Crillon to meet the Americans. I actually met Colonel House. He's a shifty bastard. But damn smart. He spoke with me, didn't give a shit that the attackers were Bolsheviks. He planned on using my saving the prime minister to leverage concessions from the French in the peace negotiations. He backed my story with the French though."

Mitchell shook his head in amazement.

"Unfortunately," I continued, "the French think I work for him, and they asked him if they could borrow me for some mission they've got going on."

"You could just leave, Griffin."

"No. House would find a way to make my life miserable, even in the States, and Raux threatened Eugene and Kiki if I didn't help. And I've got nothing better to do."

Mitchell nodded. "What does he want you to do?"

"I have no idea."

Miss Clarke stepped into the room.

"Miss Clarke, please meet my good friend, Will Mitchell. I served with him."

Mitchell turned, offered the nurse his hand, and when she took it, he kissed the back of hers. "It's a pleasure, Miss Clarke. Griffin has told me that you are taking fine care of him," he lied.

She blushed as she took her hand back. She looked at me and blushed some more. "It's a pleasure to meet you, and I'm just doing my job," she claimed, dropping her eyes.

"Well, thank you. Griffin is my very best friend, and I'd hate to lose him."

I found myself warmed by his claim.

"I hope your visitor isn't tiring you, Mr. Griffin," she said sternly as she stepped to my bed. "It's nearly time to change your dressings, and the doctor will want to check your wounds."

"If you need any help changing his dressings, I'm happy to help," Mitchell volunteered. "It wouldn't be the first time I've had to dress wounds."

"He was a navy corpsman during the war, Miss Clarke," I explained.

"Thank you, but I will be fine. Major Ryan is on his way here now," Miss Clarke told us. She turned to Mitchell. "Unfortunately, Mr. Mitchell, you will need to wait in the hallway while the doctor is here."

Major Ryan entered, and after introducing himself, Mitchell stepped out of the room.

"Morning, Griffin, how are you feeling?"

"Fine, Major. In pain, as you would expect, but fine."

"Call me doctor. I'm a major by the grace of the army, a doctor by virtue of hard work."

Miss Clarke wheeled a trolley to the bedside and helped me sit upright. She began to unwind the bandages starting with my chest. The doctor leaned over my bed, sniffing the medical gauze covering the wounds as they were revealed. Carefully but still painfully, he tugged away the gauze. Unfortunately, I knew the pain coming would be worse.

"Good. No infection. Your side looks good. The chest could use some attention," the doctor said, looking up at Miss Clarke. "We'll need to do a little cleaning here and here." He indicated for Miss Clarke where he would be cleaning.

"How long will I be here, Doctor?" I asked, trying to take my mind off the inevitable agony of the debridement and antisepsis solution.

"With no setbacks, two, maybe three weeks. Then you'll need to rest for about a month. Light exercise. Nothing too strenuous. We'll cover all this when the time comes. Of course, with setbacks, you'll probably be dead in a week," he said with a sly smile.

"Doctor!" Miss Clarke said with outrage.

"Griffin knows I'm kidding. Don't you, son?"

"Sure, Doc. Nothing to worry about, Miss Clarke."

The next fifteen minutes were spent in agony as the doctor

methodically debrided the wound in my chest and then cleaned both my chest and hip with antisepsis solution.

By the time Dr. Ryan and Miss Clarke left the room, I was completely exhausted. Mitchell returned and pulled a chair to my bedside. He didn't speak. He knew exactly how painful the dressing change had been.

I was not dead. The pain proved that. I might wish I were. With Sarah gone, I felt a gaping hole in my life. But despite my misery, I couldn't help being curious about what Raux had in mind for me. Yes, I was a pawn—a broken and brokenhearted pawn. But I still had my friend, William Mitchell. And a few more friends besides. I was surprised by that thought. Madeline, Kiki, and Rachel. Eugene, Walt, Charles, and even Henry. I had lost Sarah, but just having her at all had been an unimaginable gift. And I still had the others, and maybe Patricia too. Handy to have a murderer in your corner, I thought with a smile.

# NOTES

## Chapter 2

1. Wendell Cushing Neville. May 12, 1870–July 8, 1930. Commandant of the Marine Corps. Congressional Medal of Honor winner.

## Chapter 3

1. God with us.
2. Pronounced *shō shas*.

## Chapter 5

1. To die.

## Chapter 10

1. You are young and strong. You must stay in Montmartre. Many women, eh, many beautiful girls.
2. The Green Fairy, absinthe.
3. Alice Prin aka Kiki of Montparnasse. October 2, 1901–April 29, 1953. Entertainer and entrepreneur.
4. A little bit.
5. Walter Elias Disney. December 5, 1901–December 15, 1966. Cartoonist and entrepreneur. Disney came to France with the Red Cross after armistice and returned to the United States in November 1919.
6. Three bottles of red wine please.
7. Joey Zelli. December 1888–December 12, 1971. Club owner, grifter.
8. Eugene "Jacques" Bullard. October 9, 1895–October 12, 1961. Boxer, musician, club owner, war hero.
9. A carafe of water and a coffee please.
10. Espresso please.

## Chapter 11

1. He owes me money.
2. Bastard.
3. Trains to Italy do leave from Gare de Lyon but so could trains from Gare d'Austerlitz.
4. Get out of here!
5. Apologies by wine maybe?
6. Okay.
7. The Fabian Society was founded in England in 1884 to spread socialist principles peacefully without the need of revolution.


## Chapter 12

1. The Two Treasures.
2. Three absinthes.


## Chapter 13

1. *Juggernaut.* Directed by Ralph Ince. With performances by Anita Stewart and Earle Williams. 1915.
2. Georges Benjamin Clemenceau. September 28, 1841–November 24, 1929. Two-time French Prime Minister.
3. Candy.


## Chapter 14

1. An expresso with a dash of milk.
2. We'll be back. Soon.
3. Hello, beautiful, how are you doing?
4. All blood runs red. The saying painted on the fuselage of Bullard's airplane during the war.
5. My little fleas.
6. Dead.


## Chapter 15

1. Hispano-Suiza Type 32 Collapsible Brougham.

# Chapter 17

1. A draft beer please.

# Chapter 18

1. All you all right, Gavin?
2. Lenin, *State and Revolution* (1917).
3. Of course.
4. Charles Nungesser. March 15, 1892–May 1927. French combat pilot, aviator, daredevil.
5. Henry Johnson. July 15, 1892–July 1, 1927. Croix de Guerre and Posthumous Congressional Medal of Honor Winner (awarded June 2, 2015).
6. No offense taken/none taken.
7. He had been wounded twenty-one times in a single action in June 1918.

# Chapter 19

1. Johnson did, in fact, return with the 369th Infantry Regiment in February 1919, but for purposes of this story, he remained in France recuperating.

# Chapter 20

1. Now he only buys cheap cigars.
2. What did you see in the truck, little one?
3. Tell him, Marie.
4. I saw two men smoking. They did not speak. They just sat there.
5. When they saw me watching, they told me to go away. They were mean.
6. What did they look like?
7. Old, but not as old as my uncle. Old like you. Tired and sad.
8. Madame, please do as I ask. It is for your own good.
9. Are you all right?
10. I am sorry, Claude. What a waste.
11. Of course.
12. Edward Mandell House. July 26, 1858–March 28, 1938. Political advisor to President Wilson and key treaty negotiator for the United States.
13. Fernand Raux. May 25, 1863–February 23, 1955. Prefect of the Paris Police from November 23, 1917–May 13, 1921.
14. Get him a coffee and a cigarette. He may use the toilet if he needs it. He is not to leave until I return. Understood?

## Chapter 21

1. Yes, he is a real cowboy!
2. This is true?

## Chapter 22

1. Good morning, my name is Griffin, I'm the American who was here yesterday. With the prime minister.
2. What do you want?
3. Colonel House remains worried about the prime minister's safety. Is it quiet?
4. Yes, everything is quiet.
5. Good. I am going to look around the area. Okay?

## Chapter 23

1. Alma A. Clarke. June 10, 1890–March 16, 1963. Appears to have returned to the US on July 28, 1919.

# ACKNOWLEDGMENTS

Before acknowledging the many books and gracious support I've had in writing this story, I must make clear that all the mistakes in language, grammar, and historical accuracy are mine and mine alone.

Many have helped me bring Griffin and Mitchell to life:

My lovely wife, Michelle, who everyday demonstrates the value of "outkicking your coverage."

My children, Katharine, Michael, and William, whose day-to-day verbal jousting provided the spirit for much of the dialogue.

My editors and mentors (although they would likely cringe at the "mentor" label), my sister Elizabeth Christy, and her friend and author Debbie Garner at DeborahGarner.com.

For review of the French language, I must thank my friends Jean-François and Catherine Poupeau (really, Catherine did all the work).

I have tried to stay close to verifiable facts in connection with the historical background of the story, whether it be the baseball discussion (yes, the Yankees really did move to New York City), the Battle of Belleau Wood, or the words or attitudes attributed to Colonel House, Georges Clemenceau, and others. In seeking this accuracy, I relied on many books, articles, and letters, including Margaret MacMillan's wonderful book, *Paris 1919: Six Months That Changed the World*, John W. Thomason's descriptions in *Fix Bayonets*, General James Harbourd's book, *The American Army in France,* and Alice Prin's autobiography, *Kiki's Memiors.* For baseball history, I relied on numerous sources, including www.baseball-reference.com. For all subjects, I explored the *New York Times* archive. I was introduced to Eugene Bullard through the University of Houston, *Engines of Our Ingenuity* (No. 997), which led me to *Eugene Bullard: Black Expatriate in Jazz-Age Paris* by Craig Lloyd, and to Henry Johnson through the United States Army website on the Medal of Honor, https://www.army.mil/medalofhonor/.

I have also strived to keep the language and attitudes in the book consistent with the times. This may offend some, but I believe it is important to understand the past in order to improve the future.

# ABOUT THE AUTHOR

Alex Juden is a former law firm gopher, pretrial interviewer, naval aviator, trial lawyer, corporate compliance lawyer, and public company general counsel. He studied history and political science at Rice University. He lives in Houston with his wife and one child, who will shortly graduate from high school, following his two older siblings into the wider world.

 twitter.com/acjuden
instagram.com/acjuden

Made in United States
Orlando, FL
26 July 2023

35466589R00189